Louise Brindley was born in Darlington, County Dur-
ham, and at the age of four moved with her family to
Scarborough in North Yorkshire. All Louise Brindley's
writings reflect her knowledge of, and deep affection for,
North Yorkshire, where she still lives.

STARLIGHT

Louise Brindley

CORGI BOOKS

STARLIGHT

A CORGI BOOK : 0 552 14044 9

First publication in Great Britain

PRINTING HISTORY
Corgi edition published 1994

Set in 9½/11pt Monotype Plantin by Kestrel Data, Exeter

Corgi Books are published by Transworld Publishers Ltd, 61–63 Uxbridge Road, Ealing, London W5 5SA, in Australia by Transworld Publishers (Australia) Pty Ltd, 15–25 Helles Avenue, Moorebank, NSW 2170, and New Zealand by Transworld Publishers (NZ) Ltd, 3 William Pickering Drive, Albany, Auckland.

Reproduced, printed and bound in Great Britain by Cox & Wyman Ltd, Reading, Berks.

For Audrey and Jessie Willings,
and Margaret Johnson,
with my love.

PART ONE

Chapter One

'Are you awake, Miss Georgina?' Bridget Donovan swept aside the bedroom curtains. 'You've chosen a lovely day for the wedding. Better make haste and drink your tea. Madam's on the warpath!'

Georgina stirred and sighed, imagining her mother up and doing since the crack of dawn, getting in everybody's way, upsetting the cook – a woman not to be trifled with under normal circumstances, let alone today. Her wedding day . . .

She had not been asleep when Bridget came in with the early morning tea and the weather forecast, just lying perfectly still with her eyes closed, trying to imagine sharing a bed with Harold Bickley.

She longed to see Paris, the Île de la Cité, Notre Dame, the River Seine, which she could envisage from the pictures she had seen, the books she'd read. Her imagination stopped short of undressing in a strange hotel bedroom in front of a man whom she had always regarded as a brother, never a husband.

It struck her as being a bit indecent, standing in front of Harold in her chemise and knickers. But surely he wouldn't watch as she struggled into her white lawn nightgown. Or would he? She had no idea what he would expect of her on their wedding night. Something rather unpleasant, she suspected.

Memory drew her back to childhood days when they had played together on summer holidays in Scarborough, along with Harold's sisters, Josie and Letty, and her brother Thomas – whose nasty habit of destroying their carefully built sand-castles had driven Harold wild with rage on one occasion. Seizing her hands in a vice-like grip, 'If you don't stop that insufferable brat knocking down my sisters' castles, I'll box his ears for him!'

'And if you don't let go of me, I'll kick you hard on the shins!' Her mane of red hair streaming in the wind. 'Tommy's my brother. How dare you call him a brat?'

'He *is* a brat,' Harold shouted, 'a spoilt mama's darling who enjoys making little girls cry!'

'And you are a bully, Harold Bickley. Just because you're older and stronger than I am. But Tommy is still my brother.'

'*You* box his ears, then!'

'Don't worry, I *will*!'

'Then why are we fighting?' Harold had laughed suddenly, releasing his grip.

'Because you are so – so – *bossy*!' She had hated Harold Bickley at that moment. But childhood quarrels were soon forgotten.

The summer of 1910 that must have been, Georgina considered, counting back the years. They had not known then that their days in the sun were numbered, that soon would come a war destined to change all their lives.

Curling up her toes beneath the lavender-scented sheets and feather eiderdown, more recent memories came back to Georgina. One day in particular, in the summer of last year, when she had gone to Bradford station along with members of her own family and Harold's, to wave him goodbye before he set sail for France with his regiment, handsome and immaculate in his lieutenant's uniform.

'Will you write to me, Georgina?' he'd asked her at the last minute. And, 'Yes, of course I will, if you want me to,' she replied.

'Take care of yourself.'

'You too, Harry.' Her eyes had filled suddenly with tears at the thought of her childhood playmate going off to fight for his country. At the same time, she could not help thinking that his going to France would somehow tip the scales in favour of the Allies, and she had not been far wrong.

Five months later Peace had been declared, the Armistice signed, and Harold had returned to the bosom of his family without a scratch on him, looking just as immaculate as he had done that day at Bradford station, when she had done her best to comfort his distraught mother and sisters who had wept buckets of tears as the train drew away from the platform.

Overjoyed by their son's safe return Harold's parents, Mary and Jack Bickley, decided to throw a welcome home party and dance at Merlewood, their sprawling stone mansion overlooking the Calder Valley. It was named after the village of Merlewood, with its ancient church and woods in which, according to legend, Merlin the Magician had once sought shelter on his way to the Court of King Arthur – although it seemed more likely that the woods had been named after the blackbirds that whistled there at dusk, filling the air with the sweetness of their song.

'It will be lovely to have the house full of laughter again,' Mary Bickley confided in Georgina's mother one day over afternoon tea. 'Oh, I'm so glad that dreadful war is over at last. I nearly went out of my mind worrying about poor Harold. Another cup, dear?' She continued dreamily, 'We're having a dance floor in the conservatory, and Chinese lanterns. And I thought a buffet – so the young people can help themselves. You and Owen will come, won't you, and Georgina and Tommy?'

The Bickleys and the Brett-Forsyths had been friends and neighbours for the past 25 years: mill owners, people to be looked up to, competitors in one sense, yet bound together by their unassailable position in society, their friendship cemented by shared family interests: those summer holidays in Scarborough when the children were growing up; Christmas and birthday parties at both Elmhurst and Merlewood; Sunday School outings, dancing classes, and summer fêtes on the vicarage lawn. In any event, Jack Bickley and Owen Brett-Forsyth had never seen themselves as business rivals, especially during the war when, their order books depleted, they had been obliged to turn to the manufacture of shoddy as a means of survival.

Following her tea-time conversation with Mrs Bickley, Agnes Brett-Forsyth's thoughts turned, as a matter of expedience, to what her daughter would wear to the Bickley soirée. The girl had grown much taller and thinner during the war, so that none of her old party frocks would do, Agnes decided, emptying the contents of her daughter's wardrobe.

'Mother! What on earth . . . ?' Entering her bedroom, Georgina stared in amazement at the heap of dresses on the bed. When Agnes explained, 'But I couldn't care less what I wear to the dance,' Georgina said, inclined to laugh over such an unimportant matter. 'No-one will care tuppence how I look anyway.' Working at the mill during the war, she had not cared two hoots about dressing up, as long as she looked neat and felt comfortable.

'Then you *should* care,' Agnes said forcefully, nursing a secret ambition to bring about an engagement between her daughter and young Bickley. 'We'll go to Bradford first thing tomorrow morning to see Miss Datchett. We can buy the pattern and the material beforehand.'

'Mother! You know that's not possible. I have a job of work to do.'

'Nonsense,' Agnes said briskly, 'you must tell your father you want the morning off.' Never had she approved of Georgina's role as Owen's secretary, which she regarded as a 'come-down' for a girl in her position, who might have done her war-time duty in a more genteel manner. Josie and Letty Bickley, for example, had been content with rolling bandages at the local hospital, serving cups of tea and knitting Balaclava helmets.

But Georgina would not be swayed. 'Father relies on me to take his dictation and typewrite his letters in time for the midday post,' she said firmly. 'The dress can wait.'

In view of Georgina's stubbornness, the shopping expedition had taken place the following Saturday afternoon, when the mill was closed for the weekend. Dejectedly, Georgina had trailed in her mother's wake to the drapery department of Messengers' Emporium in the main street, and watched with a sinking heart the unfurling of a bolt of pink satin which she knew, deep down, she'd be lumbered with, despite her protests.

12

'Oh *please*, Mother,' she said, *sotto voce*, 'if I'm to have a new dress, couldn't it be green? Pink clashes horribly with my hair.' But she knew she was wasting her breath.

'You fuss too much about your hair, Georgina. Pink is a sweetly pretty colour, very ladylike and genteel.' Agnes knew that Harold liked pink, because his mother had told her so.

And so Georgina had turned up at the dance dressed overall in pink satin. A typical Miss Datchett creation, she thought disgustedly, with lots of flounces and trimmings added at the elderly seamstress's discretion. *Discretion*. Not that Harold appeared to notice her discomfort when he asked her to dance with him. 'You're looking very demure tonight, Georgie,' he said. 'What have you done to your hair, by the way?'

'Oh, nothing.' She wasn't about to divulge that she had applied a quarter jar of her father's pomade to her hair to darken it and squash it down. Red hair was bad enough; curly red hair an abomination. If only she dare have it cut short, like a boy, but her mother would throw a fit if she did.

'When are you going back to the mill?' she asked Harold as they entered the lantern-lit conservatory, where the orchestra was playing the waltz from 'The Chocolate Soldier'.

Slipping his arm round her waist, 'Not until the new year,' he said. 'I reckon I deserve a bit of fun and relaxation first before putting my nose to the grindstone. Which reminds me. What say if we go to Scarborough next weekend, now the car is out of mothballs?' Referring to his father's Vauxhall Prince Henry automobile which had been kept in the garage for the duration.

'*We?*'

'Well, you and I, Josie and Letty and their current gentlemen friends. We could stay at Fernlea. I'm sure Mrs Woodbridge would be pleased to see us again.'

Fernlea. A memory of the tall boarding-house on Scarborough's fashionable South Cliff, and its formidable owner, Florence Woodbridge, crossed Georgina's mind.

And yes, she thought, it might be fun to go back there, to walk along the promenade, look at the sea, and visit the Children's Corner near the Spa, where they had once built their sand-castles and scrambled over the rocks to find tiny crabs lurking in the trapped pools of sea-water. The war had been so long and dreary, so dark too, especially in winter with the street lamps extinguished and everyone worried sick as the war news worsened and the latest casualty figures were announced in the morning papers.

'Was it very awful – in the trenches, I mean?' Georgina asked wistfully as the waltz ended, and they threaded their way through to the dining-room to partake of the lavish buffet provided by the Bickleys. But Harold had refused to talk about it.

It might have been better had he done so, she thought, getting up, when Bridget had gone, to look out of the window at the view she had grown up with – the long, softly undulating line of hills on the far horizon, the great granite blocks of the woollen mills in the valley below – the Brett-Forsyth and Bickley mills dominating the clusters of slate-roofed houses where the mill workers lived. A harsh, Brontë-esque landscape, dour and unyielding to the eye of a stranger, perhaps. But then, a stranger might never see the swathes of heather empurpling the hills as summertime progressed to autumn, or notice the Merle Woods where the blackbirds shrilled their songs at eventide.

At times Georgina had loathed Elmhurst for its smug Victorian pretentiousness of stained glass windows, oak panelling, monumental fireplaces and massive furniture. Today she could scarcely bear the thought of leaving it to begin a new life as the wife of Harold Bickley, of returning after her honeymoon to live with her in-laws at Merlewood, until the house Harold had bought was ready to move into. What on earth would she do with her time as a guest beneath the Bickley roof, with nothing of importance to occupy her mind? But Harold had remained adamant that she must give up her job as Owen's secretary after the wedding.

14

'But Harry, I *want* to go on working,' she'd protested, but to no avail. She had seen then the same look on his face that she had done the night of the dance, when he refused to talk about his war-time experiences, as if a shutter had come down between them. And yet he had been quite affable during that weekend in Scarborough, when they had walked arm-in-arm along the promenade; watched the fishing-boats setting sail from the harbour in the lee of the Castle Hill, and seen the shore lights, at dusk swimming down into the dark, mysterious water of the South Bay. She had felt totally at ease with him then, her familiar, childhood companion of long ago.

'Damn it all, Georgie,' he'd said coldly, when she had mentioned keeping on her job as her father's secretary, 'I am quite capable of supporting you after we're married, and I dare say your father will easily find someone to replace you. A war widow, perhaps, who really needs to earn her living.'

His argument had made sense. It was Harold's lack of understanding that bothered Georgina. Moreover, her mother had absolutely forbidden her to take with her to Merlewood her old favourite dark green dressing-gown, because of its worn collar and cuffs. This meant that she would be deprived of its comforting warmth when she would need old, familiar things to cling to.

Forgetting to drink her tea, and wearing the green dressing-gown, she peeped round the door to make certain the coast was clear before hurrying along the landing to the bathroom. Various aunts and uncles had come for the wedding, and she did not want to bump into them in her old robe and slippers. Nor, she imagined, would her father's sisters wish to be seen in a state of *déshabillé*, without their false hairpieces.

The bath resembled a white enamelled sarcophagus. In keeping with the rest of Elmhurst, with its highly polished silver, sparkling mirrors and immaculately starched and ironed napery, the bathroom reflected her mother's love of good management. The towels were as white and fluffy as driven snow, the mahogany lavatory seat polished to the sheen of horse-chestnuts.

Filling the bath with steaming hot water, Georgina saw these things with a feeling of nostalgia, an awareness of how much she had taken for granted. Slipping into the bath, she noticed the way her slim young body seemed to tremble and dissolve beneath the weight of water – like that of the drowned Ophelia in a painting she had seen in the Leeds Art Gallery. Poor Ophelia, driven mad by love – or the lack of it. Closing her eyes she quoted softly: ' "There's rosemary, that's for remembrance: pray you, love, remember . . ." ' Ah, such exquisite sadness. Tears welled up beneath her closed eyelids.

Her father had taken her to a matinée performance of *Hamlet* on her fourteenth birthday, to her mother's disgust, who had protested violently that a visit to the theatre was scarcely suitable for a child of that age, especially to see one of those nasty Shakespearean plays. But how grown up she had felt, sitting beside her father, waiting for the curtain to rise, enchanted by the red plush seats and the brass rails edging the balcony, the footlights; the costumes, the make-up, the words that tripped from the players' tongues like music, the applause when the play ended and the actors lined up to take their bows.

An insistent knocking on the door jerked her back to the present. 'Georgina! You really must hurry! You've been in there a quarter of an hour already.'

'Yes, Mother. I'm coming.' Guiltily, Georgina stepped out of the bath.

Turning away to hurry downstairs Agnes Brett-Forsyth, a tall, well-corseted woman in her forties, wondered what young people were coming to these days. Really, they had no idea what planning a wedding entailed – neither Georgina nor her brother Tom. Where was the wretched boy anyway? But even as she thought of her son, Agnes' heart melted towards him. If only he realized his importance as the heir apparent of the Brett-Forsyth mill when his father retired, of Elmhurst too, when she and Owen were dead and gone. Not that she had any thought of dying just yet, and of course Thomas must finish his education before coming into the family business.

Sweeping into the dining-room, Agnes cast her eagle eye over the vast collection of cold food, the rose-bordered plates, silverware, and sparkling glasses arranged on a crackling white damask cloth: the Yorkshire ham perched atop its white china stand, the plates of sliced roast goose, the hand-raised, glossy-turreted game pies, glazed tongues, chickens and cheeses, the plethora of pickles in gleaming cut-glass dishes, the quivering jellies and the custard- and cream-covered trifles adorned with blanched almonds and strips of angelica. Above all, the three-tier wedding cake with its crowning silver vase of lilies-of-the-valley, which Georgina and her bridegroom would cut when the speeches were over and the champagne glasses raised to toast the future of the happy pair.

Harold Bickley, Agnes considered, surveying the results of her careful planning, would bring Georgina down to earth with a bump once they were married. She blamed Owen for encouraging the girl to learn shorthand and typewriting, for taking her on at the mill when his old secretary had retired at the outbreak of war, for filling Georgina's head with weird ideas: supporting her strong leaning towards the suffragette movement, for instance, which Agnes saw as a messy political issue totally out of keeping with a woman's main purpose in life – to marry, have children and learn the art of home management.

Quitting the dining-room, Agnes swept into the kitchen where the cook, Mrs Crabtree, and the three housemaids, Bridget, Polly and Gertrude, were attending to their work quite satisfactorily without her interference. 'Don't forget, Bridget, that breakfast is to be served in the study this morning,' she said in a booming voice, causing Polly to drop the pan she was holding.

'No, ma'am. That is, I hadn't forgotten.' Bridget exchanged glances with the cook, whereupon Mrs Crabtree, less in awe of the mistress of the house than poor Bridget and Polly were, said forcefully that the breakfast-table had

17

been set since the crack of dawn, and breakfast would be served at nine o'clock sharp, as ordered.

'Yes, well, I am naturally concerned that all runs smoothly today,' Agnes blustered, knowing she had met her match in Mrs Crabtree.

'If you don't mind my saying so, madam, things *are* running smoothly.' Daisy Crabtree bridled, ready to do battle. 'The time is now half-past eight. I just hope that when breakfast *is* served, everyone will be down on time to eat it!'

'That is scarcely your concern.' Agnes knew when she was beaten, but authority must be maintained. 'Have you seen my husband and Master Thomas?'

'I saw Mr Brett-Forsyth in the conservatory a little while ago, when I went through to mend the drawing-room fire,' Bridget ventured. 'As for Master Thomas, he's still in bed. Leastways he was when I took up the morning tea.'

Oh God, Agnes thought, crossing the drawing-room in search of her husband, why this feeling of disaster? Despite all her careful planning, something was sure to go wrong at the last minute.

Opening the glass-panelled doors leading through to the conservatory where the wedding presents – a formidable collection of sheets, pillow-cases, blankets, china, cutlery, clocks and ornaments – had been arranged on a series of tables amid an oasis of potted palms and glossy-leafed aspidistras, 'Oh, there you are, Owen,' she said accusingly, furious that he should be standing in an attitude of silent contemplation, placidly smoking his pipe on this, of all days, when she desperately needed his help and support. 'Have you any idea of the time?'

Consulting his pocket-watch, 'It is exactly twenty-five minutes to nine,' he said amiably. 'Why do you ask?'

'For heaven's sake, man! The wedding's at eleven. Georgina has just come out of the bathroom, there's no sign of your sisters and their husbands, Tom is still in bed and you are not properly dressed yet!'

'It won't take me more than ten minutes to put on my finery.' Carefully considering his wife, Owen Brett-Forsyth,

18

a spare, still-handsome man with greying hair, kindly eyes and a charming smile, wondered why he had married her. Of course, she had been quite pretty a quarter of a century ago, when he had brought her to Elmhurst as a bride, and he had found her bossiness amusing at the time. But the years had not dealt kindly with her. Her hitherto slender waist had disappeared beneath a solid wall of flesh, and her chin had gone forth and multiplied. More distressingly, her youthful forcefulness had developed into an armour-plating of self-righteousness.

'Well, are you going to stand there doing nothing?' Agnes demanded.

'My dear, what should I do? Drag Tom out of bed? Round up the family by force?' Owen asked mildly, knocking out his pipe in a brass plant holder.

'I might have known I'd be wasting my breath talking to you,' his wife retorted, feeling like a captain whose crew had abandoned ship in mid-Atlantic. 'You don't *care*, that's your trouble!'

'But surely everything's under control?' Owen stuffed his pipe in the pocket of his tweed jacket. 'There's enough food to feed an army. Tom will appear as if by magic when he catches a whiff of bacon and eggs, and my sisters and their spouses have never been late for a meal in their lives, so why not relax?'

'*Relax!*' Agnes' temper erupted. 'Talk sense, Owen! How can I relax?' She clicked her teeth in annoyance. 'You don't seem to realize . . . In two hours from now the house will be like bedlam. The bridesmaids are coming at a quarter past ten, not to mention Florrie, Arthur and the children, who will want refreshment after their journey, I dare say. It's too bad of you to stand there leaving everything to me.'

Owen sighed deeply. 'You have rather rushed things, my dear.' He meant that the wedding might well have taken place at two o'clock rather than eleven, but Agnes read a deeper meaning into his mild rebuke.

'*Rushed* things? Oh, is that what you think? Well, I wasn't going to sit back and let some other girl get her claws into

Harold Bickley. They were round him like flies when he came back from the war. I wasn't having *my* daughter overlooked!'

'You mean that you . . . ?' Owen's lips tightened. Of course, how stupid of him not to have realized that this rushed wedding had been his wife's doing. Puzzling incidents slotted together suddenly in his mind to form a picture of an over-zealous mother pushing her daughter into a marriage of convenience. How could he have been so blind, so obsessed with business matters not to have seen what was happening?

'You seem to forget that Georgina is my daughter, too,' he said angrily. 'I had far rather she'd made up her mind in her own good time, than – *this*!'

'This – *what*?' Agnes rounded on her husband. 'The girl has made a splendid match! Harold Bickley is a fine young man. Left to her own devices, Georgina would have let him slip through her fingers. I had no intention of allowing that to happen. I wanted to see our daughter happily married.'

'And are you so sure that she will be happy?'

'Of course. Why ever not? What that girl needs is a firm hand, a good husband – children.' Agnes' chins trembled with the force of her argument. 'I've no patience with you, Owen! I know you think the sun shines out of Georgina, but she isn't at all a pretty girl, with that red hair of hers, her pale skin and – freckles! Not to mention her odd political beliefs, and all those damn silly books she reads – poetry and the like – and not caring two hoots how she looks. If you had a ha'porth of sense, you'd see how lucky she is to be getting married at all!'

Turning on her heel, Agnes marched out of the conservatory.

Alone in her room, Georgina looked thoughtfully at her wedding dress, a satin and lace confection hanging from her wardrobe door alongside her lace wedding veil with its circlet of seed pearls which, clamped down on her mass of red hair, would give her head the appearance of a carrot pudding ready for the pot.

Soon her two bridesmaids, Harold's sisters Josie and Letty, would arrive to dress her – like a sacrificial virgin – in her satin and lace finery, to pin up her hair, with a great deal of laughter, not realizing that she had never felt less like laughter in her life before. How could she? The kind of love she had read about in the Thomas Hardy and Brontë novels, the poetry of Elizabeth Barrett Browning, had not happened for her.

It had all escalated so suddenly: Harold's homecoming, the dance at Merlewood, the trip to Scarborough; the beginning of the courtship. She had not even realized that she and Harold were courting, at first. The thought had never crossed her mind. Why should it? She had seen his frequent appearances at the Elmhurst dining-table as perfectly normal, the fuss her mother made of him as a sign that she was pleased he hadn't been killed, maimed or wounded in the war. In any case, Harry had always treated Elmhurst as a second home.

Looking at her wedding dress, events seemed lumped together in Georgina's mind. That Christmas party at Merlewood, for instance, when Harold had drawn her under the mistletoe and kissed her. Not a lingering kiss by any means, which had nevertheless surprised her, because he had never attempted to kiss her before.

Thereafter, she had found herself increasingly alone with Harold Bickley, as though some plot was afoot to leave them alone together whenever possible. Or was she just being fanciful? Apparently not. Even so, in her innocence, she had not realized what was happening . . . Not until, after the Easter Morning service in the parish church, on their way to Merlewood for luncheon, Harold had drawn her aside and asked her to marry him.

Startled, to put it mildly, her eyes wide with disbelief, 'Marry you, Harold? But I . . .' Words had failed her.

'Oh, come on, Georgie,' he said briskly, 'you can't be all that surprised. After all, we've been seeing a lot of each other lately.'

'What's unusual about that? We've always seen a lot of each other, ever since we were children.'

21

'I've bought you this,' he said, producing a morocco-leather box from an inner pocket. 'Well go on, open it. It's your – Easter egg!'

'A – ring?' She stared in amazement at the diamond cluster scintillating against a blue velvet pad.

'More than just a ring, Georgie. An engagement ring. Come, try it on, see if it fits; but I expect it will. Your mother told me the size.'

Aghast, 'You mean my parents know about this?'

'Of course. I had to ask your father's permission to speak to you. Give me your hand. There now, it fits perfectly.'

'Just a minute, Harry! What did my father say?'

'That he had no objection to me as a son-in-law!' Put out by Georgina's lack of enthusiasm, 'Why? What did you think he'd say? After all, I'm not some fly-by-night, someone he scarcely knows!'

'No, of course not.' Staring at her ring finger, 'I didn't mean to offend you, it's just that I had not considered the possibility of marrying anyone just yet,' Georgina said truthfully. 'There's so much I want to do with my life.'

'What, for instance?'

'Well, I'd like to travel. See something of the world.'

'Oh, is that all?' Harold laughed, filled with renewed confidence. 'Then what's to stop us? I'll take you to Paris on our honeymoon. Gay Paree!'

'But do you really care for me?' Georgina asked wistfully, meaning did he love her.

'Of course I do. I wouldn't have asked you to marry me otherwise, now would I?'

'I suppose not.' But the magic was missing.

'Then will you or won't you?'

And so, because it was Eastertime and the world seemed filled with new promise after four years of war, and because Georgina was a tender-hearted girl who could not bear the thought of making anyone unhappy on this joyous Easter morning, 'Oh, very well then,' she said resignedly. 'If you really want me to.'

Entering the Merlewood drawing-room, holding Georgina's hand firmly in his, 'I have asked Georgie to marry me, and she has said yes,' Harold announced triumphantly.

Suddenly they were surrounded with a crowd of well-wishers. Jack Bickley uncorked a bottle of champagne. How odd, Georgina thought, that champagne and glasses were to hand, as if everyone knew why Harry had dawdled her here from the church, and what he had said to her near the rhododendron thicket at the gate. 'Oh, my dear child,' Agnes cried, sweeping Georgina into her arms, a relieved expression on her face.

Later, the mysterious chemistry which existed between Georgina and her father had drawn them apart from the rest. Facing Owen, 'I think you might have warned me beforehand,' she said quietly.

'I wanted to, believe me, but I was sworn to secrecy.' His eyes betrayed the shame of his coercion.

She understood her father's quest for peace at any price, her mother's upper hand in the husband-and-wife relationship. 'Just tell me one thing, Father. Are you pleased about Harold and me?'

Owen said solemnly, 'All I care about is your happiness, my dear. It is up to you to decide where that happiness lies.' He had not, until that moment, begun to realize the extent of his collusion in all the secrecy and subterfuge leading to his daughter's engagement to a man she was not in love with. He now knew the shame of not being entirely honest with her, of participating in a silly charade at her expense. He should have known better.

Sending word by Bridget that she was not hungry, and would not come down to breakfast, Georgina knew that her mother would come upstairs to find out what ailed her – if she was simply nervous, or sickening for something.

'Georgina,' Agnes cried, rustling into the room, 'are you ill?'

'No, Mother, I'm perfectly well, thank you.' Turning away from the window, gathering up her courage, 'I'd like to talk to you, that's all. It's very important.'

'My dear, you cannot possibly go to the church without

eating. At least have a lightly boiled egg and a slice of toast,' Agnes insisted, turning a deaf ear. 'I expect you are feeling nervous. Every bride does on her wedding day. You'll feel much better after the ceremony, I dare say.'

'Please, Mother! I *must* talk to you.'

'Later, Georgina not now. I have a thousand and one things to see to downstairs. Your Aunt Florrie, Uncle Arthur and the children, will be here at any moment.' She turned at the door. 'I'll send Bridget up with a breakfast tray, and you had better take a Daisy powder, just in case you are sickening for something.'

'*Mother!*' But Agnes had hurried away, closing the door firmly behind her, unwilling to find out what Georgina wanted to talk to her about.

Minutes later Bridget appeared with the breakfast tray which she plonked down firmly on the bedside table. 'Mother of God,' she cried dramatically, 'there's all hell let loose downstairs! Your aunts are flapping about like chickens with their heads off. Master Thomas has sliced into a game pie in the dining-room, and Mrs Crabtree's talking of handing in her notice. I say, miss, are you all right? You're as white as a sheet.'

'Tell me, Bridget, have you ever been in love?' Georgina asked unexpectedly.

'Why yes, miss. Once, a long time ago.' Bridget, a dark-haired Irish girl with a wild-rose face and blue eyes, 'put in with a sooty finger', puckered her forehead. 'Why do you ask?'

'How did it feel? Being in love, I mean.'

'Feel? Why, I don't know that I can rightly explain, miss.'

'Please try.'

'Well, all mixed up. Kind of happy and sad at the same time.' Bridget shook her head confusedly. 'His name was Keiran. He was my childhood sweetheart back in the old country. Leastways he was until . . . Oh, I expect it was all my fault. I didn't know when I was well off. Forever tormenting him I was, so proud, so cocksure of myself, thinkin' he'd stand for coals breakin' on his head, until the silly fool went an' married someone else.'

'Please, go on.'

'That's why I came over here, to England, to make a fresh start, to forget about him . . . The trouble is, I can't forget, an' I don't suppose I ever shall. That's what it's like to be in love, wanting a man so much you'll die if you can't have him. Only you don't die, you just go on living from one day to the next.'

The Irish blue eyes filled with tears. 'The truth is, I'd go to the ends of the earth and back to be with him, if he wanted me. I'd throw myself at his feet an' beg him to forgive me. I'd do anything at all to make him love me again.' A shuddering sigh escaped her. 'I'm sorry, miss, but you did ask.'

'I didn't mean to upset you,' Georgina said gently.

'Oh, don't worry about me, miss. It's just that I can't help wishing it was me, not you, setting off to the church, to find Keiran waiting for me. Will that be all, miss?'

'Yes. Thank you, Bridget, that will be all.'

About to leave the room, the girl said simply, 'It's not for the likes of me to tell a lady like you what to do, but my grandma's a wise woman, an' I know what her advice would be: when in doubt, say No. After all, a lifetime's a very long time to go on regretting a mistake, to keep on paying for it over and over again, and I should know.' And then she was gone, regretting her own mistake in not keeping a still tongue in her head, certain sure she'd get the sack if the mistress found out she'd spoken her mind so boldly. Then what would become of her if she was dismissed without a reference, and not a penny to bless herself with?

At a quarter past ten Georgina's bridesmaids appeared to help her into her wedding dress – thankfully not a Miss Datchett creation. Calling out, 'We're here,' they burst into the room in a flurry of lemon taffeta run through with fine gold-thread embroidery, silk flowers in delicate pastel shades adorning the flounced skirts, wearing wide-brimmed leghorn hats bound in pale green satin ribbon. Both were fair-haired, fashionably slender, with shapely bosoms; self assured, inured to the good things of life, attractive to the opposite sex, keen on dancing, clothes and parties. Rich enough to fritter their time away.

Letty, the younger sister, flung her arms round Georgina. 'Isn't it exciting?' she chortled. 'Just think, from now on we'll really be sisters! Why, what's wrong, Georgie? You're shaking like a leaf. You're not going to faint, are you?'

'Oh, for God's sake, Letty, have a grain of sense! I expect she's nervous,' Josie, the harder of the two, observed. But Letty was right, Georgina looked as if she might pass out at any moment, and how *thin* she was. Scarcely a picking on her. Dare she suggest tucking cotton-wool into her bodice to give her a bit of shape, a touch of rouge to put colour in her cheeks? But no, better not, she decided. Georgina had a prickly side to her nature. She just hoped that Harry knew what he was doing, marrying a redhead with strange ideas about the emancipation of women. And why all the rush to get married in the first place? She doubted if Harry would have thought of marrying Georgina had it not been for 'Aunt' Agnes' unsubtle approach in throwing them together at every possible opportunity. She liked Georgina well enough, but was Harry in love with her? Oh well, no use worrying on that score. No skin off her nose, Josie decided. A very *pretty* nose, she thought, catching sight of herself in the dressing-table mirror.

'Your dress is a *dream*,' Letty enthused, helping her sister to settle the folds of heavy white satin about Georgina's slim legs, glancing admiringly at the skirt with its silver-thread embroidery and cascade of lace ruffles. 'Harry's eyes will pop out of his head when he sees you in this! Now for the veil. Better sit down, Georgie, you're far too tall standing up.'

Obligingly, Georgina sank down on the dressing-table stool, taking care not to crease the dress, and watched, in silent dismay, her bridesmaids attempting to tame her riot of curly red hair. Never before had she realized so acutely what a plain girl she was, with her high cheekbones, green eyes, wide mouth, pale skin and freckles.

'I think that riding to the church in an open carriage is

a lovely idea,' Letty babbled, jabbing pins into Georgina's hair. 'And it's such a glorious day for a wedding, isn't it, Josie?'

'Yes,' Josie said absent-mindedly, clamping the circlet of seed pearls on the bride's forehead, thinking that the veil and headdress would at least hide most of Georgina's hair.

'You look simply gorgeous, Georgie,' Letty said ecstatically, clasping her hands. 'Gorgie Georgie!' She burst into a peal of laughter at her clever play on words.

'Oh, do stop twittering,' Josie interrupted. 'Look at the time! A quarter to eleven. High time we were off.' She paused momentarily to apply a soupçon of powder to her retroussé nose, to smooth her hair and re-settle her hat, before heading for the door with her sister in tow. 'Well 'bye for now, Georgina. See you in church,' she called, with a wave of her hand. 'Oh, do come *on*, Letty!'

When they had gone, Georgina clenched her hands till the knuckles showed white, then, very slowly, she took off her engagement ring to leave the third finger of her left hand unencumbered to receive her wedding ring, that small circle of gold which would bind her to Harold Bickley more powerfully than the chains that had bound the suffragettes to the railings of number 10 Downing Street during the war.

Covering her face with her hands, 'Oh, dear God,' she prayed, 'please give me a sign. However small or insignificant, please give me a sign.'

If only she could have talked quietly to her mother, told her how uncertain she felt about this wedding. But she had never come close enough to Agnes to reveal her secret fears and emotions. Realizing how uneasy she felt about marrying Harold Bickley, a more understanding mother might have told her to cancel the wedding, but understanding had never been her mother's strong point, and she had been unwilling to listen in any case.

At that moment Agnes entered the room, resplendent in her wedding finery – purple ankle-length dress and a matching toque smothered in artificial violets, a *lavallière* of pearls holding her chins in place; black patent leather shoes too pointed for comfort, grey antelope suede gloves, dangling pearl earrings and a silver fox fur complete with dead paws, ears and brush.

'Oh, my dear child, how lovely you look!' Agnes enfolded her daughter in a cloud of Devon Violets perfume as she kissed the air with her lips. 'Now, do remember to hold yourself erect when you walk down the aisle, and for heaven's sake don't be late for the ceremony! Oh, my goodness, is that the time?' Yet again the door closed firmly behind her.

Slowly, Georgina walked downstairs, her white satin skirt brushing the red staircarpet. Owen was standing in the hall below, holding her bouquet of pink roses and trailing maidenhair fern. Looking down, she saw that his eyes were misted with tears, that the servants – the cook, the house-maids, the gardener and the stable-lad – were lined up beside him to wish her luck on her wedding day. She knew and liked all of them so well: Mrs Crabtree, Adam Dickenson the gardener, whose son Peter would drive the carriage to the church, Bridget and the other two maids, whom she regarded as friends, to the disgust of her mother who felt that a dividing line a mile wide lay between those who did the work and those who paid their wages.

'Thank you all so much,' Georgina said softly as Owen handed her the bouquet, and she walked down the front steps to the waiting carriage.

It was a glorious day, the blue sky touched with feather-light puffs of cloud sailing in the breeze, an unmistakable scent of springtime in the air. She had been unable to explain to her mother the reason why she wished to drive to the church in an open carriage rather than a motor car, but her father understood why – because she loved freedom, the feel of the wind on her face.

A rare girl, Georgina, thought Owen. He held her hand, wishing he knew what to say to make the coming ordeal easier for her, hating his own weakness in allowing his wife to hold sway over his less forceful character. But old habits died hard. He said simply, 'You look lovely, my darling. Tell me, are you – happy?'

28

'No, Father, not very.' Georgina attempted a smile. 'Not now, at any rate, but I expect I shall be in time, when all this fuss is over and done with. I just wish—'

'What, my dear? What do you wish?' Tightening his clasp on her hand, 'Please, tell me.'

'That this journey might last for ever!'

Oh God, Agnes thought as the minutes ticked by without a sign of the bride, what on earth had gone wrong? She glanced anxiously over her shoulder. What would people think, being kept waiting like this, especially poor Harold whose face had frozen into a mask of scarcely concealed irritation as he flicked over the pages of a hymn book. Had one of the carriage-horses cast a shoe? Had Georgina tripped over the hem of her dress and sprained her ankle?

The bridesmaids were beginning to flutter like yellow butterflies in a lepidopterist's net, the organist had almost run out of improvisations. Then, ah, thank goodness! Here at last was the bride, entering the church on her father's arm. Fifteen minutes late. She would speak to Owen about that later.

Dismounting from the carriage, which her father had ordered to drive twice round the village green, Georgina paused awhile to survey the wealth of lilac bushes growing near the lych-gate, as if she was seeing everything of beauty for the last time, as though, after today, she would cease to exist as a person in her own right, cease to inhabit her intensely private world of literature and dreams. The man she was about to marry cared nothing for literature, art, the theatre, poetry, or dreams, come to that. All Harold cared about was how quickly the builders would finish re-pointing the walls of the Bradford house, and how soon they could move into it after the honeymoon. But she had promised to marry him, and the time had come to fulfil that promise.

Standing still as the bridesmaids spread out her veil on the cold stone slabs of the porch, Georgina sensed rather than saw the congregation flanking the red-carpeted aisle. Keeping her eyes firmly fixed on the stained glass window above the altar, she saw the white dove – symbolic of the Holy Spirit – outlined against blood-red glass, high above the white-robed clergyman waiting to join her in Holy Matrimony to Harold Bickley.

'Ready, my dear?'

'Oh, yes.' Tucking her hand in her father's arm, Georgina heard the strains of the Wedding March, the rustling sound of the rising congregation.

Thankfully, the church was familiar to her, a place of worship since childhood. Walking down the aisle, she remembered herself as a child in a white muslin dress with a sash tied in a bow at the back, making her first Communion, wearing the single row of pearls her father had given her for her twelfth birthday. She now wore them as the 'something old' which tradition demanded a bride should wear on her wedding day. Not a fine, grand necklace by any means, but infinitely precious to her because of the giver.

Turning his head, Harold could scarcely believe that the vision of loveliness coming towards him was really Georgina. The girl walked like a queen, so remote and so distant that he felt he scarcely knew her at all, and wondered if he had ever really known her, this mysterious, veiled Georgina whom he now saw as a stranger.

Stepping forward to take her hand, certain misgivings he had kept strictly to himself about marrying someone he had known all his life suddenly took flight. Of course, 'Aunt' Agnes was right in predicting that theirs would be a brilliantly successful match, a means of securing the future of the mills, of strengthening the ties between the Bickleys and the Brett-Forsyths.

'Dearly beloved, we are gathered here in the sight of God, and in the face of this congregation to join together this man and this woman in Holy Matrimony, which is an honourable estate . . .'

'Wilt thou, Harold Ewart, have this woman to thy wedded wife . . . and, forsaking all other, keep thee only unto her, so long as ye both shall live?'

'I will.'

'Georgina, wilt thou have this man to thy wedded husband . . . ?'

At that moment a trapped sparrow fluttered down from the rafters and came to rest on the altar – a tiny, terrified creature with a swiftly beating heart beneath its breast feathers, uncertain which way to fly, to find release from its imprisonment.

Georgina saw in that bird an answer to a prayer.

'. . . Wilt thou obey him and serve him, love, honour, and keep him, in sickness and in health, and, forsaking all other, keep thee only unto him, so long as ye both shall live?'

The time was now or never. The choice seemed obvious. Imprisonment or freedom. As the sparrow took wing, 'I'm so sorry, Harold, please forgive me,' Georgina whispered. Then, gathering up her skirts, she ran. Ran from the church into the sunlight of a fresh May morning, arms outspread to encompass the loveliness of the world. *Her* world.

Hastening down the path to the lych-gate, her flowing veil, lifted by the breeze, caught on the branch of a lilac tree, releasing her mass of red hair to float free in the sweetness of a new beginning.

Entering the waiting carriage, tossing aside her veil, 'Drive me home, Peter,' she said breathlessly. 'I – I couldn't go through with it at the last minute.'

Peter smiled. Chucking the reins over the horses' backs, 'I never thought you would, Miss,' he said. 'But there'll be hell to pay later.'

'Yes, I expect you are right,' Georgina admitted, wondering how she would face the onslaught of her mother's anger.

Chapter Two

Agnes stood as one petrified, unable to take in the enormity of what had happened. One thought burned into her brain like a branding-iron. What would people *say*? In a split second of realization, she saw herself as a laughing stock. Worse still, an object of pity.

How *dare* Georgina have subjected her to this humiliation? Legs buckling, she sat down abruptly, aware that the congregation were turning to each other to discuss the dramatic turn of events, whispering behind her back. Oh God, how would she live down the disgrace of it?

Adding insult to injury, the Reverend Simmons had approached the stunned bridegroom and his family to offer his sympathy. So that was the way of it, Agnes thought bitterly. Sympathy for the Bickleys, none for herself. And why was Owen standing there like a graven image, looking intently at Mary Bickley, doing nothing to support her in her hour of need?

Of course, all this was his fault. He must have said something on the way to the church to put Georgina off getting married. Why else would they have arrived so late?

Later, during a sleepless night, Agnes would recall the scene: the Bickley family, *en masse*, rallying round Harold, Georgina running up the aisle in a flurry of white satin, leaving her dumb-struck bridegroom on the steps leading up to the altar: jumbled impressions out of sequence, each one more disturbing than the last. The bridesmaids staring at each other in dismay, Thomas grinning as if the whole thing was a joke, Owen gazing at Mary, a faraway look on his face, Mary Bickley's hastily averted eyes as she hurried forward to comfort her son, as if she, Agnes, were a leper.

Well, she would see about that! In full possession of her pride, Agnes rose to her feet, a towering presence in her purple wedding ensemble, and butted her way up the aisle, brushing aside Owen's hand on her arm as she stormed down the path between the gravestones.

Sobbing, Georgina laid her head against Daisy Crabtree's comforting shoulder. 'I couldn't go through with it, I just couldn't,' she wept.

'I know, my lamb.' Daisy spoke softly, patting the girl's heaving shoulders. 'Mr Harold's a nice enough young man, but we all knew he wasn't right for you. Come on now, dry your eyes and let me help you out of your dress. Then into bed with you. What you need is sleep.'

'*Sleep!* How can I sleep? Don't you realize what I've done? My mother will never forgive me!' Georgina imagined Agnes coming up to her room to give vent to her wrath, demanding to know why she had left Harold standing at the altar. At that moment she half wished she hadn't. But Mrs Crabtree was right, she did need sleep.

The past weeks had been a nightmare, deciding who to invite to the wedding; that trip to London to choose the dresses, with Agnes in charge of the expedition, and worrying about the house that Harold had bought for a knock-down price on the outskirts of Bradford – a grey stone villa with cold, dark rooms and mottled marble fireplaces.

'Don't fuss so, Georgie,' he'd said impatiently when she had expressed her doubts about living there, 'I know what I'm doing. The place is a bargain.' An ugly bargain, Georgina thought, wondering how she would be able to live in a valley with practically no view at all. But the builders had been slow to proceed, with so much other renovation work on hand. Then Harry had told her they would be living at Merlewood for the time being, until the house was ready to move into.

'Perhaps we could postpone the wedding,' Georgina had suggested hopefully, bringing down her mother's wrath on her hapless head. 'Don't be so ridiculous! The invitations have been sent out, the church has been booked, the honeymoon arranged.' She had felt then that a trap was closing in on her. No wonder she hadn't been able to sleep properly.

Too tired to think any more, Georgina slipped into bed and watched, through heavy eyelids, as Mrs Crabtree hung up her wedding dress and veil. When the cook quietly drew the curtains, she was already half asleep.

Agnes entered the house in a towering temper. For two pins she would have swept the food from the dining-table with the flat of her hand. Summoning Mrs Crabtree, she told her to clear everything away, not stopping to consider that those arriving back from the church might feel in need of sustenance. She merely saw the table with its vast collation of food that would never be eaten by the Bickleys and their entourage of wedding guests, as an affront to her pride.

'Very well, madam. Am I to take it, then, that you will make other arrangements for luncheon?' Mrs Crabtree enquired calmly.

Incensed by the woman's air of disapproval, 'You may take it that I expect my orders to be carried out at once! When I have decided what to do about luncheon, I will let you know. Now you may send Bridget to Miss Georgina's room and tell her that I wish to see her in the study within the next five minutes. Is that clear?' Turning to face her husband, 'You, too, Owen!'

Closing the study door firmly behind her, 'Now, Owen, I want the truth! What did you say to Georgina to prevent her marrying Harold Bickley?'

Deeply resentful of his wife's hectoring tone of voice, the implication that he was responsible for the present crisis, 'There was nothing I needed to say to her,' he responded sharply. 'The girl made up her own mind. Quite rightly, in my opinion.'

Taken aback, 'You dare to stand there and tell me . . . My God, Owen! You do realize what this means? Georgina's outrageous behaviour has made fools of us, enemies of the Bickleys. Did you see the way Mary looked at me?'

'Oh come now, Agnes, keep a sense of proportion. The Bickleys have been friends of ours too long for one storm in a teacup to make any difference to that friendship. Georgina knew all along that she wasn't in love with Harold. If you hadn't pushed her so hard, none of this would have happened.'

Feeling that she was being slowly strangled by the *lavallière* of pearls at her throat, her face suffused a dull red, '*Love,*' Agnes uttered contemptuously. 'You and your high-flown ideas on *love*! Georgina would have come to love Harold in time, when the children began to arrive, and think what it would have meant to the future of the mills to have an up-and-coming generation of mixed Brett-Forsyth and Bickley blood to carry on when we are dead and gone, to support Thomas in the years to come. That is why I wanted Georgina to marry Harold Bickley, to carry on a tradition, to make certain of the future. Now, thanks to the whim of one stupid girl, everything I worked so hard to achieve has been lost, squandered, thrown away!'

'So you were prepared to sacrifice our daughter's happiness for the sake of some business arrangement in years to come? My God, Agnes, what kind of a mother are you?' Deeply disturbed by his wife's revelation, Owen turned away in disgust.

At that moment, Bridget Donovan knocked at the door and entered the room. 'I'm sorry, Madam,' she said nervously, 'but Miss Georgina's fast asleep, and I hadn't the heart to disturb her.'

'*Asleep!* Well, I'll soon see about *that*.'

Sweeping past her own and her husband's relations standing uncertainly in the hall, Agnes trod heavily upstairs to her daughter's bedroom.

About to begin clearing the dining-table, Daisy Crabtree stood back in dismay as Thomas Brett-Forsyth, a heavily built youth of fifteen, thick-lipped, with an insatiable appetite, preceded his cousins into the room to attack the food.

'*Master Thomas!*' This was the last straw. 'Madam gave me clear instructions to clear the table at once,' Mrs Crabtree protested.

'Oh, stuff and nonsense,' Thomas said airily, knowing he could twist his mother round his little finger if necessary. 'We're hungry.' He added, impertinently, 'In any case, that's what we're doing, isn't it? Clearing the table?' Winking at his cousins, 'Go away, Mrs Crabtree. You may clear what's left of the grub later, when we've finished eating.'

She returned to her kitchen, trembling with rage. Things had come to a pretty pass, Mrs Crabtree thought, for a woman of her age and experience to have her authority flouted by a fifteen-year-old boy. The sooner she handed in her notice, the better. She had felt inclined to do so earlier in the day when madam had barged into the kitchen to harp on about the breakfast. Indeed, there had been many occasions during the past year when she had felt inclined to leave Elmhurst, and she would have done so had it not been for Mr Brett-Forsyth and Miss Georgina. But now things had gone too far.

The past year had been well nigh unbearable, with the housework to oversee as well as the cooking, with never a word of thanks from the mistress. Well, one could stay in a job too long. Moreover, she had not been engaged as a housekeeper. The extra duties had been piled on her when the *bona fide* housekeeper had departed twelve months ago, on the understanding that a new housekeeper would be appointed in due course. But Mrs Brett-Forsyth had not even bothered to advertise for a new housekeeper, Daisy thought bitterly. A case of the 'willing horse'.

Finding another job held no terrors for Mrs Crabtree, who knew her worth. When she had worked her month's notice she would pack her trunk and return to London, to stay with her sister until she had found something more suitable. She was fed up with the West Riding in any case, would never have come here in the first place had she not married a Yorkshireman. But her husband had been dead and buried these many years past, and she would be glad to go back to her roots. Perhaps she would find a job as cook with a London family – at one of those posh houses in Eaton Square.

'I'm sorry, Mother,' Georgina said wearily, 'I did try to tell you how I felt about getting married, but you wouldn't listen.'

'That's right, blame me! And sit up when I'm talking to you. Why you came to bed in the first place is a mystery to me. How could you think of sleeping at a time like this?' Agnes gave full vent to her feelings. 'Well, you had better get up at once, go to Merlewood, see the Bickleys and set this matter straight. Tell them you were ill, temporarily deranged. Tell them anything you like, but make certain they understand that I had no part in this shameful affair.'

Looking up at her mother, the truth flooded in on Georgina. 'But you *did*! You planned the whole thing. You even told Harold my ring size. Perhaps you even went with him to choose it!'

'How dare you speak to me like that!' But the barb had gone home. While Agnes had not been with Harold to choose the ring, she *had* suggested a diamond cluster.

'I'm sorry, I didn't mean to be rude, and I will go to Merlewood if you like. I owe Harold an apology. Besides, I must give him his ring back.'

'And that will salve your conscience, I suppose? But the matter doesn't end there. What about the wedding presents, the house, the honeymoon?'

'Don't worry about the presents, I'll return them myself. As for the house, Harold will sell it at a profit once the repairs are done.' Thank God, she thought, that she would never have to live there – all those sunless rooms and potted brawn fireplaces. She added, 'One of these days Harry will find a girl to suit him as I never could. When that happens he will thank his lucky stars that I gave him his freedom.'

'Very well Georgina, if that is your attitude, I wash my hands of the whole sorry affair. But mark my words, you'll live to regret what you've done.'

'No, Mother, I don't think so.'

'Oh, *you* don't think so. Well I do! You are a selfish, ungrateful girl, in my opinion.' Giving up the battle of wills, Agnes swept out of the room, along the landing and down the stairs to the dining-room where, to her horror, she discovered members of her own family, and Owen's, making inroads on the wedding buffet which she had specifically ordered Mrs Crabtree to clear away.

The sight of guests beneath her roof tucking into the repast without a by your leave, deeply shocked Agnes, who had expected to find them sitting in the drawing-room, as subdued as mourners at a funeral, out of respect for her feelings.

Sweeping into the kitchen to confront Mrs Crabtree, trembling with rage, 'So, you took it upon yourself to disobey my orders?' Agnes said hoarsely. 'Very well then, you may pack your belongings and leave this house the first thing tomorrow morning!'

'That, Mrs Brett-Forsyth, will be my pleasure entirely.' Unharnessing her pinafore, 'I was about to hand in my notice in any case. But I'll not wait until tomorrow morning. I'll leave today, by the three o'clock train from Bradford Station.'

'But you can't go now. There's luncheon to see to. Dinner to cook.'

'Strikes me that lot in yonder won't be needing anything more to eat when they've finished stuffing themselves,' Mrs Crabtree observed coolly, 'and *I'm* not to blame for that. It's a pity, madam, that you haven't taught that son of yours how to behave properly. But then, you can't make a silk purse from a sow's ear. As for dinner, as I see it, you have two choices. Either let your guests finish what they've started, or cook the dinner yourself!'

Head held high, Mrs Crabtree walked out of the room. Seldom, if ever, had she felt happier, except that she would miss her fellow workers, the master and Miss Georgina.

Should she say goodbye to the girl? No, better not, Daisy decided. The poor child had enough to contend with at the moment, without an emotional farewell from an old and trusted servant. She would leave her a note with her London address.

Georgina walked to Merlewood alone, at dusk, past the church and the lilac trees in bloom, seeing, as a dark blur, the woods where Merlin had once sought shelter. Not that she believed a word of that old legend, but she wanted to – desperately needed to believe in something beyond her present unhappy state – that miracles did happen. But why should she doubt it? Had not that sparrow, fluttering down to the altar in time to prevent her making the mistake of her life, been a small miracle? But she scarcely thought that the Bickleys would understand if she told them that she had turned her back on Harold because of a sparrow.

Approaching the house, her courage almost failed her. The drawing-room lights were on, which meant that the family had finished dinner and were most probably gathered round the fire, discussing the events of the day.

The manservant who answered her ring stared down at her, obviously taken aback by her appearance. 'Miss Georgina,' he said lamely.

'I'd like to speak to Mr Harold.' Looking past the servant, she saw Josie on the landing, her face grim and unsmiling.

'All right, Johnson,' Josie said, 'I'll deal with this.'

When the servant had hurried away, 'I wonder you had the nerve to come here, Georgina,' Josie said coldly. 'You can take it from me that Harold does not wish to speak to you – ever again.'

'I'd rather hear that from him, if you don't mind. After all, what happened today concerns us, no-one else.'

'You're a fool if you think that.' Josie came downstairs to face Georgina. 'Mother is in a state of shock. The doctor had to be sent for. My father is seriously worried about her, so are we all. If you had no intention of marrying my brother, why did you become engaged to him in the first place? How do you imagine *he* feels? A broken engagement would have been better than leaving him at the altar.' Her eyes flashed contempt. 'But then, you always did have a flair for the dramatic. Wanting to be different.

'During the war,' Josie scoffed, 'you couldn't be content with helping at the hospital. Oh no, you had to throw in your lot with the working class. I suppose you thought the mill workers would admire you. The wonder is that you didn't go to work in clogs and a shawl!' Her voice had risen alarmingly.

'What on earth's going on?' The drawing-room door opened and Harold walked out. 'You might keep your voice down, Josie, with Mother upstairs in bed – Oh it's you Georgina. Well, what do *you* want?'

'To talk to you, in private.'

'I should scarcely have thought that necessary,' he said icily, 'since you made your feelings for me perfectly plain in public.'

Georgina knew that she deserved his condemnation, but she had not realized how deeply it would hurt. 'Please, Harry,' she said in a low voice, 'we must talk sooner or later.'

'Oh very well then. We'd better go into the study.' Turning, he led the way to a room across the hall. Closing the door, he walked to the fireplace and stood with his back to it, not inviting her to sit down, an indication that he intended to keep the interview as short as possible, making her feel like a servant about to be dismissed for stealing.

'Perhaps I shouldn't have come,' she conceded, 'but I wanted to set things straight between us, and to give you this.' She handed him the morocco box containing her engagement ring, which he received in stony silence and stuffed into the pocket of his dinner jacket.

Unnerved by his dismissive attitude, the hostile expression on his handsome young face, Georgina considered leaving unspoken her regret that she had not felt able to go through with the wedding ceremony. But she must say what she had come to say, whether or not he chose to listen.

'Harold,' she began haltingly, 'I shall not attempt to make excuses for my bad behaviour. I know I behaved badly, and that is my punishment – knowing that I have made you, and a lot of other people, unhappy. Such was not my intention. You must believe that. I meant to go through with the wedding. Then, at the last moment—'

'At the last moment – *what*?' Taking a step forward, Harold gripped her by the shoulders, feeling that he would like to shake, until her teeth rattled, this red-haired girl who had made a fool of him in front of a church full of people.

'I had the sense to realize that you are no more in love with me than I am with you. Now would you mind letting me go?' A memory arose of a fair-haired boy and a red-haired girl struggling on the beach at Scarborough, what seemed like a million light years ago, her threat to kick him on the shins if he continued to bully her. And this, perhaps, was the crux of the matter, Georgina thought as he relaxed his grip on her shoulders, that she could not have faced a lifetime married to a man whose bullying instincts would have dominated her every thought and action.

Allowing his hands to fall to his sides, 'That's all very well,' he said sullenly, 'but there are more important things than love of the kind you mean – the flowery, romantic stuff. Ours would have been a great match so far as the mills are concerned. Besides, I'd have shown you a good time in Paris. Huh, we might have been on our way there now, if you hadn't been so stupid. What a waste of money!'

Money. Was that all that mattered to Harold? Knowing she was wasting her time, turning away, laying her hand on the doorknob, 'I came here to say I'm sorry, to ask your forgiveness in the hope that we might at least remain friends. I see now that is impossible.' She opened the door. 'Don't worry Harold, I am quite prepared to pay the penalty of my bad behaviour. As soon as I've decided where to go, what to do, I'll be leaving Elmhurst. When I'm gone, perhaps my parents and yours will be able to forget about – all this; become friends once more. I sincerely hope so.' Her voice catching on a sob, 'Goodbye, Harry.'

'And so you see, Father, that I must go away, for the time being at least?'

41

Understanding his daughter's need to escape, Owen said heavily, 'Yes, I suppose that you must,' wondering how he would be able to live without her. 'But where will you go? What will you do?'

'I'd like to go to Scarborough,' Georgina said thoughtfully, remembering her childhood days, the thrill of the tide washing in on the shore, the crying of the seagulls overhead, the curious amalgam of woods, grass and seashore, the Italian Gardens, the intermingled fragrance of roses and seaweed, the tall, majestic buildings on the South Cliff, the ancient ruins of a Norman fort on the Castle Hill. 'I can type and take shorthand, so I'm certain to find some kind of job.'

'My dear child, that won't be necessary. I will make you an allowance.' Owen could scarcely bear the thought of his daughter going to work in some strange office far away from home, but Georgina shook her head. 'No Father. Thank you, but I would rather earn my own living.'

Blaming himself for his ineptitude, impatient with his lack of initiative, 'I should have gone with you to Merlewood this evening,' he said, 'talked to Jack and Mary Bickley, made them understand that what happened today was inevitable.'

'No Father, the breach will heal quicker when I'm out of the way. Please don't worry about me. I shall look upon it as an adventure.'

How young, bright and determined she was, Owen thought, and how lovely. Despite his wife's condemnation of Georgina as 'not at all a pretty girl', he had always seen her as beautiful, reminiscent of the pre-Raphaelite painting of King Cophetua's Beggar Maid. Fashions in female form and face changed and altered with time, but Georgina's bone structure, tender mouth, her straight, finely chiselled nose, fearless eyes, and the proud lift of her head, would outlast time and fashion. Moreover, her face seemed illuminated from within.

They were talking together in Owen's study, Georgina's favourite room, with its book-lined walls, deep red velvet curtains, Persian carpet, and the comfortable wing-chairs which had once belonged to her great grandfather, Thomas Brett-Forsyth. His portrait hung over the fireplace – a fierce-looking old gentleman with a mane of white hair – except that, if one looked closely enough at the painting, one discerned a glint of humour in those piercing, grey-green eyes of his.

How she would miss this room, and her father, when she left home; but when she was gone, perhaps her parents and the Bickleys might pick up the threads of their friendship.

Owen went down to the study at midnight, to smoke a pipe of tobacco. What had gone wrong with his life, he wondered, looking up at the portrait of his grandfather who had founded the Brett-Forsyth mill, and what would happen to it when he was dead and gone? Would it continue to flourish with Thomas at the helm? He thought not. There was a streak of laziness in his son, an air of corruptness about him that worried Owen. Was he an unnatural father to dislike his own son? But then, was Agnes a natural mother to have betrayed her own daughter?

In the solitude of his study Owen wrestled with his conscience as he had so often done before. One thought emerged sharp and clear: he must help Georgina. Who did he know in Scarborough who might give the girl a job of work to do? Ah yes, of course, his old friend Cecil Colebrook, a solicitor by profession, who had his offices in St Nicholas Street. Not that they had been in close contact recently, but they had continued their habit of exchanging Christmas cards, even during the war years.

Knocking out his pipe, Owen crossed over to his desk, drew forth a sheet of paper and began writing: 'Dear Cecil, I have a favour to ask of you, concerning my daughter Georgina . . .'

'Owen! What on earth are you doing down here at this time of night?' Agnes swept into the room in dressing-gown and slippers. 'Have you taken leave of your senses?'

Laying down his pipe, thoughtfully regarding his wife,

43

'No, Agnes,' he said calmly, 'but I think it likely that you have done so.'

'Would you care to explain that remark?' Her chins quivered.

'Certainly, my dear. As if we had not enough trouble on our hands, was it sensible of you to dismiss Mrs Crabtree?'

'Nonsense,' Agnes uttered contemptuously, 'servants are ten a penny.'

'And are daughters also ten a penny?' Owen rose to his feet to confront his wife. 'My fear is that, having left home, Georgina may never come back to us. I had rather lose the Bickleys' friendship than my own daughter.'

'Stuff and nonsense! Georgina will come back, never fear. She knows where she's well off. As for the Bickleys, if their friendship means nothing to you, it does to me – although I shall make no move towards them until Mary has apologized for the way she looked through me at the church, as if I were to blame. I shall not forget *that* in a hurry! As for Georgina, it will do her good to realize there's a price to be paid for riding roughshod over people's feelings.'

Repelled by the sight of his wife standing there in her armour-plating of self-righteous indignation, her uncorseted body bulging beneath the padded dressing-gown she had on, knowing that he no longer loved her and thinking of Mary Bickley, he said, 'And have you stopped to consider the price you might have to pay for riding roughshod over Georgina and Mrs Crabtree?'

He turned away in disgust, returning to his desk. 'And now I have an important letter to write. When I have done so, I shall go to bed in the blue guest room, where I intend to sleep from now on.'

Agnes' mouth sagged open, then closed like a trap. 'I forbid you to do any such thing!' she said explosively. 'Well, if this is your idea of revenge, you are more despicable than I thought. Moreover, I refuse to be made a laughing-stock in my own home. What will the servants think?'

But she knew, even as she spoke, that Owen meant what he said, that he really intended to sleep in a guest room from now on, that she had lost her power to intimidate her normally compliant husband when, regarding her coolly, he said, 'I couldn't give a damn what the servants think. Now go back to bed and leave me in peace.'

Chapter Three

'My name's Poppy Hewitt. What's yours?'

The girl asking the question was short in stature, with dark hair, fashionably frizzed at the front, wide-awake brown eyes, full red lips, a tip-tilted nose and an air of naughtiness about her, as if she knew all about the world and its wicked ways.

'My name's Brett. Georgina Brett.'

As a matter of expedience, Georgina had decided to shorten her surname. Agnes had thrown up her hands in horror at the thought of a Brett-Forsyth working in a common-or-garden solicitor's office. What would people think? 'And why Scarborough?' she'd protested. 'Why not London, Liverpool or Nottingham, where our name is not so well known?'

'I think I'll be happy in Scarborough,' Georgina replied, adding to her mother's sense of outrage that being happy had even crossed her mind – as if she had no right to be happy ever again after what she had done to Harold Bickley. Had she declared her intention of going to Mongolia as a missionary, it would not have been right for Agnes either, in her present frenetic state of mind.

'Are you used to office work?' Poppy enquired, thinking that this new girl did not look much like an office worker, despite her plain black skirt and starched white blouse.

'Oh yes, I worked at a mill in the West Riding as a secretary during the war, typewriting, taking dictation – the usual kind of thing.'

'So what made you leave?'

'Personal reasons.' Georgina smiled, wanting to appear friendly, yet unwilling to recount the story of her life.

'In other words, why don't I mind my own business?'

They were standing in a long, pleasant room with

high windows overlooking St Nicholas Street, one of Scarborough's busiest thoroughfares, a street Georgina had often walked along with the Bickley children, long before the war, the sun warm on their faces, agog with excitement, catching the scent of salt air and seaweed as they skipped down the zig-zagging cliff paths to the sands.

Breaking Georgina's train of thought, Poppy asked, 'Have you ever been to Scarborough before?'

'Yes, quite often as a child.'

'Where are you lodging?' Curiosity may have 'killed the cat', but Poppy was not feline. She simply wanted to know more about this new girl, with her air of reticence and her startlingly red hair scragged back from her face and tied with a black velvet bow.

'At Fernlea. Which is my desk, by the way?'

'Oh, this one next to mine,' Poppy said vaguely, with a wave of her hand. 'Fernlea? Where's that?'

'On the South Cliff, overlooking St Martin's Church.' Georgina uncovered the Remington typewriter on her desk.

Poppy's eyes opened wide in surprise. 'The South Cliff? But that's where the "nobs" live!'

Mistake Number One, Georgina thought, catching the note of reproof in Poppy's voice. 'I'm not exactly *living* there,' she said desperately, 'it's just that friends of mine knew the landlady before the war, and I didn't know where else to go.' Drawing the fire away from herself, she asked, 'What about *you*, Poppy? Where do you live?'

'Down Newborough,' Poppy said, pulling a face, 'in a basement room with cockroaches. Ugh! Nasty little brutes. But my landlady's not a bad old stick. She doesn't mind me staying out late on Saturday nights, and I had a kipper for breakfast this morning. Ain't life grand?' She added brightly, 'I could put in a word for you, if you like. The room next to mine's coming vacant next week.'

'Thank you, Poppy.' In for a penny, in for a pound, Georgina thought. Having thrown in her lot with the 'working class', she might just as well live as they did. She was not proud. 'I'll leave it to you, then, to have a word with your landlady.'

47

Curiously drawn to her new workmate, Poppy said confidentially, 'A word of warning: Mr Colebrook's a good sort, Mr Mainwaring isn't bad if you get the right side of him, but watch out for Mr Petch. He'll make a pass at you if you're not careful. And him a married man with four children!'

'Thanks, Poppy. I'll remember.'

The door opened at that moment to admit Patience, the office junior – a plain, fat, fifteen-year-old girl with blocked sinuses, and Jimmy, the messenger boy, a lanky sixteen-year-old youth with acne who, sent out on the simplest errand, would remain absent for as long as possible.

'One of these days, you'll get here after Mr Colebrook, then you'll find yourselves in trouble,' Poppy reprimanded them severely. 'And don't think I'll stick up for you, because I won't. This is Miss Brett, by the way, the new shorthand typist.'

'Gosh,' Jimmy said admiringly, 'you can blot my copy-book any time you feel like it.'

'Don't be so cheeky. Oh, heck! Here comes Mr Colebrook now. Sit down, all of you, and try to look busy.' She added, *sotto voce*, to Georgina, 'First he'll hang up his hat and walking-stick in the outer office, then he'll go through to his office and ring his bell, wanting to see you, I dare say. But you needn't worry, he won't bite you.' She started counting, 'Five, four, three, two, one . . .' At the sound of the bell Poppy giggled, rose to her feet and scooted towards Mr Colebrook's inner sanctum. Emerging seconds later, 'I told you so,' she said breathlessly, 'it's you he wants to see.'

Cecil Colebrook, a genial, white-haired man, rose to his feet as Georgina entered his office. 'So you are Owen's daughter,' he said warmly. 'I can see the resemblance. But I understand that you wish to be known as Miss Brett. May I ask why?'

Standing erectly, her hands folded on her skirt, 'I'd rather not trade on the family name, nor your long-standing friendship with my father, if you don't mind,' Georgina said quietly, unwilling to admit that her mother had jibbed at the thought of a daughter of hers working in a common-or-garden solicitor's office. In any case, there was nothing in the least common-or-garden about her employer's office, she decided, with its vast mahogany desk, leather chairs, and the impressive array of well-thumbed law books, arranged on the floor to ceiling shelves.

'Very commendable.' The lawyer's eyes twinkled. 'Your father wrote me that you had been his secretary during the war. Tell me, were you a good secretary?'

'My father seemed to think so, but he may have been biased.'

'Quite so.' Colebrook chuckled. 'Well, we shall see. Just remember that accuracy is more important than speed when it comes to typewriting legal documents.'

'Thank you Mr Colebrook. I'll remember.'

'Where are you staying, by the way?' Colebrook recalled that the last time he had seen this girl she could not have been more than eight years old, a scrap of a red-haired child clinging to her father's hand after Sunday morning service at St Martin's Church, when the Brett-Forsyths and the Bickleys were on holiday in Scarborough in the summer of – 1908? Was it really as long ago as that?

'With Mrs Woodbridge at Fernlea, for the time being, until I find somewhere closer to the office. Miss Hewitt's landlady may soon have a vacancy.'

Colebrook frowned, worried at the thought of a girl of Georgina's upbringing forsaking Fernlea for some dubious lodging house in a poor part of town. 'Would that be entirely wise, my dear? I hardly think that your parents would approve.'

Clasping her hands together more tightly, 'Thank you for your concern, sir, but I came to Scarborough with the intention of making my own way from now on. I can't afford to put up a social barrier between myself and my fellow workers. Life would be impossible for me if I did that.'

'I see.' Colebrook sighed, then smiled, liking the girl's honesty and lack of snobbishness. 'Very well, my dear, you must do as you think best; but please remember that I am your friend if ever you should need help or advice.'

'That's extremely kind of you, sir. And – thank you for giving me this job. I'll do my best to please you.'

'Well, what did he say to you?' Poppy asked, eaten up with curiosity. 'I thought you'd taken up residence in there!'

'Oh, he just emphasized the importance of accuracy rather than speed, and wanted to know where I'm staying.' Georgina summarized her conversation with Mr Colebrook as succinctly as possible. Sitting down at her desk, 'What would you like me to do first?'

'Here. Best make a start on these.' Poppy handed Georgina a sheaf of foolscap paper with lists of names and addresses.

'What are they?'

'Oh, just something to do with the electoral roll. Mr Colebrook's standing for Parliament at the next election.' Poppy said airily. 'And where do you think you're off to, Jimmy my lad?'

'To the post office,' Jimmy said jauntily, 'with a couple of letters that got missed out of last night's post-bag.'

'All right, then. But if you're not back in ten minutes, you'll be in trouble. Serious trouble.'

'Shall I buy you a penny bun on my way back?' the lad asked cheekily. 'You know, one of them you like, with pink icing on top?'

'I'll give you a penny bun!' Poppy called after him as he went down the stairs, whistling. 'Honestly, that boy gets worse every day. But I can't help feeling sorry for him. His father was killed in the war.'

Georgina's heart warmed towards Poppy who, despite living in a cockroach-infested basement, thought life grand because she had been given a kipper for breakfast, and cared deeply about her fellow human beings.

A few minutes later Mr Mainwaring and Mr Petch entered the office. Glancing up from her typewriter, Georgina saw that Mr Mainwaring was very tall, with a fringe of mouse-coloured hair straggling about the dome of his otherwise bald head, wearing pince-nez spectacles which had cut red furrows into the bridge of his nose. His drooping suit of clothes sported a wilting flower on the left lapel of his pin-striped jacket.

Petch, on the other hand, resembled a lion, all compact muscle and sinew, so that one could fairly discern the rippling biceps beneath the material of his lightweight brown suit. Tawny hair brushed back from his forehead, and a bristling moustache, emphasized his resemblance to the king of beasts. Georgina disliked him on sight. There was something predatory about him which repelled her, a certain boldness in his glance which made her feel that he was mentally undressing her as he paused near her desk to exert his charm on her.

'Ah, you must be Miss Merrill's replacement,' he said smoothly. 'Miss – Brett. Am I right?'

'Yes, sir.' Georgina shuddered slightly.

'Very good. I'll send for you later, to take my dictation.'

'He's taken a fancy to you,' Poppy said, when Petch had departed, 'the randy old goat! God, he makes me sick, he really does. Just you watch him, that's all.'

Georgina awaited miserably the flashing light on the indicator board that would summon her through to Petch's office. When the summons came, picking up her pad and pencil, and taking a few deep breaths, she entered the 'lion's den'. She envied young Patience, whose duties included nothing more demanding than sharpening pencils, making tea, and showing clients to the various offices, or the waiting-room, depending on the passage of time – some clients being more long-winded than others.

'Sit down, Miss Brett.' Leaning back in his leather chair behind a vast expanse of desk, Petch noticed the way Georgina moved – as lightly and elegantly as a ballet-dancer.

Fingering his moustache, observing her closely through narrowed eyelids, he experienced a familiar movement in the region of his crotch, the usual manifestation of manhood that the sight of a beautiful girl evoked in a male of his calibre. Not that this glorious creature made the most of herself by any means, he considered, imagining that shining mass of auburn hair floating loosely about her naked shoulders.

'I'm ready when you are, Mr Petch,' Georgina said coolly, realizing too late the implication of her words, unable to prevent a hot tide of colour rushing to her cheeks. How could she have been so stupid? Petch, she knew, had read a *double entendre* meaning into her innocent remark. 'To take your dictation, I mean.'

'But of course,' Petch smiled, aware of her discomfort, convinced that before very long he would be able to persuade her to have dinner with him, if he played his cards carefully. He knew, from long experience of the opposite sex and their foibles, that he must not rush his fences with this particular girl if he hoped to get her into bed with him, which he intended to do in the fullness of time. In the meanwhile, what pleasure he would derive from the chase, what satisfaction from her ultimate submission.

Flicking over a page of her notebook, Georgina thought that if Mr Petch got up from his chair and took so much as a step towards her, she would kick him hard on the shins, as she had once attempted to kick Harold Bickley.

'Well, how did you get on with old Petch?' Poppy enquired breathlessly when Georgina emerged from his office. 'Did he try to pinch your bottom?'

'No. I rather think that Mr Petch has other, more involved plans for me than that,' Georgina said, unable to control a sudden upsurge of laughter. 'Oh, Poppy, do you know what I said to him?'

'No. What?'

'I'm ready when you are.'

'You *never*!' Poppy's eyes opened even wider. 'Gina, that's priceless. It's a wonder you came out of that office in one piece!'

'What did you call me?'

Poppy wrinkled her forehead. 'Gina. Why? Do you mind?'

'No. It's just that no-one has ever called me that before.

I rather like it.' Gina Brett, she thought, feeling like an entirely different person.

The morning passed quickly for Georgina, in her strange new surroundings. This was a busy office, with clients coming and going – mainly well-dressed men and women arriving by motor car or carriage, to consult one of the partners on matters pertaining to property, wills and so forth.

The chambers of Colebrook, Mainwaring and Petch occupied the whole of the building above a branch of Woodall and Hebden's Bank. The space occupied by Poppy, Georgina and Patience was central to the partners' offices. Jimmy, on the other hand, occupied a cubby-hole along a draughty passage leading to a series of back rooms where the files, important documents and deed-boxes were kept under lock and key. In this cubby-hole he dealt with the outgoing post, took furtive puffs at forbidden cigarettes and read penny dreadfuls avidly. There was also a kitchen with a gas-ring, a kettle, and cups and saucers, where Jimmy and Patience ate their lunch-time sandwiches at 12 o'clock, an hour before Colebrook, Mainwaring and Petch went out to lunch at the Royal Hotel to partake of roast beef and Yorkshire pudding, roast lamb and mint sauce, or whatever.

'Now it's our turn,' Poppy told Georgina, when the trio had departed. 'Come on! Let's eat our sandwiches on the sea-front!'

'Sandwiches? I haven't brought any sandwiches,' Georgina admitted.

'Never mind. You can share mine.' She hurried through to the cloakroom with Georgina in tow, pinning on a brown velvet tam-o-shanter in front of a cracked mirror. 'They're only bloater-paste, and the bread's like doorsteps, but what won't fatten will fill.'

How sweet and clean the fresh air felt on her face, Georgina thought as she and Poppy hurried along St Nicholas Street towards the sea-front. How good it felt to be alive and young on this glorious day in May, with the sea and the sky so blue, and the Corporation workmen busily preparing the town for the coming holiday season – the first since the outbreak of the 1914–18 war – when the front had been closed to holidaymakers: the whole of Eastborough and the foreshore barricaded with coils of barbed wire. Not that those feeble barricades had proved the slightest use when, in the winter of 1914, the German warships *Von der Tann* and *Derrflinger*, had bombarded Scarborough from the sea, an event which had shocked an entire nation to an awareness of what enemy action really meant.

Sitting beside Poppy, looking out to sea, Georgina imagined those German warships opening fire on a sleeping town in the early hours of a December morning; imagined the flashes of gun-fire, the populace racing for cover; the dead and the dying . . . But how different everything looked now, with the Will Catlin building adorned with its post-war crop of bunting fluttering in the breeze of a perfect early summer afternoon.

'Here, have a sandwich,' Poppy invited, opening a brown paper bag to reveal several doorsteps of bread and margarine so thinly spread with bloater-paste that the brown thread of colour was scarcely discernible between the roughly cut chunks of bread. But, digging her teeth into one of Poppy's sandwiches, Georgina felt that she had never tasted anything so good before.

'What are you going to do tonight?' Poppy asked.

'I hadn't thought about it. Go to bed early, I expect, with a good book.'

'Read, you mean? What a waste of time.' The pleasure of reading any kind of book lay beyond Poppy's power of comprehension. 'Why don't you take a walk along the Foreshore? That's what I'll be doing with my gentleman friend.' She added archly, 'He's an artist, you know, and very well educated.'

'How interesting. What's his medium?'

'Eh? He's an artist, not a clairvoyant.'

'I meant does he paint in oils or watercolours?'

'Oh, anything,' Poppy said expansively, proud that a poorly educated girl like herself had an artist for a friend.

Not that she knew what he was on about most of the time, he used such high faluting words. 'I'll introduce you, if you like. His studio's just across the way from the office, near the Royal Hotel; it's an attic really, with a big glass skylight.'

'What kind of pictures does he paint?' Georgina asked.

'Mainly what he calls seascapes. Pictures of the sea, you know? He sits on the end of the pier in all weathers; doesn't seem to feel the cold. But then he's got plenty of meat on his bones.' Poppy giggled self-consciously. 'Can't think what I see in him really. He's nearly old enough to be my father, and he's not what you'd call good looking. It's just that I've never known anyone like him before.'

'What's his name? Perhaps I've heard of him before?'

'His name's Rab. Don't ask me his last name 'cos he's never told me. To be honest, I don't know where he came from or anything else about him. He won't talk about his past. And the way he dresses! You can tell he's an artist by looking at him. And that studio of his is like a padden-ken.'

'How did you come to meet him?'

Standing up to brush crumbs from her skirt, an indication that it was time they were getting back to work, Poppy replied, 'Oh, the girl you replaced, Connie Merrill, introduced us. She took me up to his studio one Saturday afternoon.' Poppy's colour heightened suddenly. 'He sent her across to the cake shop to buy cream buns for our tea. The minute she'd gone, he kissed me. I knew he would. I wanted him to.' Mistily, 'I've never been kissed like it before.' Settling her hat, 'I expect you'll think I'm awful!' She added primly, as they began the stiff climb up the zigzagging paths to St Nicholas Square, 'But he didn't care for Connie all that much anyway.'

Owen had driven Georgina to Scarborough the day before, thankfully unaccompanied by Agnes. The coolness of her mother's goodbye had seemed like a slap in the face to Georgina. Nevertheless, as the journey progressed, she felt grateful that she and Owen could spend a little time together before the final separation, without Agnes' overwhelming and disapproving presence in the motor-car.

Upon their arrival at Fernlea, Mrs Woodbridge, an imposingly tall woman with iron-grey hair dressed Pompadour-style, wearing a black ankle-length skirt and a matching bombazine blouse with a high-boned collar, Whitby jet earrings and a jet mourning brooch mounted with a likeness of her dear, departed husband, accorded Owen and Georgina the accolade of afternoon tea in her private sitting-room. It was an overfurnished apartment, cluttered with Goss china ornaments, horsehair sofas and armchairs; occasional tables and what-nots lumbered with shell-framed family photographs, and a depressing screen pasted with cut-out pictures depicting, among countless others, the Death of Nelson, the faithful Welsh hound Bethgelert being stabbed to death, Queen Victoria on her deathbed, Gordon of Khartoum stalwartly facing his executioners, and a blind beggar-girl staring sightlessly at a rainbow.

Georgina thought, at first, that the grey parrot perched near the lace-curtained bay window was stuffed, until the maid-of-all-work brought in the tea-things. These included a plate of mustard-and-cress sandwiches, scones and a chocolate cake. The bird suddenly uttered a piercing shriek, causing her to slop her tea into the violet-patterned saucer, a social gaffe which she felt her prudish landlady would not easily forgive.

At that moment Georgina resolved that she would not stay at Fernlea a minute longer than necessary.

When Owen had driven away, she had gone upstairs to her room to shed tears of loneliness, of homesickness, despite her smiling assurance to her father that she was happy; looking forward to starting work the next day.

Quickly drying her tears when the dinner-gong sounded, she had hurried downstairs to the dining-room, to sit alone at a window table, feeling herself far distanced from her fellow boarders. These were an elderly ex-army Colonel and his wife, an ageing spinster intent on guzzling her soup before making inroads on the roast beef and Yorkshire pudding, and another elderly gentleman, so deaf that the waitress was obliged to shout into his ear-trumpet to make herself heard.

Georgina made her way back to Fernlea, her first day's work at Colebrook, Mainwaring and Petch behind her. Standing near the window of her room, she went over in her mind her meeting with Poppy Hewitt, the partners, Patience and Jimmy. She had possibly been reckless to consent to Poppy's 'putting in a word' for her with her landlady, with a view to moving to a cockroach-infested basement in a poorer part of town where, presumably, she would be obliged to exist on a diet of kippers and bloater-paste sandwiches.

Strangely, she did not care tuppence how inferior her future lodgings might be, as long as she felt free to live her own life from now on.

It occurred to her that Georgina Brett-Forsyth seemed like a shadow of her former self, that Georgie Bickley had ceased to exist from the moment she had left Harold standing at the altar . . . On the other hand, Gina Brett might just stand a chance of survival in a future which seemed to lie before her as brightly challenging as the Golden Road to Samarkand.

Chapter Four

'Mrs Potts – she's my landlady – said you could look at the room this afternoon,' Poppy told Gina. 'We can go when the office closes, if you like.'

This was Saturday morning. It had been a pleasant week on the whole. The warm, sunny weather had continued, and the two girls had been to the sea-front every day to eat their sandwiches. Gina had found the work interesting, the coming-and-going of the clients fascinating to watch. Now she was looking forward to the weekend and moving her belongings into the room next to Poppy's – when she had made the necessary arrangements. The only fly in the ointment was going to be telling the formidable Mrs Woodbridge that she was leaving Fernlea.

At one o'clock the girls walked along St Nicholas Street and turned right into Newborough; this was a continuation of the main street, with no demarcation line since the old Newborough Bar had been demolished. And yet a world of difference lay between the elegant Westborough with its fashionable shops, leafy squares and privately-owned villas, and Newborough with its bustling street markets, pubs and lodging houses.

If streets were people, Gina thought, Westborough would be a discreet, well-mannered elderly lady, Newborough a fun-loving whore, raucous, coarse, and down-to-earth. The old Bar may have been demolished, but the social barrier still existed.

'Well, this is it!' Poppy sounded apologetic.

Looking up at the house, Gina saw that the windows were reasonably clean and the steps to the front door had been sandstoned. Other steps, she noticed, led down to a basement area where the dustbins were kept. A ginger cat was sitting on the top step, sunning itself, oblivious to the cries of the stallholders shouting their wares, the laughter and music issuing from the open doors of a public house further down the street.

'Come inside,' Poppy said eagerly, 'I'll tell Mrs Potts you're here. An' don't worry too much about the noise – it's only twice a week, on market days.'

A faint smell of leaking gas and fried kippers permeated the entrance hall, with a hint of boiled cabbage thrown in – a smell that would send her mother into a decline if she caught a whiff of it, Gina thought. But then every house possessed its own particular smell. Elmhurst, for instance, smelt of Monkey Brand soap, starch and beeswax furniture polish; Merlewood of pot-pourri, Josie and Letty's expensive French perfume, and Jack Bickley's pipe-tobacco.

Poppy's landlady, almost as broad as she was long, with iron grey hair twisted into a knot on the top of her head, and kept in place with a fearsome array of ironmongery and back-combs, led the way down to the basement. 'As you can see, it's all nice and clean,' she said, throwing open the door of the room overlooking the dustbins.

The room was large, and not as dark as Gina had imagined it would be, because of the bay window. The furniture was shabby, the carpet threadbare in places, but despite its obvious defects, she liked the room far better than the clinically clean guest-room she occupied at Fernlea, with a list of rules and regulations pinned to the back of the door.

'The rent is ten shillings a week, payable in advance,' Mrs Potts told Georgina. 'That includes breakfast, an evening meal and sandwiches, clean bedding once a month, and use of the bathroom. As you can see for yourself, there's a nice clean bed, a gas-fire and ring, and a slot-meter near the fireplace.' She added firmly, 'I'm giving you the first refusal on Miss Hewitt's recommendation, so you'd oblige me by making your mind up right away.'

Georgina, whose mind was already made up, opened her purse to find a ten-shilling note. 'Thank you, Mrs Potts,' she said, 'the room will suit me fine. When may I bring my belongings?'

'You can move in whenever you like.' Tucking the note down the front of her blouse, Mrs Potts felt its satisfying warmth between her ample breasts, and bestowed a gracious smile on her new lodger. 'Now, if you'll come upstairs to my private apartment, I'll give you the rent-book and key.'

Poppy, who had been hovering anxiously in the passage, breathed a sigh of relief when she saw the ten-shilling note change hands, and tacked on to the procession to the Potts' rooms on the ground floor – close enough to the front door to enable the landlady to keep a sharp eye on her female lodgers. (She wasn't having any hanky-panky under *her* roof!)

The transaction of the rent-book and key completed, Georgina decided to go to Fernlea at once to fetch her belongings and to face Mrs Woodbridge. No use delaying the dreaded confrontation. The sooner she got it over and done with, the better.

'I'll come with you,' Poppy said, 'to give you moral support and help with your luggage.' She had never been inside one of those posh houses on the South Cliff, and couldn't wait to find out what Fernlea was like inside.

Blimey, it *was* posh. Too posh for the likes of her, Poppy decided, waiting in the drawing-room for Gina to emerge from Mrs Woodbridge's office. She had never seen anything like it before, and didn't altogether like what she saw – all those prickly horsehair sofas and chairs, lace antimacassars, beaded cushions, ugly ornaments, and that bearskin rug with snarling yellow teeth and a nasty expression in its glass eyes, as if it were contemplating taking a bite out of her leg if she ventured any closer.

Cocking an ear, she heard Mrs Woodbridge say, in an accusatory tone of voice, 'Very well then, if that is your decision, though I think it hardly likely that your parents will approve of your leaving me in the lurch like this.'

'I'm sorry, Mrs Woodbridge,' Gina replied, 'I am moving into town to be closer to my place of work.'

'Your place of work indeed,' Mrs Woodbridge retorted.

'Huh, why a girl in your position should feel it necessary to work at all, is beyond me.'

On entering the drawing-room, the unpleasant interview over, Gina said urgently, 'Please, Poppy, let's get out of here as quickly as possible. My luggage is in the hall. We'll take a cab into town. There's a rank just round the corner.'

'Mrs Woodbridge didn't sound too well pleased that you were leaving,' Poppy observed, lugging Gina's hat-box and one of her suitcases round the corner into Ramshill Road.

'You're right. She wasn't!'

'Well, for what it's worth, I'd far sooner live down there than up here,' Poppy said disgustedly, meaning that she would far rather live in Newborough than here on the South Cliff. 'Talk about airs and graces! But,' her curiosity getting the better of her, 'what did Mrs Woodbridge mean about a girl in your position?'

The horse-drawn carriage creaked and swayed as the girls got into it and the driver hefted aboard the luggage. It was then, as the horse clip-clopped its way across the Valley Bridge into town, that Georgina told Poppy something of her past life, that she had left her home in the West Riding under a cloud, which Poppy thought highly romantic.

'You mean you actually left your young man standing at the altar?' Poppy asked, wide-eyed, regarding Gina as the heroine of one of those new-fangled picture shows she adored; conjuring up the scene in her mind's eye – a lovely bride, dressed all in white, running up the aisle of a church the size of Westminster Abbey, the pale, distraught bridegroom wringing his hands in despair.

'We're here, Poppy,' Gina reminded her as the cab drew to a halt.

And, 'Oh, so we are,' Poppy said hazily, gathering her wits together to help Gina hump the luggage downstairs to her room.

When the suitcases had been emptied, and Gina's clothes hung in the wardrobe, 'I could murder a cup of tea,' Poppy said plaintively. 'I know. Let's go round to Rab's studio. He'll make tea for us in two shakes of a lamb's tail.'

'But I couldn't possibly intrude,' Gina demurred,

disliking the idea of playing gooseberry. But Poppy wouldn't take No for an answer. 'Don't talk so soft,' she said airily. 'Besides, I want you to tell me what you think of him.'

The stairs leading up to Rab's studio were narrow and twisting. Georgina heard the creaking of the stairs with some trepidation. It seemed to her that the building might collapse at any minute from age and neglect. But Poppy, who had obviously trodden these stairs many times before, seemed impervious to the creaks and groans. 'Coo-ee,' she sang out on the top landing. 'It's me, Rab! I've brought someone to see you.'

The door facing them opened to reveal a stockily-built man whose appearance gave the impression of immense physical strength.

At first glance he seemed to Gina disproportionately built, as though his head and shoulders were far too big for his body, an ugly man, and yet as she moved forward to shake hands with him, that first overall impression was forgotten as he looked at her, and smiled.

'This is my friend, Gina Brett, the one I told you about,' Poppy said artlessly. 'She's just moved in next door to me, and we're gagging for a cup of tea.'

'In that case you had better sit down and I'll put the kettle on to boil.'

'Sit down where I should like to know,' Poppy reprimanded him severely. 'Honestly, Rab, this place is like a pigsty! Why don't you tidy up once in a while?'

Rab laughed, revealing strong white teeth. 'And deny you that pleasure?'

The room they were in was of unusual length, with two windows, one at the sitting end of the apartment, overlooking St Nicholas Street, the other a huge skylight at the far end, beneath which stood an artist's throne and a paint-daubed easel. A swathe of turquoise material draped carelessly over the throne suggested that a female model had recently posed there, an impression strengthened by the lingering scent of some exotic perfume – musk or sandlewood – and a few oddments of womanly apparel: a diamanté-edged Spanish comb, a book of *papier-poudre* tissues, a box of rouge, a scattering of hairpins and an embroidered hanky on a shelf beneath a gilt-edged mirror.

The bare wooden floor at the studio end of the room was splashed with dried oil paints, as colourful as confetti. The walls were stacked with canvases of varying size, some framed, some not, their backs to the room. A rough bench near the easel was littered with artists' materials, palettes, knives, bottles of turpentine, paint tubes and brushes in stone jars. Opposite the window stood a brass and iron bedstead, the mattress covered with what looked like horse or army blankets, a colourful knitted counterpane and a number of cushions, silk-covered, trimmed with tarnished gold braid. On the floor beside the bed was a pile of books, some novels, others books on art, poetry and music. At the foot of the bed stood a black, hoop-topped cabin trunk.

In one corner of the living end of the studio was a pot-bellied black stove, unlit on this warm May day, the black hearth covered with a film of wood-ash, in front of which was a shabby, cretonne-covered couch and a table littered with newspapers, a tobacco-jar, pipes, ashtrays and drifting petals from a stoneware pot of white lilac. Watching with some amusement Poppy's attempts to create order from chaos, Rab moved towards a long farmhouse table on which stood a paraffin stove, kettle, milk-can, cups and saucers, and various tins containing tea, sugar and coffee-beans, which he ground himself.

The room fascinated Gina. 'To make one little room an everywhere'. Those words by John Donne took on a new meaning, for here under this roof was everything a man needed, not merely as a means of survival but an enrichment of the senses. The room was the man. Everything about it suggested that he had come to terms with himself in shrugging aside the trappings of orthodoxy to live as he pleased.

She could not begin to guess his age. In a sense, he was ageless. She had seen faces like his in biblical paintings – strong faces with fearless eyes, olive-skinned faces crowned with abundant dark hair – a suggestion of gipsy blood running through his veins.

His clothing, as unorthodox as the wearer – moleskin trousers, loosely-fitting fisherman's jersey, open-toed sandals – emphasized his masculinity. And yet his movements were controlled, peculiarly graceful, his hands long and slender with well-manicured fingernails. Disturbed by his powerful male sexuality, Gina knew that, left alone with this man, she might find him as impossible to resist as Poppy had done. She had, moreover, the distinct impression that he knew what she was thinking.

'Honestly Rab, how you manage to live in such a muddle is beyond me,' Poppy chuntered, sweeping the fallen lilac petals into the palm of her hand and looking round for somewhere to put them. 'And I'll bet any money you haven't bought any grub for the weekend.'

Rab laughed. 'Don't worry, I'll go down to the market before closing time for some meat and vegetables.'

'And bread. Don't forget to buy a loaf of bread,' Poppy reminded him.

'Ah yes, the staff of life, to keep body and soul together. A strange anomaly don't you think, Miss Brett; the age-old assumption that the soul of man is contained within the often grotesque human body? I prefer to think of mine floating somewhere above my head, sailing free in the wind and the rain, above and beyond the temptation of a loaf of bread or a scrag end of mutton stew.'

He smiled then, that slow dawning smile of his, reminiscent of a string drawn back from a bow before the arrow was fired, with deadly accuracy, to find its mark.

Poppy hadn't the faintest idea what he was on about. She had never heard the word anomaly before.

'You mean – a free spirit?' The idea appealed strongly to Gina.

'Exactly so.' Their eyes met.

'I wish I knew what you two were on about,' Poppy broke in, flummoxed that her mention of a loaf of bread had resulted in a dissertation on the subject of the soul. And this, she realized, was where she came unstuck with Rab:

64

that she didn't know what he was driving at half the time, except when they were in bed together. She knew what he was driving at then, right enough. 'Here, let me make the tea.'

Warming the pot, Poppy wondered if Rab was really in love with her. He had never said so. Perhaps he saw her as a bad girl, but she wasn't a whore, and she had never loved any man before the way she loved him.

The tea made, Poppy handed round the cups, wishing that Gina and Rab would sit down to drink it on the space she had cleared on the sofa.

They had apparently taken to each other, and Poppy was pleased about that. Truth to tell, she'd been worried that Georgina, a lady born and bred, might feel out of place in Rab's studio, so different from that posh home of hers in the West Riding. But she needed to know what Gina thought of Rab, to gain her approval of the man she one day hoped to marry.

'Is this – yours?'

'Yes. Do you like it?'

Gina frowned, tilting her head. 'I'm not quite sure. I've never seen a painting quite like it before.'

'Stand back from it a little.'

Gina stepped back, then suddenly she saw, she *knew*. 'Oh yes,' she said, 'of course!'

Rab said, enigmatically, 'One should always stand back a little, I've discovered, from life as well as art.'

Aware that Rab was looking at her intently as he packed his pipe with strong tobacco, 'Tell me, are you engaged in anything special at the moment?' she asked.

Despite the ambiguity of her question, he knew what she meant. 'Nothing of importance.' Striking a match, 'Mainly small seascapes.' He lit his pipe. 'A local gallery sells my work on a commission basis. It's hack work, but at least it keeps body and soul together.'

Poppy groaned. 'Oh, don't start on about souls again! What about tonight? Shall we go for a walk along the Foreshore?'

'That depends.' The smell of Rab's tobacco mingled

oddly with that trace of exotic perfume and the aroma of coffee beans in the air. 'Our guest may prefer a quiet walk through the Italian Gardens and along the cliffs to Holbeck, if she would care to join us, that is.'

Poppy's face fell. 'Thank you, but I have other plans for this evening,' Gina said, determined not to play gooseberry a moment longer than necessary. 'I'm going to the theatre.'

Startled. 'Who with?' Poppy asked.

Gina smiled. 'I'm going alone.'

'*Alone?*' Poppy's eyebrows disappeared into her hair.

'Yes. There's a play I particularly want to see, and tonight is the final performance.'

'A – *play?*' Poppy's mind boggled. A trip to the theatre to see a good musical or 'turns' she could understand, but a play with actors spouting yards of dialogue seemed a poor substitute for a good laugh and a bit of a sing-song. Besides which, the idea of a girl going to the theatre alone – or anywhere else for that matter – seemed as inimical to the gregarious Poppy as staying indoors to read a book. 'Well, rather you than me, that's all.'

'I think I know the play you mean,' Rab said. 'I saw it last Tuesday or Wednesday night, I forget which.'

'You did?' Poppy bridled, seriously put out. 'You never told me! You might have asked me to go with you. Why didn't you?'

'My dear girl, because I knew you wouldn't be interested,' Rab explained patiently. 'In any case, you were washing your hair. Remember?'

'Oh yes,' Poppy said grudgingly, 'but I could have washed my hair another night, if I'd known.' The thought of Rab going anywhere without her was more than she could bear. But she knew in her heart of hearts that, despite their physical intimacy, there were secret, hidden areas of his life that she could never begin to share, to even understand. The thought depressed her, but not for long. After all, she had tonight to look forward to.

Linking Gina's arm as they walked along St Nicholas Street together, 'Well, what did you think of him?' Poppy asked.

Gina was at a loss for words. 'You mean – Rab?'

'Of course I mean Rab! Who else?'

'He seems very – charming.' What else could she say? Poppy was the last person on earth she could confide in. Even the broad-minded Poppy might be shocked if she told her the truth – that she thought Rab the most exciting man she had ever met. More than that, the stunning impact of their meeting had aroused feelings she never knew existed before, until he looked at her and smiled. Then it seemed as if the world had tilted suddenly on its axis, that the universe, sun, moon and stars were spinning about her in glorious confusion, and the two of them were standing alone together on some high pinnacle of awareness above and beyond the confines of earthly existence.

Poor Poppy would think her mad if she attempted to put into words the way she felt now, as if her feet were scarcely touching the pavement, as if her vision was suddenly much clearer, so that she saw each colour, the contour of every leaf on every tree in Woodall Gardens with a heightened awareness of their form and beauty. Perhaps she *was* mad. Mad to think that Rab felt the same way about her. And even if he did, what then?

Glad of the privacy of her basement room, closing the door behind her, she stood with her back to it, overwhelmed by the enormity of what had happened, lost in memories of that one short hour of her life which had brought her face to face with her own sexuality, a grown woman capable of wanting a man so much it hurt.

Common sense told her that the sooner she put Rab out of her mind, the better, for her own sake and Poppy's. But what had common sense to do with the fast beating of her heart? At the same time, she could not help wondering how many women had shared Rab's bed beneath that glass skylight.

The theatre smell was unmistakable – a warm fugginess tinctured with perfume and cigar smoke – the distillation of a thousand audiences of fashionably dressed women and men of the kind who were making their way up the broad marble staircase to the Dress Circle.

Owen had insisted on Georgina's acceptance of twenty pounds the day he had brought her to Scarborough and, to please her father, she had not refused the gift. But despite the amount of money in her purse, enabling her to afford a seat in the Dress Circle, Gina wanted no part of the snob aspect of the theatre audience.

Paying sixpence for a ticket, she made her way up a narrow staircase to the gods, and found herself a seat in the front row. Leaning her elbows on the red plush, gazing down at the Orchestra Stalls, Gina imagined her mother's horror if she could see her now, a well brought-up young lady – a Brett-Forsyth – sitting alone in the cheap seats of a provincial theatre, rubbing shoulders with the 'great unwashed'.

But this was part and parcel of the reason why she had left Harold Bickley at the altar, this need of freedom, of self expression. And this, she knew, lay at the heart of her admiration for Rab, because she had glimpsed, in his unorthodox lifestyle, the same need of freedom, his refusal to conform to the standard patterns of social behaviour.

If only she could get him out of her mind, forget the way he had looked at her, the curious longing she had seen in his eyes: Forget the studio, the white wood-ash in the hearth, those drifting lilac petals, the smell of the place – that tantalizing amalgam of paint, coffee and perfume – the purposeful litter, the dust-motes dancing in the rays of sunshine streaming in through the skylight window. Forget the way he moved, spoke and laughed; the feeling she had, having met him, that she could never live without him.

But live without him she must – for Poppy's sake.

The drama of unrequited love and passion unfolding on-stage seemed less potent to Georgina than the drama of real life. Looking down from her seat in the gods, she experienced a thrilling commitment to the theatre, as if she belonged down there, on the stage, behind the footlights, as if the theatre was in her blood. But the leading lady was wooden, the underlying reason why the play failed to capture her full attention.

If only the actress, playing the part of a woman accused of killing her lover, had let go her inhibitions in the final court scene, had truly believed herself to be a murderess on trial for her life, and had made her impassioned plea for mercy in a voice hoarse with emotion, she might have had the audience on its feet, applauding her performance.

Walking back to her lodgings after the performance, Gina thought how differently she would have played the part if she were an actress. In that final scene, for instance, at that supreme moment when the prosecuting counsel asked her, 'Did you or did you not murder your lover?', she would not have shouted the reply, 'Yes, I killed him because he didn't deserve to live!' Rather, she would have paused a moment or two, then whispered brokenly, clasping her hands together, 'Yes . . . I killed him . . . You see, he didn't deserve to live.'

Lighting the gas, hearing the hiss of the mantle, undressing ready for bed, feeling homesick in her new surroundings, battling with her conscience, her mind in a turmoil, Gina saw a cockroach scuttling towards the haven of the skirting board. It would have been so easy to end its poor little life with the sole of her shoe. Instead, she burst into tears.

Too tense to sleep, tossing and turning in bed, she heard, beyond her basement window, the hoarse cries and music and laughter of the world outside, the sounds of this alien new life of hers which she had embraced with so much girlish optimism and blinkered courage before realizing what she might be letting herself in for.

Much later, when the night sounds – the music and the laughter – had died away, still wide awake, she heard the creak of the stairs as Poppy returned to her room.

After their lovemaking, Gina wondered, had she and Rab lain together in each other's arms, looking up at the stars, the wash of moonlight on the skylight window? She had never experienced the pangs and pain of jealousy before, because she had never met a man capable of stirring so terrifying an emotion.

Thinking back, she remembered poor Bridget Donovan's stumbling attempt at describing what it felt like to be in love – 'All mixed up. Kind of happy and sad at the same time.' And, 'That's what it's like to be in love, wanting a man so much you'll die if you can't have him. Only you don't die, you just go on living from one day to the next.'

She had never thought to ask Bridget what it felt like to be jealous.

Now she did not need to ask anyone. She *knew*.

Chapter Five

The painting was finished. Rab stepped back from the easel to consider his work, deriving no pleasure from it. The picture, that of a dark-haired girl of gipsy appearance, with pouting lips and smouldering eyes, her head resting against a cushion, naked apart from a swathe of turquoise silk artfully arranged to reveal the seductive curves of her body – leaving nothing to the imagination – filled him with a scourging sense of shame. Not because the girl was naked. He had painted too many nude women before to be titillated by the anatomical details of the female form, but because he had painted the picture for money. Corrupt money.

He knew the painting would sell. There was a steady market for this kind of junk, which the gallery owner kept in a backroom to show to a coterie of elderly male clients who came to view after hours – pathetic voyeurs of the kind who probably also enjoyed pornographic literature and paid young women to submit to their futile fumblings in bed.

Had it really come to this, Rab thought, the bastardization of art for the sake of money to keep a roof over his head? If so, he might as well be dead and buried. Perhaps he would have been by now, had he been captured by the Germans, had he not made his desperate bid for freedom after that vital shot at Sarajevo had been fired, when hatred and suspicion had turned friends into enemies, and foreigners were being rounded up as spies. But he dare not think of that.

Turning away from the canvas, Rab thought instead of a picture he would dearly love to paint. A portrait of Gina.

His mind suddenly clear and lucid, untroubled by images of the past he wished to forget, he remembered the proud uplift of her head, that amazing bone structure beneath the flawless ivory skin, the dusting of freckles, tender young mouth, the play of light in her hair, those wing-like eyebrows, dark lashes. And there was something more difficult to pin-point, almost impossible to portray – a quality of innocence laced with strength, a kind of sadness in those arrestingly beautiful green eyes of hers, a sadness mitigated by the radiance of her smile.

Yesterday he had met the woman of his dreams. Last night, because of Gina, he had taken Poppy to a picture show, treated her to a meal afterwards, then escorted her back to her lodgings.

Naturally, the girl had been upset that their evening together had not ended in physical intimacy. Her despairing cry, as she clung to him, weeping, had touched him to the heart. 'Don't you want me any more? Is that it?' Poor, kind-hearted Poppy! How could he have possibly told her that the only woman he would ever want from now on was Gina? That would have been too cruel.

Afterwards, lying in bed, looking up at the night sky beyond the skylight window, he had realized the in-escapability of his past life, the impossibility of reaching an untouchable star. He had never known, never experienced, a love like this before. All he knew, with any degree of certainty, was that he would love Gina till the day he died.

Getting up on Sunday morning, he made coffee the way he liked it, hot and strong, from freshly ground beans, the way Mrs Steiner used to make it in Germany before the war. The whole house had been permeated with the scent of it bubbling away on the kitchen stove when her family came down to breakfast, her husband Otto and her two sons, Friedrich and Gunter. How lucky, how fortunate he had been to be regarded as a member of that family with whom he had spent so many summers, a poor art student with scarcely a couple of coins to rub together.

Early Sunday mornings were precious to Rab, when the streets of Scarborough were empty and quiet, and he could walk along the sands without meeting a soul. Then, he found peace of mind, and his memories seemed less painful.

Later, he knew, Poppy would come to the studio in her best Sunday clothes. Perhaps today she would bring Gina with her. He prayed that she would.

Gina was still sleeping when Poppy came to her room and knocked at the door. 'Are you awake? Can I come in?' She knocked again.

'Oh, Poppy! Yes. I'm sorry. Do come in.'

'I can't *get* in! The door's locked.'

'Just a minute.' Getting out of bed, Gina shrugged into her old green dressing-gown and opened the door.

'Do you always lock your door? I don't,' Poppy said plaintively.

'Not as a rule. Why? Is anything the matter?'

'I want to talk to you, that's all.' Poppy perched on the end of the bed.

'What about?' Gina sensed that something was wrong with the girl.

'The theatre.'

Gina looked at Poppy in surprise. A discussion of the theatre at seven o'clock on Sunday morning was the last thing she had anticipated. 'What about it?'

'*I* don't know. I want *you* to tell *me*.'

Difficult to believe that she had felt bitterly jealous of Poppy last night, Gina thought. By the light of early morning, poor Poppy looked like a bird with ruffled feathers. Lost, bewildered. Unhappy.

'I expect you'll think I'm daft,' Poppy continued. 'Maybe I am, but it cut me up a bit when Rab said he'd been to the theatre without me because I wouldn't be interested. The truth is, I'm pig sick of being ignorant. Mind you, there's not much wonder. I left school at eleven – when my ma died. Someone had to look after our Alfie and Frankie, and there weren't no-one else. Our da didn't give a damn about us kids . . . I'm sorry, I don't suppose you're interested.'

'Of course I'm interested. Please go on.' Gina sat up in bed.

She had been born in Hartlepool, the eldest of five

children, two of whom had died in infancy. Her mother had worked as a chambermaid in a seafront hotel before her marriage to Albert Hewitt, a jack-of-all-trades, master of none.

'Ma might have thought better of getting married at all if she'd known what she was letting herself in for. I don't suppose she would have, only – she found herself in a bit of a fix.' Poppy flushed. 'Of course Da wasn't bad looking in them days, judging by the wedding photograph Ma showed me. I expect that's why she fell for him.

'After the wedding they went to live with my Grandma Hewitt until I was born. Poor Ma told me what a dog's life she had there. Grandma was always throwing it up at her that she'd had to get married – as if Da had nothing to do with it. Well, things got so bad that Ma threatened to leave and take me with her if Da didn't find somewhere else to live.' She sighed deeply.

'That's when we moved to a couple of rooms over a barber's shop. Da started out doing shaves, soon he was cutting hair, not that he knew a blind thing about cutting hair to begin with, but he was as sharp as a tack and had the cheek of the devil. He'd have gone to London and cut the king's hair if he'd been asked.' She paused reflectively. 'So that's where I grew up, in two crummy rooms over a barber's shop. Then Alfie was born, and I started putting two and two together about all them funny noises—' She stopped speaking abruptly.

'What kind of noises?' Gina asked gently.

'Well, I slept on a couch in the living-room, but I'd wake up in the night and wonder what was going on next door. I'd think Da was poorly the noise he was making, all that puffing and grunting. How the baby slept through it I don't know. I didn't cotton on to what was happening until Ma fell pregnant again with Frankie.' Poppy's voice quavered. 'Da never gave her a minute's peace. One day I came home from school early an' – he was standing behind her with his braces dangling. He didn't even stop what he was doing when he saw me, but poor Ma burst out crying . . .'

'Please, Poppy, don't upset yourself. There's no need to go on.'

'But I *want* to talk about it. It's been burning a hole in my brain all these years. I want you to understand why I am as I am, why I don't know how to speak proper.

'Well, Da got the sack from the barber's, an' we went to live in a basement near the docks.' Poppy smiled crookedly. 'Seems that's all I'm fit for, living in a basement. Anyway, Ma had to take in washing and scrub floors to make ends meet. And what did my father do? I'll tell you. He got her pregnant twice more, when she hardly had the strength to stand up. No wonder those poor bairns didn't live very long. Girls, they were. She christened them Lily and Violet. She always did like flowers.'

'Oh, Poppy. I'm so sorry.'

'Yes, well poor Mother never got over losing them. She took poorly all of a sudden, as if the heart had gone out of her. I reckon she was just too tired to go on living any more. She weighed six stone when she died. The doctor said it was cancer, but I think she died of a broken heart.

'So then it was up to me to take care of Da and my brothers. Not that he was bringing home enough money to feed the cat. Worst of all, I knew he didn't care tuppence about us. All he cared about was going to the pub to drown his sorrows. *His* sorrows! I didn't mind so much about myself, but I did worry that the kids hadn't decent shoes to go to school in. When I tackled Da about it, he hit me in the face and told me to shut my bloody mouth or he'd give me a taste of what he gave Ma. I was so frightened I ran to my room and locked the door. After that, I daren't turn my back on him in case he came up behind me. I'd catch him looking at me, and I knew what he was thinking.' Poppy's eyes filled with tears. 'He wanted me real bad. His own daughter!

'I was glad when war came and he went into the army.' Bitterly, 'I suppose he was glad to turn *his* back on us. I can see him now, standing there in his uniform, telling us we were going to live with our Aunt Charlotte – Ma's sister.

'That was the best thing that ever happened to us. She

was good to us. The boys went to school with decent shoes on their feet, and she made me learn shorthand and typewriting so's I'd be able to earn a living.' Her face crumpled suddenly. 'When the telegram came saying our Da had been killed in action, I wasn't sorry. I was glad. I thought, Yes, serve you right, you bloody bugger!'

'Oh, Poppy.'

'So now you know why I want to better myself. Will you help me? Will you correct me when I say things wrong? Will you take me with you to the theatre and explain about the plays and everything? I'm sick of feeling shut out. I want Rab to respect me. I want to read books and newspapers like he does. I want to be a lady – like you.'

'Of course. I'll help you in every way possible.'

'Something else is bothering me,' Poppy said. 'I'm worried that Rab has someone else on the go. Did you notice all that stuff on the shelf – that Spanish comb and rouge – and what about that perfume? The place reeks of it! Oh, I know he uses models now and then, but he never lets on who they are, and he won't show me the pictures. Why is he so secretive if there's nothing going on?'

These were questions that Gina could not answer, and so she kept silent. But Poppy's story had touched her to the heart, and she meant what she said. She would do everything she could to help her.

Hearing footsteps on the stairs, Rab quickly covered the painting. When Poppy gave her usual 'Coo-ee' on the landing and entered the studio alone, his heart lurched with disappointment that she had not brought Gina with her. His greeting lacked enthusiasm, the kiss he gave her was perfunctory – as if they were friends, not lovers, Poppy thought jealously, having got it firmly into her head that some other woman had taken her place in his life, someone he was seeing behind her back. More specifically, the model who had left her personal belongings on the shelf beneath the mirror and filled the air with the reek of her rotten perfume. Moreover, she had known last night that Rab's

76

mind was not on making love to her. For the first time ever, he had not even wanted to kiss her.

Now, watching him closely as he turned away and began scraping a palette as though his life depended on getting it clean, she felt as if a thorn hedge had sprung up between them. Then, her anger rising, and on a sudden impulse, she uncovered the painting on the easel.

'What the hell do you think you are doing?' Striding towards her, seizing her arm. 'How dare you look at my work without permission?'

'Some – *work*!' Poppy's face puckered. 'I *knew* it. You – *bastard*! Who is she? What's her name? I suppose you've slept with her, and I'll bet any money you didn't go to the theatre alone, that she went with you.'

Relaxing his grip, by nature a non-violent man, 'My life is my own, Poppy,' Rab said, holding his anger in check. 'You'd do well to remember that. I went to the theatre alone.'

Poppy was on the verge of tears. 'But you *have* slept with her, haven't you?'

Rab sighed deeply, tired of the questioning, the intrusion into his private affairs. 'That is my business,' he said abruptly, turning away. But Poppy would not let well enough alone. Incensed with anger, 'I want the truth!' she cried hoarsely. 'I have the right to know. It's my life too. I'm tired of being shut out! What are you trying to hide? All this time, and I don't even know your bloody last name!'

'Very well then, if you really must know, her name is Harriet Cohen. She's a professional model. And yes, I did sleep with her on several occasions, as I have slept with many women in the past. But that was a long time ago. I make no apology for that, why should I? I'm a man, not a plaster saint.'

Sinking down on the couch, Poppy burst into floods of tears. 'And I thought you cared for me,' she sobbed.

He crossed towards her, gently touching her shoulders with his fingertips. 'I *do* care for you Poppy, a great deal, because you have brought laughter into my life.'

Staring up at him, her eyes wet with tears, she cried,

'Yes, and don't forget what else I've given you, the way I've looked after you, tidied up for you – everything a woman has to give when she loves a man the way I love you! But you don't care tuppence about me really, do you? Not really . . .'

'You push me too far, my dear.' He ran his fingers through his hair wearily, his brain tormented with thoughts of Gina, unable to think clearly, feeling himself caught in a trap from which there was no escape. Gina, Gina, Gina . . . the one woman on earth he really wanted. The one woman on earth he could never have, and he knew it.

The down-to-earth Poppy, drying her eyes, said angrily, 'Push you too far? That's a laugh!' Getting up from the couch, standing strong and firm on her own two feet, her best Sunday hat slightly askew, 'The trouble with you, you ain't been pushed far enough. You're an artist, a good artist, even *I* know that. So why waste your time painting muck like *that*?' She pointed towards the easel. 'Why don't you stop fiddling about with those seascapes of yours and paint something decent for a change? A really *good* portrait.' The idea came to her in a flash of inspiration. 'Why don't you paint a portrait of Gina?'

Turning his face away to hide his emotion, Rab said carefully, 'That's a brilliant idea – but would she consent to sit for me?'

'She would if I asked her to,' Poppy said, 'she's my best friend, remember?'

Rab remembered.

The simple act of buying a morning newspaper on her way to work had a tonic effect on Poppy. Gina, she knew, would help her with the hard words and explain the things she didn't understand – the pronunciation of Versailles, for instance, where the Peace Treaty with Germany had been signed.

'But the war was over ages ago, and we won, so why bother with a Peace Treaty?' As far as Poppy was concerned, on the eleventh of November last year, when the guns had stopped firing, the Armistice had been signed, and when people had stopped being killed, that was it.

She was far more interested that rising hemlines and a lighter look were the keynotes of the Paris fashion shows. After all, she had a good pair of legs and trim ankles that would show to better advantage in shorter skirts.

To her surprise, Gina had jibbed at the idea of sitting for Rab when she broached the subject. 'Why ever not?' Poppy asked perplexedly. 'Don't you like Rab? Is that it?'

When Gina reminded her that Rab was *her* friend, and she didn't wish to intrude, Poppy gave a snort of laughter. 'Oh, *that*! Where's the harm in a cup of tea and a bit of a chat? Come with me to the studio this afternoon and talk to him about the portrait. He really would like to paint you.'

'I can't think why.' Her mother had dinned into her since childhood what a plain girl she was, and Georgina saw no reason to doubt that what Agnes said was true. She laughed. 'What a waste of paint.'

'Huh, not such a waste as the last picture he painted. We had a real dust-up when I saw it, but I think it did him good. He's been nicer to me ever since I dragged things into the open; and I was wrong about that – model. They did have a bit of an affair a long time ago, but it's over now. Leastways, he said so and I believed him.' Poppy's voice quavered, 'I *had* to believe him, I daren't do any other. The truth is, I'd put up with anything rather than lose him. I couldn't bear not being with him. I think I'd die if he finished with me. It's awful loving a man so much, more of a pain than a pleasure.' She paused self-consciously, 'Hark at me. And he said he liked me because I brought laughter into his life.'

'I'm sure that's true.' Gina turned to tidy the dressing-table which didn't need tidying, shaken by Poppy's revel-ations about the depth of her feelings for Rab, so poignantly expressed, knowing exactly how she felt, keeping her face turned away to hide her own emotions.

'Oh please come with me,' Poppy said persuasively, 'for my sake. I *want* Rab to paint your picture. It was my idea, as a matter of fact. I want him to stop wasting his time painting rubbish. Besides, you're my best friend, and I want you to be Rab's friend too. I suppose I'm daft, but I've got it into my head that you don't like him very much, despite what you said about him being charming.' She added astutely, 'That's the kind of thing people say when they don't know what else to say, isn't it?'

'Damning with faint praise, you mean?' Gina smiled sadly, straightening her brush and comb, knowing how much she wanted to return to the studio – that little 'everywhere' which had never been out of her mind for a moment – as a means of exorcism, perhaps, to convince herself that it was just an ordinary room, Rab an ordinary man. 'Very well, then,' she said, 'I'll come with you.'

'Oh, good.' Poppy smiled blissfully.

Walking towards the studio, Gina dreaded seeing Rab again, afraid that he might read in her face the mental torment she had suffered since her first visit, the sleepless nights, the jealousy, the pretence of not caring when Poppy mentioned his name.

She had heard of love on the rebound. Possibly, having left home under a cloud, riddled with guilt over Harold Bickley, recalling the love poems of Elizabeth Barrett Browning, and feeling that the magic of love had not happened for her, she had seen in Rab the romantic figure of her imagination, the kind of man she had secretly wished to fall in love with. As a growing child she had fallen in love with Sir Lancelot of the Round Table, had imagined herself as Queen Guinevere, just as, lying in the bath on her 'wedding' day, she had imagined herself as Ophelia – dying for love, or the lack of it.

More realistically, more likely, Gina thought, as she climbed the stairs to the studio, since she had not been in love with Harold Bickley, she was suffering not from love on the rebound, but dreams on the rebound.

Even so, she dreaded the opening of the landing door, the possible shattering of her illusions. Even worse, their confirmation. She would know, the minute the door opened, if the impact Rab had made on her at their first meeting was a dream or reality.

The door opened, and she *knew*. No dream this.

'Well, here we are,' Poppy said artlessly. 'I've brought Gina to talk about the portrait. Shall I put the kettle on to boil?'

Chapter Six

Summer was fast slipping into autumn. The moors above the Calder Valley were ablaze with patches of purple heather.

Looking out of the study window, Owen scarcely noticed the swathes of colour, the curving driveway flanked with regiments of rigidly pruned laurels, or the line of elm trees from which the name of the house derived. The garden, robbed of natural beauty, reminded him of Agnes, whose obsession with order and neatness was evident outdoors as well as in. The wonder was that she had not forbidden the birds to build their nests in the trees bordering the stone wall at the garden's end.

His wife's attitude towards Georgina and the Bickleys had not softened. Indeed, she seemed more deeply entrenched in self-righteousness, and kept harping on about that look Mary Bickley had given her in church. In these circumstances it seemed unlikely that the breach would ever be healed, and Georgina would continue to shoulder the blame for the sorry state of affairs.

Owen's allegiance to his daughter remained rock solid. He did not blame her for leaving Fernlea, although her letter saying that she had moved into a basement room in Newborough had given rise to a battle royal between himself and Agnes, when she had condemned the girl as a traitor to her class, finding her own level in the gutter.

Deep in thought, Owen realized how wise Georgina had been to leave home, where the atmosphere was heavy with Agnes' hostility to the world in general and himself in particular. At least he was now spared the unpleasantness of sharing a bed with her, but he knew she would never forgive him for continuing to sleep in a guest room, forsaking his marital duties.

A cook had recently been appointed to take the place of Mrs Crabtree, following a series of disastrous experiences with a string of local women who had come up daily from the valley to face his wife's rejection of the lot of them as incompetent fools who could not even peel a potato properly, much less cook to the standard she required.

In his continuing state of dejection since Georgina left home, Owen cared little about food. If potatoes stared up from the plate and pie-crust sank wetly in a sea of lukewarm gravy, he had scarcely noticed.

Owen missed his daughter and deeply regretted the loss of the Bickleys' friendship, which meant a great deal to him. Especially Mary's. He missed the company of the young Bickleys, too, who had brought life and laughter into the house. But Agnes had steadfastly and stubbornly refused even to write to Jack and Mary expressing the hope that in time their friendship might be restored. Standing on her dignity, she expected an apology from them.

Saddened and bewildered by recent events, Owen saw himself as lacking in moral fibre. Despite his stand against his wife's physical domination, he continued to let her dictate to him in other ways, as a matter of expedience, unwilling to make public their private differences of opinion. With this in mind, he treated Agnes with consummate courtesy in front of the servants and the new coterie of friends – ladies of the various charitable organizations to which she belonged – whom she had taken to inviting to Elmhurst for afternoon tea: gossipy women who would have made a meal of any sign of dissension between husband and wife.

Where would it all end? Owen wondered, as the breakfast gong sounded. Turning away from the window, he walked slowly towards the dining-room to face his wife across the toast-rack and teapot, knowing that to attempt a bite of food would choke him. Catching sight of Bridget Donovan carrying a tray laden with plates of bacon and eggs, his gorge rose suddenly at the thought of watching Agnes masticate her food with those strong yellow teeth of hers.

So he told the girl to explain to her mistress that he had received an urgent call from the mill and had decided to forego having breakfast this morning. 'I'm sorry to ask this of you,' he said contritely, 'but . . .'

'Don't you worry, sir.' Bridget nodded understandingly. '*I'll* tell her. Now, hadn't you better hop it through the side door while the coast is clear?'

'Bridget, you're a gem.'

Silently leaving the house by the side door, Owen drove down to the mill where he felt himself to be the captain of his soul, master of his fate, where comfort lay in the noise and rattle of the looms, the flying shuttles, and the chatter of the men and women attending to the many complicated rituals necessary to textile manufacture. They were producing miles of glowing, brightly coloured tweed and the softly muted, speckled cloth for which the Brett-Forsyth Mill had become famous as far afield as Italy, Spain and France, before frontiers had been closed to international trade. That was when the mill had perforce turned out, not endless streams of heather-purple, lovat green, soft pinks, restrained greys and blues, but uncompromisingly ugly khaki material to clothe the British soldiers fighting and dying for their country on the battlefields of Europe.

Hearing the clatter of the looms, Owen remembered the days long ago when, entering the family business as a young man fresh from university, his father had put him through every phase of textile production, from the unloading of the raw wool from the horse-drawn wagons which had lumbered up the steep main street to the factory yard, to the packing-shed from which the finished product was despatched to the various destinations.

His apprenticeship had been long, hard and thorough. Given a broom, he had been told to sweep up the horse-droppings in the yard; made to clean and oil the machinery under the supervision of the works' foreman who had treated him as he would have done any other lad learning the trade. He had carded, spun and dyed, returning home to Elmhurst dirty, tired, with stained hands and aching feet; but he had never been happier in his life than he was then when, sharing his dinner breaks with his fellow workmen, laughing at their tales uttered in a broad Yorkshire dialect, he knew that he had been accepted as one of them, not merely tolerated because he happened to be the boss's son.

Then his mother had died, and the neighbouring mill, a mile down the valley, had changed hands, bringing into his life Jack Bickley, son of the new owner, with whom he had struck up an immediate friendship.

Thereafter, where Jack Bickley led Owen had followed, liking Jack's devil-may-care attitude to life, admiring his much stronger, outgoing personality. He wanted to be like Jack, to the extent that when young Bickley had confided his interest in a girl – Mary Baines – whom he had met at a dinner-dance in Bradford, and intended to marry, if she would have him, Owen had begun to think it was perhaps time that he too found a partner in life. But he was by nature much shyer than Jack, and tongue-tied in the presence of attractive girls of marriageable age, who obviously preferred more dashing escorts.

Then, shortly before the sudden death of his father, he had met Agnes Mirfield, daughter of a Leeds clothier, at a lantern lecture in the Town Hall, a pert young woman who, in vulgar parlance, appeared to have her eye on him as she sat down opposite to partake of coffee and biscuits after the lecture. Owen had quickly realized that he need not attempt to make conversation – Agnes never stopped talking.

On the steps of the Town Hall she had suggested they might meet again soon – the following weekend, perhaps, for Sunday lunch at her parents' house near Roundhay Park.

Overwhelmed by the girl's self-confidence and lack of inhibition, basking in the glow of her evident preference for himself rather than any other unattached male who had attended the lecture, he had gladly accepted.

That meeting was destined not to take place. On the Saturday night Owen's father had suffered a brain haemhorrage and had died in the early hours of Sunday morning, expunging all thoughts of the luncheon invitation from Owen's mind. Lost and lonely after the funeral, he had suddenly remembered, with a deep feeling of guilt, that he owed Agnes Mirfield and her parents an apology, and had sat down forthwith to write them a letter explaining why he had not been able to visit their home.

Next day, to his surprise, Agnes had come to Elmhurst to offer her sympathy and support. Bossing him prettily, she had asked if he had eaten since the funeral. When he admitted that he had not, she had taken it upon herself to cook him an omelette, brushing aside the cookhousekeeper's indignation at having her kitchen invaded by a complete stranger.

Looking back, Owen realized that it was Agnes who had done all the courting. That she had married him for his money had not occurred to him at the time. Now he realized how cleverly she had seized the opportunity of becoming the mistress of Elmhurst. It was Agnes who had chosen the engagement ring, and placed the announcement in the *Leeds Mercury*, who had suggested holding the reception at the Griffen Hotel after the wedding ceremony in Leeds' Moortown church, and a honeymoon in Bournemouth.

And so, after the honeymoon, Owen had brought Agnes back to Elmhurst as his bride. Mary, the wife of Jack Bickley, had been pregnant with Harold at the time.

Thankfully, the two women had struck up an immediate friendship, by nature of their circumstances – two young brides sharing the novelty of becoming the mistresses of the two great houses, Elmhurst and Merlewood, the acknowledged leaders of local society, the mothers of an up-and-coming generation of Bickleys and Brett-Forsyths.

But Mary was ever the softer and kinder of the two, Owen thought, entering the mill, the one who had grown older more gracefully, who had perhaps come too late to the realization – as he himself had – that Agnes was to blame for the wedding fiasco which had placed their friendship in jeopardy.

' 'Morning Maister Forsyth,' old Ben Adams, the doorkeeper said, as Owen passed by his cubby-hole. 'I hear tell that yon Mrs Bickley has tekken a turn for the worse, that t'doctor had to be sent for in't middle o't night.'

Owen turned back in alarm. 'Are you quite sure?'

'As sure as ah'm standin' here,' Ben nodded. 'They do say as 'ow she's on her way out o' this vale o' tears, the poor wumman. Echt, but it'll be a grand funeral, I'm thinkin', wi' her so well respected an' all.'

Without a moment's hesitation, Owen hurried back to his car, one thought in mind. He must go to Merlewood at once.

The long drive curved up to the house, scene of so many happy Christmas and birthday celebrations. Less pretentiously furnished than Elmhurst, he had found the atmosphere of Merlewood more relaxing, and the gentle Mary had a special way with flowers, bringing indoors every bloom under the sun, from the earliest daffodils to the last of the great, bronze and yellow chrysanthemums. Agnes abhorred indoor flower arrangements: falling petals made such a mess on the carpets.

Nearing the house, Owen saw that two cars – those of the doctor and the parson – were parked on the gravelled forecourt. Sick at heart, he walked up the steps to the front door and rang the bell. The manservant, Johnson, appeared in answer to the summons. 'Please tell Mr Bickley I wish to see him,' Owen said quietly.

'Very good, sir, I'll tell him you're here, if you would care to wait in the study.'

'Tell me, how is Mrs Bickley?' Owen knew it was infra dig to question a servant but, unlike Agnes, he had never stood on ceremony with what she termed the 'working class', and he had to know.

'I cannot say, sir,' the man replied woodenly. 'If you'll follow me, I'll show you to the study.'

'There's no need, Johnson. I know where it is. I *have* been here before.'

'As you wish. I'll tell the master.'

Entering the study, Owen remembered the many evenings he and Jack had spent here together when their wives were otherwise engaged. How cosy the room had seemed then, with a fire in the grate and the curtains drawn against the outside world. Now the room seemed cold and inhospitable, with no fire, and a feeling of chill in the air. Owen shivered slightly, as though a goose had walked over his grave.

The door opened, and Jack Bickley came in, a tall figure, unsmiling.

'Jack, my dear fellow!' Owen stepped forward, hand extended. 'I came as quickly as I could, to offer my help and support in any way possible.'

Ignoring the outstretched hand, Jack said heavily, sarcastically, 'As *quickly* as you could? Four months, and not a word of explanation or apology, and you came as *quickly* as you could?' He turned towards the fireplace and rested his hands on the mantelpiece, staring into the empty grate.

'Jack, I'm sorry, believe me, I—'

'Oh, I know, it wasn't your fault. It never is.' Bickley turned to face Owen. 'Now you've come to offer your help and support, whatever that may mean.' He laughed bitterly. 'Tell me, Owen, how you propose to help and support me? I'd really like to know.'

Owen said quietly, 'I heard that Mary was seriously ill – that's why I came.'

'And what of your lady wife? Hasn't she come with you to offer *her* help and support?' Jack's sarcasm was cutting.

'Agnes doesn't know I'm here. Please, Jack, you must know how I feel about you and Mary—'

Jack interrupted, 'There's little point in discussing that now. I'm sorry, Owen, you've come at a very bad time. I'll speak plainly, then I must go. What happened between Harry and Georgina was unfortunate. The girl might have had the decency to break off the engagement beforehand if the thought of marrying my son was so repugnant to her; but far greater damage than a public humiliation was done that day, when Mary was brought face-to-face with the realization that a long-standing friendship with someone she trusted, had ulterior motives.' He turned to face Owen. 'I'm sorry, things might have been different had Agnes come to see Mary to apologize for her meddling, in forcing an engagement between Harry and Georgina. Had that

88

happened, if Agnes had possessed enough humility and wisdom to shoulder the blame for her mistakes, Mary might have recovered.'

'Might have . . . ?' Owen's heart lurched.

'Mary died an hour ago,' Jack said.

Mary Bickley's funeral service took place in the Merlewood Parish Church.

The Bickley and the Brett-Forsyth mills had closed for the day as a mark of respect. The route from Merlewood to the church was lined with silent men and women gathered together to watch the passing of the cortège – the hearse drawn by two black horses, the coffin piled high with wreaths of autumn flowers.

Absent from the floral tributes was the wreath of white chrysanthemums sent by Owen, bearing the inscription, 'With deepest sympathy from Agnes, Owen, Georgina and Thomas Brett-Forsyth'. Harry Bickley had tossed it on to a slow-burning bonfire in the kitchen garden of Merlewood, filled with a deep and burning hatred of the Brett-Forsyths who had killed his mother as surely as if they had thrust a knife into her heart.

'The Lord is my Shepherd, I shall not want . . .'

Sitting alone at the back of the church, Owen covered his face with his hands as the funeral service proceeded, knowing that it was Mary he had loved all along. Gentle, sweet Mary with her love of flowers, birds in flight, the sound of the sea foaming in on the shore in those happy, carefree days in Scarborough when the children were young, and his eyes had met hers across their jealously-guarded sand-castles, so soon to be washed away by the relentless, incoming tide.

'The Day Thou gavest, Lord, is ended . . .'

As the organ swelled, Owen prayed that his girl was happy in her new life, that he might live long enough to induct his son into the complexities of running the mill after he was dead and gone, and wished with all his heart that it was Georgina, not Thomas, who would one day step into his shoes.

* * *

If asked why he felt unwell, Owen could have given no clear indication of what ailed him. His symptoms were mental rather than physical: a constant feeling of worry and exhaustion, a lack of interest in life now that Georgina had gone away, the underlying blame he attached to himself for the death of Mary Bickley, the relentless pressure of his life with Agnes, his increasing dislike of his son and heir, whose presence at Elmhurst during the school vacation had proved an added burden.

The boy was totally out of hand, lazing in bed till midday, wanting breakfast in his room, appearing at lunch to gobble his food in complete silence and generally causing more work for the servants. He treated Owen, Agnes and the servants with careless contempt, and would absent himself from the house for hours on end without a word of explanation. He invariably returned home for dinner, after which he would either go through to the billiards-room or slouch idly in the drawing-room, refusing to engage in conversation about his school work, and pulling a long face if his father attempted to talk to him about his future at the mill.

One evening in the drawing-room, after Thomas had dawdled off to bed, facing Agnes squarely, Owen had laid down the law. 'Can't you see, Agnes, if that boy is not brought to the realization of what the future holds for him, I might just as well sell out to the highest bidder?' He paced the room, his nervous system strung to fever pitch. 'You know as well as I do that Thomas will never make university. It's all there in his school reports: "Uninterested in his lessons, Lacking in discipline, Slothful, Disobedient, Unruly!" I warn you, Agnes, if there is no marked improvement next term, I shall take him away from school and send him into the Navy – as a stoker, if necessary!'

Agnes ranted and raved, to no avail. Owen remained adamant.

Knowing when she was beaten, next morning she trod heavily upstairs to her son's room, on the pretext of taking him a cup of hot chocolate. She began haltingly. 'Now,

Tommy dear, I think it's time we had a little talk together about – your future.'

Sitting up in bed, bleary-eyed, Thomas regarded her balefully. 'What about my future? I ain't finished school yet.'

'Haven't, Tommy dear, not ain't,' Agnes reproached him mildly. 'You must remember that you are a Brett-Forsyth, heir to the mill, of Elmhurst too, when your father and I are dead and gone.'

'And suppose I don't fancy being the owner of the rotten mill? Suppose I don't want to spend my life sitting cooped up in an office all day like Pa?' Thomas said sulkily.

'*Thomas!*' Agnes looked at him, aghast. In a split second, seeing all her hopes and dreams of the future in danger of collapse, she lost control. First Georgina, now Thomas! Was there no end to her children's ingratitude for all the hard work and planning she had done on their behalf?

For the first time in her life, she spoke sharply to her son, her anger at full throttle. 'You dare to lie there and tell me that you have no interest in your inheritance?' Eyes blazing, Agnes drew herself to her full height, a formidable figure in her grey morning dress, beneath which the bones of her corsets were clearly visible, giving her the appearance of an armour-plated Valkyrie. 'Are you completely witless? Haven't you the sense you were born with, you stupid child? Can't you see what is being handed to you on a plate – money, power, a secure place in society!'

She glared at him, her bosom heaving. 'Make no mistake, I have worked hard all my life to give you every advantage. Throw it away now, and I wash my hands of you. You can go into the Navy, for all I care!'

So saying, she swept out of the room on the full tide of her wrath.

God, Thomas thought, staring after her in amazement, the old girl had really got it in for him. Startled, he lay back against the pillows, shocked at last into an awareness of his future role in life, filled with horror at the very thought of entering the Royal Navy, at the beck and call of a lot of jumped-up officers. Besides which, he hated the sea, had

91

always hated it. He briefly re-lived being sick over the side of a rowing boat on a fishing expedition in Scarborough's South Bay: the constant rolling motion of the waves, the taste of bile in his mouth as he had brought up the contents of his stomach to feed the fishes in the quivering water beneath the prow of the boat . . .

Lurching out of bed, he vomited his chocolate drink into the 'jeremiah', then lay spreadeagled on the bed, turning over his mother's words in his mind: 'Money. Power. A secure place in society.'

And yes, why not? Thomas thought greedily. Everything he wanted handed to him on a plate, if he played his cards right. So what did it matter if he muddled his way through his school work, gained poor marks, and failed to enter university? As the son of a rich man his future was assured provided he toed the line, pretended a devout interest in the boring business of textile manufacture. All he had to do was lie convincingly to his parents, tell them he'd had a change of heart about the mill, and in time reap the full benefits of his role as the inheritor of the Brett-Forsyth fortune.

Later, Thomas went down to his father's study, and knocked at the door.

'Come in.' Owen looked at his son in surprise. Seldom had the boy entered this room of his own volition. Rather he had entered it under duress, to be given a sharp reprimand for some misdemeanour or other during the course of his sulky, rebellious childhood.

'I fear the Greeks, even when bearing gifts.' The quotation sprang unbidden to Owen's mind as the boy stood rigidly in front of the desk, giving the appearance of a juvenile St Paul who had suddenly seen the light on the road to Bradford, not Damascus.

'Well, what can I do for you?' Owen injected a note of heartiness into his voice. Doubtless the boy wanted more money to spend on tuck next term. He was amazed when Thomas said, 'If you are going to the mill this afternoon, Father, I'd like to go with you.'

'You would? May I ask why?'

The unexpected question threw Thomas momentarily. 'I'd like to have a look round,' he said lamely.

'Why today in particular?'

'I'll be back at school next week.'

'To waste more of the money I am spending on your education?' Owen's mistrust of the boy came uppermost. Never before had Thomas expressed the remotest interest in the mill. Why now?

'I'll try to do better next term,' Thomas said, remembering his mother's threat to put him into the Navy. Dread of that possibility lent a note of desperation to his plea. 'I really mean it, Father.'

'Very well, then. Of course you can come with me.' Possibly he had misjudged the boy, Owen thought, willing to give him the benefit of the doubt.

Rewarded by his father's smile and nod of approval, God, Tom thought as he quit the study, it had been as simple as falling off a log. He'd quite enjoyed pulling the wool over the old man's eyes.

Chapter Seven

It had been, for Gina, a summer of change, of discovery, of passionate awareness, deep emotional involvement and self-denial, as Rab painted her portrait.

First had come the initial charcoal sketches, the light blocking in of her face seen from different angles – the right profile, then the left, finally the full face drawn from a soppy angle, in Poppy's opinion, as Rab, sitting at Gina's feet, captured on paper her downward glance, the faintly quizzical expression in her eyes, the amused smile hovering about her lips.

'But it doesn't even *look* like Gina,' Poppy said forthrightly. 'It could be – *anybody*.' The subtlety of the sketch evaded her entirely, but Gina knew what Rab was driving at. The portrait was meant to convey womanhood incarnate, every woman on earth who had ever looked down and smiled at a child – or a lover.

That love existed between herself and Rab had been evident from the moment she came to the studio to discuss the portrait. No need of words, their eyes had said it all. In that brief yet clearly defined moment in time, relief had washed over Gina like a tide, so strong and deep a feeling that she was afraid Poppy would sense it. But Poppy had her back to them, filling the kettle at the cracked stone sink in a corner of the living area, lighting the paraffin stove, opening the tea-caddy, setting out the cups and saucers.

Poor Poppy had quickly tired of the mechanics of portraiture, what she thought of as the fiddle-faddle of all those sketches of Gina's hairline, nose, ears, mouth and eyes. As she had seen no point in the signing of a Peace Treaty with Germany when the war was over and everyone knew who had won, she grew increasingly impatient with

Rab's tardiness in picking up his paintbrush and palette and getting on with the job in hand. And so, as the summer progressed, she had taken to shopping and visiting the penny library on Saturday afternoons, leaving Gina and Rab together for an hour or so.

The first time that happened, alone with Rab, Gina said uncertainly, 'I wish Poppy had not talked me into this.'

Sensing that she was afraid of him, afraid of the strong physical attraction between them, 'You are free to leave if you wish,' he replied coolly, lighting his pipe and shaking out the match. Making no move to touch her, speaking without due emphasis, wanting to reassure her, yet knowing that certain things must be said for his own sake as well as hers. 'You realize, of course, that I am in love with you? You'd be a fool not to know how much I want you. I'd be an even greater fool to imagine—'

'Please, *don't*!' Gina covered her mouth with her hands, afraid of saying something she might regret, of admitting her own feelings.

'These things cannot be swept under the carpet, my love.'

Rising hurriedly to her feet, legs shaking, facing Rab squarely, she replied, 'In this case they must be, for Poppy's sake. The girl's in love with you.'

'And you imagine that I am in love with her? Is that it?'

In the grip of a powerful emotion which she knew not how to express or contain, 'I can't answer that,' Gina said hoarsely. 'You have – made love with her, that much I know.'

Rab smiled sadly. 'And that, in your opinion, is an infallible guarantee of love? The acid test? What a child you are! I have slept with many women, have loved none of them – until now. As I was about to say, I'd be a fool to imagine that I could ever have *you*. Do you think I don't know that if I attempted to hold you, to kiss you, I would risk losing you? Call it my punishment if you will, for a life misspent, of searching for the one woman to give meaning to an otherwise hopeless existence.' He laughed bitterly. 'Ironic, don't you think, that having found that one woman, my wicked past has caught up with me at last.' Turning away, knowing that if he continued to look at her a moment longer he might find himself unable to resist the longing to take her in his arms, he said tautly, 'Please, Gina, please go now.'

Her escape route was clear, unimpeded. All she had to do was gather together her belongings, open the door and run down the stairs to the street below. But she knew she could not; knew that her destiny was linked to this man; knew that every word he said was true.

In a blinding moment of truth, she did not care tuppence about his past, how many women he had slept with. She was as powerless to leave him now as the sea, running in on the shore, was powerless to resist the pull of the moon.

'Rab,' she said urgently reaching out to him for understanding, knowing she was in his hands, that if he wanted her as much as she wanted him, he had only to put his arms about her, bend his lips to hers, and she would be lost.

Deliberately, he turned his back on her, on his own instincts and desires; in what he would think of, forever afterwards, as the most unselfish moment of his life. 'I'll make some coffee,' he said, 'the way it used to be made in Germany, before the war.'

The one gift he had to lay at Gina's feet was his refusal to take advantage of her innocence. It had been different with Poppy and the many other women he had used for his sexual pleasure. He was not ashamed of his sexual appetite. A strong man, hungry for life, which he had lived to the full, he was as God had made him, unashamedly male and virile. Now, the love he felt for Gina outweighed all thoughts of conquest. Wise men did not attempt to touch an unreachable star, to sully or debase a perfect human being.

Standing close behind him, 'I love you, Rab,' she whispered. 'I had to tell you, just this once. I wanted you to know.'

Standing still, head upraised, surprised by the sudden rush of tears to his eyes, he willed himself not to turn. 'And I love you, Gina. More than you'll ever know.'

And, 'Yes,' she sighed, suddenly at peace. 'I know that now.'

As the summer blossomed, Gina came to realize the power of Rab's intellect, his interest in art, music, literature and the theatre, which they discussed in depth as the portrait took shape.

That he had travelled widely became evident when he talked of the Uffizi Gallery, the Louvre, the Metropolitan Museum of Art, from first-hand experience. And yet he remained an enigma, as though his life were a jigsaw puzzle with the vital pieces missing.

She knew that he had lived in Germany before the war from his reference to the coffee. He had talked briefly of Dresden and Paris as people speak with affection of places in which they have lived and known well. Yet he dwelt on none of these things, apart from the theatre, and literature – her own great passions.

Inevitably, their conversation ended when Poppy burst into the room with her library books and her bass shopping bag lugged up from the market, containing a few fresh vegetables, a bit of meat or fish she had bought to replenish Rab's store cupboard. Suddenly the studio would be filled with her ebullient presence. At such moments, Gina would notice the tightening of Rab's lips, the way he bit harder on the stem of his pipe, and guessed why. His relationship with Poppy had altered since she came into his life. They were no longer lovers.

Curiously, Poppy appeared not to care, or pretended she did not. Her self-imposed task of bettering herself had become the dominant factor, imparting a new sense of purpose, so that she seemed more self-assured in Rab's company. A brave performance. At Gina's suggestion, she had started reading Dickens. So far, she had read *A Tale of Two Cities* and *David Copperfield*. Quite an achievement for a girl who had never read a book from cover to cover before.

*   *   *

One Saturday afternoon, bursting into the studio, Poppy stopped abruptly on the threshold. 'What's going on?' she demanded.

Self-consciously, Gina put down the book she was holding, a copy of Shakespeare's *Antony and Cleopatra*. 'I was reading aloud,' she explained.

'Oh! Well, carry on. Don't let me stop you.'

Gina laughed. 'I'd nearly finished anyway. Shall we have a cup of tea?'

'Yeah, sure thing. I'll put the kettle on.' Unpinning her hat, Poppy sped towards the living end of the room. 'I've brought some iced buns from Bonnets for us teas. I mean, our teas!' Filling the kettle, 'What was you reading?'

'Nothing very exciting. Just something from Shakespeare.' Gina caught Rab's eye. She felt suddenly, deeply ashamed of herself. Guilt-ridden. A traitor to both Shakespeare and Poppy. Shakespeare whom she revered; Poppy, because the girl was her friend who trusted her implicitly.

The following Saturday afternoon, when they were alone together, Rab said, 'Tell me, Gina, have you ever thought of becoming an actress?'

'Well, yes, the idea has crossed my mind from time to time,' she admitted.

'Then why hold back? Gina, you're a beautiful, talented woman. You have it in you to become a great actress. Can't you see, my love, you were born for better things than a solicitor's office? You don't belong behind a desk, a typewriter, not to simply a handful of people, but to the great, shining world of the theatre. No, please let me finish. Think of it Gina: the footlights, the music, the power of the spoken word.' He paused. 'You were born to be loved by all mankind, not by just one man with nothing to give you but his heart.'

'And if I told you that is all I want, all I have ever wanted?' She stepped down from the dais, felt the trembling of her limbs as she moved towards him. Laying her hands on his arms, she said, 'I don't want the love of all mankind, just *your* love. I'm not asking for the moon, only to stay near you, to share even the smallest corner of your life. Is that too much to ask?'

A vision of Paris rose up in his mind. Shaken by an overwhelming desire for escape, he thought of shore lights swimming down in the River Seine by night, the tree-lined boulevards and pavement cafés, the drifting of autumn leaves in the Tuileries gardens. How rich, full and exciting the future would be with Gina beside him. He imagined a rented apartment in the student quarter where they could live together as man and wife . . .

Slowly, regretfully, the vision faded. He could never subject Gina to that kind of existence. Nor could he shrug off certain responsibilities which lay on his conscience like a dead weight. How could he live with himself, or Gina, if he allowed his selfish desires to overrule his innate sense of decency and honour?

He said quietly, 'You will always be a part of my life, but I beg of you not to squander your talent, as I have mine. Please, darling, let me write you a letter of introduction to the London School of Dramatic Art. The director, George Landis, is an old friend of mine.'

Gina's eyes filled with tears. 'So you don't want me near you?'

Rab's self-control broke suddenly. Throwing aside paint-brush and palette, sweeping her into his arms, he kissed her as he had always wanted to kiss her, passionately, almost savagely, full on the lips.

'Now do you know how much I want you?' he muttered hoarsely, feeling the soft, womanly shape of her in the circle of his arms. 'I love you, Gina Brett, as I have never loved a woman before, and never will again. But you must do as I ask. Look to the future. *Your* future. Promise?'

Almost too breathless to speak, 'I promise,' she whispered.

Memory drew her back to that first night, when she had gone to the theatre alone, how she had placed her own interpretation on the way a certain line should have been spoken to gain the full dramatic impact. This she had known instinctively, but so much more was involved than an instinctive feeling for words. Realistically, what use a whisper if no-one beyond the front row could hear it?

To become an actress, she would have to learn how to project her voice so that even a whisper could be heard in the back row of the gods, how to walk properly, how to use her hands – and so much more. Stagecraft was tantamount to witchcraft, for when an actress who had mastered her profession came on-stage, what happened between that actress and the audience was akin to witchcraft, a kind of magic. The girl who had played Ophelia at the Bradford Alhambra all those years ago, had possessed that magic, Gina remembered.

Now that the end was in sight, as the final brush strokes were laid upon the canvas, Rab knew that he had created his own particular masterpiece. The composition of the painting was stunningly simple. Wanting nothing to detract from the loveliness of Gina's face, he had painted her against a background of subtly blended shades of grey and blue, reminiscent of a winter sky.

Against that deceptively simple background, Gina's hair burned like a flame. Strongly resisting the temptation to paint her with her hair down, she wore it drawn back from her temples, revealing the delicately planed cheekbones and softly smiling mouth. Easier by far had he asked her to look straight ahead, as if posing for a camera, but he wanted to capture the veiled mystery of the downward glance, to emphasize the wing-like eyebrows, the sweep of her lashes.

Her eyes, he had discovered, were not the green of any paint he had ever applied to his palette, not the colour of green glass, nor jade, and so the experimentation had begun, the mixing and testing until he had the colour he wanted. Then had come the delicate stippling of the freckles high on her cheekbones, reminiscent of a light dusting of pollen on a hazel catkin.

But every moment he had spent agonizing over the

portrait had been worthwhile, Rab thought, laying down the tools from which he had created the portrait of the woman he loved.

Smiling, he considered the master-stroke to be the high-necked white blouse with its prim edging of lace and narrow black velvet bow. Once again he had resisted the temptation of romanticizing the subject with clouds of tulle. He now knew, with a deep feeling of pride in his work, that he had been right in painting her the way he had first seen her. And whatever happened, he would never part with his Portrait of Gina.

In time to come, Gina would remember this summer of the portrait with mixed feelings of joy and sadness, a time of awakening, a watershed in her life – a summer on which, ultimately, the whole course of her future would depend. Her love for Rab deepened with every passing minute. She lived each moment with an underlying awareness that she might never again be as happy as she was then.

Young and in love, she noticed everything about her – flowers, trees, buildings, even passers-by, with a new clarity of vision, as if she were garnering each colour, each memory, into the storehouse of her mind against those times when colours would seem less vibrant, less beautiful. She knew the completion of the portrait would mean the end of her precious hours alone with Rab, and so she had wished that time would slow down a little, that the summer would never end. But summer was fast edging into autumn, and soon, Gina thought, the heather would be in bloom on the moors above the Calder Valley, signalling the end of summertime, the beginning of winter, as frost nipped the air and the bracken turned brown.

The letter Rab had handed her from George Landis, saying he would be delighted to audition Miss Brett, and looked forward to meeting her if she would care to write to him, remained unanswered. A letter from Owen, however, breaking the news of Mary Bickley's death, received an immediate reply.

'Dear Father,

You must not blame yourself for the death of Aunt Mary. Rather blame me. What happened was my fault entirely. I know now that I should have told her, quietly and sensibly, that I was uncertain about my engagement to Harold. She would have understood and advised me, I'm sure . . .'

Staring into the past, pen in hand, Gina thought that even had she done that, would not the rift between the two families have happened anyway? Knowing her mother so well, would not Agnes have regarded Mary Bickley's interference as an insult? Of course she would have. As for herself, Agnes would never have forgiven her for going behind her back to seek Mary's help and advice. So whichever way she had turned she would have been in the wrong.

Reading between the lines of Owen's letter, Gina guessed that her father had been in love with Mary Bickley, and her heart went out to him. She missed him so much, and longed to see him again, to feel his arms about her, to pour out all her troubles to him as she had done as a child. But she was a grown woman now. Even so, she wished with all her heart that she might go back in time to those carefree days before the war, of laughter in the sun, long before she had known the joy and the pain of love.

Packing his cabin trunk with his meagre belongings, Rab knew how deeply he would regret leaving this studio in which, for a short space of time, he had lived as a free spirit.

Now the time had come to take up the burden of his old life, he could only hope and pray that Gina and poor little Poppy would understand why he could not have borne to say goodbye to them. Better, he considered, simply to leave. No tears, no recriminations.

Poppy, he knew, would fall on his neck and weep if she knew he was leaving, and beg him not to go. He couldn't bear that. Gina, on the other hand, would stand tall and proud, saying nothing. But, reading the anguish in her eyes, he might waver in his duty.

Planning ahead, he had made a deal with the owner of the local gallery who bought, for a song, the many canvases stacked against the walls of the studio, many of which he had painted in his student days in Paris: pictures of the River Seine by night, the Île de la Cité at daybreak, others of the Steiner home in Dresden, of scarlet geraniums blooming on a kitchen window sill; a tall woman with dark hair grinding coffee beans near an open window, a view of the street beyond. But the one picture the greedy gallery owner really wanted, the Portrait of Gina, was not for sale, Rab told him, not at any price.

The cab he had hired to drive him to the station arrived punctually at seven o'clock that September Saturday morning. After helping the driver downstairs with the cabin trunk, Rab returned to the studio for one final moment of farewell to all he had known and loved during his brief sojourn in Scarborough.

Standing on the threshold he saw the great skylight window, the iron bedstead, the long, empty tables, the pot-bellied black stove near the sagging couch, the confetti-like splashes of dried paint on the bare wooden floor close to the raised dais on which Gina had sat to have her portrait painted. The room had seemed alive at that moment, with unforgettable memories of the past few months which he would remember until the end of time.

How he could bear to close the door on all those memories, he scarcely knew. But he *must*.

The landlady was waiting in the hall below to accept the key to the studio. Bidding her a hurried farewell, Rab got into the cab. As it moved away from the pavement, he turned his head for a final upward glance at the skylight window.

Mysteriously, importantly aglow, Poppy scuttled about the office, clearing up for the weekend. Mr Colebrook and Mr Mainwaring had already left, but Petch was still on the premises. 'I wish he'd hurry up and go,' Poppy said glancing up at the clock.

'Well, I'm off,' Jimmy announced, emerging from his cubby-hole. 'Come on, Patience.'

'You'll go when I say so, not before. I'm in charge here,' Poppy reminded him sharply. 'It ain't – isn't one o'clock yet.' She grinned at Gina, pleased that she had corrected her grammatical error without being reminded.

'It's five to,' Jimmy said impudently, 'an' there's nowt much you can do in five minutes.'

'Oh, isn't there?' Poppy said grimly, keeping a straight face, 'You'd be surprised. It wouldn't take me more than five seconds to give you a clout round the earhole!'

'I'll tell me ma!' Jimmy dodged behind a desk, laughing, as Poppy bore down on him. 'Come on, catch me if you can.' His laughter dried up suddenly as Petch came out of his office.

'A moment please, Miss Brett,' Petch said, 'I have a very important letter to dictate, if you wouldn't mind staying on for a few minutes. The rest of you may go.'

Giving Poppy an anguished look, Gina picked up her notebook and pencil. A request from one of the partners was something she could not refuse, but she felt nervous at the thought of being alone with the man after office hours.

'Sit down, Miss Brett, this won't take long,' Petch said smoothly when she entered his office. 'May I say how well you are looking? Apparently the sea air agrees with you. You are positively blooming.'

'If you don't mind, sir, my landlady will be expecting me at a quarter past one.' Mrs Potts provided her lodgers with soup and bread in lieu of sandwiches, at the weekend.

'Oh, come now, Gina. I may call you Gina? When we've finished here, I'll take you across to the Royal for lunch.'

'That won't be necessary, thank you. Now, may we get on with the dictation?'

'Oh, damn the dictation!' Petch moved swiftly to the door and stood with his back to it as Gina rose hurriedly to leave.

'Please let me pass,' she said calmly, unwilling to let him see how frightened she was. But Petch stood there smiling down at her, blocking her way with his strong, tautly muscled body, wetting his lips. 'Don't be a silly girl,' he said thickly, 'give me what I want and you'll be well off, I promise. You can have anything you like – nice clothes, a gold bracelet—'

Suddenly his arms were about her, his lips on hers. Thick, wet lips. She could tell by his breath that he had been drinking. Useless to struggle, he was far too strong. Instinctively she raised her right knee to the crotch of his trousers and drove it hard into his groin. Uttering an obscenity, he doubled up with pain. Seeing the way clear, Gina tugged open the door and fled through the outer office and down the stairs, pausing only to snatch up her handbag from her desk.

Breathless and shaken, she ran along St Nicholas Street into Newborough, aware that people were turning to look at her, hatless and dishevelled.

Mrs Potts was in the hall, looking displeased. 'Where have you been, Miss Brett? I expect my lodgers to be on time—' As Gina brushed past her with a murmured apology, 'Is anything the matter? *Miss Brett!*'

In the safety of her room, Gina stood with her back to the door. Then, crossing to the wash-stand, she scrubbed her face with the flannel to remove every trace of that wet kiss Petch had planted on her mouth, shuddering at the memory of his body close to hers, the smell of drink on his breath, her violent reaction to his embrace. How could a professional man of his standing have done such a thing? How could she, a well brought up young lady, have reacted so violently? So far, she had been happy at Colebrook's, but what of the future?

It was then that she remembered the letter from George Landis in her handbag, the chance of an audition at the London School of Dramatic Art. Her mind made up, getting out her writing pad and pen, she wrote to him suggesting a date for their meeting, and hurried out to post the letter before she could change her mind.

Poppy was in her room when she got back, looking worried. 'Hey,' she said, 'what's up? Mrs Potts said you looked dreadful when you came in. Did old Petch make a pass at you?'

'I'm afraid so.' Poppy would have to know sooner or later.

'The old devil! I thought he was up to something. Huh, he wants striking off, and he's going the right way about it. Are you going to complain to Mr Colebrook?'

'No, Poppy. The last thing I want is to cause trouble.' Gina sat down on the bed, her legs still shaking.

'*You* cause trouble? It's old Petch that's caused the trouble as far as I can see! What – what did he *do*?'

'I'd rather not talk about it.'

'I bet I can guess. Did he try his standing with his back to the door routine? I thought so. He tried that on with me once.'

'What did you do?'

'Do? I told him if he didn't let me out, I'd tell his wife. The drunken pig! You know he keeps a bottle of whisky hidden behind those books of his?'

'No, I didn't know that, but it explains why . . .' Gina attempted a smile. 'Let's not talk about it any more. Are you seeing Rab this afternoon?'

'Yes, and you're coming with me. I'm not leaving you here on your own.'

Poppy's championship warmed Gina's heart. How funny – and dear – she looked standing there, arms akimbo, wearing her best straw hat trimmed with artificial flowers, the size of two-pennorth of copper, as fierce as a tigress guarding its cubs, the closest friend she'd ever had.

'Come on, get changed,' Poppy advised, 'and let's get going. Rab will make us some tea, and I'll nip across to the cake shop for some of them – those cream cakes he likes.'

Gina changed in to a fresh blouse and skirt, pinned on her hat, and walked along St Nicholas Street arm-in-arm with Poppy, to the studio, thinking how pleased Rab would be that she had replied to Landis' letter. She would tell him when Poppy nipped across the road for the cream cakes.

Entering the building, they walked up the twisting stairs

106

to the top landing. 'Coo-ee,' Poppy sang out as usual, laying her hand on the doorknob, expecting the door to swing open, to see Rab standing there, a welcoming smile on his face.

'That's funny.' Poppy frowned. 'He must have gone out. The door won't budge.' She laughed suddenly, 'Oh, I expect he's gone down to the, er, "throne room". There's only one, you know. He'll be back in a minute. Let's sit on the stairs and wait. But why lock the door? He knew I'd be coming.'

Sitting on the stairs, the girls waited five minutes, ten, then fifteen. At twenty past three they knew, by the creaking of the stairs, that someone was coming. 'It's him!' Poppy cried joyfully, scrambling to her feet. 'I expect he's been out shopping.'

Gina also stood up, a gnawing feeling of unrest deep inside her. She had half guessed the truth before the landlady appeared on the lower landing, before she heard her say, 'It's no use hanging about here, you two. The artist feller's gone. He left early this morning.'

'*Gone?*' Poppy's cry of anguish touched Gina to the heart. 'But he *can't* have! I mean, he *will* be coming back soon, won't he?'

'Not so far as I know. Leastways he never said nothing about coming back. All I know is, he hired a cab to drive him to the station, settled up with me, and went. I've just hung a "Flat to Let" notice in the downstairs window.'

'But surely,' Poppy wailed, beside herself with grief, 'he must have said where he was going? Left a forwarding address?'

'No, miss, I'm sorry, he did nothing of the sort. He seemed in a bit of a hurry. Now, if you don't mind moving, I want to clean up a bit in there before the next tenant moves in.' Hefting her bucket and broom up the last few stairs, producing a key from her apron pocket, she entered the studio, and closed the door firmly behind her.

'Come on, Poppy,' Gina said gently, helping the weeping girl to the street below, one arm firmly anchored about her waist. 'Rab's sure to be in touch with you soon.' What else could she possibly say? She must give poor Poppy at least a shred of hope to cling to. But, strangely, Poppy would not be comforted. 'No,' she said hoarsely, 'it's no use pretending. He never really loved me, I knew that all along. He just wanted rid of me, only he hadn't the guts to say so! I expect he's gone away with – *her* – that model.'

'No, Poppy, I'm sure that's not true. I just know it isn't true.' But Poppy wasn't listening. From the depths of her despair she said slowly, heedless of the tears streaming down her cheeks, 'The awful thing is, I'm going to have a baby. Rab's child. The poor little bastard!'

Chapter Eight

Gina put Poppy to bed, and drew the curtains. The light hurt her eyes, she said, and Gina could see why. The girl's lids had puffed to twice their normal size from all the tears she had shed. Curiously, Poppy's distress strengthened Gina's resolve not to betray her own emotion. No use attempting to solve the riddle of Rab's hasty departure, of putting forward possible reasons why he had gone away without a word of explanation. She simply hoped that he would write soon to put Poppy out of her misery.

Sitting beside the bed where Poppy lay with her head buried in the pillows, Gina asked her gently if Rab knew she was pregnant. 'No, I never let on,' she sobbed. 'I was going to tell him tomorrow.'

Relief washed over Gina that Rab had not gone away, like a thief in the night, to escape his responsibilities. Had he done so, her trust in him would have been shattered. Smoothing Poppy's hair, she applied a cold water compress to her aching forehead. But where had he gone to, and why?

'The truth is,' Poppy said brokenly, 'I wanted to get pregnant. I thought if I did Rab would marry me. I wanted that more than anything, to be his wife, to take care of him. Well, I've landed myself in a right mess, haven't I?' She clutched Gina's hand, her body racked with sobs. 'Now what will happen to me? I'll have to give up my job, leave here. Mrs Potts will give me notice when she finds out!'

'Don't worry, I'll take care of you,' Gina promised, unable to foretell that her promise would change the whole course of her life.

'But why should you? What am I to you that you should be stuck with a daft lass like me?' Poppy asked, choking back a sob.

'You are my friend,' Gina said simply. She could have

109

said much more, remembering the way Poppy had taken her under her wing when she first came to Scarborough, the sharing of her dinner-time sandwiches, the way she had stood by her when she went to Fernlea to confront Mrs Woodbridge, and so much more. Because she looked upon Poppy as the sister she had always longed for, and never had.

Supper was served at six o'clock in the small dining-room on the ground floor, next to the kitchen, at a long table to accommodate all her lodgers. No separate tables nonsense for Mrs Potts, who believed in keeping things simple – including the meals.

The menus never varied. She had the bills worked out to a fine art to save a penny here, tuppence there. Porridge, potatoes and kippers were cheap to buy, so were beef sausages and faggots. The Sunday roast, usually belly-pork, or mutton, which Mr Potts sliced to transparent thinness with a well-honed, cut-throat razor. Thereafter the meat would appear in various guises, mainly hashed or rissoled. Brawn was another great standby, as was the stock-pot. Potts, who worked as a sweeper at the market, would bring home with him parcels of bones and left-over vegetables when the market closed on Saturday night, to ensure a continuing supply of 'Brown Windsor'. Puddings were invariably rice, tapioca, bread and butter, or stodgy wedges of boiled flour and suet served with a scraping of jam and thin, lukewarm custard.

When Gina asked if she could bring down her supper on a tray, Poppy retched feebly at the thought of tackling a slice of quivering brawn and lumpy mashed potatoes. 'No,' she whispered, pressing her hanky to her lips. 'Just tell Mrs Potts I'm not feeling well, tell her I've caught a cold, only don't let her come down to see me. I couldn't bear anyone near me, only you.'

Making her way upstairs to the dining-room, knowing that Mrs Potts would be suspicious if neither of her basement lodgers put in an appearance, Gina sat down at the table as the gong sounded and the other residents, mainly shop-assistants, appeared, laughing and talking. 'Where's Poppy?' one of them asked, just as Mrs Potts arrived with a tray of food.

Hearing Gina's explanation that Poppy had caught a cold and was staying in bed, 'Huh,' the landlady said, 'just as well. I'm sure *I* don't want any of her germs. I've enough on my plate as it is.'

Looking at the plate Mrs Potts put down in front of her, Georgina felt a burning sense of injustice on Poppy's behalf. Not a word of regret that the poor girl was ill. The sooner she removed herself and Poppy from this place the better, she thought, prodding at the brawn, an idea formulating in her mind. If only they could find a small house to rent. A two-up, two-down would do, where they could be alone and independent when Poppy's waist began to thicken, and she could no longer keep secret the fact that she was going to have a child.

Oh God, Rab, where are you? Gina thought despairingly. But some instinct told her that he would not come back for a very long time, perhaps never. The same instinct told her that he had gone away, without explanation, because he could not have borne to say goodbye. This she understood, remembering the day Harold Bickley went off to war, all the futile things one said at the last moment to fill in time. 'You will write to me, Georgina?' he'd asked, and yet he had never bothered to reply to her letters. She wondered, vaguely, why not.

Looking in on Poppy, she saw that the girl had cried herself to sleep, and went to her own room, glad to be alone at last, drained and exhausted from the necessity of keeping a firm grip on her emotions.

Lying face down on the bed, the held-back tears came as a relief. Exploring the long corridor of memories, she recalled every word she and Rab had said to each other from the moment they met, remembered the way he smiled, the sound of his voice, the richness and scope of his intellect, the way he had fired her imagination with his talk of the theatre, of books, poetry, art and music, his concern for her future. She then remembered the letter she had posted to George Landis earlier that day, and knew that she had wasted a stamp. She could not leave Scarborough now, with Poppy dependent on her for help.

Nor, she thought wearily, could she remain at the office after what had taken place between herself and Basil Petch. She must hand in her notice to Mr Colebrook the first thing on Monday morning, find herself another job. Or, if she found a place for herself and Poppy, they could possibly earn a living by taking in work.

Sitting up, drying her eyes, and fired with renewed hope, Gina crossed swiftly to the sideboard drawer where she kept her writing materials. Sitting at the table, nibbling the end of her pen, she knew what she must do. Setting pen to paper, she wrote: *'Dear Father, I need your help. Please come if possible, as quickly as you can . . .'*

The letter sealed and stamped, Gina made her way to the post-box on the corner for the second time that day.

On Monday morning, she walked with Poppy along St Nicholas Street to work. Nearing the office, she noticed that poor Poppy kept her eyes straight ahead, as though willing herself not to look up at the studio skylight catching the sunlight of this early September morning. Her eyes were filled with tears.

'Try not to cry any more,' Gina murmured sympathetically, holding her arm. 'Think of the baby.'

'Think of the baby,' Poppy said irritably. 'I've thought of nothing else but the blessed baby for weeks now. I'm sick and tired of thinking about it. I wish it had never happened, and that's a fact. And if I could lay my hands on Rab, I'd choke the life out of him!' So saying, she marched up the stairs like *The Fighting Téméraire*. And anger, Gina thought, was the best, possibly the only, antidote to grief. Rather Poppy snappish and irritable than Poppy defeated.

She had made no mention of her hazy plans for the future, nor the fact that she had decided to hand in her notice, thinking that Poppy had experienced enough emotional upheaval for the time being. Thankfully, Poppy

112

was in the cloakroom when Colebrook hung up his hat and walking-stick. 'May I have a word with you, sir?' Gina asked breathlessly.

'Of course, my dear. Come in. What can I do for you?' A sharp observer of his fellow humans, Colebrook knew at once that the girl was about to impart bad news.

She said slowly, 'I wish to hand in my notice. Of course I'll stay until you have found a replacement, but . . .' her voice faltered.

'Sit down.' The old man regarded her thoughtfully. 'Now, what is all this about, eh? You are not happy here, is that it?'

'No, sir, not entirely,' Gina confessed, unwilling to go into details.

'The work is too hard for you, perhaps?' Colebrook persisted.

'No, not at all. I just want to leave, that's all.'

Petch, Colebrook thought angrily. Petch had been up to his old tricks again. But he had to be sure.

'Then you feel, possibly, that you have been harassed in some way? By myself, for instance?'

'Oh no, not by you, sir. You have been kindness itself. You mustn't think that.'

'Then by some member of my staff?'

A tide of colour stained Gina's cheeks as she recalled the unpleasant incident in Petch's office. 'I'm sorry,' she said, 'I can't answer that question.'

So it *was* Petch, the bloody fool! Well, he had been warned that further harassment of the female staff would not be tolerated. Colebrook was at a loss to understand why a man of Petch's professional standing, with a wife and children, should play fast and loose with every attractive female that crossed his line of vision. Tapping his fingers on the desk, 'Have you another job to go to?' he asked.

'No, but . . .' remembering that Mr Colebrook had once told her she could turn to him for advice, 'that is, do you think I could earn a living by taking in typing?'

Colebrook considered the question carefully. 'I don't see

113

why not. Good stenographers are few and far between. I, for one, would be willing to entrust important documents to someone of your calibre working away from the office, and I dare say many of my colleagues would feel the same. A busy office with clients coming and going all day long is not conducive to concentration.' He smiled. 'May I ask where?'

'I haven't got as far as that yet. I'd thought of renting a furnished house or rooms, if possible.'

A thought teased Colebrook's mind. Now where on earth? He'd seen a flat to let recently. Ah yes, of course, in the house next to the Royal, when he'd gone to the hotel to dine with his wife on Saturday evening. How convenient it would be for Jimmy to slip across the road from the office to deliver and collect confidential legal documents, if Georgina decided to go ahead with her typewriting agency. Of course the place might not be suitable, but he could at least mention it.

When he did so, the colour in the girl's cheeks drained away as quickly as it had risen. Had he said something to upset her? When he asked her, 'Oh no,' she said quickly, 'it's just that someone I – knew – once lived there, and I . . . Well, it isn't quite what I had in mind.'

'In that case, I suggest that you contact Mr Marshall, an estate agent friend of mine in Queen Street. I'm sure he'll be able to help you.'

'Thank you, Mr Colebrook, you have been most kind.'

When she had gone, Colebrook sent for Jimmy. 'Has Mr Petch come in yet?' he asked.

'Yes, sir, a few minutes ago.'

'Then tell him I wish to see him immediately.'

'Yes, sir.'

When Jimmy had hurried away, Cecil Colebrook sat back in his chair to await his confrontation with the lecherous Basil Petch, to which he looked forward with a certain degree of grim satisfaction.

After reading Gina's letter, Owen set off for the mill as usual, dealt with the post, dictated replies to his new secretary, then he left quietly to drive to Scarborough to see his daughter.

'Well, Father, what do you think of it?'

Glancing round the studio, 'I'm not quite sure,' Owen said. 'I find it somewhat disturbing.'

'In what way?'

'I don't know.' Looking up at the skylight, he added, 'I thought you were happy with Mr Colebrook. What happened to change all that?'

'It's a long story.'

'Even so, I'd like to hear it.'

And so Gina told her father about Rab, Poppy, the portrait, Petch and Mrs Potts, holding nothing back, confiding in the one person she knew she could turn to for love and understanding.

'This girl Poppy must mean a great deal to you,' Owen remarked when Gina had finished speaking.

'Yes she does. You see, I've never had a real friend before.'

Owen said gently, 'And the artist, Rab? You say you are in love with him. Doesn't it worry you that Poppy is expecting his child?'

'In one sense, yes, of course it does, but – oh, how can I explain? What Rab and I shared was far more than a physical relationship. I mean, there are different dimensions to love. It is possible, isn't it, to love someone deeply without physical contact?'

Remembering Mary Bickley, Owen knew exactly what she meant. He too had loved someone in the same, non-physical way and this, he knew, was the rarest, the most precious love of all, to enter the mind and the soul of a beloved person with no thought of sexuality to destroy or to mar the quintessential purity of love.

'So this is where it all happened?' he said softly, realizing why the room had so disturbed him – because the man who had once lived here had imbued the very air about them with the power of his unorthodox personality.

115

'You think I shouldn't take it?' Gina's voice betrayed her uncertainty.

'Not without asking Poppy,' Owen said. 'Has it occurred to you that she might find her memories of the past too painful to bear? Your own memories also?'

Gina shook her head. 'Not my memories, Father. I was a little unsure at first, how I'd feel crossing the threshold – not seeing Rab standing at his easel. But not now, because he's still here, and always will be.' She smiled sadly. 'But you are right, it must be Poppy's decision, not mine.'

'She knows nothing about all this?'

'No. I wanted to talk it over with you first. Not that I had thought about coming here to live when I wrote you that letter, only about setting up a typewriting agency, of finding a place for Poppy and me where we could live and work together until the baby's born.'

'And after the baby's born?'

'I don't know, Father. I just want to see her through the worst time. If she doesn't want to come here, then I'll find somewhere else.'

'In that case, you'll need financial help,' Owen said. 'No argument!' Getting out his cheque book and pen. 'For one thing you will need a typewriter, possibly two; money for food and clothing; items of furniture. I must be sure in my mind that you and Poppy will not go hungry, that the child she is carrying will not suffer any ill effects.'

The way her father included Poppy warmed Gina's heart. She had never loved him more or felt so close to him as she did then.

Next day, 'You mean you've handed in your notice without telling me? Huh, you're a dark horse, and no mistake.' Poppy tossed her head, hurt to the quick by what she saw as her friend's betrayal.

They had walked down to the seafront to eat their sandwiches. The season was almost over now, but the bunting still fluttered about the Arcadia building, and a few late visitors were strolling along the Foreshore enjoying the

116

sunshine and sea air. Suddenly Poppy's eyes filled with tears as she recalled the many evenings she had walked this way with Rab. With her hand tucked into his arm, wearing her best blouse and skirt and her straw boater with the floating red ribbons, she had chattered nineteen to the dozen stepping along proudly beside him; pausing now and then to lean on the railings to watch the Pierrot show on the sands, or chivvied him to buy her a knickerbocker glory in one of the ice-cream parlours across the road.

'Don't be angry, Poppy. I had no choice after what happened with Mr Petch. Besides, I have an idea.' Treading warily, 'I'm thinking of starting a typewriting agency.'

Smarting from the injustice of life, 'Oh well, that's fine, isn't it?' Poppy retorted. 'I wish you luck, I'm sure. I suppose that means you'll be leaving Mrs Potts as soon as you've found somewhere better to live?' Tears spilled down Poppy's cheeks. She had never felt so miserable, so unwanted in her life before. In vain she fiddled in her handbag for a hanky.

'Here, have mine. Dry your eyes, blow your nose, and listen,' Gina said. 'We are *both* leaving Mrs Potts. Unless you don't want to come in with me.' That thought had never crossed her mind until now. Perhaps she had taken too much for granted?

'Not *want* to?' Poppy blew her nose hard. 'Oh, Gina, I'm sorry. I thought—'

'I know what you thought, but you were wrong. I would have told you before, but it all happened so quickly. Yesterday, you know when I said I couldn't have lunch with you? Well, my father came over to see me. I needed to talk to him, to make sure he approved.'

'And did he?'

'Yes.' Gina drew in a deep breath. Now for it. 'Of course, we'd need to find suitable premises—'

Poppy said mistily, interrupting the sentence, 'I know where I'd like to be, given the choice.'

'Oh? Where?'

Eyes shining through her tears, Poppy said, 'The studio, Rab's studio! I mean, it is to let, isn't it?'

'You really wouldn't mind going back there?'

'*Mind?* It's the only place on earth I want to be. I never stop thinking about it, dreaming about it. I mean, who knows, Rab might come back to the studio one of these days. Just think how surprised he'd be to find me there, waiting for him!'

Forever after, for the rest of her life, Gina would look back on the time she and Poppy had spent together in the studio with mixed feelings of happiness and regret.

Growing older, in rare moments of solitude snatched from her pressurized life, she would remember the way she had felt, lying in bed and looking up at the moon and stars through the skylight window. As autumn deepened into winter, the lashing of rain against the windows, the shadows cast on walls and ceiling by the brightly burning wood fire in the stove, the distant, mournful sound of the fog-horn on the lighthouse pier, the view of the sea from the living-room window: the clatter of typewriter keys as she and Poppy strove to cope with the piles of legal documents on their desk.

But above and beyond all that, lingered the fragrance of freshly ground coffee, pipe tobacco and perfume, of the herbs that Rab had once used liberally to spice the food he had cooked for himself in the small Dutch oven adjacent to the stove, so that the air about them seemed permeated with memories of the man who had left his bold, unorthodox imprint on both their lives.

How happy she had been then, Gina remembered, taking care of Poppy, making certain that she ate a proper breakfast and a nourishing evening meal. Living under the same roof, how well she had come to understand her friend's strengths and weaknesses, likes and dislikes, moods and machinations.

There had been times when Poppy's rapid mood changes had driven her almost mad with frustration. But, making allowances for the girl's condition and her occasional bouts of depression when Rab's defection and her natural dread of the ordeal facing her, came uppermost,

118

she had managed to keep the peace between them by the simple expedient of listening, of saying nothing until the storm had blown itself out. Then Poppy would say tearfully, 'I don't know how you put up with me, Gina, I really don't. I'm nothing but a fat, ungrateful pig! Why don't you tell me to clear out, and have done with it?'

'What? And do all the typing myself? No fear.' Never once had Gina said, 'I put up with you because I love you, because my life would seem empty without you.' But there was no need of pretty speeches. They had both known how much they meant to each other.

Poppy's baby was due in March. As the winter progressed, she would sit on the shabby settee in front of the fire knitting a shawl for it, puzzling over the pattern, dropping stitches, while Gina cooked their evening meal and busied herself with the washing up afterwards, telling Poppy not to worry, that she wanted her to rest as much as possible; to get on with her knitting. She wondered what Rab would think if he could see the place now, surprised to find that she had inherited some of her mother's housekeeping skills in wanting to keep the studio as clean and tidy as possible, although she had never felt inclined to scrape up the confetti-like paint stains on the floor where his easel had once stood.

The long, rough farmhouse tables were scrubbed now to pristine cleanliness, one of which they used as a desk, their typewriters standing where Rab's paintbrushes, stone jars, paint tubes and bottles of turpentine had once taken pride of place.

Rab's bed, in which Georgina now slept, was covered with more orthodox clothing than old horse and army blankets, and Owen's cheque had made possible the purchase of a comfortable bed for Poppy on the far side of the room, in the living area close to the fire, a less draughty position than Gina's.

Increasing bulkiness made Poppy diffident about being seen in broad daylight, and so Gina did the shopping and brought home books from the penny library for her friend to read when she grew bored with dropping stitches. But the girl could not stay indoors all the time, and so Gina would persuade her to walk round St Nicholas Square when darkness fell and the residents of the tall houses surrounding the square had drawn their curtains for the night. The crisp, cold air blowing in from the sea did Poppy good, and helped her to sleep better.

Deeply ashamed of her condition, she had not told her Aunt Charlotte in Hartlepool that she was pregnant, knowing she would throw up her hands in horror at the very idea of her niece giving birth to an illegitimate child. Gina tried to persuade Poppy to write to her aunt telling her the truth, but Poppy would not hear of it. 'I don't want her to know,' she said stubbornly. 'Besides, she has enough on her plate looking after my brothers.'

'But she is your next of kin, and she's bound to find out sooner or later,' Gina pointed out. But Poppy remained obdurate. 'I'll cross that bridge when I come to it,' she said.

As Christmas approached, Gina experienced a tug of homesickness for Elmhurst, and would hurry downstairs each morning in the hope of finding a message from Agnes on the doormat. A tuppenny Christmas card would have sufficed, a few scrawled words as a sign of reconciliation at this great Christian festival of forgiveness. But no card from Agnes arrived to grace the holly-decked mantelpiece.

Even so, Gina decided to make this a Christmas to remember, for Poppy's sake, to which end she bought colourful candles, tinsel and baubles to decorate the Christmas tree. She had lugged it home from the market along with great bundles of holly, a sprig or two of mistletoe, and a shopping bag filled with fresh vegetables, cheese and the small duck they would have for their Christmas dinner.

Enchanted with the Christmas tree, Poppy clipped the wax candles to the branches, hung the baubles, and looped up the tinsel as eagerly as a child, nursing the secret of the present she had bought for Gina.

She had actually braved an appearance in public on the Saturday before Christmas losing herself in the crowds of shoppers thronging Westborough. Hearing the carols played by the Salvation Army Band Poppy was caught up in the excitement, and dropped sixpence into a collecting-box. She entered a stationers to choose a pen and pencil set in a presentation box with a red silk lining, priced one-and-sixpence, purchasing, at the same time, affectionately-worded Christmas cards to send to Aunt Charlotte and her young brothers, Alfie and Frankie, and a special one for Gina. Then she had gone into a bazaar in the main street to buy Ludo and Snakes and Ladders games to send to her brothers, and a pair of warm woollen gloves for her aunt. She was uplifted by the feeling of Christmas in the air; the wet pavements beneath her feet which reflected circles of light cast by early blossoming gas-lamps.

And yet, from all this was missing the one person on earth that Poppy yearned after day and night. Where was Rab now, she wondered, trudging home with her purchases. Why had he gone away so suddenly without a word of explanation? Why had he not written to her? Or perhaps he had sent a Christmas card and a letter to her old address in Newborough, and Mrs Potts had not bothered to send them on to her. But even as these thoughts crossed her mind Poppy knew in her heart of hearts that her child would be born fatherless. She would give birth to the baby without a wedding ring on her finger; would carry the stigma of an unmarried mother for the rest of her life . . . unless . . . Somehow, she could not believe that Rab would not come back to her.

The candlelit Christmas tree shone brightly in a shadowy corner of the room as darkness fell on Christmas Day. The wood in the stove sank slowly to ashes as the two girls made ready for bed, but Gina knew that happiness could not be conjured from the trappings of tinsel and holly. Only love

121

and forgiveness could have imbued this day with any real meaning. Looking up at the frosty stars beyond the skylight window, she thought that a message from Rab, a word from Agnes, would have made all the difference to herself and Poppy, dispelling the deep well of loneliness beneath their pretended gaiety.

Chapter Nine

January came in on clouds of whirling snow, settling and deepening as soon as it fell, which transformed the town overnight into a fairyland of white, muffling the sounds of traffic in the street below, blanketing the light from the overhead window.

The studio was intensely cold. Twice daily Gina went down to the wood-shed in the yard to fetch fuel for the stove, lugging the weighty skeps upstairs, her fingers numb, hair tucked up beneath a green woollen hat. Poppy, depressed by the cold and the lack of natural light, and bundled up in clothes, huddled near the stove to keep warm, uncaring that her legs were becoming scorch-marked as she hitched up her skirts to savour the heat on her shins.

But it wasn't just the cold and the lack of daylight that depressed Poppy. In a few weeks from now she would have to face the greatest ordeal of her life. The thought of giving birth filled her with a nervous terror as she recalled the agony her mother had endured bringing her children into the world. And to think that she had brought this trouble on herself. A love child, she thought bitterly, conceived without love on Rab's part. What a fool she'd been to want a baby by him, to take the initiative in their lovemaking, rousing him to a passionate awareness of her sturdy young body, using every wile known to woman to make him respond to her overtures, even when she had known, deep down, that he would have responded – as any hot-blooded man would have done – to any desirable female who had so wantonly begged him to make love to her.

Now she was paying the price of her folly. The sight of her bloated, ugly body in the gilt-framed mirror above the shelf where the model Harriet Cohen's items of makeup and lace-edged handkerchief had once lain, filled her with a burning sense of shame.

As January wore on, Poppy became more depressed and irritable. Even when the snow on the skylight window began slowly to melt, she could not bring herself to tackle the ever-increasing piles of legal documents which flooded in daily from various solicitors' offices. All the typewriting was left to Gina who, despite her sympathy for Poppy, could not cope with that amount of work on her own.

One day she said quietly, 'Look Poppy, I need your help.'

Up in arms in an instant, 'Oh, so you're calling me a lazy good-for-nothing, are you?' Poppy retaliated, her colour rising.

Gina sighed deeply. 'I said nothing of the kind. I just think it can't be good for you sitting still all day, brooding—'

'A fat lot you know! You're not the one having a baby,' Poppy said explosively. 'You might come down off your high-horse if you were – if you felt as miserable, fat and useless as—' Suddenly, clutching her stomach, she uttered a low-pitched cry of pain. Then, 'Oh God,' she muttered, 'it's started. Gina, help me. *Please* help me!'

The memory of the hours that followed would remain as a series of rapidly changing events in Georgina's mind, a meaningless jumble of images linked to the knowledge that Poppy was desperately ill.

In time to come she would scarcely remember pulling on her outdoor clothing, racing downstairs to alert the landlady, asking her to stay with Poppy until the doctor arrived, hurrying along to Queen Street, where the doctor had his surgery. Mounting the front steps, she had hammered at the door-knocker, begging the maidservant who answered to tell the doctor that he was needed urgently to attend to her friend who had gone into premature labour, who was bleeding badly, and in great pain.

All that Gina would clearly remember was the expression in the doctor's eyes when later, at the hospital, he came into the waiting-room to tell her that Poppy was sinking fast following the birth of her child. Despite all their efforts, they had been unable to stop the bleeding. His softly uttered words, 'You may see her now. She has been asking for you,' struck terror into Gina's heart.

The room in which Poppy lay was small and cold, smelling of chloroform and disinfectant.

Approaching the bed, 'I'm here, darling,' Gina whispered, holding Poppy's hand.

'I knew you'd come.' Poppy smiled serenely, as if she knew that her brief sojourn through life was almost over. 'You've been so strong – the only real friend I've ever had.'

'Oh, Poppy!' Gina bent her head to hide her tears.

'Hey, come on now!' Clasping Gina's hand, 'I'm not afraid of dying. I thought I would be, but I'm not. I mean, it won't be all that different from going to sleep, and I'm so tired . . .' She was speaking in little more than a whisper, pausing for breath. Her hand felt weightless, her face looked grey. Poppy was dying, and she knew it, but her eyes in the pale mask of her face were still curiously alive as she struggled to say what was on her mind. 'Promise me you'll take care of my baby.'

'Yes, darling. I promise.' Tears trickled down Gina's cheeks.

'Call him – Oliver – after that boy in the book I read. Remember?' She closed her eyes. Gina sat beside her, stroking her hand, unaware that Poppy had slipped away from her. Even when one of the nurses came to look at Poppy, and said quietly, 'She's gone, I'm afraid,' Gina could not believe that she was dead. A burning anger rose up inside her. 'No!' she cried sharply. 'She hasn't. She can't have. I'd have known.'

'Please, Miss Brett. I know how you feel, but there's nothing more you can do for her now. Come with me. Doctor Banting would like a word with you.'

Turning at the door and looking back, Gina saw, through a mist of tears, Poppy's serenely sleeping face upon the pillow; seemed to hear her say, down the misty corridors of time, 'I had a kipper for breakfast this morning. Ain't life grand?'

Now all that remained of Poppy was a tiny bundle of humanity she had promised to take care of.

A boy called Oliver.

Doctor Banting's questions were gently put yet deeply probing. Gina, in a state of shock, answered as one in a dream, wishing he would go away and leave her alone with her memories of Poppy.

'Tell me, Miss Brett, were you and Miss Hewitt related in any way? Cousins, perhaps?'

'No,' Gina replied dully. 'Poppy was my friend. She asked me to take care of her baby.'

'Forgive me for asking but had she any family? Next-of-kin?'

'An aunt and two young brothers in Hartlepool.'

'The aunt must be notified.'

'Of course. I'll send her a telegram.'

'Miss Brett, I know you are very upset, but the situation is this.' He paused, 'About the baby. If Miss Hewitt's aunt wishes to adopt it, there is nothing to be done about it.'

Once more came the burning feeling of anger. Where was the justice in all this? Where the God of mercy she had learned about at her confirmation classes, the trusting child in the white muslin dress? 'But you *don't* understand! I gave a solemn promise. Poppy asked *me* to take care of her baby.'

'I am very sorry, Miss Brett. I understand how you feel, but—'

'*Understand?* How could you possibly understand?' What price women's emancipation now, when men apparently had all the say? Her anger encompassed Rab, also, who had left Poppy to face living, and dying, without him. Now here was this man, this doctor, telling her he understood her feelings when she scarcely knew them herself; brushing aside Poppy's dying wish as if she had no right to bequeath the most precious possession she had ever owned to the one she had chosen to receive that legacy.

Dr Banting said quietly, 'I was merely pointing out that, legally speaking, you have no claim to the child. If the mother's wishes had been made plain in writing, and properly witnessed—'

126

'The mother was bleeding to death, doctor!' Gina's voice caught on a sob.

Banting's heart went out to the girl. Anger, he knew, was a normal shock reaction to sudden bereavement. He said, 'In any case, the child will have to remain in my care for the time being. A baby born eight weeks prematurely has its own battles to fight.'

'You mean he may not – survive?' She stared at the doctor with frightened eyes.

'There is that possibility, I'm afraid. He is very tiny, extremely weak.'

Gina would remember for the rest of her life the sudden upsurge of love she had experienced the moment she saw Poppy's baby, a tenderness she had never known before.

Mrs Reece – Poppy's Aunt Charlotte – came at once in response to Gina's telegram. She was a plump little woman in her early fifties, decently if shabbily dressed, wearing a black armband as a sign of mourning. Obviously shocked by the news of Poppy's death, she sat in front of the stove sipping the tea Gina had made for her after the train journey from Hartlepool.

'But I don't understand what happened, how Poppy came to die so suddenly,' she said. 'I heard from her at Christmas, and she said nowt about feeling poorly. It's beyond me.'

Gina said compassionately, 'Poppy died of a haemorrhage. You see, she had given birth to a baby.'

Charlotte Reece clattered down her cup, slopping the tea into the saucer; eyes wide with shock. 'A baby? But I didn't even know she was married.'

Drawing in a deep breath, clasping her hands, 'She wasn't,' Gina said quietly.

There was no harm in Mrs Reece. She was simply the product of an older generation of women who regarded illegitimacy as a sin.

'I might have known!' Mrs Reece said bitterly. 'Like father like child.' Unclasping her handbag, she felt for a handkerchief. 'I warned my sister not to marry that man, but she took no notice. Well, she rued the day, poor soul! But I did my best for her. I sent her money when she hadn't two brass farthings to rub together. Oh yes, and when Albert joined the Army, after poor Belle was dead and gone, I did my duty by her children. But the fact is, I never took to Poppy from the word go.' She wiped her eyes. 'There was too much of her father in her for her own good. All those fancy ideas of hers about wanting to get on in the world. Well, a fine end she's come to, I must say.'

Fighting the battle on Poppy's behalf, 'Poppy *did* get on in the world,' Gina said. 'We were in partnership together – a typewriting agency. She was good at her job, highly thought of by Mr Colebrook. Please, you mustn't think unkindly of her. She told me, had it not been for you she would never have learned shorthand and typing, that her brothers would not have had decent shoes to their feet. But all that matters now is the future of her child.'

Charlotte Reece stared up at Gina in dismay. 'You don't expect me to look after it, do you? What about the father? Let him take care of it. He had his pleasure, now he must take the responsibility. I want nowt to do with it. I have enough on my plate as it is, looking after the boys.' Her attitude softened a little. 'I'm sorry about what's happened, but all this has come as a shock to me, Poppy dying so suddenly an' all, and I'm not as young as I was.'

The moment had come. Gina said carefully, 'I am willing to take care of the baby, if you have no objection.'

'*You?*' Mrs Reece appeared bemused. 'Why you're nowt but a girl! What do you know about taking care of a baby?'

Gina smiled. 'About as much as Poppy would have done, had she lived, but . . .' trading for once on her background, 'I am not without means. Little Oliver will be well taken care of, I assure you.'

'Oliver? Is that its name?' Charlotte puckered her forehead. John, James, Thomas, even Eustace, she would have understood and accepted, but Oliver. 'Where did Poppy come by an outlandish name like that?' she asked in amazement.

'From a book she'd just read,' Gina replied. '*Oliver Twist,* by Charles Dickens.' A note of pride entered her voice, remembering the way poor Poppy had avidly read that book, not as a mind-stretching exercise, but eagerly, because she had enjoyed it.

'Well.' Out of her depth, Mrs Reece gave up pondering the bewildering complexities of the situation. 'If you're willing, take the child, and welcome, I'm sure. But what about the funeral?' Expense stared her in the face.

'I'll gladly make the arrangements, and pay for it, if you wish,' Gina said gently, facing the realization that she was now virtually Oliver's mother, unless Mrs Reece changed her mind at the last moment.

'Oh, very well then.' Overawed by Gina's command of the situation her integrity, her beauty, Mrs Reece capitulated. Here was a lady and no mistake. The thought occurred that Poppy must have come well up in the world after all, to have had a friend of this calibre. The tears that flowed then, to Charlotte's credit, were born of regret that she had not come closer to her niece, that her staunch Christianity had never come to terms with the fact that Poppy had been conceived out of wedlock.

Later that day Gina sent a telegram to her father. The message read briefly, 'Please come at once. Desperately in need of help'.

Owen came.

'I am the Resurrection and the Life, saith the Lord, he that believeth in me, though he were dead, yet shall he live, and whosoever liveth and believeth in me shall never die.'

Had poor Poppy believed in life after death? Gina wondered as the coffin was lowered into the ground. Religion was a topic they had never discussed. Probably Poppy had never stopped to think what she believed in, a 19-year-old girl in love with life.

She would have been pleased, Gina thought, to know how many friends she'd had. Cecil Colebrook had closed the office for the day as a mark of respect, and came to the funeral with Mr Mainwaring, Patience and Jimmy. Poppy's fellow boarders had arrived together, wearing their Sunday best coats and hats. Dr Banting had taken time off from his busy practice to attend the service at the Dean Road cemetery. The landlady of the studio was also at the graveside, standing close by Mrs Reece and Poppy's brothers, Alfie and Frankie – both of whom resembled Poppy, especially Frankie, whose eyes were exactly the same colour as his sister's.

Clinging tightly to her father's arm, it seemed to Gina that despite Poppy's short time on earth, she had somehow touched upon the real purpose of life – to bring happiness into the lives of others.

Stepping forward, when the service was over, Gina saw the handful of snowdrops she scattered on the coffin as a symbol, not of death, but of hope for the future – a reminder of the coming springtime which, God willing, along with many another springtime, Poppy's child would see with his own eyes.

After the funeral, Owen said quietly, 'When Oliver is strong enough, I shall come for you, take you home with me.'

Daylight was fading, the corners of the studio were dim, with flickering shadows dancing on walls and ceiling. Gina noticed, with tear-dimmed eyes, Poppy's smoothly made bed, the shawl she had been knitting for the baby tucked behind a cushion of the chintz-covered settee.

Imagining Agnes' reaction if she turned up at Elmhurst with Poppy's child in her arms, Georgina shook her head. 'I'm sorry, Father, that is out of the question. I must stay here, take care of Oliver in my own way.'

'But there are no facilities,' Owen reminded her. 'Forgive me, my darling, but you'll need hot water, drying space, a garden. You cannot, with the best will in the world, keep a child cooped up indoors all day long. Nor could you look after a baby and run a business at the same time. One or the other would be bound to suffer.' He paused briefly. 'Besides, I *want* you to come home, where you belong.'

The things he said made sense, even so she could not

see her mother jumping for joy at the return of the prodigal daughter.

Owen said eagerly, 'I have been thinking that those rooms on the top floor of the west wing would make ideal nursery quarters. They are seldom in use nowadays, and you could make use of the back staircase to ensure privacy.'

'Mother may not approve,' Gina said slowly.

'Perhaps not at first,' Owen conceded, 'but it's high time that what happened last May was put aside and forgotten. The whole thing has blown up out of all proportion, but we have the child's future to think of now, and I intend seeing that he has a fair start in life.'

Gina bowed her head. 'Very well, Father, I'll do as you ask.'

Agnes received the news of Georgina's homecoming in icy silence followed by an outburst of fury at what she termed her husband's disregard for her feelings. The further revelation that their daughter would be bringing a child with her produced a reaction tantamount to shell-shock. Literally trembling from head to foot, she stared at Owen in utter amazement, seemingly robbed of speech, her mouth contorted as if she had suffered a stroke. But her voice, when it returned, was more powerful than ever.

'So that's it!' she raged, incensed with anger. 'I might have known. I said the girl would sink to her own level, and she has.'

Owen frowned, seriously perplexed. 'What are you talking about?'

'Ha! I see she has managed to pull the wool over your eyes, but not mine. I warn you, Owen, if you bring that wretched girl and her bastard here to Elmhurst, I shall leave!'

Sick at heart, 'My God, Agnes, how could you think such a thing of Georgina? The child is not hers. Even if it were, what kind of mother would turn away her own flesh and blood?'

'Oh, trust you to whitewash the whole sordid affair, as

131

you did when she left poor Harold Bickley at the altar! Have you no sense of shame?'

'*Shame?*' He suppressed a strong desire to shake his wife till her teeth rattled. 'Georgina has done nothing to be ashamed of.' His anger rising, 'Had you thought more of our daughter and less of young Bickley, that episode would not have been blown out of all proportion and Mary Bickley might still be alive!'

Rounding fiercely on her husband, 'Oh, so now you are blaming me for the death of Mary Bickley!' Agnes' eyes narrowed. She said jealously, 'But then you always did have a soft spot for her. Don't think *I* didn't notice. A man of your age making a fool of himself over a married woman.'

Owen knew, then, the underlying reason why Agnes had stubbornly refused to patch up her quarrel with Mary. The extent of her bitter jealousy and lack of humanity shocked him deeply. He said heavily, 'I intend having my own way in this matter, Agnes, and there's an end of it.'

'In that case, I shall pack my belongings and go to stay with my sister and her husband until Georgina is out of this house. Is that perfectly clear?' Turning away abruptly, seething with self-righteous anger, Agnes stalked out of the drawing-room where the confrontation had taken place, and went upstairs to her room to begin emptying drawers and wardrobes like a woman demented.

Watching her go, Owen wondered if he had done the right thing in suggesting Georgina's return to Elmhurst. Had he been too eager to drag her away from the roots she had established in Scarborough? Was he nothing more than a meddling old fool in wanting to give his daughter and Poppy's baby the care, understanding and love to which they were entitled?

Switching off the lights, making his way upstairs to his solitary room on the second floor, he reflected sadly how little one really knew about one's children, and made ready for bed.

Curiously, the thought of Agnes leaving Elmhurst came as a relief to him. But might not Georgina view her mother's defection in a different light? As a slap in the face?

* * *

The baby felt as soft and weightless as thistledown in her arms. Walking up the front steps of Elmhurst Gina noticed, with an uprush of love, the tiny tuft of dark hair above the beautifully modelled face of the sleeping infant.

Then, nestling little Oliver closer to her heart she saw, through a mist of tears, the familiar patterns and colours of home – the stained-glass lights of the vestibule windows, the mosaic patterns of the tiles beneath her feet, the red staircarpet. The polished newels and banisters exuded a whiff of beeswax polish as she stepped across the threshold into the oak-panelled hall.

But why was everything so hushed and silent, as though there had been a recent bereavement in the house? Where were the servants? Where was her mother?

Asking that question, Gina knew by Owen's tone of voice when he told her that her mother had gone to Doncaster to stay with Aunt Florence and Uncle Arthur, that nothing had changed between herself and Agnes, that her re-appearance at Elmhurst with Poppy's baby had deepened, not healed, the rift between them, to the extent that Agnes apparently could not bear the sight of her.

Owen had gone to a great deal of trouble to refurnish rooms on the top floor as a nursery suite, and he had been right in saying the studio would not be the place in which to bring up a baby, but she had turned her back on it with a great deal of regret. Now she must not let him see how deeply this strange homecoming had affected her. But how could he not know? They had always been so close, so aware of each other's feelings.

He said gently, 'I thought I had found a solution for you and Oliver. Now I'm not so sure. I allowed selfishness to override my better judgement.'

'Please don't, Father.' Georgina thought how tired he looked. 'We are home now.' She smiled. 'What a lovely cradle. Where did it come from?'

'Young Peter made it,' Owen said, referring to the gardener's son, 'and I have asked Bridget Donovan to act as nursemaid to help you take care of the baby.'

'How long will Mother be gone? Did she say?' Gina laid down the sleeping child in the warmly blanketed cradle, keeping her face turned away, not wanting Owen to see how deeply she minded that Agnes had not been there to meet her.

'I'm not sure. She said – indefinitely.' Owen's voice faltered. 'I'm so sorry, my darling, I thought . . .' How could he put into words his fervent hope that their daughter's homecoming would have healed the breach between them? That time and common sense would have softened his wife's attitude to Georgina?

Straightening up, facing her father, Gina said compassionately, 'All this is my fault, not yours. You mustn't blame yourself.' She added wryly, 'There are times when I wish that I *had* married Harold Bickley. Had I done so, none of this would have happened.'

'Oh no, my dear, you mustn't say that. You mustn't even think it.' Owen stepped forward to clasp her hands. 'Do you imagine I could have borne seeing you married to a man you were not in love with?' His voice roughened, 'I gloried in your independence and, so far as I am concerned, you made the right decision. What I regret most deeply is that I did nothing – nothing – to help you reach that decision.'

Georgina said quietly, 'That is water under the bridge. What we must face now is the future.'

When he had gone downstairs, Gina sat down on the window-seat and leaned her head wearily against the cold glass. Looking out at the misty twilight pierced with pinpricks of light, she tried to imagine that future in a place she no longer thought of as home, her heartstrings drawn back to a room beneath the stars, an old black wood-burning stove, a scattering of paint drops on bare floorboards, knowing instinctively that her return to Elmhurst had driven a further wedge between her parents, and that Agnes would not come home while she was in the house.

A knock came at the door. Bridget Donovan entered the room. 'Oh, Miss Georgina, it's pleased I am to see you,' she cried, hurrying forward.

'Bridget!' Gina held out her arms to the girl. In the twilit room it might have been Poppy standing there with all her well-remembered warmth and charm. Tears ran down her cheeks unchecked, to Bridget's consternation. 'There, it's tired out you are after all the worry,' she said. 'The master told me you'd lost your friend. But it's home you are now. May I look at the baby?' Bending over the cot, 'Ah, he's a fine boy, right enough.' Smiling at Gina, 'I'll help you to look after him. The master sent me to stay with him while you're at dinner. There's a little kitchen through yonder where I can warm the milk for his bottle.'

'Thank you, Bridget.' The girl's charm and spontaneity, her very presence, had brightened Gina's outlook. Unpacking her cases, choosing the dress she would wear for dinner, washing her hands and face, brushing her hair, listening to the soft lilt of Bridget's Irish brogue as she chattered on about the new cook, and life in general at Elmhurst, pausing now and then to look at the sleeping baby, she began to feel happier, more confident of the future. Possibly she had been wrong in supposing that her mother's absence was more than a coincidence.

Bridget was right, she *was* tired, both mentally and physically, worn out with the horror of Poppy's death, the funeral; worrying that Oliver might not survive the trauma of his premature birth, that Poppy's Aunt Charlotte might change her mind about the adoption when it became clear that the child would live. All these things, combined with constant, underlying pain of Rab's disappearance, the longing for him which never eased, allowed her no peace of mind; had brought her to a low ebb. In such a state, shadows became threatening storm clouds, draining life of all its colour, joy and optimism.

Owen was in the drawing-room, awaiting her arrival. As he poured a glass of Madeira, she noticed that his hand trembled slightly on the decanter, and felt a surge of pity for this man, her father, whose gentleness had been his undoing, whose life had been overshadowed by her mother's far stronger personality.

Shivering slightly despite the warmth of the fire, sipping

135

the wine, glancing round the over-furnished room in which, despite her mother's absence, her dominant personality seemed to hold sway, Gina knew that she had outgrown her past life, her youth and childhood at Elmhurst, that there could be no happiness, no future for herself and Oliver under this roof.

As if Owen had read her mind, he said as they went into the dining-room together, 'The future you spoke of so bravely: you can tell me, I'll understand. All I ask is that you will stay here for at least a little while. Then, whatever you choose to do with your life when you leave Elmhurst will lie in your own hands. One thing I beg of you, don't shut me out of your life. Promise you'll let me help you in any way possible.'

'Oh, Father! You know that I could never shut you out!'

Through a mist of tears she saw the long, polished dining-table set at one end with heavily embossed silver cutlery, starched dinner napkins, polished glass goblets, and tapering candles burning in a heavy, silver candelabrum. The maid, Gertrude, in her best bib and tucker, was standing near the kitchen door, ready to serve the soup, roast lamb and apple tart, and bobbed a curtsey at their entrance. And Gina knew that she had no choice other than to give her father the little space of time he had asked for. As for the future – who knew where that might lead her?

It was then that she remembered the letter from George Landis, at the London School of Dramatic Art.

Chapter Ten

The journey had been a nightmare. Slumped in the corner of a third class carriage, Rab had seen with a heavy heart the passing of familiar scenery as the train jogged west towards St Just.

Throughout his sojourn in Scarborough, he had known that he must return here one day, consequently he had made no promises that could not be kept, had lived each day as it came in his attempt to prove to himself, at least, that he could earn a decent living as a painter. He had proved nothing of the kind. His had been a hand-to-mouth existence fraught with failure and disappointment – apart from his portrait of Gina.

Gina!

The unexpected, the unbelievable had happened when he had fallen in love with her, and this was the bitterest blow of all, that he had been forced to turn his back on the one woman on earth who had brought a sense of purpose into his life.

The pain of leaving her without a word of explanation ground into him as he watched the evening shadows falling over the Cornish countryside. What must she be thinking now? And what of Poppy?

Never at any time had he told Poppy he loved her; even so, he should have discouraged her frequent visits to the studio. A man of the world, he had known how Poppy felt about him. He should have told her from the beginning that he could not return her love, but poor little warm-hearted Poppy had fulfilled an urgent need in his life, that of physical release, without which, at times, he would have felt less than a man.

The journey ended, he climbed down wearily from the train to stamp his feet on the platform. Then, feeling a little less cramped from lack of exercise, he went along to the guard's van to help the man off-load his cabin trunk. Eleanor had stated, in her last brief letter, that she would send the carriage from Bourne House to meet him, but there was no sign of it yet.

The wayside station, with its wavering gas-lamps and a capricious September wind blowing fallen leaves along the platform, seemed a lonely, inhospitable place to be once the train had departed, but Eleanor would relish the notion of keeping him waiting. Not that he harboured a desire to cross the threshold of that curiously sinister house perched on the cliffs above the restless waters of White Sand Bay, a house totally lacking in warmth, charm or freedom.

Suddenly he heard the wheels of an approaching carriage, and turned to see the driver stiffly dismounting from his seat to give him a hand with the luggage.

The cabin trunk stowed away, Rab leaned his head against the upholstery and thought about journey's end, of Eleanor Marquiss tall, thin, unbending, whose passionate dislike of him was all too apparent beneath her coldly formal exterior, and of her father, Phillip Marquiss, equally tall and thin, who ruled the household with a rod of iron; of Marguerite, the younger daughter, his wife, Marguerite Romer, for whose sake he had returned to Cornwall.

When the carriage entered the driveway of Bourne House, Rab knew the time had come to face his inquisitors, to confess that his brief spell of freedom had ended in failure, that he was no more capable now of supporting and caring for his wife than he had been that fraught day in 1915, when he had brought her safely home despite the frontiers and battlefields of war-torn Europe.

Eleanor Marquiss was in the hall to meet him, an unsmiling, ramrod figure in black lace, a lorgnette on a moiré ribbon about her neck, a cameo brooch pinned to the bodice of her high-necked evening gown. Slightly inclining her head, 'I trust you had a pleasant journey,' she said. 'I have given you a room on the second floor. Dickens will take up your luggage. Doubtless you will wish to change for dinner. Father and I will wait for you in the drawing-room.' Turning, she seemed to glide rather than walk towards the drawing-room, leaving Rab to help the servant upstairs with the cabin trunk. His penance had begun.

Dinner in the lavishly appointed dining-room was both meagre and tasteless: watery soup followed by stewed mutton, soggy vegetables and rice pudding, a meal which, Rab thought grimly, reflected the outlook and nature of the chatelaine of Bourne House. Not that the master of the house, seated at the head of the table, immaculate in a faultlessly cut evening suit, appeared to find the food inferior as he devoured each course without speaking to either his daughter or their guest.

And this was the man, Rab thought bitterly, to whom he owed fealty for having married his younger daughter at a time of crisis when, alone and afraid in Germany at the outbreak of war, she had turned to him for help. That marriage of convenience, which he had never intended to consummate, had cost him his freedom – too precious a thing to be thrown away for the sake of a girl with whom he was not in love. But Marguerite had felt differently about him.

Covertly watching Phillip Marquiss across the dining-table, noticing the way each mouthful of food was tucked inside the narrow-lipped slit in the lantern-jawed face, the man's cold, grey, heavily-lidded eyes, high-domed forehead and the thin, bony fingers manoeuvring the cutlery, Rab recalled a satirical drawing he had once seen entitled *Skeleton at the Feast* in a left-wing newspaper during his student days in Paris.

The Marquiss family fortune had derived from tin and clay mining, and had spread tentacles into other areas of enterprise: export, banking, fishing, farming. Which cog in the Marquiss machine he would be forced into, Rab had no idea. Nor, he imagined, would the choice be up to him. He guessed, moreover, that Phillip's silence at table was merely the lull before a storm. His assumption proved correct. The storm broke in the drawing-room when the servant who had brought in the coffee withdrew, closing the door behind him.

Marquiss, a towering colossus, standing with his back to the fire, regarded his son-in-law coldly. 'Sit down, Romer,' he said peremptorily.

'Thank you, I prefer to stand.' Rab's hackles rose. 'I should also prefer the use of my christian name or, as a matter of courtesy, the prefix Mister.'

The protagonists faced each other across the hearthrug. Rab continued, 'I came here for a specific reason. Why cloud the issue with personal abuse?'

'Very well then, I shall not prevaricate. What I have to say to you is short and to the point. The time has come for you to get your back into some work, for a change, to shoulder your responsibilities towards Marguerite, and I intend to make certain you do just that.' Marquiss was speaking quickly, decisively, scornfully. 'You have wasted enough time as it is, and where has it got you? Look at yourself! Hardly the picture of a successful artist.' He began pacing, gesticulating to emphasize his words. 'Not one penny have you contributed to my daughter's upkeep during the past years. You have proved yourself a coward and a weakling. Words cannot express my disgust of a man incapable of honouring his moral obligations.'

Interrupting Marquiss' flow, Rab said wearily, 'Then why do you imagine I came here? As for Marguerite, I never deluded her into believing I loved her. She accepted that the marriage would be dissolved – if and when we got back to England.'

'And yet you took advantage of her youth and innocence.' Marquiss stopped pacing. 'Well, I'll tell you this, Romer, under different circumstances I would have paid you handsomely to keep away. But I hold you responsible for my daughter's state of mind, and I intend to see that you pay for the harm you have caused her.' He stared contemptuously at his son-in-law. 'God knows what she sees in you, or why your presence here should be necessary to her welfare. All I can do is accept the specialist's verdict that this is the case, her only hope of recovery.'

Eleanor, who had remained seated during the exchange, got up from her chair by the fire. 'If you will excuse me, Father, I must go up to Marguerite now.' Glancing coldly at Rab, she added, 'No doubt you will wish to continue your conversation alone.' Again that curious gliding walk of hers as she left the room.

Taking the chair she had vacated, pressing his fingers together, 'And now, Romer,' Phillip Marquiss said, 'sit down and listen carefully . . .'

Later, in his room, it occurred to Rab to leave Bourne House at first light. Why stay in a place he loathed to suffer further humiliation at Marquiss' hands? What did he know or care about tin mining? Explosively he had rejected his father-in-law's dictum as monstrous, totally unfair, unthinkable. Even more unthinkable was the prospect of living under the same roof as Phillip and Eleanor Marquiss.

Pacing restlessly, he wondered why had he come here in the first place. But deep down he knew why: because of the past he could not forget, memories of a house in Dresden of which Marguerite had been an integral part. She was a child in his eyes, albeit a charming, talented child, dark-haired, with a merry laugh, a kittenish face and dancing eyes – who had seemed like a sister to himself and the Steiner brothers, Friedrich and Gunter.

Looking into the past, he remembered the first time he had seen her. Back from Paris for the summer vacation, after warmly greeting Frieda Steiner whom he regarded as a mother, and depositing his mound of luggage on the kitchen floor, he heard the strains of Chopin's *Revolutionary Study* from Otto Steiner's studio. 'Who is that playing?' he asked, listening intently.

'Go through and see for yourself,' Frieda suggested, 'while I make some fresh coffee.' And so he had opened the glass-panelled connecting door between the house and the studio, to see a young girl with dark hair tied back with a blue ribbon, her full-skirted blue dress cascading about the piano-stool, seated at the keyboard of a Blüthner grand piano, deeply absorbed in the score propped open in front

141

of her, her eyebrows drawn together in a fierce scowl of concentration.

The intensity of her playing, her mastery of the keyboard under Herr Steiner's patient yet exacting tutelage had amazed him. Then suddenly, apparently having lost her concentration, or having misread the score, she struck a series of wrong notes, pulled a face and burst into tears. Then, very gently, Otto had pointed out her mistake, told her not to cry, and suggested that she repeat the passage at a slower tempo, until she had played it correctly. 'You see, my child,' he said in his inimitably charming way, 'music is like horsemanship.'

'Horsemanship? I don't understand.'

'It is quite simple, really. The sooner the thrown rider gets back on the horse, the better, otherwise the beast will gain the upper hand and throw the rider whenever he wishes.'

'Oh yes, I think I see what you mean.' Drying her eyes, the girl had finally, triumphantly mastered the complex series of notes which had thrown her.

Turning to the window, looking up at the stars bright and shining in the autumn sky, Rab remembered the house in Dresden – a barn of a place with cluttered rooms overflowing with books and music scores. The furniture was shabby but comfortable – his idea of home – where every room was lived in, in the truest meaning of the word, as places for formulating ideas, hopes, dreams. Here the Steiner family would gather round the circular dining-table each evening to air their views on art, politics, music, the theatre; to eat the food Frieda had prepared for them, in an atmosphere of relaxed gaiety and laughter; to wash down the food with quantities of wine or freshly-ground coffee.

But possibly neither he nor those treasured companions of pre-war days had realized how soon would come an end to their laughing camaraderie once that fatal shot at Sarajevo had been fired, plunging the whole of Europe into a bloody Armageddon of hatred and injustice, pillage, murder and retribution.

Turning away from the window, slumping down on the

edge of the bed, covering his face with his hands, Rab fought hard to expel from his mind the memory of the Steiner family being herded like cattle into a truck drawn up at the front steps of the house in Dresden. The German guards had rifle-butted them into that truck. He remembered the exquisite courtesy of Frieda when she had pointed out to one of the guards that she could not move any faster because he was standing on the hem of her dress.

He and Marguerite had gone out shopping earlier that day, he recalled, because she wanted to buy a birthday present for her sister Eleanor. They had been standing at the street corner, helpless onlookers, as the Steiner family were forced into the transport and driven away at high speed to an unknown destination.

Lunging forward, determined to follow that truck, to run after it until his heart burst if necessary, he had been checked by Marguerite's anchor-hold on his arm, her hoarsely whispered words: 'No! Don't. Please, I beg of you. Can't you see that we are both in danger now? If we are caught we may be shot, starved, beaten, tortured. Oh God, I can't bear it! We must get away from here as quickly as possible. Please, *please* say you'll help me!'

And so the die had been cast. But not until he had known for certain that the day's roundup of 'spies' had been lined up against a prison wall, and shot.

It was impossible to go back to the house, then under constant surveillance by the Germans. Beside himself with grief, a wanted man in the city he had regarded as home, with a desperately frightened girl dependent on him, the only hope of escape, he realized, were forged papers. Speaking German and French fluently, he might just make it to the coast of France if luck was with him. But Marguerite had only a smattering of German and the *plume de ma tante* schoolgirl French which would scarcely suffice under duress. And so as a matter of expedience he had married Marguerite.

Now, running his hands wearily across his face, rising unsteadily to his feet, recalling the horror of the past, the apparent futility of the future, Rab opened his cabin trunk in which lay his Portrait of Gina. Propping up the picture on the dressing-table, remembering everything about her, a feeling of peace washed over him, a renewed sense of purpose. Looking intently at the portrait he knew beyond a shadow of doubt, that had he confided in Gina, had he broken down and confessed the reason why he must leave her, she would have said, in that calm, wise way of hers, 'But of course you must go back to Cornwall, face your responsibilities, take care of Marguerite.'

She would never know – how could she – how much he dreaded living beneath the same roof with the wife who seemed little more to him now than an unreal shadow from the past.

Chapter Eleven

The Merle Woods were misted over with new green foliage, lilacs in the churchyard were coming into bud – reminiscent of that other springtime, a year ago, which had changed the course of her life, Gina thought as she walked among the trees, catching the bittersweet scent of fading bluebells.

Viewing her life objectively, would she have been happier now, had she married Harold? But had that happened, she would not have met Poppy or Rab, nor experienced the intense joy and pain of living – experiences which had coloured her days; had sharpened her awareness, her need for independence. Not for her the aimless yet frantic existence of Josie and Letty Bickley whose lives revolved around a constant whirl of social activities, the dances, house-parties and holidays abroad to which their father's wealth had accustomed them.

With Oliver to bring up and care for, she could not take advantage of her father's generosity indefinitely, nor could she bear the thought that her homecoming had been the cause of a further, more serious, rift between her parents.

Since her return to Elmhurst she had spent her time taking care of the baby, glad of the seclusion of the nursery wing which had provided a resting place, a caravanserai. But often, in moments of solitude, she yearned for the studio, the freedom and independence she had known there, the joy of earning her own living, the necessity of facing up to life – however sad or difficult it may have been.

Stirring last year's fallen leaves with the toe of her shoe, hearing the dry crackle of those remnants of a dead, yet haunting, period of her life now over and done with for ever, she knew the time had come to take a brave step forward into the future. So far she had not been to church, or to the mill, preferring to stay close to home, afraid of curious glances, of meeting the Bickleys face-to-face, providing food for gossip. Her mother's prolonged absence from Elmhurst would, she knew, have provided wagging tongues with more ammunition. Speculation would have run rife among the mill workers as to why Mrs Brett-Forsyth had left home so suddenly prior to Miss Georgina's arrival with a baby.

Possibly they believed the child to be hers, Gina thought, going upstairs to her room. Well, why not? Oliver *was* hers. And this was the crowning happiness of her life, her reason for living: that it lay within her power to care for the infant whom Poppy had handed into her keeping, a child that was an integral part of the man with whom they had both been in love.

Now, every time she held the child in her arms, in the darkness of his hair and eyes, his lust for life – evident by the way he had grown in strength and stature since the day she had lifted him gently from his cot in the hospital and brought him to Elmhurst – reminded her of his parentage, of the two people, apart from her father, she had loved best on earth. And every time Oliver looked up at her and smiled, kicked in his bath, or lay asleep in his cot, she saw in him a continuation of life and love: a hope, a challenge for the future, herself as the keeper of a flame of love that would never die during her lifetime.

Whether or not she would meet him again during that lifetime made no difference to the way she felt about his child. Indeed it seemed to her, in quiet moments of reflection, that her love for Rab had reached a spiritual climax in the love she gave so unstintingly to his son.

Florrie Kershaw, Agnes' younger sister, faced her husband Arthur in the privacy of their bedroom – the only sanctuary left to them since Agnes had appeared, uninvited, to make their lives a misery.

Arthur, well up in the world nowadays since his appointment as senior accountant at the Bessacre Colliery, had had his fill of his sister-in-law, and said so in no uncertain terms as he made ready for bed.

146

'Oh, do keep your voice down,' Florrie begged him, 'she might hear you.'

'I hope she bloody well does hear me,' Arthur muttered rebelliously, savagely attacking his thinning hair with the ivory-backed brushes his wife had given him for Christmas, vaguely wondering why there was more hair in the bristles than on his head. 'Just how long does she intend to stay here? That's what I want to know.'

'Then why don't you ask her? After all, you're the man of the house.'

'Why don't *you* ask her? She's your sister.'

'I know, dear. But you know what she's like when she's crossed.'

'*Crossed?* Why can't she go home to be crossed?' Seriously put out, Arthur flumped down on his half of the feather mattress, beat the pillows with his fists and glared up at the ceiling. 'I'm telling you, Florrie, she'll have to go – the sooner the better!'

'Very well, dear, I'll have a word with her.' Getting into her side of the bed, Florrie's heart quailed at the prospect of asking her formidable sister when she was thinking of returning to Elmhurst. But Arthur was right in saying the sooner Agnes went home, the better. The trouble was, she would *interfere* so, and she was so dogmatic, so bitter – still harping on about the wedding fiasco last spring – as if herself or Arthur, or anyone else for that matter, cared tuppence that Georgina had decided at the last minute not to marry the pompous young ass Agnes had set her heart on. Trust Agnes to make a mountain out of a molehill. Florrie sighed deeply, thinking that her sister had always been her own worst enemy. Even as a girl she'd had this strange propensity to put people's backs up, and there had been no holding her when she had married money.

Switching off the bedside light, Florrie recalled the day Agnes came home, triumphantly flashing the diamond ring on her engagement finger, to announce that she had landed Owen Brett-Forsyth – as if the man were a fish, not a human being.

From the beginning Florrie had felt sorry for Owen,

destined to live his life in her sister's shadow, a quiet man destined 'until death do us part' to listen to Aggie's loud, abrasive voice issuing orders; laying down the law on every subject under the sun which, however vaguely or remotely, had a bearing on her own life and those of her husband and children. So why had Owen married Agnes in the first place? Possibly, Florrie thought, listening to Arthur's gentle snoring, forerunner of the *Rossini Overture* to come, because men of his gentle, unassuming nature felt in need of a strong hand to guide them.

Well, the poor man had paid the price of his folly and so, apparently, had Georgina. As for young Thomas . . . if Agnes imagined for one moment that she and Arthur would be prepared to have the lazy, objectionable young beast under their roof for the Easter vacation, she had another think coming, and that was that.

Agnes was deeply shocked at what she termed Florrie's heartlessness in daring to suggest that she was no longer welcome under her roof; but Florrie wasn't standing any nonsense. 'Look, Agnes,' she said, amazed by her own temerity, 'you appeared out of the blue – how long ago was that? Well, never mind, but if you've had a fall-out with Owen, it's high time it was settled. All you've done so far is hint about what's gone wrong, but you're not some daft lass having a lovers' quarrel. You've a home of your own to see to, and all I can say is, you'd best go and see to it.' She added, less forcefully, 'In any case, Tommy will be home from school soon, and you'll want to make sure he's taken care of.'

'Well, I shall certainly not stay where I'm not wanted!' Agnes bridled. 'I shall go upstairs and pack.'

'There you go again,' Florrie said heatedly, 'taking umbrage when there's no need, like that silly business of the wedding. Just because Georgina didn't fancy being tied for life to that feller you picked out for her. What a fussation! The poor lass.'

'I'll thank you to mind your own business, Florrie Kershaw! There are things you don't know about Georgina.

She has always been a trial to me with her queer, headstrong ways. What she needed was a good husband to bring her to her senses.' Agnes' chins quivered. 'But no, she wouldn't hàve that. Instead she made a laughing stock of me in front of the world and his wife. I shall never forgive her for that. Poor lass, indeed. Well, that's not all. Perhaps you'll change your mind when I tell you that she turned up at Elmhurst with an illegitimate child. That's why I left. So now you know!'

Memories crowded in on Gina as she walked into church beside her father, her head held high, knowing that her appearance in the place she had left so abruptly almost a year ago would not go unnoticed. She had, however, no intention of slinking in, head bent, or sitting at the back of the church. Drawing back her shoulders, she walked proudly, uprightly to the Brett-Forsyth pew near the lectern, aware that all eyes were upon her. And possibly this was the way actresses felt on the opening night of a play, she thought, intent on giving a good performance, pretending not to notice the blur of faces 'beyond the footlights'.

From the Bickley pew across the aisle came a sudden sharp intake of breath, Josie Bickley's harshly whispered comment: 'Well, really! Of all the nerve. Today of all days.'

This Gina had expected, that the Bickley family would regard her presence in church as a breach of good taste. Keeping her eyes fixed on the stained glass window above the altar, remembering the sparrow, she wondered what their reaction would be when she brought Oliver to the church to be christened.

Oliver. The thought of him brought a smile to her lips. In time to come, when he was old enough, would he understand when she told him about today, that it was for his sake she had braved the 'slings and arrows of outrageous fortune'?

Later she realized that she *had*, unwittingly, breached the bounds of good taste when, after the second Lesson, the Reverend Mr Simmons announced publication of the Banns of Marriage between Harold Ewart Bickley of Merlewood Parish and Susanna Crighton, spinster of the parish of St Jude, Middlesbrough. This was the first time of asking.

Oh God, what had she done? Gina thought desperately. Not for the world would she have come here to embarrass Harry in such a way, had she known. Glancing sideways she saw him seated, frozen-faced, beside an elegantly dressed young woman with fair hair drawn back in a heavy chignon, on whose head was perched a green hat trimmed with a cascade of shiny black coq feathers, apparently Harry's bride-to-be . . . exactly the type of girl she had hoped he would one day marry. Surely Harry could not believe that she had come to church, today of all days, to cause him embarrassment. But, inadvertently catching his eye, she knew that he did think so. What she read in his face was not dislike, but hatred.

Agnes made Thomas the excuse for her return to Elmhurst. As she had departed, so she arrived: full of wrath, the injured party. Not that she would ever admit to Owen that she had been given her marching orders. The first he knew of his wife's homecoming was when a message was passed on to him by his secretary, requesting the car be sent to Bradford Station to meet the four o'clock train.

Innocently, Owen imagined his wife returning in a mellow mood following a period of reflection. His hopes were short-lived. One look at her face convinced him that for whatever reason she had decided to come home, charity had nothing to do with it.

'So, you're back, Agnes,' he said pleasantly, helping a porter to stack the mound of luggage on the platform on to a hand-barrow.

'So it would appear!' she snapped. 'I have been waiting here for ten minutes or more.'

'I'm sorry, my dear. I did my best to be on time.'

'Apparently your best was not good enough.'

'Please, Agnes,' he said unhappily, helping her into the car, 'must we quarrel? I had hoped, for Georgina's sake,

150

that this would be a pleasant homecoming. She is so looking forward to seeing you—'

'I came home for Tommy's sake, not Georgina's,' Agnes interrupted harshly, having convinced herself that she was speaking the truth, that she had left Doncaster of her own volition. 'The boy will be home next week from boarding school. My place is with my son.'

'And your daughter? What of her?' Owen felt his anger rising, experienced yet again the old familiar feeling of frustration which his wife's inability to see reason invoked in him, accompanied this time by an unfamiliar, nagging pain in his chest.

'As far as I am concerned, I have no daughter,' Agnes said stonily, staring ahead at the road.

Gina came down to her father's study at midnight, as she had done before, almost a year ago. Looking up at her from his wing-chair near the fire, Owen knew why she had come, knew that he was about to lose her. Time had turned full circle. She had come to tell him she must leave Elmhurst. Now, as then, how could he blame her for wanting to leave the scene of so much unhappiness?

Kneeling at his feet, 'I want to go to London,' she told him quietly.

His heart lurched. 'Why London?'

Handing him the letter from George Landis, she said, 'This will explain why.' Cradling her head wearily in his lap, 'Please don't be angry. This is something I need to do, a chance I have to take.'

Smoothing her hair gently back from her tear-stained face, 'I'll help you in every way possible,' he promised. 'But I never knew, never guessed that you had even thought of becoming an – actress.'

'It was Rab's idea,' she said softly, thinking back to that day in the studio. 'It was Rab who persuaded me to write to Landis about an audition. I gave up the idea for Poppy's sake, but now . . .'

Drawing in a deep breath, Owen knew that the time had come to put aside his own feelings and desires for the sake

151

of his child. Perhaps he had realized all along that she no longer belonged here at Elmhurst, that despite his longing to have her near him, this was a selfish manifestation of his own grief, pain and loneliness since the death of Mary Bickley.

Cupping Georgina's face in his hands, he said levelly, 'I understand, my darling. Now tell me what you have in mind.'

Georgina told him.

A week later she left Elmhurst for London, taking with her little Oliver, and Bridget Donovan, to face an unknown future.

Triumphantly, Agnes watched their departure from an upstairs window. It pleased her to think that she had not spoken a word to Georgina since returning home from Doncaster, and had flatly refused even to look at the baby.

Chapter Twelve

'Holy Mother of God,' Bridget gasped, 'I've never seen stairs like that before. If the nursery's on the top floor, I'll be dizzy by the time I get there! This is a queer place we've come to, and no mistake.'

The estate agent who had let them into the house and handed over the keys said, a trifle acerbically, 'The staircase is unique, madam, designed by the gentleman who built Welford House when Hampstead was little more than a village.'

The staircase to which he referred, a delicately spindled spiral, wound upwards like a convolvulus to the floors above.

'I might add that the nursery suite is the sunniest in the entire house,' the agent said defensively.

'Well it would be, wouldn't it,' Bridget commented, 'being that much closer to the sky.'

Tired and anxious after the long train journey south, during which Oliver had been unusually fretful, Gina wondered if she had done the right thing in coming to London on an impulse. What if George Landis, whom she had not yet contacted, advised her to give up all thought of an acting career? Now here they were in this tall, narrow house with the nursery on the top floor and the kitchen in the basement, their luggage stacked in the hall, daylight fading, and with a hungry baby to feed, bathe and put to bed. Bridget's forthright, 'This is a queer place we've come to, and no mistake,' had hit the nail on the head, but they must make the best of what appeared to be a bad job.

Her father, Gina knew, had moved heaven and earth to find decent furnished accommodation in a respectable area of London, with a nursery and a garden, after she had told him of her plans that night in the library, and Welford

153

House, the owners of which had gone abroad for two years, had been the answer to a prayer. Owen had negotiated quickly and efficiently with the firm of estate agents handling the lease, and so the deal had been concluded. Impossible to turn round and tell him now that she wished she had not come to London after all, had never set her sights on becoming an actress.

She felt miserably unhappy tonight, in a strange bed, staring up at the pattern a street lamp cast on the ceiling, hearing unfamiliar street sounds outside the window, thinking of other lights on other ceilings . . .

Up early next morning, wandering from room to room by the light of a new day, her opinion of the house changed dramatically. Oddly shaped it may be, but its owners had come to terms with its architectural defects in not over-crowding the rooms with heavy furniture. In the drawing-room she saw a deep, comfortably cushioned couch and matching armchairs upholstered in moss green velvet, brightly coloured rugs of Oriental origin and design; above the mantelpiece, a Degas painting of ballerinas in a gilt frame.

Last night she had slept in a front bedroom on the first floor. Crossing the hall, opening another door, she knew where she would sleep from now on. She was standing in a room with a double bed, wardrobe, dressing-table and a chaise-longue – a dainty, very feminine room – with french windows leading on to a wrought iron balcony overlooking a long, walled garden.

Opening one of the windows, stepping on to the balcony, she saw lilacs in full bloom, azaleas and blood-red rhodo-dendrons amid a wilderness of crazed paths, weeds and burgeoning trees. Accustomed to the neatly mown lawns and the soldierly ranks of well pruned laurels at Elmhurst, the splendid untidiness of this garden slightly shocked her at first glance, it was so unexpected.

Apparently the gentleman who had built Welford House had harboured a fondness for wrought iron and spiral stairs, Gina observed, trailing her hand on the railing of the twisting steps leading down to the garden. He had also cared a great deal about privacy, judging from the height of the wall he had erected about his property.

Her heart lifted suddenly to the clear call of a blackbird from the branch of a sycamore tree. A feeling of peace washed over her. She felt alive again, imbued with fresh hope and renewed vitality.

Returning to the house, she heard Bridget calling to her from the kitchen, 'Miss Georgina! Breakfast's on the table,' and went downstairs to find the scrubbed-wood table set with blue-and-white willow-pattern china, with tea, toast and honey; and Bridget, fresh-faced after a good night's sleep, in a rocking chair near the fire, the baby on her lap.

'Ah, Miss Brett. We meet at last. Romer spoke highly of you. Now I can see why. So, you want to become an actress?'

Landis, bearded, informally dressed, referred to as 'maestro' by his students, due to the fluidity of his hands which he used expressively as if conducting an orchestra, regarded her thoughtfully. 'Trust Rab! He always had an eye for a beautiful woman.'

'Yes. I . . .' The mention of Rab's name had brought colour to her cheeks. She longed to hear more about him. 'Rab told me you were old friends. Did you meet here, in London?'

'No. We met in Paris, before the war. We shared the same *pension*. Rab taught art at a small academy in Montmartre, I was a member of a Paris-based theatre group. We were both as poor as church mice.'

He smiled reflectively. 'Not that lack of money prevented us living life to the full. Ah, they were good days. The nights were even better. When the theatre closed, Rab and I would meet in one of the little bistros near the Sacré Cœur for a meal and a drink. Afterwards, we would wander the city by night, not caring where we were going, talking about everything under the sun – art, music, politics, or whatever, until the crack of dawn.

'We'd go back to our lodgings, then, too tired almost to

climb the stairs to our rooms, trying not to make a noise in case the *concierge* heard us and demanded the rent money.' He chuckled deeply. 'Didn't Rab tell you?'

'No. But he showed me his paintings of Paris.'

Landis sighed. 'He has great talent. Who knows what might have happened had it not been for the war? Things might have been far different had he not gone back to Germany that summer. But that's water under the bridge. Tell me about yourself.'

'There's not much to tell. I've been earning a living as a stenographer, but I've always loved the theatre. Rab persuaded me to contact you. He – he seemed to think I had – talent.' Her colour deepened.

'We shall see,' he said warmly, thinking that here was a girl with star quality. Charisma. A shining air of – starlight – about her. 'Now, what have you brought to lay at my feet?'

'I don't understand,' she said simply.

He used his eyebrows expressively. 'Oh come now, Miss Brett, you mean that you have come unprepared for your audition? Have you not memorized Portia's speech from *The Merchant of Venice*? Cleopatra's death scene?'

'I'm afraid not. I . . . I didn't know quite what to expect.'

'No matter. Come with me.' Throwing open a door, he led the way to a room with curtained windows and a small spotlit stage at the far end. 'Now, this is your theatre, that is your stage, forget about me, get up on that stage and recite anything that comes to mind – "Little Bo-Peep" if you wish, I don't care what, only do it, Miss Brett! Do as I ask you.'

Mounting the stage, she stood there in silence feeling that her tongue had stuck to the roof of her mouth. Her mind had gone blank.

'Don't worry, take your time. Say whatever comes into your head.'

' "There's rosemary, that's for remembrance. Pray love, remember," she whispered, "and there is pansies; that's for thoughts . . . There's fennel for you, and columbines; There's rue for you, and here's some for me . . . I would

156

give you some violets, but they withered all when my father died. They say a made a good end . . ." ' Sinking to her knees, she buried her face in her hands and wept, thinking of her father in whose eyes she had read despair when he said goodbye to her.

My God, Landis thought, electrified by her performance, the girl was a born actress, a potential leading lady. The amazing thing, in his view, was that she appeared to be without vanity. Most young women who stood on the audition platform did so with the intention of making a good impression, knowing exactly what they were going to say and do: posturing dramatically, declaiming rather than speaking the lines they had learned for the occasion. But *this* girl. She was actually crying! He said calmly, approaching the stage, 'Thank you, Miss Brett.' Offering his hand, he helped her down the steps. Hers was ice-cold, trembling. 'Come back to the office, I'll make some tea.'

The thought occurred that he could do with a stiff drink, whisky – possibly even champagne. He felt like celebrating.

Gina had imagined that a school of dramatic art would be an imposing building, not a rambling Victorian villa down a side street, stripped of all but essential furniture. The rehearsal room on the first floor – presumably once the drawing room – was uncarpeted and unfurnished, apart from a few hard chairs and a table piled with dog-eared manuscripts, from which focal point the maestro conducted the proceedings. Not that he remained still for long. Having set the scene and explained what he wanted the actors to do, he would move rapidly among them picking up mistakes, manoeuvring them physically into position if necessary, calling out instructions: 'Concentrate on what you're doing! You must keep on acting all the time when you're on-stage. Act with your eyes, your hands, your shoulders. Act with the back of your head. It is not enough to learn your lines. You must speak them as if what is written on the pages had sprung from your own mind, not the author's.'

His vitality was amazing. Despite the heaviness of his

build, he moved gracefully. In common with his hero, David Garrick – of whom he might well have been a reincarnation, and whose life and work he had studied intensely – Landis' eyes were dark and penetrating, his features 'plastic and accommodating', his voice 'natural in its cadence, and beautiful in its elocution'. Watching him at work, Gina wondered why so gifted an actor had chosen to squander his talent in teaching others how to act.

She quickly learned, however, that the man was a harsh disciplinarian, a hard task-master, almost impossible to please; a strict time-keeper, insistent that his students appear in the rehearsal room at nine o'clock sharp.

Never in her wildest imagination had she begun to realize the sheer hard work involved in learning how to act. Natural talent was not enough, it seemed; the ability to memorize lines was not enough. Having learned them, one apparently must forget the fact of having learned them at all, and say them as if they had been dredged from the subconscious.

A tiny, effervescent Frenchwoman, Giselle Gautier, purported to be Landis' mistress, in charge of makeup, wardrobe and properties, appeared at intervals to claim the maestro's attention. She was a woman of enormous chic, with greying hair drawn back from an angular face – unremarkable apart from the size and luminosity of her eyes and the sensuality of her full, pouting lips. When Madame Gautier entered the rehearsal room, everyone stopped what they were doing to look at her. In Gina's case, to try to fathom the reason why a severely dressed older woman, far from beautiful in the accepted sense of the word, radiated an aura of beauty. Had it to do with the way she used her hands, the turn of her head, the mobility of her mouth when she spoke? The pout of her lips, Gina decided, derived from those splendidly strong, slightly prominent teeth of hers; the dramatic impact of her eyes from the subtle use of kohl. Above all, Madame Gautier appeared beautiful because she thought of herself as a beautiful woman, so that charm and self-possession radiated from that belief. The students adored her. Gina was fascinated by her.

*　　*　　*

She had been at the school almost three months when Landis invited her to dine with him one evening at a French restaurant in the West End.

At first, Gina had felt disinclined to accept his invitation. Who knew what she might be letting herself in for? Her fellow students might resent her being singled out for the maestro's attention if they found out. On the other hand, Landis' friendship with Rab may lead her to further discoveries about the man with whom she was in love. But it seemed unfair to go out in the evening, leaving Bridget alone in the house with a baby to take care of.

Strung on the horns of a dilemma, she left the decision up to Bridget, who told her, in no uncertain terms, to go out and enjoy herself. Even so, Bridget was spending too much time alone, to the detriment of her high spirits. What she needed was another woman in the house to talk to, someone compatible to share the burden of housekeeping, cooking and nurse-maiding, which had fallen too heavily on one pair of shoulders.

Getting ready for her dinner appointment with Landis, and sitting in front of her dressing-table mirror, brushing her hair, she remembered Daisy Crabtree, whose letter, following the *débâcle* of her – Gina's – wedding day, and Daisy's departure from Elmhurst under the cloud of Agnes' dismissal, she had kept ever since.

But what if Mrs Crabtree had found other, more congenial employment? It was hardly likely she would feel inclined to come to Welford House to work. But that was beside the point. She would never forget how, on her return from the church that fateful morning, she had cried on Daisy's shoulder. For that reason alone she would write to the address Mrs Crabtree had given her, saying how much she and Bridget looked forward to seeing her again; inviting her to supper one evening when Oliver had been settled for the night.

Laying down her hairbrush, and staring at her reflection in the mirror, Gina thought that she would rather have supper with Bridget in the basement kitchen of Welford

House, than dinner at a French restaurant with George Landis.

How plain she looked, how dull, in her high-necked white blouse, with her hair scraped back from her forehead – the antithesis of a budding actress. In view of the struggle she was having to keep up with her studies, to absorb even the simplest instructions fired at her regarding the up-staging of her fellow students, she felt the time had come to tell the maestro that she had decided to give up all thought of acting as a career.

The restaurant, small and dimly lit, smelt different from any restaurant she had been in before – of strange herbs and spices, and Gauloises cigarette smoke. A far cry from the Kardomah Restaurant in Bradford where she had lunched occasionally with her father, against the back-ground noise of clattering plates, and a trio of elderly ladies playing Mendelssohn's 'Spring Song'.

'This place reminds me of Paris, of a certain bistro on the Left Bank where the students would gather to drink wine and eat the most delicious food imaginable,' Landis observed when they were seated at a candlelit table. 'French cookery is the best in the world, in my opinion, so simple yet . . .' he bunched his fingers expressively to his lips and blew a kiss, '*formidable!*'

'I've never been abroad,' Gina confessed, looking at the menu, wondering what to order, feeling out of place, aware that Landis was staring at her intently. 'Perhaps I never shall now.'

'Why not? Why not – *now*?' The innocence of the girl never ceased to amaze him. Did she not realize her potential? Was she blind to her beauty? Had she not noticed the way heads turned to look at her when they entered the restaurant? Apparently she had not.

'It's hard to explain.' Laying aside the menu, she propped her chin on the linked fingers of her hands, her eyes betraying a nameless longing which he could not fathom.

'Perhaps you have no wish to travel, to see the world?' he suggested.

'Ah, but I have. That's just it! I long to see the world, but—'

'But *what*?'

The time for honesty had come. Clenching her fingers more tightly, she said softly, 'I once had a dream of becoming an actress, but that was a long time ago. My father had taken me to a performance of *Hamlet* at the Bradford Alhambra. I came away from the theatre with a headful of dreams. Then the war came – not a dream but a terrible reality.'

'Go on,' Landis urged quietly.

'I kept that dream at the back of my mind for a very long time, pushed out of sight – the way that children push aside forgotten toys – until someone,' her voice faltered, 'someone came along to remind me of that old, half-forgotten dream of mine.'

'You mean Romer? Rab Romer?'

'Yes.' Her voice sank to a whisper, her eyes swam with tears. She pressed her hands to her lips momentarily. 'But I know now he was wrong in thinking that I might become an actress. The harder I try, the more I fail. I've tried my best to learn, to please you, but I'm wasting my time and yours.' Blinking away her tears. 'I can't accept the discipline of learning how to act. I'm sorry, I've tried, but I can't. You've told me over and over again how to use my hands, but they appear to have a will of their own. Then, when I try to remember your instructions, I find I've forgotten my lines, and my tongue seems frozen to the roof of my mouth.'

'Oh, God,' Landis said wearily, 'I should have realized. I should have known.'

'That I'd never make an actress?' Gina laid her hands quietly on the table, awaiting the maestro's final adjudication of her faults and failings as a student, which she richly deserved.

'*What?*' Leaning forward, he seized her hands in his. 'No, no, that's not what I meant. All this is my fault, forcing you into a mould. I should have known that you cannot be taught in the same way as the others.' He said eagerly,

161

'Don't you see, Gina, you *are* the mould!' Beckoning the waiter, 'We must have some wine. Better still, champagne.'

'I've never drunk champagne!' Caught up in his excitement, uncertain why he was so excited, Gina laughed.

'Then it's high time you started.' Raising his glass, he toasted her. 'Here's to the good things of life, to fame, and fortune, and success! From now on, you will be coached privately by Madame Gautier.'

'Madame Gautier?' Gina wrinkled her nose against the rising bubbles in her champagne glass, not quite sure if she was on her head or her heels, thinking how different champagne tasted from the occasional glass of sherry or Madeira she had drunk at Merlewood or Elmhurst.

'Yes, Giselle Gautier. The finest actress I have ever worked with.' Landis' eyes kindled with remembrance. 'You should have seen her as *La Dame aux Camélias* in Paris before the war. She was too old for the part, of course, but the moment she went on-stage she was youth personified: ageless, exquisite.' He leant back in his chair. 'Giselle will teach you how to make the most of your looks, how to dress, move, walk and speak far better than I ever could, and it is this more personal approach you need above all. If you'll forgive my saying so, your choice of clothes leaves much to be desired, and that trace of a West Riding accent must be got rid of. These lessons usually come later in the curriculum – deportment, makeup, speech training and so on. In your case, however, there seems little point in going against the grain.' He smiled, thinking how lovely she looked by candlelight. 'I have great plans for you, my dear.'

'Plans?' The maestro's words and the champagne had gone to her head. The thought of being coached privately by Madame Gautier appealed to her far more than appearing daily in the dreaded rehearsal room alongside the dozen or so other students in the class, all of whom seemed much less inhibited than herself. 'What kind of – plans?'

At that moment a waiter brought to their table the food they had ordered. When the man had gone, tucking in his serviette, Landis, appreciative of the authentic French aroma of the *boeuf bourguignonne* on his plate, said, 'We'll discuss that later, if you don't mind. For the time being, let us eat, drink and be merry, as Rab Romer would say.'

Rab! Gina looked down at the food on her plate unseeingly at the mention of his name, her lighthearted mood of a moment ago suddenly forgotten.

'You're not eating.'

'I'm not very hungry.'

Landis said quietly, 'Of course, I should have realized. You're in love with Rab, aren't you?'

Raising her head, 'Yes,' she said.

'Oh, you poor child.' Landis laid down his serviette. He stretched his hand across the table. 'Forgive me, but didn't he tell you he was married?'

'*Married!*' She felt the room spinning round her. Her face drained suddenly of colour. She felt sick. Rising quickly to her feet, she gripped the edge of the table to steady herself. She had to get out of this place into the fresh air. Now! As quickly as possible.

Galvanized into action, Landis took control of the situation. Placing a steadying arm about her waist, he led her to the door, pausing momentarily to pay for the food they had not eaten.

Her head was against his shoulder. He felt the trembling of her body as he pushed open the door and guided her to the pavement's edge where he summoned a passing taxi. Deeply shaken, cursing himself as a fool, holding her close on the back seat of the taxi, 'Forgive me,' he said hoarsely, 'this is all my fault.'

'No. Not your fault, but mine. I should have known. I should have guessed when he went away so suddenly without a word of explanation. It was all so obvious; but you see, I thought he was in love with me. I never dreamt that he was – lying.'

'Gina! Gina, my dearest girl, any man in his right senses would love you. How could they help it? You are the most beautiful, the most desirable woman any man could wish for.' He spoke from the heart, from the strong feeling of desire for her that threatened to overwhelm him at that moment, as he held her close to his swiftly beating breast.

Struggling hard to gain control, she murmured, 'I'm sorry. The champagne must have gone to my head.'

'That's what champagne is for,' he reminded her unsteadily, resisting a strong urge to kiss her, knowing how futile that would be, simply glad that she trusted him enough to allow him to hold her on the back seat of the taxi.

But ah, dear God, if only he had been Rab Romer holding Gina in his arms . . . how differently she might have reacted to his closeness.

Chapter Thirteen

The weight of the books on her head forced Gina to walk very slowly and carefully the entire length of the room, lest they slipped from their precarious position and ended up on the floor, which eventually they did.

Giselle Gautier laughed. 'Tomorrow,' she said, 'you will carry on your head a jug filled with water. Perhaps a good soaking will teach you to keep your head erect.'

Picking up the books, 'My head *was* erect,' Gina said mutinously.

'In that case, why are the books on the floor?' Giselle sighed deeply. 'What is wrong with you, *chérie*? Is it that you enjoy, perhaps, wasting good money on lessons that you are too – how do you say – pig-headed to learn? Or do you think yourself too perfect to profit from my instruction?'

'I? Oh no! Please, you mustn't think that. It is just that I . . .' Gina covered her face with her hands.

'That you are very unhappy, *n'est-ce pas*? Very uncertain of yourself, of the future? I know, believe me,' Giselle said gently, 'but if – how shall I put it – if you can garner strength from unhappiness, blend that strength with humility, then and only then will you become an actress of any importance, provided that you are willing to learn all the tricks of the profession. If not, then I suggest that you stop wasting your own time, and mine. The choice is yours entirely.'

Standing upright, poised and calm, Madame Gautier continued proudly, 'You see, *mademoiselle*, acting is a way of life; a torment at times, but a necessary torment to those who have known, as I have, the glory of the footlights, the thrill of an audience in the palms of ones hands: the ability to move that audience to tears or laughter by the merest gesture, a certain inflexion of the voice. This is a gift bestowed by God, worth every moment of the hard work involved in developing that God-given talent, which has been bestowed on you in full measure. If only you had the sense and humility to learn how to bring that talent to fruition. More than this I cannot say. Well, *Mademoiselle* Gina, what is your answer?'

Gina said simply, 'I should like to try the water-jug test now.'

Giselle smiled. 'Now there is no need of such a test. From henceforward you will walk with an imaginary pitcher on your head. The lesson has been learned.'

What Madame Gautier said was true. Gina was unhappy, uncertain of herself and the future. Landis' revelation that Rab was married had thrown her off-balance, imbuing her with the feeling that nothing in life really mattered, except Oliver. Her dreams and ambitions had turned to dust in her hands, throwing her into a mental turmoil from which there had seemed no escape until Giselle, in her wisdom, had brought her face-to-face with her shortcomings, her pig-headedness and lack of humility.

Alone in her room, staring at her reflection in the mirror, Gina knew that she must pick up the pieces of her shattered life and put them together again. She was not the first woman in the world to have suffered the heartbreak of an abortive love affair nor, her common sense told her, would she be the last.

Given a chance against the world in learning how to become an actress, she now stood in danger of losing that chance by her own stupidity, her own folly, if she failed to respond to Giselle Gautier's coaching. This much seemed certain, unless she threw herself, heart and soul, mind and body into the bewildering world of the theatre, unless she learned how to 'garner strength from unhappiness', as Madame Gautier had suggested.

So what should she do? Start another secretarial agency; spend the rest of her life typing long, boring legal documents to earn a living, or undergo the mental and physical torment of learning how to walk, move and speak correctly in the hope of one day appearing behind the footlights of a West End theatre?

The choice was obvious.

Next day she went to her tutorial with the clear intention of working hard, or the money her father had spent in underwriting this venture would be wasted. Worry about Owen had formed part of her depression; guilt at having left him, knowing how much he had wanted her at home. The tears she had shed at her audition had been inevitable. The words, 'They say a made a good end' had brought vividly to mind the realization that he was no longer a young man, that the death of Mary Bickley had had a profound effect on his health and strength. She must not add to his burdens. For his sake as well as Oliver's she must work hard to repay his kindness to her.

Walking towards the school she experienced, for the first time, a frisson of pleasure in the realization that the pavements beneath her feet were London pavements, that she was here in one of the great capital cities of the world, facing the greatest challenge of her life so far. The success or failure of that challenge lay in her own hands.

Two days later, the letter she had written to Daisy Crabtree, in care of her sister, Mrs Stephenson, came back unopened and marked 'Address unknown'. Someone, presumably a neighbour, had scrawled beneath her own address on the back of the envelope, 'Mrs Stephenson passed away last year. Mrs Crabtree in service up West. Don't know where. Yours truly, L. Pritchard.'

Bridget said, when Gina showed her the envelope, 'Poor Mrs Crabtree. She thought the world of her sister. But if it's me you're bothering your head about, you needn't. You'd be surprised the friends I've made out shopping with little Oliver in his pram, or wheeling him up on the Heath. There's one girl I like especially, called Rosie – a nursemaid like me – who works for a posh family just round the corner.' She laughed. 'Truth to tell, Miss Georgina, I'm beginning to like this place. It isn't half as bad as I thought it would be at first.'

*   *   *

'Ay Ee Eye O You. Tay Tee Tar Toe Tum. Repeat after me, please! Good. And once again.'

Gina laughed. It seemed so odd, a Frenchwoman teaching an English girl how to speak English correctly. But then, Giselle Gautier was a remarkable woman who spoke English with hardly a trace of a foreign accent. But possibly a purist who knew nothing of regional dialects was the best person to teach the language as she had been taught it, by a professor of English at the Paris Conservatoire of Music and Dramatic Art where she had studied as a girl.

Looking fondly at her protégée, Giselle thought how well she had progressed in her studies since that fraught day last spring, when she had seemed so at odds with the world. Madame had known then that the girl possessed that *je ne sais quoi* which set her apart from her fellow students, and Landis had been right in thinking she would gain more from private coaching than joining in with the rest.

She remembered what he had said to her when he had asked her to take on the role of private tutor: 'This girl is a born actress. Her talent must be nurtured gently, it cannot be forced. She has faults, of course, but inability to act is not one of them.' Pacing the room excitedly, waving his hands, 'She is strong-willed but immature, totally lacking in self-confidence. She is also deeply unhappy – an affair of the heart – but her face is exquisite.'

'You are not falling in love with her by any chance?'

'In love? Don't be ridiculous, Giselle! I am not a boy to be seduced by a pretty face . . .'

'An exquisite face, then?' Giselle queried gently, recalling that her own face had once been described as exquisite by Landis, a long time ago, when he had cupped her chin with his hands and leaned forward to kiss her. The fact that he did not remember that kiss or her passionate response to it, caused her momentary pain, but that was all in the past. She doubted if he even knew that she was still passionately in love with him now, as she had been then: the reason why she had given up her acting career to come with him to England, before the war, to help him establish his School

168

of Dramatic Art. But it pleased her to think that the many embryo actors and actresses who had come and gone during the past decade, believed her to be his mistress. If only that were true.

Shrugging aside her own feelings, she had to admit that Gina Brett's face *was* exquisite. But she had much still to learn about clothes and makeup. Madame had considered the matter carefully and come to the conclusion that the girl had no dress sense. Her clothes, though of excellent quality, lacked style and movement, but this was an exciting time in the world of fashion, with rising hemlines and lighter, softer, more colourful fabrics coming into vogue, and to make the necessary impact on casting directors it was important for a budding actress to dress well. The initial impression was vital, and the time was fast approaching when she must make her début. Also, something must be done about her hair. The colour was glorious, but there was too much of it.

The end of the war had brought a resurgence of the old flair and gaiety to the great Paris fashion houses. Bizarre, even outrageous and revolutionary, was this new concept of fashion, influenced by the magic of Diaghilev's Ballets Russes with its exotic sets and costumes, which had captured the imagination of the war-weary masses who witnessed its swirling movement and colour.

A girl of Gina's height and slenderness would wear to perfection the softly draped, low-necked dresses, dramatically flaring wide-collared coats and head-hugging hats which had taken Paris by storm – hats which called for shorter, neater, face-flattering hairstyles. But Madame knew from experience that the last thing most women wished to part with was their crowning glory, and so she must tread warily. It was one thing to teach deportment and voice production, to encourage the learning of a foreign language, to recommend the reading of classic plays, apart from those written by William Shakespeare, to touch upon the history of the theatre and stimulate discussion on the various aspects of play production, quite another to ask a young woman to part with her hair; to contemplate the stripping away of the old in favour of an entirely new and different personality. On the other hand, she knew this must be done if Mademoiselle Brett was to make the impact her talent demanded.

Men, as Madame Gautier knew to her cost, especially those of the theatrical fraternity, were not normally impressed by talent alone. The packaging of that talent was all-important – a certain gloss or mystique, an air of chic, an aura of perfume, of sophistication. Then, and only then, did they sit up and take notice. And she intended that they should sit up and take notice of Gina Brett, who reminded her of herself when she was young.

She said, 'I want you to come to Paris with me.'

'*Paris!*'

'It is important that you should. A necessary part of your education.'

'I'd like to, Madame, but it is not as simple as that.'

'I have friends there with whom we could stay quite cheaply, so money need not concern you—'

'It isn't that,' Gina said, knowing she could well afford the trip. 'You see, I have a child to consider. My son Oliver.'

'A child?' Giselle's eyes opened wide in surprise. 'I had no idea. How old is he?'

'A little over seven months.'

'My dear girl, why have you never mentioned this before?' This explained many things, Madame thought. Gina came to the school in May, it was now early September. A recent pregnancy and the broken love affair at which the maestro had hinted, would account for her springtime depression, especially if the child was illegitimate.

'There seemed no reason why I should.' Gina bit her lip. 'I'm sorry, but I have always regarded my private life as my own.'

'How very wise of you.' Giselle smiled wistfully. 'I, too, have kept my own secrets during my lifetime, the reason why, perhaps, I sublimated my personal sorrows in acting. Hiding my face behind a mask, as it were.'

Drawn to the realization that here was someone she could

170

trust implicitly, Gina said, 'Oliver is my son by adoption, a legacy entrusted to me by his mother, whom I loved dearly.' Her self-control almost broke. 'It's a long, complex story, but it would be unfair of me to expect his nursemaid to shoulder the full responsibility for his welfare during my absence. So you see, Madame Gautier, the reason why I cannot accept your invitation.'

'Yes, of course. But it seems a pity, a great pity that you could not trust Oliver's nursemaid to take care of him for, say, four or five days at the most. Or perhaps she is an untrustworthy person?' Giselle raised her eyebrows enquiringly.

Falling into Madame's cleverly worded trap, Gina sprang immediately to Bridget's defence. 'To the contrary, Madame Gautier, my son's nursemaid, Miss Donovan, is a trusted friend of long standing who came with me to London to look after my son.'

'My apologies to Miss Donovan,' Giselle smiled. 'I had not, of course, realized that she was so well known to you. I imagined her to be someone you had engaged through one of those "Situations Vacant" advertisements so prevalent in the London newspapers nowadays.'

'*Touché*, Madame Gautier!' Gina laughed suddenly, knowing she was being gently teased, glad that Madame knew about Oliver. 'Very well, then, you win! I will go to Paris with you, if you think it necessary.'

'More than that, *chérie*, it is essential. Besides, it will do you good to see something of the world. The saying goes, "See Naples, and die". I prefer, "See Paris and live!"' Giselle's eyes sparkled.

Paris burst upon her senses with all the brilliance and excitement of a fireworks' display. The colours of autumn changing the trees from green to gold, the blue sky and the dazzling displays of flowers for sale on the street vendors' barrows, painted a striking backdrop against which the city glowed like a jewel.

From the moment of their arrival at the Gare du Nord, Gina was caught up in the feeling that she had stepped into a dreamworld of new sights, sounds and colours, of movement and laughter never before experienced. 'Gay Paree', Harry Bickley had called it. Now she knew why. There was a sense of excitement more potent than wine in the air. From the back seat of a honking taxi, she saw the landmarks she had read about: spacious tree-lined boulevards, pavement cafés, striking displays of autumn clothes in the windows of the great department stores, hurrying crowds of people thronging the pavements, all of whom seemed imbued with a sense of purpose lacking in the populace of London.

Deciding against staying with friends, Giselle had booked rooms at an hotel near the Rue de Rivoli. Time was of the essence. Shrewdly, she had planned exactly how to spend the three days available to her to bring about the necessary changes in her protégée's appearance. Window shopping came high on her list of priorities. At first the merest subtle suggestion that this or that outfit would suit Gina to perfection, then would come the visit to the gown department to try on the garments, the casual remark that she would need a special dress for their first night theatre outing to see a performance of *Petrushka* by Diaghilev's Ballets Russes; on the second night of their stay, a production of *La Dame Aux Camélia*s: on their final night in Paris, dinner with Madame's friends at a fashionable restaurant in the Champs Elysées. Quite how she would persuade Gina to have her hair cut off, Madame had not yet decided.

Forever afterwards, with a bursting feeling of pride in her heart, a mist of tears in her eyes, Giselle Gautier would remember the sublime moment when Gina had stood on the threshold of that restaurant in the Champs Elysées, a dazzling, radiant figure in white, her shining cap of red hair cut in the latest fashion, the way all eyes had turned to watch her as she walked between the tables as upright as if she were carrying a pitcher of water on her head.

Never had Gina worn such a dress before, of softly draped chiffon, with crystal beads about the low-cut bodice, and the new length hemline – a gift from Madame which she had been loathe to accept, it was so expensive. But Giselle's generosity had not ended with the gown alone. She had also insisted on giving her a pair of white satin evening shoes, and a matching pochette with a silver chain.

'But I cannot possibly accept so many expensive gifts from you,' Gina had demurred in the gown department of the Galeries Lafayette. 'Why on earth should you spend so much money on me?'

'Let us say that I was more than relieved when you sat, like a lamb, to have your hair cut off.' Giselle laughed. 'This is your reward.'

'Oh, *that*?' Gina smiled reflectively. 'Would it surprise you to know that I would have had it cut long ago, had it not been for my mother? Frankly, Madame, I have always loathed and detested the colour of my hair. Would you believe that I once tried to darken it and squash it down with my father's pomade?'

'Knowing you as well as I do now, *chérie*,' Giselle said, tongue-in-cheek, 'nothing would surprise me.' Yet even as she spoke Madame Gautier realized that her remark was not entirely true, that she knew almost nothing about her protégée's past life. She simply knew, and accepted, that here was a girl destined to become a very great actress. Her faith in that belief was intensified when Gina had entered the restaurant in the Champs Elysées, like a queen.

The wonder was, Giselle thought afterwards, that the diners in that brilliantly lit, red-carpeted room, had not risen to their feet to applaud her entrance.

Chapter Fourteen

During Georgina's absence, Bridget had been staying with the mother of her nursemaid friend, Rosie, at Walthamstow. This arrangement had been made when Gina had flatly refused to leave Bridget and Oliver alone in the house at night. Then, Rosie's mother, Mrs Adams, who had small children of her own, had offered to let Bridget sleep in Rosie's room, and provide a cot for the baby.

Returning to Welford House by taxi, Gina paid the driver who had helped her up the front steps with her luggage. Stepping into the hall, she called out, 'Bridget, I'm home!' She hurriedly peeled off her gloves and placed them on the hall table. 'Where are you?'

'Down here, Miss Georgina,' came a voice from the basement.

'I'm coming!' Lightly she tripped down the stairs, eyes glowing at the thought of holding Oliver in her arms; forgetful of her new clothes.

'Holy Mother of God!' Bridget stared in amazement at the new-look Georgina, taking in every detail of her elegantly cut tweed coat with its ocelot trimmed collar, in the new length, her peach-bloom velour cloche hat, glossy leather shoes with triangular flaps about the ankles, matching exactly the colour of her handbag. 'What have you done to yourself? What have you done to your hair?'

Gina laughed. 'Make me a cup of tea and I'll tell you all about it!' She threw her arms about Bridget, bewildering the girl's senses with the discreet yet heady perfume of Patou's *Joie de Vivre*. 'How's my precious boy?' Lifting Oliver from Bridget's arms into her own, she saw with delight, his smile of recognition and noted with deep, inward satisfaction, the sturdiness of his limbs, the chubbiness of his fists against the softness of the ocelot collar, as she sat down in the rocking chair near the fire to nurse him.

'Should you be doing that in your fine new clothes, Miss Georgina?' Bridget asked anxiously, pouring boiling water into the teapot.

'The day I care more about clothes than my son,' Gina said softly, 'is a day I never wish to see.' She smiled wistfully. 'All this was not my idea, Bridget, believe me.' After a slight pause. 'I gather that you don't entirely approve?'

'No, it isn't that, Miss Georgina,' Bridget said worriedly, creasing her forehead, 'you look wonderful. But I have the feeling – well, that you are not my Miss Georgina any more. You seem – forgive me. You seem like a stranger to me now.'

It was then Gina realized that she felt like a stranger to herself – and yet, Madame Gautier had assured her, in Paris, that to change her style of dressing completely was essential to her future success as an actress, and she had gone along with that, trusting entirely to Giselle's judgement. Besides, it had been easy to shed her old image in the pulsating atmosphere of the fashion departments of the shops she had visited, with their breathtaking displays of gowns by Schiaparelli, Lelong, Worth and Chanel. Not that she could have afforded couture clothes, but the flow and cut of the gowns had convinced her that her own style of dressing was dull and *passé*.

Moreover, there had been less expensive versions of the designers' art on show, in exciting fabrics and colours – evening dresses in crêpe-de-chine, ninon, velvet, chiffon and brocade, day dresses, costumes and coats expressing, in their imaginative cut and design, the beginning of a new era of fashion which, in history books, would be known as 'The Roaring Twenties', the age of the Flappers, the Bright Young Things who, having cropped short their hair, also cropped short their skirts to reveal their silk-stockinged ankles.

'There's a present for you in my handbag,' Gina said, 'I hope you'll like it. Open it, I have my hands full at the moment.'

175

'Perfume!' Bridget regarded the contents of the small package she had taken from the handbag, with obvious delight. 'Real French perfume! What a treat.' Pouring the tea she had made, 'Tell me, Miss Georgina, what is Paris really like? Where did you go? What did you do? What did you see?'

Sitting by the fire in the basement kitchen, Gina conjured up her countless impressions of the city which had fired her imagination, re-living the joy of walking beside the River Seine after dark, seeing the myriad shore lights swimming down mysteriously into the dark water; the colourful passage of the brightly lit *bâteaux mouches* past the Île de la Cité. She thought of how she had felt entering Notre Dame cathedral, hearing her footsteps echoing on the grey stone flags, the sense of peace and holiness she had sensed there, how she had knelt down and prayed for guidance, the courage to face the unknown future as it should be faced, realistically, without self-pity: the wisdom to lay aside, without bitterness, unhappy memories of the past.

She wondered if Rab had come to this place to gain information for his work, and pictured him in a quiet side chapel, sketch-book in hand, capturing on paper the delicate bosses and roof traceries. Many of the paintings he had shown her at the studio had been of Paris, and her imagination had led her to believe that they would one day visit Paris together as lovers, walking beneath the trees in the Tuileries Gardens: standing, perhaps, in the Louvre, looking at the works of those great artists whose names he revered: Titian, Rembrandt, Caravaggio. A dream, but a beautiful dream while it lasted. That dream was over now.

Rab had told her that day in the studio, when he had urged her to think of becoming an actress, that they had no future together. If only he had told her then that he was married. She would far rather have heard the truth from his lips, face-to-face, when they were alone together, than have heard it from George Landis across a candlelit table in the unreal atmosphere of a French restaurant.

Oh, Rab, she had thought, that day in Notre Dame, why

didn't you trust me enough to be honest with me? You told me you loved me, and perhaps you did according to your light, possibly not more, but differently from the way you loved Poppy.

In any event, she had thought, rising to her feet, in the long run both she and Poppy had been expendable in Rab's life. And it was this feeling of rejection she could not come to terms with.

The ugliness of the scene struck anger into his soul. How could mankind desecrate the natural beauty of so rich and varied a landscape?

Looking down at the Marquiss Mine from a high vantage point, Rab saw that the cliffs fringing the curling, sapphire blue sea had been scarred by outcrops of headgear and pumping equipment, engine-houses, chimney stacks; the raised tracks on which the wagons were lumbered to the dressing frames, that the ground was pitted with great earth weals, as if some colossus had scourged the land with a rawhide whip.

Then, seeing a straggling line of tired-faced miners emerging from the wooden-gated stockade with its 'Keep Out' warnings, men filthy and exhausted from long hours spent underground, he realized, with a feeling of shame, that, to those men, the mine meant shelter, food and clothing for their wives and families. His bitterness was directed, not towards those poor devils obliged to work in the bowels of the earth to earn a living, but towards men like Phillip Marquiss whose affluence had been derived from greed, made possible by the miserable wages they paid their workforce.

Hands clenched into fists, he thought how devilishly cruel and clever his father-in-law had been in condemning him to work in a place of such brutal ugliness. Marquiss had judged precisely the demoralizing effect of this hell-hole on someone like himself, whose life so far had been dedicated to art: his love of beauty, of colours captured on canvas.

Lifting his eyes to the far-flung horizon, his face drawn

with pain, he suddenly remembered the painting of the blue interior of the Sainte Chappelle he had shown to Gina at their first meeting – an enigmatic picture at first glance, unless, standing back from it, one realized that the criss-crossing rays of light, in varying shades of blue, were meant to convey the shafts of light streaming down from a glorious blue, stained-glass window. He remembered the words he had said to her that day: 'One should always stand back a little, I've discovered, from life as well as art.'

He now knew, despairingly, that henceforward there could be no standing back from either life or art, because of Marguerite, whose helplessness had moved him to tears when he had entered her room last night . . .

'Rab, my darling! I knew you'd come back to me! I told them you would, but they didn't believe me.'

She had fluttered across the room to him, arms outspread to embrace him, as fragile as a moth or a butterfly in her white peignoir, her long dark hair spread about her shoulders. 'They think I'm mad, you see.' Puckering her forehead, she added, 'Well, perhaps I was for a little while, when our baby died . . . such a lovely little boy . . . but I'm not now – now that you've come back to me.'

She whispered eagerly, 'Now we can have another baby, can't we? *Can't* we? All you have to do is to make love to me once more!' Staring up at him with frightened eyes, 'You *do* love me, my darling, don't you? Please, *please* tell me that you love me, that you will sleep with me tonight; I want you to give me another baby!'

The trained nurse, standing in the shadows of the room, ready to administer a sedative if her patient became too distressed, glanced at Rab with pitying eyes, knowing as well as he did that his wife had never given birth to a child, that her pregnancy had been a figment of her imagination.

Never in his life had Rab felt more helpless than he did when, quitting the room, he heard Marguerite begging him piteously not to leave her, to sleep with her, to make love to her, followed by her high-pitched scream of anger, her flow of invective when, after the nurse had quietly asked him to go away, he realized the extent of Marguerite's mental illness.

Holding his hand to her lips, she had bitten savagely into the flesh. Tears streamed down his cheeks as, finding a handkerchief to bind the wound, he saw the blood stains welling up through the clean linen.

'You will do as you are bloody well told, Romer,' Phillip Marquiss said hoarsely, his cheeks empurpling with rage. 'I am the master here!'

'Oh no, Marquiss,' Rab regarded the man disdainfully, 'not in this instance. I have no intention of taking the job you've in mind for me.' He smiled grimly. 'I dare say it would suit your purpose to have the men despise me, to have them call me – whatever they would call an over-seer totally lacking experience of the work involved. If I attempted such a thing, they would have every right to call me your puppet – or worse, your spy! It would please you, wouldn't it, to have me report to you every word they uttered behind your back, to hold me personally responsible for a fall-off in production, to hand me an invisible whip with which to thrash the latecomers, the absentees, no matter how valid their reasons. Well, I'm telling you here and now, Marquiss, you've chosen the wrong man to do your dirty work!'

'I might have known it,' Marquiss said bitterly. 'Might have known that you would cringe away from your respon-sibilities like a beaten dog.' His lips curled back from his strong, yellowing teeth, in a sneer of contempt for his son-in-law's cowardice when it came to earning a living. 'This means, I suppose, that you intend to return to your old, feckless, irresponsible lifestyle? To turn your back on my daughter?'

'No, not at all,' Rab said calmly, repelled yet fascinated by the bubbles of saliva at the corners of the man's mouth. 'It simply means that I wish to earn the respect of the men – as one of them.' Looking down at his injured hand, he continued, 'You needn't worry, I shall do all in my power to help Marguerite. But in my own way, not yours.'

'Don't be a fool, Romer!' Visibly startled, Marquiss brought his fist down on the desk in front of him. 'If you imagine for one moment that I intend to be made a laughing stock in the eyes of my workforce, I advise you to think again. Mock heroics will not work with me as they did with my daughter.' Again came the salivating sneer. 'You'll discover there is precious little glory in hewing rocks for a living, and you thrive on glory. I saw with my own eyes how much you enjoyed the adulation showered on you when you brought Marguerite back to England, how besotted she was with you, how you had influenced her to the extent that I scarcely knew her as my own daughter, the happy young girl I left in charge of that wretched Steiner family . . .'

A sudden spring, and Rab was at the man's throat, murder in his heart. He felt the scrawny windpipe beneath his trembling fingers and saw the abject terror in Marquiss' eyes as he forced him down on the desk. 'You – bastard,' he muttered thickly.

Grappling with Rab's hands, 'For Christ's sake!' The words came jerkily, spasmodically, from Marquiss' mouth, as he gasped for air, his head rolling from side to side; eyes bulging as the pressure on his windpipe increased.

Then, 'Get up,' Rab said contemptuously, seeing that the man had urinated. 'Stand up, and be thankful that I didn't put an end to your miserable existence.' His hands were still shaking, his mouth was dry. 'Next time, I may not be able to prevent myself!'

He walked unsteadily from the room.

At least by mining for a living he would be in contact with something real – Nature, rocks, earth. Working underground, he would not be aware of the desecration of the landscape. Hard, physical labour would bring about the benison of exhaustion of mind and body, of deep, dreamless sleep. Working alongside the men of the Marquiss Vor, he might gain not merely the respect of the miners, but self-respect, a kind of absolution for the hurt he had caused Gina, Poppy, and Marguerite . . .

Marguerite: he would never again enter her room without

180

fear, never again leave without sadness and regret – and fear for her future; irredeemable sorrow for the past, all the complex, interwoven strands of his life which had brought him to the realization of his failure as an artist and a human being.

Chapter Fifteen

Harold had met Susanna Crighton at a house party in the Lake District. Since the death of his mother, he had grown increasingly introspective and irritable. At breakfast with his sisters when the invitation arrived, he had refused to listen to Letty's persuasive voice telling him that he should accept, that it would do him good to have a change of scenery.

'Who are these people anyway?' he demanded crossly, helping himself to bacon and kidneys. 'I don't know them from Adam.'

'Of course you do.' Letty pulled a pet lip. 'We met them at the Claytons' dance last summer. I think it's very kind of them to ask us to their house-warming party, and I think you are being disagreeable and horrid.'

Josie said scathingly, 'Letty's right. You're like a bear with a sore head these days, but all the bad temper in the world won't bring Mother back. As for that wretched affair of the wedding, you should thank your lucky stars you weren't saddled with Georgina. She wasn't right for you, and you know it. You'd never have thought of marrying her in a million years if it hadn't been for that interfering mother of hers.'

'*Josie!*' Letty looked shocked. No-one had dared mention Georgina's name to Harold since the evening she had come to Merlewood to return the engagement ring.

Josie continued relentlessly, 'Hurt pride's one thing; to carry it round with you like a banner for all the world to see displays remarkably bad taste, in my opinion – a complete lack of *real* pride.'

Oh God, Letty thought, glancing fearfully at her brother, now there'd be ructions. Trust Josie to march in where angels feared to tread. But no. Surprisingly, Harry seemed chastened. All he said was, 'All right, then, I'll go to the bloody house party, but I'll bet any money they'll have some horse-faced girl lined up for me to partner.'

She was wearing a long-skirted costume in subtle shades of lilac and pink tweed, he noticed, a shell-pink blouse and a straw hat trimmed with pink artificial roses. Pink – his favourite colour. Lustrous fair hair winged out beneath the hat brim; her eyelashes, thick and dark, made little fans on her cheeks when she looked down, which she did quite often, then up again, very quickly, so that recipients of her upward glances were bowled over by the look of innocence in her widely spaced blue eyes.

What an attractive girl, Harry thought, acknowledging the introduction with a brief handshake and a murmured, 'I'm delighted to meet you, Miss Crighton.'

'Please, you must call me Susanna.' Smiling up at him from her basket chair on the terrace, 'Won't you sit down, Mr Bickley, and let me pour you some tea? You must be fearfully thirsty after your journey.'

'Why, yes, I—'

'Isn't this a lovely house?' Pouring the tea, she said, 'Helen Donaldson is my cousin. She and Gareth lived in Stockton before they came here. They couldn't believe their luck when Gareth's bank sent him here. If you've been to Stockton, you'll know why. Hardly a beauty spot. But *this*. I mean, imagine waking up in the morning to a view of Lake Windermere.' She sighed prettily, fluttering her lashes. Harold looked at her bemusedly as she prattled on.

'Shall I let you into a secret? I was so afraid they'd find someone frightfully old and boring to be my escort at dinner, I very nearly changed the place-cards. I'm glad now I didn't. Your names on the guest-list sounded a bit formidable.' She laughed deliciously, dimpling her cheeks. 'The Misses Josie and Letty, and Mr Harold Bickley! I imagined your sisters would be at least sixty, grey-haired, wearing black lace, and *pince-nez* spectacles. But they're charming, aren't they? Certainly Frank and Charles Considine appear to think so.'

Turning his head, Harold saw his sisters, perched on the stone balustrade edging the terrace, chatting merrily to a couple of dark-haired young men alike enough to be twins. Unreasonably angry that they were making a spectacle of themselves, he said coldly, 'Apparently so. I apologize on their behalf, Miss Crighton.'

Wrinkling her forehead, 'But why on earth should you? We're here to enjoy ourselves, aren't we? Don't tell me you're a prude, Mr Bickley!'

Sensing her disapproval, 'No, of course not,' he said quickly, 'it's just that, well, our mother died recently.'

'Oh, how sad! I'm so sorry, Harold.' Leaning forward to touch his hand sympathetically, 'I may call you Harold, mayn't I?' she asked.

'Of course.' He paused, searching for words. 'I'm sorry if I gave you the wrong impression, I . . .'

'Were you in the war, Harold?'

'Yes. The Army. Why do you ask?'

'I think that we should forget about being sad and enjoy life,' she said. 'There is nothing wrong in being alive and young. The Considine brothers were in a German prison camp for a whole year.' She shuddered. 'Think how dreadful that must have been. Can you blame them for flirting with your sisters?'

Regarding him shrewdly, she liked what she saw. Broad shoulders, fair hair brushed back from a high forehead, straight nose, firm mouth. He might be great fun, she considered, if he learned to relax more. Moreover, he possessed a certain arrogance of bearing which sprang from a secure, moneyed background. His clothes were faultlessly tailored, his movements co-ordinated, so that nothing about him jarred on her. Susanna liked well-polished, handsome men of her own social standing. Sadly since the war unscarred heroes, the leaders of men into battle, were thin on the ground. Had not the Considine brothers been imprisoned by the Germans, for instance, they might well have been killed – worse still, maimed for life – returning home minus an arm or a leg. Physical disability in any shape or form was repugnant to Susanna. She could never bring

184

herself to marry a man less perfect than herself, and she desperately wished to be married.

Seated next to Harold at dinner, she regaled him with fascinating glimpses into her background: her home, Acklam Grange, near Middlesbrough, her first pony, summer holidays abroad with her parents, before the war. How, during the war, she had served mugs of tea at Darlington Station, to servicemen alighting from the troop trains because, she explained, she felt that she must do something positive towards the war effort – thinking it best not to mention that her burst of patriotic fervour had fizzled like a damp squib when she discovered that the weary soldiers queueing up for tea could not have cared less who served it, as long as it was sweet and hot.

Returning to Merlewood in a dreamlike state of enchantment, Harry remembered dancing with Susanna, how neatly she had fitted into his arms, her hand poised as delicately as a butterfly on his shoulder, the soft womanly shape and fragrance of her, the billowing of her rose-pink evening gown as they swirled to the *Merry Widow* waltz played on a gramophone.

More than a mere change of scenery, he had experienced a change of heart, an uplifting of the spirit in Susanna's delightful company, so that the dour Harold Bickley who had travelled under duress to that weekend party no longer existed.

In love for the first time, he viewed his future through rose-tinted glasses. From then on his life had been imbued with a new sense of purpose. Besotted with Susanna, he had begun travelling to Acklam Grange practically every weekend, except on those occasions when she came to Merlewood to enchant everyone, his father included, with her charm and vivacity.

During this time, his sisters had become engaged to marry Francis and Charles Considine, to Jack Bickley's bemusement, who viewed with some trepidation the dissolution of his family. Not that he had any fault to find with his prospective sons-in-law, whose family credentials were impeccable. Both were bright young men with good prospects. But, bereft of his wife and daughters, Merlewood would seem an empty shell.

Christmas brought an invitation to the Bickleys to spend the holiday at Acklam Grange in the company of the Considines, the Donaldsons and various other members and friends of the Crighton family – an invitation which Jack Bickley accepted as an alternative to spending Christmas alone.

It was there, on Christmas morning, that Harold proposed marriage to Susanna. They were walking in the grounds at the time. A thick, hoar frost had turned the grass to the crackling consistency and colour of icing on a wedding cake. Their breath whirled away like smoke in the thin, cold air as, drawing her close to him in the sanctuary of a woodcutter's shelter, fragrant with the scent of sawdust and oak chippings, he asked her to be his wife, half afraid of her answer, pushing to the back of his mind the sour memory of Georgina's reluctance to become engaged to him that Easter morning in the garden of Merlewood. *Georgina*, damn her! Georgina whose shadow continued to haunt the recesses of his mind no matter how hard he tried to forget her. Georgina who had shamed him in front of a church full of people, whom he held responsible for the death of his mother. Georgina whom he had treated as uncivilly as a servant the night she came to Merlewood to return the engagement ring he had placed on her finger . . .

'Harry, darling, of course I'll marry you!'

'You will? Oh, thank God!' Thankfully, he pressed Susanna closer, in a great upsurge of mingled joy and relief. 'I'll do everything in my power to make you happy. Oh, darling, I love you so much.' Tilting back her head, he smothered her face with kisses.

When he had finished, 'Haven't you forgotten something?' Susanna asked, straightening her hat.

'Forgotten . . . ? Oh, lord, yes! I'm sorry, my darling.' Unearthing the half-hoop of flawless diamonds he had chosen as her engagement ring, from his waistcoat pocket,

'I do hope you'll like it,' he murmured, slipping it onto the third finger of her left hand.

'Like it. Oh, Harry, it's beautiful! Simply glorious!'

The ring, she thought, catching sight of the fire and colour at the heart of the exquisitely cut stones, must have cost a small fortune. Her heart leapt with joy. She had wanted Harold from the moment she met him. Now he was hers, all hers, putty in her hands.

She had everything clear cut in her mind. Visiting Merlewood, charmed by its potential, she had seen herself as the undisputed mistress of the house. Once Josie and Letty were safely married and out of the way, she would be given free rein to do exactly as she wished by way of alteration and refurbishment. Harry's father would welcome her presence as the chatelaine of the house. She liked Jack Bickley, and realized that he had a soft spot for her. Soon she would persuade him to hand over the running of the Bickley Mill to his son.

For the time being, she was content to return to Acklam Hall hand-in-hand with Harold, her cheeks stung crimson with fresh air and kisses, to announce their engagement and to drink champagne in celebration of the most successful day of her life. Champagne which she had advised her father to order beforehand, in anticipation of Harry's proposal.

Harry could not quite believe his luck when Susanna told him that she wanted to live at Merlewood after the wedding. 'You're sure you won't mind living under the same roof as my father?' he asked anxiously.

'Darling, of course not! After all, it *is* his roof, and he's rather a pet, isn't he?' Susanna laughed. 'We can't leave him all on his own, the poor lamb, when Josie and Letty have gone to Newcastle.' She added, patting her hair into place in front of the drawing-room mirror, 'They will soon be getting married, won't they?'

And, 'Oh yes,' he replied cheerfully, placing his arms about Susanna's waist, 'as soon as they've found somewhere to live. Knowing them, they'll have a double wedding.' Happier than he had ever been before, turning his bride-to-be away from the glass, he kissed her more deeply than usual. Shock waves ran through him when he felt Susanna's warm tongue in his mouth.

Later that morning, they had gone to church to hear the Banns read. 'How dare you not have told me about that, that woman?'

'I'm sorry. It didn't seem important.'

'Not important? You were on the verge of marrying the wretched creature!'

'I told you, darling, she was just someone I'd known all my life. It was an arranged marriage. Please believe me, Susanna, Georgina meant nothing to me. Ask my father, my sisters, ask anyone you like. I'm telling you the gospel truth.' Ashen faced, he pleaded, 'For God's sake Su you *must* believe me! It's you I love. You, and only you.'

'Don't touch me, Harry. Go away. Leave me alone.'

'I'm damned if I will!' Striding towards her, seizing her shoulders, his temper coming uppermost, 'You'll listen to what I have to say, and stop behaving like a child. I repeat once more, and for the last time, that Georgina Brett-Forsyth meant nothing to me. Quite obviously, the lack of feeling was mutual. Now are you satisfied? If not, I suggest that *you* should be the one to go!'

Passers-by in the street, particularly drably dressed women wheeling prams, stopped to watch the parade of elegantly garbed wedding guests entering the portals of St Jude's. Agog with excitement, the throng of onlookers awaited the arrival of the bride.

A young mother whose baby had started to bawl, picked up its dummy from the grimy pavement, and stuck it back in its mouth. Straining forward, craning her neck, she saw a vision in white satin emerging from a limousine, trailing clouds of cobweb-fine Honiton lace from a wreath of orange blossom; holding a bouquet of pure white lilies in her gloved hands, and caught, as the bride walked up the steps on her father's arm, the lingering scent of *Muguets des Bois* perfume.

Standing ramrod straight beside Susanna, scarcely daring to look at her, gripped with an appalling sense of fear that she might pick up her skirts and run away from him at the last moment, Harold felt his legs trembling, a wave of heat running up his body, beads of perspiration breaking out on the palms of his hands, a curious dryness of the mouth, a constriction of the throat, so that he could scarcely reply to the parson's solemn question, 'Wilt thou, Harold Ewart, have this woman to thy wedded wife . . . ?'

Then came the moment he dreaded.

'Wilt thou, Susanna, have this man to thy wedded husband, to live together after God's ordinance in the holy estate of Matrimony . . . ?'

'I will,' Susanna replied in a clear, firm voice.

Harold felt faint with relief.

Owen knew that his wife's brooding had now become an obsession, motivating her every thought and action, a kind of illness. Reading an account of the Bickley–Crighton wedding in the social column of *The Leeds Mercury* had brought on an outburst of temper so violent that he feared for her sanity. 'For God's sake, Agnes, calm yourself. Do you want the servants to hear?'

Shaking off his restraining hand on her arm, 'Calm myself! How can I? My life is ruined, and you tell me to calm myself! I shall go off my head one of these days what with one thing and another. First Thomas, now this.'

Yesterday had come a letter from their son's headmaster saying that Thomas' bad behaviour and lack of academic achievement, culminating in his verbal abuse of the maths master, had resulted in the Board of Governors' decision to expel the boy forthwith. He would be pleased, therefore, if arrangements could be made to collect Thomas and his belongings at the earliest opportunity.

Owen had sympathized with his wife's reaction to the

headmaster's letter until she had started blaming everyone except the culprit for what she termed the Board
of Governors' high-handedness in daring to treat poor
Tommy in such a fashion. Well, she would see about that!
Her colour rising with her temper, she would go to the
wretched school, demand to see the governors and tell them
exactly what she thought of them. As for the headmaster,
hanging was too good for him!

'You'll do nothing of the kind, Agnes,' Owen said
wearily, sick and tired of the constant war of nerves with
his wife. 'I shall go to Leeds the day after tomorrow, bring
Thomas home, and then we will decide what to do about
his future.'

Her eyes widening in horror, 'Decide what to do about
. . . !' Turning on her husband in a fury, 'If you think for
one moment that I would consent to my poor boy entering
the Navy. I warn you, Owen, I shall fight you tooth and
claw. The child's place is here, with me.'

'The "child" as you choose to call him, is nearly
seventeen years old, on the brink of manhood. It is high
time he started behaving like a man.'

The scene that followed had left Owen weak and shaken.
Later that day he had made an appointment to see his old
friend, Doctor Willis, who had brought Georgina and
Thomas into the world.

'Tell me, Owen, how long have you been so short of
breath?'

Dan Willis, white-haired, on the verge of retirement,
applied his stethoscope to Owen's chest.

'Oh, I don't know. I can't remember exactly how long.'
Attempting a smile as he buttoned his shirt, 'Why? Is it
important?'

'Fairly important, I'd say.'

'Two months, then, perhaps three.'

Raising his eyebrows, 'My own guess would be six
months, possibly even a year,' Willis said quietly. 'I'm right,
aren't I?'

'I told you, I can't remember exactly how long.'

'Then I'll hazard a guess. You have been feeling extremely unwell for some time now. Forgive me, ever since the death of Mary Bickley, in fact.'

'You have no right to assume—'

'God dammit man,' Willis interrupted, 'I'm your friend! We grew up together, remember, in this curiously enclosed little world of ours known as the West Riding. I'm older than you are, but there seemed precious little difference between us the night I came to Elmhurst when your father died, or when I brought your children into the world.' He paused. 'I'm sorry, I had no right to assume that the Bickley affair had any bearing on your illness.'

'I am – ill, then?' Owen asked quietly.

'I'm afraid so. But you knew that when you came to see me.'

'Yes, I suppose so,' Owen acknowledged. 'I simply tried to ignore it.' He smiled briefly. 'Is it my heart?'

'Yes, mainly your heart, but your lungs are also affected. The one has a strong bearing on the other. Your lung condition is called emphysema. Labouring to draw breath has weakened your heart to some extent.'

'How great an extent?'

Willis sighed deeply. 'Let me put it this way, Owen. With rest and care, if you promise to take the medicine I prescribe for you, and give up smoking that rammy old pipe of yours, you may well live to a ripe old age.'

Owen laughed. 'You mean that if I pamper myself like an old woman, give up my one bad habit and sit at home all day with my feet up, I may achieve my three score years and ten?'

'Quite possibly you might,' Willis responded warmly. 'But this is no laughing matter. I am seriously worried about you, Owen.' Drumming his fingers on the desk, 'I wish I knew how to say this without offending you too deeply, or putting our friendship in jeopardy, but couldn't you persuade Agnes to visit me? I'm sure I could help her.' He paused. 'How old is she now? Forty-six, forty-seven? A difficult age for a woman.'

Owen said dejectedly, 'That is out of the question, I'm afraid. You know Agnes.'

There was nothing more to be said on the subject of Mrs Brett-Forsyth, Willis realized. How to tell a man that his road to salvation lay in leaving his wife? As an onlooker who had seen most of the game, the doctor had watched his friend's decline into ill health with the objectivity of a physician powerless to halt that decline until expressly asked to do so. By the same token, he could not treat what he saw as Agnes Brett-Forsyth's paranoia unless she came to him for help. An unlikely event in Agnes' case, he thought bitterly, whose greatest delusion centred upon her firm belief that she was beyond reproach.

As a young doctor, he had viewed with trepidation Owen's misalliance with the daughter of a Leeds clothier, whose gents' outfitters shop in Boar Lane catered to the needs of the working class. People who, buying goods through the club-card system, paid through the nose for poor quality garments simply because they were too badly paid to afford to clothe themselves by any other means. Not that Willis was a snob, and if Agnes Mirfield had betrayed by the merest word that she shared her future husband's interest in art, music, poetry and philosophy, he would have danced at their wedding. As it was, he had seen Agnes as a shrewd, vapidly pretty young woman intent on making a good marriage, and he had not been wrong. Her saving grace was, in his view, that she had given birth to a daughter who, growing up, had fulfilled her father's strong need of intellectual companionship. A delightful girl, Georgina, who from an early age had become the butt of her mother's scarcely concealed jealousy and irritation as the bond of affection between Owen and his daughter had strengthened and deepened with the passing years.

Then young Thomas had come on the scene, towards whom Agnes had cleaved with an almost animal affection. Or was affection the right word? The mother's love for her son had been almost frightening in intensity. Holding Thomas to her breast, Agnes had resembled a lioness savagely guarding its cub. The cub had, predictably, taken after its mother.

Willis, the onlooker, throughout his long association with the Bickleys and the Brett-Forsyths, had watched with concern the domestic dramas of both families, had recognized the delicately poised, necessarily understated, yet passionate love affair of minds between Owen Brett-Forsyth and Mary Bickley. He had seen, with anguish, Owen sitting alone in the church on the day of Mary's funeral, knowing the reason why he was there alone, his head sunk in his hands, tears streaming down his face.

From that day, he had noticed, from a distance, his friend's slow decline into old age, as if his life's blood had ceased to circulate, as though the young, vital man he remembered in the heyday of his manhood, had already given up the ghost.

'Is it possible that you could go away for a short time? Get away on your own for a while?' Willis asked.

'Quite impossible at the moment, I'm afraid. Thomas is coming home tomorrow – for good.' Owen's face betrayed the shame he felt over his son's bad behaviour, but he needed to unburden himself, and Willis was an old and trusted friend. 'He has been expelled from school.'

'I'm sorry, Owen.' Willis paused. 'Does this mean he'll be joining you at the mill?'

'It rather looks like it. I threatened him with entry into the Navy if he didn't pull his socks up, but . . .' Owen shrugged helplessly, 'Agnes will not tolerate the idea, and frankly I don't feel up to another battle of wills.'

'In that case, why not leave Thomas with his mother for a while until the dust settles?' Willis suggested. 'There is nothing to be gained from your staying at Elmhurst under pressure. Take the holiday I advised. Why not visit Georgina?'

'Georgina. Yes, I'd like that.' Owen's face lightened at the mention of her name. 'She's in London now, you know, training to become an actress. Did I tell you?'

'No. I simply heard that she had left home.'

Owen said contritely, 'I'm sorry, Dan, I should have told you myself. You, of all people. What a fool I've been. What a blind, silly old fool!' He buried his face in his hands. 'The fact is, I couldn't bear to tell anyone.'

'Tell me *now*,' Willis said.

Chapter Sixteen

Gina walked with her father on Hampstead Heath every afternoon during his stay in London. Wanting to spend as much time with him as possible, she had been granted a fortnight's leave of absence from her studies.

These had been leisurely outings, of necessity, owing to his shortness of breath. During this time they had talked as they had done since she was old enough to share his ideals, to understand and appreciate the finely-honed quality of his intellect and the gentleness of his nature – which her mother saw as airy-fairy nonsense and a lack of manly fibre.

Meeting him at King's Cross, she had been shocked by his frail appearance and the slowness of his movements, even though he had warned her in a letter that his visit was in the nature of a rest-cure advised by Dr Willis.

Thinking the stairs might trouble him, she had given him her room on the ground floor, where he could sit on the balcony, if he felt so inclined, to gain as much fresh air and sunshine as possible without tiring himself too much. But he had been adamant about those afternoon strolls on the Heath, refusing to be treated as an invalid, and it had touched Georgina's heart to see him wheeling Oliver's pram, his thin hands firmly gripping the handle.

Overjoyed at seeing the master again, Bridget had not been able to do enough for him, taking breakfast to his room and beguiling him with her artless chatter, telling him about her friend Rosie, and how much she enjoyed living in London now that she had got used to it, pretending not to notice how ill he looked and how rapidly he had deteriorated since the last time she had seen him.

One day in the kitchen she said passionately to Gina, 'It's all wrong, so it is, a good soul like him put through so much misery with Madam! I'm sorry if I'm speaking out of turn, but what I say is true.' Clattering pots and pans, 'I wish we could keep him here with us, take care of him as he should be taken care of.'

'So do I. But he would never agree to that. Duty, to my father, is what bread is to the starving. He would never forsake that duty.'

'I guess you're right, miss. All the same, I can't help thinkin' what a tussle he'll have training Master Thomas to take over from him when the time comes.'

Gina made no reply. Bridget's outspoken comments reflected her own anxiety about her father's future; a sick man faced with the task of inculcating a sense of responsibility into someone incapable of shouldering that responsibility.

At that moment she remembered Thomas as a child, wantonly destroying Josie and Letty Bickley's carefully built sandcastles; Harold's angry words, 'If you don't stop that insufferable brat knocking down my sisters' castles, I'll box his ears for him!'

She had sprung to her brother's defence on that occasion, simply because Tommy *was* her brother, and family loyalty ran deep, though she had known that what Harold said was true.

If she had been born a boy, Georgina thought, carrying the lunch tray to her father's room, she would have gloried in taking over the mill – that towering edifice to industry with its rattling looms and long weaving sheds. But she had not been born a boy; had suffered, life-long, the consequences of that quirk of nature – rather like Queen Elizabeth, another redhead, she thought wryly – as she set down the tray of food on the table beside her father's chair. Poor Elizabeth, with the heart, brain and spirit of a man trapped in the body of a weak and feeble woman.

One afternoon, inevitably, the subject of Rab had arisen when Owen asked if she had had news of him lately. Sitting beside him on a bench, watching the slow fluttering of autumn leaves from the trees, she told him that Rab was married.

'I'm so sorry, my dear,' her father said quietly, holding

196

her hand, thinking how much she had changed from the happy, laughing child she used to be, and wishing he knew what to do to help her.

'You needn't be,' she said, keeping her voice light for his sake. 'It's better to know the truth than to keep on hoping. Now all I want to do is forget him.'

Looking at Oliver in his pram, Owen wondered if that would be possible with the man's child a constant reminder of the past.

On the last day of his visit, walking with his daughter in the sunshine of a 'St Luke's Little Summer', Owen told her that Harold Bickley's wedding announcement had appeared recently in the columns of *The Leeds Mercury*.

'Really? I'm so glad. I hope he'll be happy. But it's not Harry I'm concerned about, it's *you*, Father.'

'Me?' Startled. 'But why?'

'You know why! Father, must you go home tomorrow? Couldn't you stay here with me? I can't bear the thought of you going back to – I'm sorry, but I love you so much I just want you to be happy, not to have to face . . .' Words failed her, but he knew what she meant.

He said quietly, 'You mustn't fret about me, my darling. The mill is my life.'

'I know, but . . .'

He smiled wistfully. 'You are not old enough to remember your great-grandfather, who founded the mill. I scarcely remember him myself. I was little more than a child when he died, but I knew that he stood for all that was good and decent at a time when people were on the point of starvation in the West Riding, in need of jobs, food and clothing. Old Thomas Brett-Forsyth put down roots in the Calder Valley. A man of vision, he brought hope and employment to those who might well have died of hunger and neglect in the wake of the Luddite Riots. The mill is my heritage. Do you understand?'

'Yes, Father, I understand.'

She turned her face away, not wanting him to see the tears in her eyes.

Wearily, Giselle Gautier laid down her pen. She was tired, and there were times when she hated this rambling, untidy apartment of hers on the top floor, its walls pinned with memorabilia of those days when she had been the toast of Paris: posters, and photographs of herself with the crowned heads of Europe, faded reminders of glorious standing ovations, bouquets and baskets of flowers, diamonds and pearls from rich, ecstatic admirers; memories of candlelit suppers and champagne, late night parties, until she had wakened one morning to the realization of the emptiness of life without George Landis. He was the only man she had ever really loved, and for him she had given up fame and fortune for this crowded apartment which served as a studio, office and living quarters – so close to, yet so cruelly separated from the maestro's apartment across the landing. Separated, she thought wistfully, getting up from her desk to stare out of the window at the rain-swept street below, by nothing more than a few feet of wood which might as well have been the English Channel.

It was for Gina's sake that she was burning the midnight oil, with the girl's springtime audition in mind, and the work necessary to prepare her for the ordeal of standing before an audience of hard-headed agents and managers, to convince them of her potential as an actress.

In time to come, Gina would make an unforgettable Cleopatra, a wonderful Gertrude, but not until years of hard theatrical training and a wider experience of life had given her the stature to fill the stage with her presence, to take command of the audience, until her voice had gained maturity. For the time being she must concentrate on Ophelia, Juliet, Cyrano de Bergerac's Roxanne – a repertoire suited to her youth and beauty.

Vital to her success would be a good, reliable agent, someone she could trust to guide her through the contractual maze when she graduated from drama school, preferably a man of integrity and charisma. The name of TJ Power sprang instantly to Giselle's mind; Power, as he was known by the theatrical fraternity. No-one knew what the initials TJ stood for. But Power had become increasingly selective lately in view of his commitment to his list of star clients, all of whom he represented with a no-nonsense approach to work, linked to an amazing knowledge of the theatre, an almost clairvoyant instinct when it came to choosing the right play for the right person, at the right time.

Hardly likely that Power, with a full list of clients, would attend Gina's April audition. But having linked the pair of them in her mind, Giselle Gautier would move heaven and earth to bring about their meeting. She would write to Power, inviting him to the audition, she decided, using her personal influence. After all, she too had been a star.

These English springtimes were impossible, Giselle thought, dismounting from the taxi, shivering violently as a gust of wind scurried rain along the pavement, soaking her own feet and Gina's as they hurried down the narrow passage to the stage door. '*Mon Dieu!*' she cried. 'Today of all days, why could not the sun have shone?' She had so wanted Gina to sail through the foyer as trimly as a yacht, to make a favourable impression on the prosperous-looking group of men talking and smoking cigars near the ticket office. Instead, she had been obliged to hustle her away as quickly as a bride who must not be seen by the groom before the wedding.

Students from other academies of dramatic art would also be taking part in the auditions, working in groups, performing scenes from Shakespearian or Restoration plays. Landis, in charge of his students, had come to the theatre earlier to bring the costumes, wigs and makeup. Gina would be on her own, her solo appearances sandwiched between the corporate offerings to give her time to change costumes. At least she would have a dressing-room to herself. Madame had insisted on that. A *dressing room*? More of a cubby-hole, she thought in disgust, but no matter. 'Sit down, *chérie*,' she fussed, 'we must get you out of those wet shoes before you catch your death of cold.'

Unaware of the state of her feet, sitting in front of the brightly lit mirror as Madame removed her shoes and knelt down to buff her toes with a towel, this was it, Gina thought, the culmination of her year of intensive training at the School of Dramatic Art. Soon she would be called upon to face the greatest challenge of her life. How would she meet that challenge?

Seated at the back of the auditorium was TJ Power, a restless, dark-haired man in his early forties, bored to death by auditions, especially scenes from *Othello* and *Macbeth* performed by youngsters who stood little chance of success in the dog-eat-dog world of the theatre, a great pity, he thought. Obviously these students had worked hard and conscientiously to learn their lines, to memorize their movements – and it showed. Or was it his fault? Had he become so blasé, that he no longer recognized embryo talent when he saw it?

All he could clearly see in his mind's eye, as he rose from his seat and made his way to the nearest Exit, was the hard, cold expression on his wife's face when she told him that she was leaving him, going back to America where she belonged.

'But *why*?' He had failed to understand at the time, still did not understand why she had left him. So he had, possibly, been neglectful of her in attempting to build up and extend the theatrical agency bequeathed to him by his father, but this had been mainly for her sake, to ensure the lifestyle to which, in America, she had become accustomed. Her parting words, 'I'm sorry, TJ, I'm sick and tired of playing second fiddle in your life, that's all,' had seemed a betrayal of the physical love they had once shared, their passionate awareness of each other's presence across a dinner table or a crowded room.

Standing with his hand on the Exit door, he paused briefly to look back at the stage. Now what? he wondered. Naturally, some poor little ninny attempting to play Ophelia. Why did they do it? Why didn't the silly children simply go home, marry decent young men, have lots of babies and give up all thought of acting as a career? He really could not endure . . .

The girl drifted across the stage as lightly as a wind-blown petal, the fluid lines of her slender young body emphasized by the diaphanous white dress she had on, her remarkably lovely face betraying the fear and bewilderment of Ophelia in Act Two, Scene One of *Hamlet*, as she moved centre stage, and stood there, delicately smoothing the back of her left hand with the palm of the right. Then, knotting her hands together, holding the fingers of her left hand in a vice-like grip, she uttered the lines: 'And with a look so piteous in purport as if he had been loosed out of hell . . .'

A voice off-stage spoke the words of Polonius, leading the girl into the speech beginning, 'He took me by the wrist and held me hard'. The girl, at that moment, outspread her left hand as though silently appealing for mercy, as if the crazed Hamlet's hands had been at her throat, choking the life out of her.

Not a sound or movement could be heard in the auditorium. Power's hand remained on the Exit door as if soldered there. The girl stood, head bowed, awaiting her next cue.

Sinking to her knees, tears raining down her face, forgetful of the audience, Gina's voice came softly yet clearly, 'There's fennel for you, and columbines. There's rue for you, and here's some for me . . . I would give you some violets, but they withered all when my father died. they say a made a good end . . .'

Christ! Sweet Jesus Christ, Power thought bemusedly, the unbelievable, the unprecedented had happened, and he had almost walked out on the most thrilling moment of his theatrical life so far – the birth of a star.

Never before had he witnessed, and might never do so again, a company of hard-headed theatrical managers, financiers and directors, rising to their feet to applaud the performance of an unknown drama student – a slip of a girl in a white dress who, rising slowly to her feet, tears streaming down her cheeks, seemed curiously impervious

201

to the applause. Then Landis walked on-stage to lead her away from the footlights.

Plunging quickly through the Exit door on which his hand had rested for the past fifteen minutes, hurrying along the pavement towards the alley leading to the stage door, careless of the steadily falling rain, stopping briefly at the florists on the corner to purchase an armful of daffodils and a fragrant mass of violets, TJ Power's heart beat quickly in anticipation of meeting . . . Ophelia . . . face to face. The daffodils he would give to Madame Gautier, the violets to 'Ophelia'.

Maestro was kissing her hands, Giselle weeping, the stage manager smiling; students gathered in the wings were staring at her, whispering excitedly as Madame Gautier led her back to the dressing-room. Gina scarcely noticed the eager faces of her fellow students, or the smiling stage manager. Curiously drained of emotion, all she clearly remembered was a glowing gas-light in the Dress Circle, fixing her eyes on that unwavering blob of light shining in the darkness, as a navigator might fix his eyes on the Pole Star.

And then the miracle had happened. Forgetful of herself, she had become Ophelia, a tormented girl on the brink of madness. Poor Ophelia, groping in the darkness of a mind deranged for one shred of sanity to cling to, desperately offering her gifts of imaginary flowers to a faithless lover. The stultifying fear she had experienced awaiting her entrance, the sick feeling that she would forget her lines and make a fool of herself, had ceased to trouble her once she had stepped from darkness into the light. Her pride, her stubborn determination to succeed, had come upper-most at that moment. Remembering Madame Gautier's last minute instruction to find some object on which to con-centrate, she had fixed her eyes on that gas-light in the Dress Circle, until . . . Then the stage had become her milieu, the unseen audience in the darkness beyond the footlights, not enemies, but simply people to whom she owed a kind of respect in giving the best performance of which she was capable. Ultimately, had come the miracle of forgetfulness of everything else except the portrayal of a tender young girl faced with the final, solitary loneliness of death.

Now, shaken and weak from the outpouring of so much emotion, she was glad of Madame Gautier's supportive arm about her waist, bemused by the feeling that she had not yet slipped back into her own skin. Aware that the tears in her eyes were those of Ophelia, yet somehow inescapably linked with those of Gina Brett. She entered the dressing-room to see a dark-haired stranger smiling down at her from a great height, a man who, pressing a mass of fragrant violets into her hands, said simply, 'My name is Power. TJ Power. I imagine that we'll be seeing a great deal of each other from now on.'

PART TWO

Chapter Seventeen

The garden was his special, secret place. Meandering paths overhung with spreading branches and flanked with thickets of azalea and rhododendron became, at will, a dense tropical jungle; or Indian country where silent-footed Cherokee waited in ambush. A neighbourhood tom-cat, lying in a patch of sunlight, assumed the proportions and majesty of the king of beasts.

Sometimes, tired of play, he would lie on his back beneath the trees to watch the domestic affairs of the birds, admiring the energy and purpose displayed in the fetching of twigs and scraps of soft lining material to build their nests, and teaching their young to fly. When he grew up, he had told his mother, he wanted to learn all about birds. The next day she had given him a wonderful book with paintings of brilliantly coloured birds he had never heard of before – parakeets and birds of paradise, herons and kingfishers, flamingoes and oyster-catchers – a treasure-trove of birds. His favourite of all was a peacock with an outspread tail of shimmering deep blue and gold feathers.

When his mother bought Welford House from its previous owners, Bridget told him, she had given strict instructions to the foreman, whose men were engaged in laying a patio at the foot of the iron staircase, not to encroach upon the tangle of trees and shrubs further than was strictly necessary. 'I'll never forget the look on the man's face,' Bridget chuckled. ' "But, ma'am," he said, "think what a fine garden you'll have without all that undergrowth." And your mother said, "I'm thinking what a miserable time my son would have without it!" '

Oliver loved his mother with a growing male child's awareness of her beauty, knowing she was different from other mothers, that she must go away from time to time 'on tour' – whatever that meant. As a child at nursery school, he was not old enough to understand that his mother was different because she was famous, and so he had clung to Bridget who scolded him when he was naughty, and made him brush his teeth, who took him for walks on the Heath, and occasionally to matinées at the Hampstead cinema.

Bridget had started a scrap-book in which he carefully pasted the cuttings she clipped from the review columns of various newspapers, so that by the time he started prep school, he knew the reviews by heart. His favourite was: 'Miss Gina Brett's performance of *St Joan* may at some time be equalled, never surpassed. The astonishing vitality, humility, and depth of vision of this exquisite young actress brought to life Bernard Shaw's complex Maid of Orléans so powerfully that the audience rose as one to applaud her tour de force. Many, myself included, were close to tears as Miss Brett, standing alone on-stage, maintained the poise and dignity of a truly great actress.'

Somehow, Oliver had not been able to imagine the smiling mother who threaded his childhood with silver ribbons of happiness, wearing a suit of armour. There was nothing stiff and starchy about her as she fed the pigeons with him in Trafalgar Square, took him to Regent's Park Zoo, on river trips to the Tower of London to see the crown jewels, to St Paul's Cathedral and Westminster Abbey, dressed in comfortable old clothes in which she passed unnoticed in a crowd.

As time went by, he began to wonder why he had no father. When he asked Bridget why not, she told him that a lot of brave men had died in the war, and not to worry his head about such matters. Did she mean that his father had died in the war? From then on his imagination had run riot, and he had thought a lot about his father, wondering what had happened to him and why his mother had never shown him photographs of his father, withdrawing into a terrifying world of childish doubt and fear in which the adult world had seemed ranged against him in a conspiracy of silence. His mother had been away at the time. When she came home, she had taken him to her room and told him the truth.

Gina had known all along that the day would come when she must face telling Oliver that she was not his real mother. Never had she considered lying to him when he started asking questions about his father, nor could she contemplate playing traitor to Poppy, whose memory remained fresh and fragrant in her mind. When the boy was old enough to start asking questions, she must supply the answers. Anything else was unthinkable. She simply prayed that he would understand how much he meant to her.

Making no attempt to cloud his judgement with sentimentality, she told him that his real mother had died giving birth to him, and had asked her to take care of him.

'Is my father dead, too?' the boy asked hoarsely.

'No, he is still alive.'

'Then why did he go away? Didn't he like me?'

Filled with compassion for the child's bewilderment, knowing he would scarcely understand what she was about to say, 'The truth is, my love, he went away before you were born. He never knew about you.'

'Didn't – didn't my mother tell him?'

'No, love. He went away before she had time.'

'Then I hate him! I hate him!' Oliver cried passionately. 'He shouldn't have gone away when my mother needed him.' Jumping up from the chaise-longue, he rushed over to the window and leaned his head against the glass, his tender child's body racked with sobs.

'Oliver. Look at me.' Gina spoke quietly but firmly, resisting the strong temptation to hold him in her arms, to cosset and comfort him. That would come later, God willing. 'You are wrong to hate your father, to blame him entirely for what happened. There were reasons why—' She pressed her fingers to her lips momentarily, blinking back tears as she remembered the studio, the first time she had seen Rab standing there in a shaft of sunlight from the skylight window, aglow with vitality, exuding the essence of a man in charge of his own destiny.

209

Gaining control of her emotions, 'Will you believe me when I tell you that your father is not a bad man? It's hard to explain, hard for you to understand right now, but you will in time, when you're a little older. And,' her voice shook slightly, 'above all, my darling, will you believe that I could not love you more if you were my own flesh and blood?' She opened her arms to him, uncertain if he would come to her, desperately afraid that the truth might have built up an insurmountable barrier of mistrust in his mind, knowing that she was not his real mother after all.

He came to her with the swiftness of a hummingbird in flight.

Oliver liked his mother's friends on the whole, especially his Uncle Power and his Aunt Gautier, who made a great fuss of him whenever they came to Welford House to have supper on the patio, but he was not entirely sure about his Uncle George who scared him a bit at times, with his deep, growly voice and flailing arms, who had once bowled him over with a dramatic gesture of his right hand.

'My dear child, forgive me,' Landis said, to Oliver's disgust. 'That's all right, sir,' he replied stiffly, his pride wounded by the term 'child'. He was, after all, nearly 10 years old.

Allowed to stay up later than usual during the long summer holidays, Oliver absorbed the magic of the garden at dusk, loving the scent of the thickly clustered roses and lavender intermingled with the spicy odours of the parsley, sage, rosemary and thyme his mother had planted in the earthenware pots bordering the patio. Knowing why she had done so was their secret. She had told him about his mother, and their happy days in Scarborough. Parsley, sage, rosemary and thyme were reminders of the song, 'Scarborough Fair', in memory of Poppy.

When Gina knew that the owners of Welford House had decided not to return to England, she had made an offer for it. The place had become home to her. She liked Hampstead, Oliver had settled well at school, and Bridget had made friends in the neighbourhood. Power had skilfully guided her career since the memorable day of the audition and she had repaid her father the money he had loaned her, overcoming his reluctance to accept repayment by pointing out gently that she wished to stand on her own feet. This he understood.

Intensely proud of his girl, her success had lightened the burden of his own life to a great extent, had counterbalanced his anxiety over his son's reckless lifestyle and his wife's increasing paranoia. Despite his increasing frailty, he had not yet handed over to Thomas, nor would he do so as long as he had strength left in his body to prevent the dissolution of the Brett-Forsyth Mill – his grandfather's answer to the poverty and unemployment once rife in the Calder Valley – the great Brett-Forsyth Mill which had given renewed hope and self-respect to the generations of men and women who had worked there ever since.

His infrequent visits to Welford House to stay with Gina had been oases in a desert of anxiety. The special, tender relationship he had formed with Oliver, whom he regarded as his grandson, had grown and blossomed throughout the years. Grandpa Owen, the boy called him as he had shown him his treasures – his 'bird' book, his precious scrap-book, his hoard of sea-shells from the sands at Scarborough, where his mother had taken him for a holiday the previous summer.

Apart from his Uncle George's expressive hand-waving, which he took great care to avoid, seated on a stool beside his mother's basket-chair on the patio, Oliver listened enchanted to the conversation, as soft-winged moths fluttered close to the light and her guests sipped champagne – conversation which centred on the theatre, London, Hollywood and New York when his Uncle Power and Uncle George argued the merits of something called cinematography and that of the legitimate theatre.

'Sure, I'll grant that Garbo is a great actress,' Power conceded, 'but where would she be without closeups, a gauze veil in front of the camera, a minimum of lines to learn? Do you really imagine, maestro, that even the divine Garbo, faced with the reality of a sustained stage performance, could hold a candle to Gina?'

'No, of course not,' George interposed, 'but we are talking about an entirely different art form. I venture to say, the art form of the future. God dammit man, do you mean to tell me that if Gina – I beg your pardon, my dear – received an offer to star in a Hollywood film, you would not jump at the chance of seeing her face, gauze and all, on the cinema screens of the world?'

'Frankly, George,' Power said lazily, stretching his legs, 'I would far rather she appeared, as the damned good actress she is, *sans* gauze, in a Broadway production.'

The Great White Way, Giselle thought, imagining the lights of Broadway clustered as thickly as twinkling stars against a New York skyline, wishing that her lost youth might be miraculously restored to her in this exciting new era of opportunity, far beyond anything she had envisaged during her own career, long before the birth of wireless entertainment or talking pictures.

Sipping champagne, and still beautiful despite her advancing years, Madame Gautier reflected on the rapidly changing world about her. Vaguely regretful of the sacrifice of her career from some altruistic motive which no longer seemed valid or even important, it occurred to her that she had reached the stage of living her life vicariously, in the glow of other people's success – particularly Gina's. Not that she regretted her hand in shaping that success story.

The passage of time had added lustre to Gina's beauty, a certain flair and style far distanced from that of the gauche 19-year-old girl who had come to the School of Dramatic Art in the summer of 1920.

Standing in the wings, Madame had witnessed her protégée's immaculate performances as Juliet, Ophelia, Roxanne, Viola – what she thought of as the great ingénue roles, preceding the tougher testing ground of Hedda Gabler, St Joan and Phèdre. She possessed first-hand experience of what it meant to be a leading lady, the constant striving for perfection, the loneliness and fears, the self-doubt despite the applause, the bouquets, the critical acclaim.

'You are very quiet, Giselle.' Gina leaned forward to touch her arm. 'What are you thinking?'

'Oh,' Madame shrugged expressively, 'nothing of any importance. Just about time, and how quickly it passes, leaving so little behind – apart from memories.' She smiled wistfully. 'If I were young again, I should gobble up every opportunity that came my way to add to my store of memories, but the scope for an actress was more limited then than it is today. Otherwise,' she laughed, 'I would have taken Broadway, America, by storm!'

'So you think, given the chance, that I should go to America?' Gina asked.

'But of course! Live every moment of your life to the full. Make the most of your youth and beauty. Face every challenge that comes your way.'

Power knew what she meant. He said, 'I have already contacted my New York colleague, Alwyn Jefferson, regarding a suitable play for Gina. It is simply a matter of time.' His eyes dwelt on Gina. 'Well, what do you think? Are you willing to face the challenge of Broadway?'

Gina smiled, 'Forewarned is forearmed,' she said enigmatically.

Giselle wondered, not for the first time, if Power and Gina were lovers. Difficult to tell. Certainly they had everything in common. Power had guided Gina's career every inch of the way since the day of her audition, but was their close relationship merely a mirror reflection of her own long association with George Landis? A one-sided affair? Pondering the question, if they were not lovers, Giselle decided, they *should* be. Slightly tipsy from the amount of champagne she had drunk, she felt like telling them to go ahead, to make love if they felt like it, not to squander their youth and opportunities as she had done.

Oliver said, at that moment, 'I think that I should like to go to bed now, Mother.'

Returning to Welford House from her Sunday evening visit to her friend Rosie's snug little home in Golders Green, Bridget Donovan's thoughts turned, inevitably, to the one

213

person on earth she wished to forget. Where was Keiran O'Grady now? she wondered, staring at her reflection in the dressing-table mirror, envious of Rosie's uncomplicated domestic happiness with her husband and two children, the kind of happiness she might well have achieved had she not been so sure of herself as a young girl, so certain of her own beauty and power of attraction that she had lost the man she loved to a much plainer girl. Quite simply, she had failed to understand that Keiran, despite his smouldering good looks, had wanted nothing more than an obedient little wife who thought the sun shone out of him.

On the other hand, had she not emigrated to England to make a fresh start, she would never have risen to her present position as housekeeper to a famous actress, her mistress's confidante and friend, and young Oliver's refuge-cum-miracle-worker in times of trouble. These blessings, in Bridget's estimation, far outweighed her nostalgic musings on what might have been had she married Keiran O'Grady.

Her promotion to housekeeper had happened when Miss Georgina bought Welford House and engaged a cook, a housemaid and a daily woman. The former nursery had then been altered to provide private accommodation for the cook, Mrs Alderson, and a bed-sitting room for the maid, Clarice. At the same time, the unused rooms on the third floor had been altered and refurnished for herself and Oliver, in such a way as to ensure her own and the boy's privacy – although the connecting door between the two apartments stood wide open as often as not.

So all in all she had done quite well for herself, Bridget thought, unbraiding her hair ready for bed. Standing in her dressing-gown, she looked out of the window at the group on the terrace below. Clarice had cleared the supper table before going off duty – doubtless to read one of those soppy romantic novels she was so fond of, and it looked as though Oliver was saying goodnight to his mother and her guests. How gently she kissed him, Bridget thought, relieved that the boy had been told the truth about his parentage. How she had missed him when he'd started boarding school. Such a clever boy, she thought fondly, turning away from the window, wondering what he would do with his life when he grew up.

Getting into bed, about to switch off the lamp, she heard a knock at the door. 'Oliver?' She smiled at him as he entered her room, 'Are you all right?'

'Oh, Bridget!' His face crumpled.

'What is it, my lamb? Come here. Tell me what's wrong.'

Snuggling into her arms, 'Uncle Power is going to take Mother a long way away – to America,' he said.

Gina liked these lazy, relaxed summer Sunday evenings in the company of her three closest friends, far removed from the glare of the footlights.

Tonight, as usual, Power lingered awhile after the departure of the maestro and Madame Gautier. 'About America. Shall I go ahead with my plans?' he asked quietly, thinking how beautiful she looked by starlight.

'Yes, why not? You see, Power, I've always longed to travel. An ambition of mine as far back as I can remember.'

'I'd come with you, of course,' he said positively. 'New York's a frightening place for a newcomer, as I discovered the first time I went there alone.'

'I can't imagine you being frightened of anything,' Gina said.

'Can't you?' His laugh held a trace of bitterness. 'You'd be surprised. I'm a coward at heart!'

'Aren't we all?' Looking up at the stars, Gina remembered the mental agony of first nights in particular, the sick, empty feeling, the coldness and sheer panic at the thought of an expectant audience out there. But Power knew all about that. What she would have done without him these past years, she could not imagine. He had always been there, standing beside Giselle in the wings, willing her to succeed. It was Power who had recognized and done something about her inability to work with other actors as well as she should. At first she had hated the idea of spending a year with Sir Barry Jackson's Birmingham Repertory Company before attempting a role in a West

End production, but that year had been worth its weight in gold in teaching her how to integrate with her fellow performers, about stage-craft, props, lighting, makeup – and concentration.

'Broadway is no easy option,' he said, lighting a cigarette.

'But you think it's right for me?'

'Yes, I do. You need a challenge of this kind.'

She frowned, 'What's wrong, Power? You seem on edge.'

'I'm concerned about you, that's all.'

'Concerned? But why?' She looked at him in surprise. 'I'm perfectly well.'

'I didn't care for that gossip-column item about you and Wynter. He's married, you know.'

'What are you implying?' Her anger flared suddenly. 'Are you suggesting we're having an affair?'

'You can't deny you've been seeing a lot of each other lately.' Power flung away his scarcely smoked cigarette. Jealousy ate into him as he remembered the Press photograph of them dancing together at the Café Royal.

'Of course I can't deny it! He's my leading man, for heaven's sake!' Her eyes flashed fire. 'Do you really think me capable of having an underhand affair with a married man? Why, it's ludicrous! Laughable!' But she wasn't laughing.

'No, of course not. But you know what these gossip columnists are like when they get their teeth into even a hint of scandal.'

'They are not the only ones, apparently!' She turned away abruptly, deeply hurt that Power had imagined, for one moment, that she and Damian were more than friends.

She stood rigidly, her back towards him, breathing in the scent of rosemary and thyme, thinking of Oliver, whom she would never condemn to any kind of unwelcome publicity.

'I'm sorry, Gina,' Power said, 'I didn't mean to upset you. That was the last thing on my mind.' He laid a placating hand on her arm.

Turning to face him, her anger subsiding, 'I'm sorry, too,' she admitted, 'I shouldn't have lost my temper the way I did. But you know how things stand in the world of the theatre? It's like walking a tightrope at times. If I refused to attend the last night parties, the champagne luncheons in my honour, the charity balls, the Press interviews, you name it – I'd be branded difficult, temperamental, a snob!' She attempted a smile. 'On the other hand, going along with all the razzamatazz, I find myself featuring in the gossip-columns as a kind of femme-fatale.

'The fact is, I'm none of those things! Just an actress trying my damnedest to do a difficult job of work to the best of my ability.'

'Please, Gina, don't cry.' Power tightened his clasp on her arm.

'*Cry?* Who's crying?' Tears streamed down her cheeks. Suddenly, Power's arms were around her, and she was sobbing her heart out against his shoulder.

Catching the fragrance of her hair, he knew that he wanted her more than he had ever wanted a woman before, except Ruth. But Ruth was gone for ever from his life. A memory. Gina was here, now, warm, fragrant, exciting. A reality.

Cupping her face in his hands, he kissed her, a long, lingering kiss which left her breathless. When the kiss was over, 'I love you, Gina,' he said simply. 'I have loved you from that first day I brought violets to your dressing-room. Remember?'

'Of course I remember. How could I possibly forget? But I never thought, never believed for one moment that you were in love with me. How could I?'

She had to be entirely honest with him. 'I have always thought of you as my friend, my agent. Nothing more. As a very proud, rather private man.' Looking up at him, 'There were times when you appeared not to like me very much at all – you were so harsh and demanding, telling me what, or what not to do. Then suddenly there you were, a few moments ago, accusing me of having an affair with Damian Wynter!'

'Because I was jealous,' Power said stiffly, 'jealous because you had danced with him at the Café Royal, because your name had been linked with his.'

217

'For what it's worth, I danced with other men, that night,' Gina said coolly, 'just as Damian danced with other women, his wife included.' She laughed bitterly. 'You know, Power, I'm sick and tired of this kind of intrusion into my private life. I don't need it. I don't want it. I've never been a "party" person. From now on, I'm through with all the champagne luncheons, the charity balls: walking the tightrope. And if I'm seen as difficult, temperamental, a snob – well, so be it. I'm not a puppet on a string. Not a social butterfly. I'm an actress with lines to learn, endless rehearsals and costume fittings to attend. But why tell you? You, above all people, should know exactly what I mean.'

He said bleakly, 'So you don't believe I meant what I said when I told you I loved you?'

Recalling the feel of his lips on hers, her response to that kiss, compounded of a starlit summer night, a need, deep within her, to love and to be loved in return, she said quietly, sincerely, 'Of course I did. But you must give me a little more time to get used to the idea.'

Chapter Eighteen

This dinner invitation was an engagement she could scarcely refuse, Power told Gina. Sir James Adley, whose wife had died recently, had returned to London to pick up the threads of his former life.

Briefly he sketched in the background. Sir James and his wife, Lady Caroline, had gone up to Scotland in the summer of 1925 to settle his father's estate and decide what to do with Craiglachan, the house in which old Sir Edgar Adley had lived in seclusion since the end of the war.

There, Lady Caroline had suffered a massive stroke from which she had never recovered. 'It must have been hell for Sir James,' Power said, 'watching the woman he adored dying by inches, unable to speak or move, reduced to a vegetable existence, especially a woman of her calibre, a famous beauty in her day, a patroness of the arts, a brilliant hostess.' He added, engagingly, 'So you will come? Sir James assured me, when I met him for lunch the other day, that it will be a small, private dinner party at his home in Eaton Square.'

'Couldn't you go without me?' Gina sighed. 'You know how much Sunday evenings at home mean to me. I see little enough of Oliver as it is.'

She might have known that Power would not take No for an answer.

'Miss Brett, I am so pleased to meet you.'

The tall, grey-haired man who welcomed her to his home, was startlingly handsome despite his age, possessed of one of those lean, aesthetic faces which remain firm and sculpted throughout the years. Charming and charismatic, nothing about him suggested that he had suffered a recent, tragic bereavement. Obviously, Gina thought, he did not wear his heart on his sleeve. Or possibly, born and bred English gentlemen were accustomed to hiding their feelings.

'Power, my dear fellow,' Sir James said, warmly shaking his hand, 'come through to the drawing-room.' Leading the way, 'What would you like to drink? Sherry, Madeira, or something stronger? Miss Brett?'

'Sherry, thank you.'

'Please, do sit down.'

'What a beautiful room,' she said simply.

'How kind of you to say so.' Adley smiled. 'My wife chose the furnishings to complement the painting above the mantelpiece. She loved the colour blue.'

Looking at the picture, 'It's a Monet, isn't it?' Gina asked.

Intrigued, 'What makes you think so?'

'The colouring for one thing, and the subject matter. Oh, I'm sorry, Sir James, please forgive me. I'm an actress, not an art connoisseur.'

'No, please continue.'

'Well, this picture is scarcely divisible from Monet's *Train in the snow* in the Musée Marmottan in Paris,' she explained. 'There is no mistaking the colouring, the brush-work, for any artist other than, perhaps, that of Alfred Sisley.' Wishing she had held her tongue, 'Is it by Alfred Sisley? Or am I wide of the mark?'

'No, Miss Brett. The picture you are looking at was painted by Claude Monet in 1874, a year in advance of his famous *Train in the snow*. I congratulate you on your knowledge of art.'

'I had a very good teacher,' she said, remembering Rab.

Nursing his glass of whisky and soda, Power realized how little he really knew about Gina. Where and when had she studied art, for instance? And why that faraway look in her eyes when she had mentioned her teacher? Christ, but she was beautiful in her simple white evening gown – a perfect foil for her mass of shining auburn hair. So what was happening? Why the sudden, unmistakable rapport between Gina and Sir James Adley? Feeling expendable, shut-out, why the hell had he brought Gina here in the first place, he thought sullenly.

Relief washed over him when the double doors opened and Sir James' butler announced the arrival of Madame Gautier and George Landis.

Dinner was served at a polished mahogany table set with monogrammed silver cutlery, starched linen, and a centre-piece of gardenias in a shallow crystal bowl.

The food was delicious. 'You have a darned good cook, if I may say so, Sir James,' Landis commented, dwelling on the delights of the succulent roast beef and crisply roasted potatoes, the light-as-air Yorkshire puddings, slightly *al-dente* vegetables, and gravy enriched with meat juices. 'Please offer her my congratulations.'

'Thank you, George, I shall certainly do so.' Sir James acknowledged the compliment with the offer of more wine. 'My cook, Mrs Crabtree, I count as a blessing in life. She has been with me for some time now. One of the old school. An absolute gem.'

'Mrs Crabtree?' Gina's face lit up. 'Daisy Crabtree?'

'You obviously know the lady,' Adley remarked.

'Yes, she was with my family in the West Riding for some time. I'm afraid I lost touch with her after she came to London.'

'A small world,' Power commented drily.

After dinner, Sir James invited Gina to look at the view of Eaton Square from the drawing-room windows.

The fading daylight of a warm summer day had painted the London sky with flares of gold, a slip of a moon, a brushful of stars. Trees in the gardens were heavy with the weight of summer, the branches interlaced with lamp-light.

'That glow in the sky will still be there when darkness deepens,' James Adley said softly, 'a reminder of the world out there. Your world, Miss Brett. I saw you in *St Joan*. An unforgettable performance.' He smiled, wishing the brief moment might last a while longer, but the servant

221

bringing the coffee tray had departed, and his other guests were waiting.

Sitting near the fireplace, sipping coffee, Gina noticed a group of silver-framed photographs on a marquetry side-table. One in particular caught her eye, that of a beautiful, dark-haired woman, pearls about her throat. A portrait of Lady Caroline Adley, she imagined, taken at the height of her hostess days, the woman who had created this room, who had matched so perfectly the colours of brocade and velvet with those of the Monet painting over the mantelpiece, who chose, with unerring good taste, each item of furniture.

Giselle had embarked on the subject of changing fashions and hairstyles, the emancipation of women, which she saw as a step in the right direction. 'I'm sure that Gina will agree with my point of view; you too, Power.' Teasingly, 'I'm not so sure about you, George. Come now, admit it.'

Landis appeared startled. 'Why pick on me?' he rumbled. 'If women wish to crop their hair and dress like men, that's their misfortune, not mine.'

The conversation washed over Gina. Gazing up at the Monet, she remembered Rab who had taught her so much about art, to whom she owed far more than she could ever hope to repay. He would never know how much – her success as an actress, above all, his son. These were the gifts he had given her, wittingly or not, so that he would remain forever a part of her life, impossible to forget or to stop loving in memory, as she loved Poppy. But life went on, and Power was real, not a ghost from the past but a vibrant human being in whose arms she might discover – not necessarily a better, but a more fulfilling kind of love, to do with touch and warmth, and a sense of security. And if, one day, Power asked her to marry him, she would say Yes, for Oliver's sake, also. The boy needed stability, a father figure to relate to.

The future seemed golden with opportunity, as if she had struggled painfully uphill to find a different, more worth-while way of life awaiting her. Finding Daisy Crabtree again seemed a good omen. Tomorrow she would write to her;

invite her to visit Welford House on her day off. Bridget would be overjoyed.

'This has been a wonderful evening, Sir James,' she said quietly, at their leave-taking. 'I particularly enjoyed the view of Eaton Square from the drawing-room windows.'

'I thought you would, which is why I showed it to you,' he replied, lightly kissing her hand.

Next morning, Bridget brought to her room a bouquet of long-stemmed red roses. The attached card read: 'Until we meet again. Soon, I hope. James Adley'.

'Miss Georgina! Bridget! Well, I never. Fancy us meeting again after all this time.'

Daisy Crabtree had scarcely changed at all, Gina thought. She was perhaps a little stouter than before, a little greyer, but this was still the kind-hearted woman on whose shoulder she had cried on her abortive wedding day in the spring of 1919 – which seemed almost a lifetime ago.

'We tried to get in touch with you through your sister,' Bridget prattled, 'but the letter came back to us, didn't it, Miss Gina?'

'Poor Edie,' Mrs Crabtree sighed, 'she went very suddenly. So I advertised for a job. Lady Adley replied, and that was that. I never thought the poor soul would be struck down so cruelly. I went up to Scotland with them while Sir James was settling his father's estate. Quite a nice little holiday, I thought. I never dreamt I'd be there for nigh on five years, but I couldn't leave them in the lurch, and I grew quite fond of the place for all its drawbacks.

'A fine house, Craiglachan, but very draughty in winter, and stuck in the middle of nowhere. We'd be cut off for weeks at a time when the snow came. Miss Leonora, the Adleys' daughter, pestered the life out of her father to move my lady back to London. I think they had words about it, for off she went in a huff. But anyone with two grains of sense would have known such a thing was out of the question.

'Of course, Sir James had to come back to London quite often to manage his business affairs. He's a publisher, you know. I don't mean novels, but serious books on art and antiques. He and my lady were very knowledgeable about such matters. Sir James owns a picture gallery in Bond Street, and my lady once told me they had shares in some of the big West End theatres.'

'Really?' Gina's interest quickened. So that was why Power had been so insistent on accepting Sir James' dinner invitation? Wheels within wheels. Power had never hidden the fact that he considered sound financial backing of paramount importance in the world of the theatre, and of course he was right. Even so, he might have told her that her visit to Eaton Square was probably in the nature of a command performance by a wealthy patron of the arts, with a view to future investment in the TJ Power Theatrical Agency. Possibly she was wrong, but she didn't think so.

'Which reminds me,' Mrs Crabtree went on. 'I understand that you have taken up acting, Miss Georgina. What has Madam Brett-Forsyth to say about *that*?'

Gina said quietly, 'We have never discussed the matter.'

'No, well, better not, I dare say.' As Bridget went to see about afternoon tea, 'Forgive me for asking, but how did things turn out at Elmhurst?' Her face puckered anxiously. 'Did Madam make up with the Bickleys?'

'I'm afraid not.'

'Oh dear, what a rod some people make for their own back.' She smiled sadly. 'Do you remember coming home from church that day? Poor lass, how upset you were. But you did the right thing not marrying that Harold Bickley. He wouldn't have made you happy. Now look at you, so grown up and beautiful and successful—'

'Oh, Daisy!' Gina's eyes filled with tears. 'You'll never know how pleased I am to see you again.'

'There, there, my lamb. Have a good cry, it'll do you good.'

Gina shook her head, and smiled. 'There's no reason for me to cry. I'm not sad, just a bit nostalgic, that's all. Come, I thought we'd have tea on the patio, it's such a lovely day.'

* * *

When Sir James Adley invited her to lunch with him, Gina saw no reason to refuse. Scarcely prepared for Power's reaction to the invitation. 'Why, Power,' she said teasingly, 'I do believe you're jealous.'

'Jealous! Of course I'm jealous! I saw the way he looked at you the other night when you were standing together near the window. What were you talking about so intimately?'

'The view. Really! What did you think we were talking about?'

'In any case, he's far too old for you,' Power said sullenly.

Gina's patience snapped suddenly. 'Don't be ridiculous! Age has nothing to do with it. I accepted Sir James' luncheon invitation because it would have semed churlish to do otherwise—'

'And because you find him attractive? That's true, isn't it?' Power insisted.

Drawing herself up to her full height, in command of the situation, with a look of utter disdain, she said coldly, 'I find many men attractive, surprisingly, even you, Power, when you are not behaving like an immature schoolboy.'

'Gina. I'm sorry, I only meant . . . God dammit, woman! You know what I meant.' But she was gone. The door of his office slammed shut behind her as she walked away from him. My God, he thought, she was even more beautiful when she was angry.

She had never seen the countryside west of London before. Today, it was heavy with the full-leafed trees of summer, lush with rich green meadows dotted with picturesque villages; stately country houses set in acres of parkland, and with glimpses of the River Thames sparkling in the sunlight.

Sir James drove his vintage Hispano-Suiza Alfonso with consummate ease and panache towards the market town of Devizes, set like a jewel in the heart of Wiltshire – a far cry from the high-banked lanes of the Thames Valley – with rolling downs stretching to crystal-clear horizons, the air as sparkling and golden as champagne.

'Oh, this is lovely!' Gina cried ecstatically, 'so untouched, so beautiful, a bit like the moors above the Calder Valley in summertime. I had almost forgotten there was so much space, so much freedom in the world.'

How beautiful she looked, James Adley thought, in her lightweight green linen dress and wide-brimmed straw hat, her face aglow with sunshine and fresh air. The head waiter of the Bear Hotel ushered them into the dining-room overlooking the town square where the market stalls were set out with delectable piles of fruit and vegetables, and a central fountain splashed droplets of clear water into a grey stone basin.

Difficult to imagine that this unassuming young woman possessed the power, on-stage, to hold sophisticated West End audiences in the palm of her hand by the sheer magnetism of her acting ability; to wring tears from them, as she had done in the final act of Bernard Shaw's *St Joan*, when the Maid of Orléans faced the sacrifice of her life for her beliefs.

'Tell me, Gina, what are your future plans?' Sir James asked, when they had ordered lunch.

'I'm going to America,' she said simply. 'At least I hope so. Power has everything in hand. He thinks it high time I faced a new challenge. He could be right, but I'll miss my home – my son.'

'You have a son?' Sir James raised his eyebrows. 'I'm sorry, I had not realized that you were married.'

'I'm not. Oliver is mine by adoption,' she explained. 'It's a rather sad story, I'm afraid.'

Realizing that this was neither the time nor the place to indulge in unhappy memories, unwilling to spoil the mood of the day, Sir James said quietly, 'Let us dwell on happy things. There is too much sadness in life. And when you return from the States? What will you do then?'

'Oh, I'd like to study art in more detail; see more of the world. All the things I might have done sooner had it not been for the war. Above all, to make certain of my son's future, to give him a sense of security.'

A smartly dressed woman approached their table. 'Forgive me,' she said, 'but you are Gina Brett? I recognized you the minute you came in. Would you mind giving me your autograph? I thought it would be nice if you signed the menu, a memento of the place we met. I saw you in *St Joan*. You were marvellous. But you are even lovelier off-stage . . . Oh, thank you so much. I shall treasure this, believe me.' Overwhelmed by the encounter, looking up at Sir James who had risen to his feet, she babbled, 'You have a beautiful daughter, Mr Brett. You must be very proud of her.'

Deeply embarrassed, when the woman had gone, 'I can't think what made her say that,' Gina apologized.

Sir James laughed softly, 'I can. After all, I *am* old enough to be your father.' He paused. 'As a matter of fact, I half expected that you would refuse my invitation. I risked that possibility because I felt we had a lot in common. Your interest in art, for one thing, your appreciation of beauty for another, apart from the theatre – which has long been an absorbing passion of mine. I wanted to talk to you, to discover more about you.' He smiled ruefully. 'Call it the selfish desire of a lonely old man, if you like.'

'For what it's worth, I don't look upon you as a father figure,' Gina said gently. 'Anyway, age is immaterial in my opinion, something that happens to everyone in the long run – the lucky ones, that is. I am thinking of all the young men who were killed in the war, who died before they had begun to live.'

'Thank you, my dear. That is the nicest compliment I've ever had.' Gazing at her lovely face across the table, James Adley knew that he had found someone capable of filling the emptiness of his existence with hope for the future. He experienced a renewed vigour and sense of purpose, lacking since the death of his wife, whose wasted body had been laid to rest in the private cemetery at Craiglachan.

After lunch, they walked together on the downs, enjoying the sunshine and fresh air, laughing, talking of this and that, until Gina caught sight of the time. 'Heavens! I'll be late for the theatre,' she said.

Returning to the car, 'You will never know how much

this day has meant to me.' His eyes on the road ahead, 'You realize, of course, that I am deeply attracted to you?'

'Yes.' This she accepted as a statement of fact, requiring no commitment on her part.

'I'd like to think there'll be other days like this, that we shall meet occasionally to talk of – "shoes and ships and sealing-wax". Would that be possible?'

'I don't see why not.' James Adley's friendship would be an enrichment of her life, a calming influence. With Power, she often felt as George Du Maurier's 'Trilby' must have done under the domination of the hypnotist, Svengali. Even so, she had given a great deal of thought to that night on the terrace, the feelings his kiss aroused in her, his declaration of love.

With Power, she would have to face the balancing of two strong personalities. At least life would never be dull, and they had much in common. He would be jealous, demanding, but never boring, and she did care for him a great deal.

'What are you thinking?' James asked.

'About my agent. TJ Power.' She saw no reason to lie.

'I see.' A pause. 'Are you in love with him?'

'I'm not sure.'

'For what it is worth, he is certainly in love with you,' Adley commented drily. 'I saw the way he looked at you.' Reaching the outskirts of London, he asked 'Are you afraid of commitment?'

'Perhaps. Oh, I'm sorry. How thoughtless of me.'

'Not at all. I'm glad you felt able to confide in me. What are friends for?'

'James. I meant what I said. I hope we shall meet again soon.' She smiled. 'You're good for me, you know that?'

Getting out of the car, which he had parked close to the alley near the stage door entrance, on an impulse, she kissed his cheek. 'Goodbye James, and thank you again for a lovely day.'

'Where the hell have you been?' Power demanded as she entered the dressing-room. 'I've been trying to get in touch with you since four o'clock. Where did you go for lunch, for God's sake – China?'

'Not quite that far.' She lay down her gloves and bag on the dressing table, with no intention of telling him where she had been. Resentful of his hectoring tone of voice, 'I'm sorry, Power, but our friendship doesn't give you the right to dictate to me.'

'Friendship? Is that what you call it? Damn it, Gina, I'm in love with you!'

'You have a funny way of showing it. Frankly, I'm not sure that I like the idea of being swallowed up by your so-called love, in which trust, apparently, has no part to play. Now, if you'll excuse me, I'm about to get changed.'

'Gina, please! I'm sorry. You have every right to be angry.' Turning her face to his, he kissed her gently on the lips. 'I told you I'm a coward at heart. You see, my darling, I'm so afraid of losing you. A case of over reaction, I guess. My wife – Ruth – claimed that I didn't pay her enough attention—'

'Please, Power, don't say any more. You're forgiven.'

'In that case, a celebration is in order. I've booked a table for two at Florio's.' He grinned boyishly. 'I have something to tell you. Something very important. I'll see you later.'

Gina's dresser came into the room. 'Mr Power's very attractive, isn't he?' she said mistily, 'and ever so kind. Sam, the doorkeeper told me how good he'd been to him when he was laid up with bronchitis last January; making sure his wife and children had enough to be going on with.'

And kindness, Gina thought, lay at the heart of Power's charm. Despite his faults, his quick temper, his occasional moodiness and flashes of jealousy, he was a kind and caring human being.

Florio's, a small Italian restaurant off Shaftesbury Avenue, had by way of its excellent cuisine and intimate atmosphere become a favourite eating place of the acting profession, for late night suppers after the final curtain. And Florio, an astute restaurateur with an eye for business, made certain that his tables were unavailable to diners who arrived on speculation, in the hope of rubbing shoulders with the leading lights of the West End theatres whom Florio regarded as his personal property.

When they had ordered, and the wine-waiter had brought champagne to their table, 'Well, what is the important news you have to tell me?' Gina asked, leaning back, glad of the relaxed atmosphere, and thinking that her dresser had been right about Power. He *was* attractive, with his strong jawline, dark hair and tanned complexion, his face no longer boyishly smooth, but lived-in, the flesh betraying signs of the scoring which, in time, would deepen into furrows. It was the face of a man who had known suffering as well as success.

Pouring the champagne, handing her a glass, 'I'd like to propose a toast,' he said with mock solemnity, 'to the Great White Way. New York in the spring!'

'New York? You mean—?'

'I heard from Alwyn Jefferson this morning. You are to play St Joan, on Broadway. Congratulations, my darling!'

Chapter Nineteen

She had dreamed of this moment, sailing past the Statue of Liberty into the open mouth of the Hudson River, seeing the world's most famous skyline silhouetted against the luminous sky of a mild April evening.

Passengers crowded to the rails to watch the unfolding panorama of skyscrapers, Manhattan Island bathed in the mysterious glow of the setting sun, lights springing up along the shore as daylight faded.

The scene must be familiar to many of the people standing beside her, Gina thought, and perhaps these seasoned travellers had lost their keen edge of perception, had become inured to the humbling experience of a great ocean liner moving majestically towards its berth; its deep-bellied acknowledgement of the tug-boats puttering importantly ahead of the floating palace to guide it safely home. But the feelings she experienced at this, her first glimpse of New York, were too deep, too gripping, ever to be forgotten or taken for granted.

Wordlessly, she clung to Power's arm, and he smiled down at her, knowing how much this meant to her, marvelling at the exquisite curve of her left cheekbone glimpsed beneath the downswept hat-brim, the proud uplift of her chin above the collar of her tweed coat.

It had been tough for her leaving Oliver, but the boy was well settled at boarding school. Bridget would be there to look after him on his weekend exeats; summertime would bring a bird-watching holiday in the Lake District with his best friend's family, he was to have riding lessons, and Giselle had promised to take him to Paris in the fall. A good, sensible boy, Oliver, Power thought approvingly, a talented youngster to boot, displaying a remarkable talent for art, a quick and lively interest in life, a maturity beyond his years, and a well-developed sense of humour linked to a sturdy independence of spirit matching that of his adoptive mother.

Power's American colleague, Alwyn Jefferson, was at the berthing dock to meet them – a tall, gangling fellow with a balding forehead, wearing rimless glasses and a broad, welcoming smile, who had booked rooms for them at the Gotham Hotel on Fifth Avenue. He told Power on their way to Customs that he would not be able to have dinner with them that evening as he had hoped, but would look forward to meeting them again tomorrow, at his offices in Times Square. 'This has been a real pleasure for me, Miss Brett,' he said warmly, thinking that TJ had not exaggerated when he wrote to him how beautiful she was. The girl was a stunner. She'd be a sensation in Hollywood.

The Gotham proved to be a richly ornamented building, reminiscent of a ducal palace. Corinthian pillars flanked the entrance, marred by the modernistic glass portal extending to the pavement edge. Nevertheless, the spacious reception foyer, bristling with smartly uniformed bell-hops, exuded an aura of dignity and good taste, with deep, velvet-covered armchairs, discreet lighting, and potted palms.

Tired from the excitement of arrival, the Customs' check, and the cab ride from the docks, after showering and changing, they elected to dine in the air-conditioned Alpine Grill, in a less formal atmosphere than that of the Renaissance Dining-Room – where the women, in their rich furs and glittering jewellery, might well have been costumed by the wardrobe department of the Metro Goldwyn Mayer Studios, Power commented drily.

Excitement had taken away Gina's appetite. All seemed vaguely unreal. She could not believe that she was really here in New York, a city she had longed to see for herself, which she felt she knew well from her clandestine visits to the Hampstead cinema where, sitting in the darkness, gazing up at the screen, she had experienced a powerful affinity with the American way of life – its pulsating energy and freshness, rawness and vitality.

Breaking into her thoughts, 'We have a busy day ahead of us tomorrow,' Power said, 'so unless there is anything you'd particularly like to do, I suggest we get a good night's rest.'

'Yes, of course.' Standing close beside him in the elevator, 'I'm glad we've been given adjoining rooms,' she admitted. 'It means a great deal to me, knowing you are there if I need your help.'

He thought, kissing her goodnight on the landing, how marvellous if would be if, during the night, she needed not just his help, but his love. He wanted her as he had never wanted a woman before, he told himself. But was that strictly true? Time had a way of dulling even the sharpest memories. Making ready for bed, he remembered Ruth, his honey-blonde ex-wife, whom he had met in London during the war, with whom he had fallen instantly, desperately in love – an outgoing American with no hang-ups about sex before marriage.

It now occurred to him, bitterly, that he should have been satisfied with the sexual aspect of their relationship, should have let it go at that. His greatest mistake had lain in placing a gold wedding ring on her finger, in attempting to tie her down to a role which, by her very nature, she had been unable to tolerate or fulfil. Little wonder that she had returned to America to resume her journalistic career once she had discovered that in no way could she continue to play second fiddle to his solo violin performance as an up-and-coming theatrical agent.

Suddenly, the phone rang . . .

She had expected to feel dwarfed by the skyscrapers, and clung tightly to Power's arm as they walked down Broadway towards the Battery. Now she felt not merely dwarfed but overwhelmed by the impersonality of the buildings. Power laughed. 'You'll soon get used to it,' he promised. 'Everyone, except born-and-bred Yankees, I imagine, feels this way on their first trip to New York. I know I did.'

Glad of his presence, tall and commanding, his protectiveness towards her, Gina felt less insignificant, more relaxed. Looking up, she saw that the sun was dazzling on the windows of this stone-and-metal canyon, making the towering buildings seem less impersonal. Then, thankfully, the glass, stone and metal ravine behind them, they were facing Battery Park, and the great, shining breadth of the Hudson River.

Entranced, Gina saw the Island Ferry butting towards the Statue of Liberty standing guard over the entrance of New York Harbour, the distant shoreline of New Jersey, a great ocean liner moving majestically towards the open sea.

At that moment she stopped being afraid. Aglow, she experienced a surge of renewed energy and vitality. Now she wanted to visit all the places she had heard and read so much about: the almost completed Empire State Building, Manhattan Island, the Rockefeller Centre, Greenwich Village, Central Park, Above all, she wanted to ride in an elevated railway.

Vastly amused by her enthusiasm to swallow the whole of New York in one gulp, Power reminded her over lunch of their afternoon appointment with Alwyn Jefferson. Later, he promised, he would show her New York by night. First they would have dinner at Mori's restaurant in Bleecker Street, from the windows of which could be seen the Sixth Avenue 'El'. Indeed Mori's, with its stylish white portico, balconied and shuttered façade, he told her, seemed strangely out of place, an anachronism, in the shadow of a dingy overhead railway.

So this was Times Square, Gina thought bemusedly, caught up in the rush and bustle of this famous New York centre with its endless stream of illuminated news flashes running along the face of the Times Tower building: the place where, traditionally, thousands of New Yorkers gathered on New Year's Eve to celebrate the death of the old year, the birth of the new.

Jefferson's offices reflected his success as a theatrical agent. Despite his ingenuous appearance and easy-going charm, Jefferson's thumb remained firmly on the pulse of Broadway.

Entering the foyer, Alwyn might have warned him, Power thought resentfully, that Ruth was in New York, that he had given her the number of the Gotham Hotel. Her telephone call to his room the previous night had come as a shock. What was the point or purpose of reaping up old memories, he'd asked her. And, 'Oh, surely, TJ,' she replied mockingly, 'where's the harm in a drink for old time's sake? We were once married, remember?'

As if he could ever forget. He had been to hell and back on her account. 'I can't promise,' he'd said stubbornly.

'If you change your mind, darling, I'm staying at the Astor. Room 419.'

There was much to discuss, contractual details to be hammered out. *St Joan* was scheduled to open at the Bijou Theatre on 31 May. Rehearsals would begin the day after next in a room adjoining the Metropolitan Museum of Art in West Street, Manhattan. Gina would be given star billing. Already his team of publicists had been briefed regarding her sensational portrayal of the role in London's West End, Alwyn Jefferson said enthusiastically. Of course he would need up-to-date photographs of Gina for the billboards and the Press releases. 'Shall we say tomorrow morning, at ten o'clock, here, in my private photographic studio?' Jefferson suggested artlessly.

'Yes, of course,' Gina complied, 'though I must warn you, I hate being photographed.'

After dinner at Mori's they crossed the road to the Sixth Avenue 'El', mounted the steps to the ticket office, and awaited the arrival of the train.

Gina reminded Power of a child taking its first ride on a carousel. She sat with her hands tightly clasped, loving the rhythm of the train racketing along the track, seeing through the grimy windows a different aspect of the city of bright lights and glamour that Power had shown her from the back seat of a taxi. Here were the backs of tenement buildings with their lattice-work of fire-escapes, lines of washing strung out to dry, a man in the street below selling hot-dogs from a barrow; the sound of a hurdy-gurdy. A barber's shop advertising haircuts at 10 cents, shaves at 5 cents; a drunken man lurching into a liquor store.

Power pointed out a kosher chicken market, where the birds were newly killed every hour to comply with the purchasers' religious beliefs; a cigar store complete with wooden Indian; a Lebanese restaurant in the heart of the Syrian district, the windows scrawled with Arabic lettering.

She saw a pawnshop with a windowful of unredeemed pledges – rings, brooches, clothing, bits of silver – reminders of the poverty existing in the tangled maze of streets far distanced from the gracious avenues of up-town New York. Poor migrant New Yorkers, mainly old men and women, enjoying the freshness of a mild spring evening from the fire-escape landings, contemplated the blossoming street lamps as they had once, perhaps, contemplated a better way of life for themselves and their children in a land of opportunity. And possibly, Gina thought compassionately, life did seem pretty good to the youngsters making their way to the dance-halls and the cinemas where, for a brief moment in time, they might lose themselves in the magic of a Hollywood movie.

Returning to the Gotham, 'You're very quiet,' Power observed. 'Perhaps riding on the Sixth Avenue "El" wasn't such a good idea after all? Too much reality?'

'I'm not afraid of reality. It's pretence that frightens me.' Awaiting the arrival of the elevator, 'I often wonder if I chose the wrong career.'

'We need to talk,' he said brusquely, 'unless you are too tired.'

She smiled reflectively, 'I'm not in the least bit tired. I wish today would never end. One of the happiest days of my life.'

Opening the door of his room, switching on the light, 'I'll order coffee and sandwiches,' he said, 'if that's OK with you.'

236

'Very well.' She crossed to the window, looked down at the street below as Power picked up the telephone.

Despite the lateness of the hour, up-town New Yorkers were in no hurry to go to bed, it seemed, not as long as there was food, wine and music to enjoy, and this was the essence of New York, this urgency to live every moment as it came, and never mind about tomorrow.

When the waiter had gone, Power stood beside her. She trembled slightly as he slipped her evening wrap from her shoulders. Then, turning to face him, 'You said we needed to talk. What about?'

Catching the fragrance of her hair, holding her close in his arms, 'Don't you know? Can't you guess?' he whispered hoarsely. 'I *want* you, my darling. You want me too, don't you? *Don't* you?'

Trapped in his arms, bemused by New York, the feeling she had of being swept into a vortex beyond her power of control, she knew the time had come to lie warm and safe in the arms of someone whose love she had no reason to doubt or reject.

Wide awake, looking up at the ceiling, she remembered the studio, the moon, pale and high in a winter sky, silvering a skylight, long ago and far away . . .

She knew now, by the light of a new day, that she had given herself to Power from a deep need of reassurance born of loneliness and a fear of her ability to take Broadway by storm.

He had not realized – how could he – that she was still a virgin? And so he had entered her strongly, causing her to cry out with pain as he had thrust deeply into her quivering body until, finally, aware that his throbbing sexual drive and energy had failed to arouse her response to his ardour, he had known the humiliation of rejection.

She might have warned him that this was her first experience of love-making, he thought bitterly. 'Forgive me,' he said briefly, turning his back on her.

Was this painful, clumsy enjoining of flesh the culmination of loving? she wondered. If only he had been less forceful and demanding, had not turned his back on her. Sensing his humiliation, she blamed herself for the spoilation of a perfect day, her lack of wisdom in walking blindly into a situation which she had not known how to handle.

Remembering Rab, she thanked God that their love had remained on a spiritual plane. And yet she could not help thinking that she would have discovered, in his arms, not the pain and disillusionment, but the joy of being a woman.

Getting up, dressing swiftly, she went to her own room.

They ate breakfast in constrained silence. Pride forbade her referring to the subject uppermost in her mind. They should have talked last night. Impossible to ask a man, over waffles and maple syrup, 'Was it my fault?' In any case, there was no need to ask. Obviously Power's male ego had been deeply wounded by what he saw as her lack of response to his lovemaking. Or had the underlying current run deeper than that? Had he sensed her innate reluctance to give him the total commitment he had expected of her?

Glancing at his watch, swallowing the last of his coffee, throwing aside his serviette, 'We'd better hurry,' he said tautly, 'or we'll be late for the photographic session.' Rising quickly to his feet, 'I'll phone for a cab.'

'I'd rather go alone.'

'Don't be ridiculous! Of course I'll go with you.'

'There's no need. I am quite capable of taking care of myself. I'll meet you here for lunch at, say, one o'clock?'

'Just as you wish,' he said sullenly.

'Please don't be angry. I'd just like to be alone for a little while.'

'So should I, come to think of it.'

Taking her courage in both hands, 'About last night. I'm so sorry.'

'You're not the only one,' he said grimly.

Getting out of the taxi in Times Square, looking up at the ribbon of ticker-tape news' flashes streaming relentlessly above the churning mass of humanity in the square below, she read: 'Pope Pius XI declares war on Fascists. Italian leader, Mussolini, anti-Christian, says Catholic Church Supremo. Fascism entirely given over to hate, irreverence and violence . . . Spain declared a republic as King Alfonso quits office . . .'

Suddenly Gina shivered, as though a goose had walked over her grave.

Entering the lobby of the Astor Hotel, Power headed for the elevator, pressed the fourth floor button, and walked along the corridor towards Room 419.

When the door opened, 'Hello, Ruth,' he said heavily, 'you said you wanted to see me. May I come in?'

She was every bit as beautiful and desirable as he remembered, a witch of a woman with her slender, long-limbed body, heavily mascaraed eyelashes, and her shining crown of honey-blonde hair.

'You certainly choose your times,' she said huskily. 'I'm not even dressed yet. But I guess it's OK. After all, you always preferred me in a state of – *déshabillé*!' Turning away, 'Want a cup of coffee? Breakfast? If so, help yourself. I slept late. I'm not hungry anyway. I was just about to take a shower.'

'Stop it, Ruth!'

'Stop *what*?'

'You know damn well what!' he said bitterly. 'This game you're playing. It was always a game with you, wasn't it? Christ! I should have had more sense than to come here in the first place!'

Turning back to him, laying her hands on his arms, smiling up at him, her long blonde hair flowing about her shoulders, 'The truth is, I've missed you, TJ,' she confessed, 'so why don't you stop acting like a bear with a sore head, and kiss me? The way you used to kiss me, remember?'

Holding his hands tightly in hers, she drew him towards the bed and lay down, unloosing the cord of her bath-robe to reveal the full splendour of her upthrust, carmine-nippled breasts, her taut belly, slender thighs, and her incredibly lovely legs, spread invitingly apart to welcome, when it came, the urgent upthrust of his manhood.

It had always been like this with her. Urgent, necessary, intense. Too intense. Frightening. Nothing held back, except love. He doubted if they understood, or ever had, the meaning of the word. 'Why did you leave me?' he asked in a low voice.

'Because I wanted you here. I knew you'd come sooner or later.'

'You expect me to believe that?' Bitterly, 'Is that why you divorced me, because you wanted me here with you?'

Sitting up, bunching the pillows, lighting a cigarette, 'Marriage was the biggest mistake we ever made,' she said. 'Some people are not cut out for it. We weren't. Take two bloody-minded individuals, put them together in a cage, and what happens? They start fighting like hell to escape. We should have known that from the beginning. I think I knew, from the moment I left that registry office with a wedding ring on my finger, that it wouldn't work. I felt trapped. If you are honest enough to admit it, you felt the same way. Well, TJ?

'So I came back to America. Divorce is easier here, and I wanted that divorce more than anything I'd ever wanted before.' Stubbing out the cigarette, 'When you came back to me, I wanted things to be the way they were before we went into that registry office.' She smiled. 'And they are! How long did it take? Five, ten minutes? I knew, when you walked in the room, that nothing had changed between us – except that we are now two free, independent human beings. Frankly, TJ, I loathed being married to you, but I've missed, like hell, being loved by you.'

'You call what has just happened between us love?'

'Call it what you will. Love. Lust. Who cares? All I know is the way I feel right now. Alive again!' Running her fingernails down his back, 'How do *you* feel, TJ?'

Why bother to ask? She knew damn well how he felt. The way he had always felt after making love to her – drained, excited, fulfilled. All male. Lying close beside her, feeling the softness of her hair on his shoulders, kissing her full-lipped mouth, he thought briefly of Gina, the other woman in his life, whom he loved in his fashion. But not the way he loved Ruth, if all the deep and dark desires she aroused in him could be glorified as such.

The photographic session was a long, tedious affair.

Snapshots were fine, but posing for still photographs beneath a barrage of carefully angled spotlights robbed Gina of spontaneity. Her smile seemed soldered to her lips. The thought occurred, as she followed the photographer's instructions to look up then down, to lift or to lower her chin, what a boring profession film-acting must be.

Waiting for the lights to be moved a fraction of an inch, she remembered that night on the terrace when the maestro and Power had argued the merits of cinema-photography versus the theatre: Landis' remark that he considered cinemaphotography as the art form of the future; Power's reply, 'Sure, I'll grant that Garbo is a great actress, but where would she be without closeups, a gauze veil in front of the camera, a minimum of lines to learn?'

Power had been right, of course. She thought of the great Garbo, the alluring Marlene Dietrich who looked so wonderful on film. But what of the tedium involved? All the waiting between takes? The horror of a camera-crew watching every move, the team of makeup experts and hairdressers standing on the sidelines ready to dab on more powder, to twitch a stray hair back into place?

The clock had moved to one-thirty by the time the photographer was satisfied with his work. He called out to her, 'Thanks, honey, that's fine, just fine!'

Returning late to the Gotham Hotel, Gina asked the desk-clerk if Mr Power had left a message for her. Possibly he had already eaten, had gone to his room.

'I haven't seen Mr Power,' the man told her, 'but I have a cablegram for you. It arrived just after you left.'

'A – cablegram?' Quickly, she tore open the envelope. 'Not bad news, I hope?'

241

Staring into space, holding the message in her trembling hands, 'I must leave at once,' she said.

'Any way I can help?' She seemed stunned, the man thought. The colour had drained from her cheeks. 'Would you like me to get you a glass of water?'

'No. Thank you.' Gathering her thoughts, 'Would you ring the Cunard office, find out if there's a berth vacant on the next ship to England?'

'Sure thing. I'll get on to it right away, ma'am.'

Waiting near the desk, she heard the man speaking on the telephone. Minutes later, he returned from the inner office. 'You're in luck,' he said. 'I've made a reservation for you on the *Berengaria*, sailing tonight at nine.'

'Thank you. You've been most helpful. I'll be in my room if you need me.'

'Just one thing more, ma'am, you'll have to be at the docks by seven.'

'I'll start packing right away. Would you order a cab for six-thirty, and have my bill ready before I leave?'

In her room, she re-read the cablegram. 'Peter phoned. Stop. Master very ill. Stop. Asking for you. Stop. Signed, Bridget Donovan.'

She began packing. The time was now four-thirty. Still no sign of Power. Where was he?

Strapping her cabin-trunk, she remembered ringing her father before her departure to New York, his words: 'I'm so proud of you, my darling. Go with my blessing. Take Broadway by storm!'

Now, taking Broadway by storm was the last thing on her mind. Her father needed her, and she must go to him. Pray God she would be in time.

'Gina! What the hell is going on?'

Entering her room without knocking, Power stared in bewilderment at the packed and strapped cabin-trunk. 'The desk-clerk told me you were leaving. But you can't leave! Not now!'

'I'm sorry, Power, I must! My father may be dying.'

'But you have a contract with Jefferson! Professionalism is involved here. You might at least have waited, discussed things with me.'

'You weren't here!' She faced him squarely. 'In any case, the contract hasn't been signed yet.'

'A bloody lame excuse!'

'And what is *your* excuse? Where have you been all day?'

He had the grace to look ashamed. 'If you must know, my ex-wife is in New York. I've been with her at her hotel.' He could not have hurt Gina more had he slapped her face, and he knew it.

'I see.' She turned her head away.

'There's something else you should know. I'm staying on in New York.'

Startled, she looked back at him. 'But what about the agency? Your London office?'

'I haven't thought that far ahead.'

'So this is the end of the line?' She remembered the 'El' railway, racketing above the streets of down-town New York. How happy she had been then. 'You'd better leave, now!' she said. 'Goodbye, Power. Thanks for – the good times.'

'Gina,' he said helplessly, knowing he had exchanged gold for dross, love for lust, a shining star for a scattering of moondust, that he had hurt her deliberately. 'I never meant this to happen.'

'*Goodbye*, Power.' She held herself erectly, refusing to give way to tears.

When he had gone, she picked up the bedside phone, rang Alwyn Jefferson's offices in Times Square, knowing that she had turned her back on Broadway for something that meant much more to her.

Chapter Twenty

At ten minutes to one, Susanna Bickley came into the dining-room, dressed for going out, a Robin Hood-type hat pierced with a pheasant quill perched on her Marcel waved hair. 'I'll start lunch immediately,' she told the manservant, who had not yet sounded the gong.

'Yes, madam.' Jerking his head as a signal to the maid to bring in the soup, Johnson went through to the hall. Wielding the gong-stick, he derived a masochistic pleasure from the sound waves reverberating through the house, registering his disapproval of his mistress's bad manners in starting luncheon before the rest of the family came downstairs.

Older, much wiser now than he had been a decade ago, Johnson viewed the situation at Merlewood with a jaundiced eye, remembering the way things were in the old days, when Mrs Jack Bickley was alive, before Mr Harold had married the 'Middlesbrough upstart', when Mr Jack was in control of the mill; before Miss Josie had put the cat among the pigeons in calling off her marriage to Frank Considine, and returning to Merlewood to live. What ructions that had caused. Now, the happy household he had entered as under-footman, after the war, no longer existed. He wondered, watching Mr Jack Bickley coming slowly downstairs, supported by Miss Josie, if there was truth in the saying that a house divided against itself could not stand.

The cook, Mrs Whickham, never tired of recounting the tale of the row she had overheard the day Miss Josie came back to Merlewood to live, when she had told Mrs Harold, in no uncertain terms, that she was damned if she would stand for her mother's belongings being sold at auction to make room for modernistic rubbish of her sister-in-law's choosing. 'Then Mrs Harold snapped back at her, "I'll thank you to remember that *I* am the mistress of Merlewood now, and I'll do as I think fit." And, "Over my dead body," Miss Josie said coolly, "I shall prevent you from removing one stick of my mother's furniture, by legal means, if necessary. Mother left the contents of the house to be divided equally between myself and Letty!" '

' "It's a great pity, then, that you and Letty didn't take the wretched stuff to Newcastle when you got married," ' Mrs Whickham recounted. 'I could tell how upset Miss Josie was when Mrs Harold mentioned Newcastle. I thought they'd come to blows, I really did, when Miss Josie told her to mind her own damned business, that they had chosen to leave their mother's belongings at Merlewood out of respect for Mr Jack's feelings. Eh,' the cook shook her head, 'no wonder poor Mr Bickley had a stroke what with one thing and another. But perhaps it was just as well that Miss Josie came home when she did, before Harold's wife had time to take over completely.'

Re-entering the dining-room to oversee the serving of the meal, Johnson wondered why Miss Josie had left her husband so suddenly, after only a few weeks of marriage. Something must have gone radically wrong to change a formerly happy, attractive young woman into a sour-faced virago. Not that he disliked Miss Josie; indeed, he gloried in her ability to keep Mrs Harold from ruling the roost, and admired deeply the way she had nursed and looked after her father since her return.

Standing at the sideboard, and carving the roast leg of lamb as the maid removed the soup plates from the dining table – preparatory to bringing in the tureens of vegetables, Johnson heard the old master, Jack Bickley, ask querulously why his son was not present at table. 'He's at some meeting or other with his so-called business colleagues, I imagine,' Susanna said scornfully. 'Probably drinking himself blind at the Golf Club. Who cares?'

'*I* care.' Jack Buckley's stroke-misshapen mouth worked painfully to form his reply. 'After all, he is my—'

'Oh, for God's sake, Father,' Josie interrupted coldly,

'why waste breath? Can't you see how much she enjoys these petty domestic dramas?'

The grandfather clock in the hall struck the half hour as Harold entered the dining-room, grim-faced, completely sober. 'Sorry I'm late,' he said. Facing his father, 'I've just come from the mill.' He paused briefly to frame his words, 'It's bad news, I'm afraid. Mr Brett-Forsyth passed away this morning.'

What did it matter, now, he thought, that his father and Owen had drifted apart these past years? Brett-Forsyth had been a force to be reckoned with in the valley, more sinned against than sinning, a man of integrity. Remembering the wreath he had burned in the kitchen garden on the day of his mother's funeral, Harold regretted playing his part in fanning the fire of enmity between the two families.

Hurt pride and bitterness, his refusal to forgive and forget, had exacerbated the rift, Harold realized, when he might have healed the breach before it deepened into a chasm. He had blamed Georgina for the death of his mother, but was he not equally responsible in clinging to his hurt pride and bitterness, when a more mature attitude might have aided his mother's recovery?

Time had not dealt kindly with Harold Bickley, Johnson thought, carving the roast lamb. Ten years ago he had been a fine-looking fellow. Now, his once tautly-muscled body was larded with fat, and his thick crop of fair hair had begun to recede. No wonder. It must have been hell for him these past few years, living under the same roof with a sick father, a sour-faced wife and his miserable sister to contend with.

No doubt about it, Johnson reflected, serving the lamb, Mrs Harold had proved herself unpopular with the family and servants alike. Once her veneer of charm had worn thin, her true nature had come uppermost. To make matters worse, Georgina Brett-Forsyth had, by all accounts, done quite well for herself judging from a screwed-up page of a glossy magazine he had discovered in his mistress' waste-paper basket, in which a photograph of Gina Brett had appeared beneath the caption: 'West End actress to star as St Joan on Broadway.'

Jealousy had bitten deeply into Susanna. Despite Harold's assurance that she meant nothing to him, Gina Brett had been his first choice. She had only seen Georgina once, in church, the day the Banns were read, when she had taken an instant dislike to her, a dislike which had ripened through the years to the bitter hatred she now felt towards her rival; hatred exacerbated by the fact that the wretched girl had achieved fame and fortune, plus the accolade of having her photograph in *The Tatler*.

Marriage to Harold had not been the bed of roses Susanna had so fondly imagined. She had quickly realized that her husband had a short temper and a will of iron, an innate meanness when it came to spending money, and a complete lack of initiative when it came to lovemaking. Even so, she might have overcome those basic imperfections had not Josie appeared as a cuckoo in the matrimonial nest, to spoil her plans for the refurbishment of Merlewood. To add to her distress, Harold and Jack had welcomed Josie with open arms, despite her short-lived marriage to Frank Considine. It was 'poor Josie' this, and 'poor Josie' that, until she could have screamed with frustration – as she had done that day in the library, when Josie told her, in no uncertain terms, that she would not countenance the sale of her mother's furniture.

After that shouting match between herself and Josie, Susanna had demanded that Harry should purchase a home of their own, to no avail. She knew why. Harry was too mean to move away from Merlewood. 'After all,' he told her, 'it was your idea to live here in the first place.' And so, because she could not have borne being referred to as 'poor Susanna', whose marriage had ended as quickly and disastrously as 'poor Josie's', she had stayed on to make her presence felt. Despite the presence of 'poor Josie', she felt herself to be the undisputed mistress of the house, and woe betide any servant who refused to jump at her bidding.

Now here was Harold pulling a long face over the death of old Owen Brett-Forsyth. The bloody hypocrite! As if it mattered a damn. Well, she had her own fish to fry. Rising from the table, 'I'm playing Bridge this afternoon,' she announced coolly.

'You haven't finished lunch,' Harold reminded her.

'I'm not hungry. In any case, I have no desire to talk about the Brett-Forsyths.' Picking up her gloves and handbag, she walked out of the room.

The thought uppermost in Thomas Brett-Forsyth's mind was that the reins of power were now firmly in his hands. Sorely in need of ready cash to pay off his creditors – his tailor, turf accountant, wine-merchant, and the firm of money-lenders whose interest rates had risen alarmingly of late – soon, he reckoned, he would be in a position to rid himself of their stern demands for repayment.

Elmhurst he knew, had been willed to his mother, but he foresaw no difficulty in persuading her to hand over the deeds to him. Confused as she now was, she would be better off in a nursing home. The podgy boy had grown into an unattractive man. The puppy fat he had been prone to as a child had not hardened into muscle but through self-indulgence in food and drink, had degenerated to a flabbiness which even cleverly cut clothes could scarcely conceal.

When the funeral was out of the way, he decided, he would sell Elmhurst and the mill and go abroad to live, in the South of France, perhaps, Spain or Italy, as a man of means should live. Meanwhile, he would give his father a decent send-off: close the mill on the day of the funeral as a mark of respect. This, he considered, would fulfil his obligations to the man who had been a stumbling block in his path as far back as he could remember.

It had never occurred to him to inform Georgina of Owen's death. His sister had been absent from his life for so long that he scarcely remembered her existence. Certainly he harboured no sibling feelings towards her. Why should he? A girl who had left home under a cloud, with an illegitimate child to her discredit. In any case, Georgina was not mentioned in his father's will. This he knew because he had made it his business to find out. One day, alone in his father's office, he had opened the safe where Owen's private papers were kept.

Returning to Elmhurst when his father had been laid to rest, the wreath of arum lilies on the coffin bearing a card which read, 'To the memory of a devoted husband and father', had struck exactly the right note, Thomas thought. His mother had refused to attend the funeral, saying she was too ill to leave her room. He might have known, however, that she would rally sufficiently to hear the reading of the will when the handful of guests he had invited to the house for a buffet luncheon had departed. Trust Agnes for that.

Seated in Owen's favourite chair near the library fire, glancing across at his mother, there was something obscene, Thomas thought, that he had once floated embryonically in that mountain of quivering flesh, and drawn nourishment from those pendulous breasts.

When they were settled Mr Caulfield the solicitor, a lifelong friend of Owen's, opened the envelope containing the will, and began reading. First came a number of small bequests to the various servants gathered in a group near the door – the sum of £250 to each who had been in his employ for the past decade or more. When they had departed, Mr Caulfield continued reading, with grim pleasure, this new will which Owen had drafted two months ago.

Clearing his throat, he began, ' "To my wife, Agnes, I bequeath the property known as Elmhurst, plus an annuity of two thousand pounds per annum during her occupancy of the aforementioned property. If, however, she decides to sell the property, the sale price shall be hers entirely. Transfer of the deeds, however, shall not constitute a *bona-fide* sale. In this circumstance, her annuity would not be paid directly to her but revert to a trust fund in her name only, administered by the firm of Caulfield and Son, solicitors, in payment of bills incurred in matters pertaining to her health and wellbeing." '

Thomas' head rose sharply in the manner of a gun-dog

scenting danger. This was not the will he had read in his father's office. What the hell . . . ?

Caulfield continued implacably, ' "To my beloved daughter Georgina, I bequeath the contents of the library, her favourite room, in memory of the many happy hours she spent there as a child, along with my undying love and affection for all that she has meant to me during my lifetime." '

There had been no mention of Georgina in the will he had purloined from his father's safe, Thomas thought wildly.

' "To my son Thomas," ' the lawyer went on, ' "I bequeath the Brett-Forsyth Mill which, if properly administered, should provide him with a sizeable annual income providing he works hard to ensure that income.

' "Finally, I bequeath to my adoptive grandson, Oliver Brett-Forsyth, the sum of £50,000, plus the capital and interest of the various stocks and shares held in my name by the Leeds branch of Hebden and Woodall's Bank, along with my fervent wish that this bequest shall convey to him my gratitude for all the joy and happiness his presence on earth has brought to an old man in the declining years of his life." '

Incensed with anger, Thomas sprang to his feet. 'What the hell are you talking about?' he demanded hoarsely. 'My father left the mill and his money to *me*! His son, his own flesh and blood. I know, because I read that will with my own eyes, six months ago.'

Caulfield said calmly, 'Your father recently altered his will. He realized, of course, that his private papers had been tampered with.'

'To hell with all that mumbo-jumbo,' Thomas interposed strongly, facing the lawyer, his eyes flashing fire, 'what about *my* inheritance? What about that fifty thousand quid which should be mine by right? Do you mean to stand there and tell me that my sister's bastard stands to inherit all that rightly belongs to me? Well, you haven't heard the last of this. I'm damned if I'll stand by and let some snivelling little bastard lay his hands on my inheritance!'

Caulfield flinched in the face of Thomas' anger. Nevertheless, he stood his ground. 'You are, of course, at liberty to contest the will if you wish to do so,' he said coldly, 'though I daresay you'll discover that it is perfectly legal and binding in every respect. Now, if you'll excuse me, I must be on my way. A very good day to you both.'

Agnes looked shocked, as well she might. Shocked and stupefied. 'I don't understand,' she moaned. 'What does it all mean?'

'It means that father must have been out of his mind when he made that will,' Thomas said furiously. The lifestyle he had foreseen since Owen's demise had shattered like broken glass. The deeds of Elmhurst, he knew, were in the hands of the solicitor. Hatred of his father rose up like bile in his throat, almost choking him.

Slamming out of the house, he walked to the garden's end and stood there looking down at the Brett-Forsyth Mill in the valley below, seeing it, not as a surety of his own future means of support if, as his father had suggested, he worked hard enough to ensure a sizeable annual income, but as a stumbling block to his ambitions. The mill had meant the world to Owen; it meant nothing to Thomas in terms of family pride and historical significance. Looking down, the sooner he got rid of it, the better, he decided, glorying darkly in the thought that revenge was sweet. So much the better if he sold the mill to Harold Bickley.

Opening the paper she had bought from a news-stand in Leeds Station, Gina read, in the obituary column, a glowing tribute to her father, penned by someone who had evidently known him well during his lifetime.

Tired out after her fruitless journey from New York and this abortive train journey north, the print blurred before her eyes. The realization that her father had asked for her in vain, that she had not been there when he needed her, was more than she could bear.

The branch train to Bradford was due to leave in ten minutes. Turning away, folding the newspaper, carrying her small suitcase, she walked out of the station, hailed a taxi and asked the driver to take her to the Griffen Hotel. There, she booked a room for three nights. Alone in that room, she broke her heart with weeping. Then, undressing and getting into bed, she slept exhaustedly until the early hours of the next morning.

In the clear light of day, she realized the futility of attending her father's funeral. Had she arrived in time to see Owen alive, she would have stormed a citadel to be by his side. Now she wanted to visit his grave, quite alone. Not for her the outward show of grief. Nor could she bear the expression of assumed grief on the face of her brother Tom, who had never cared tuppence about his father, and of her mother, whose selfishness had made his life a misery.

And so she stayed in Leeds, until the funeral was over, scarcely leaving her room, having her meals sent up. On the fourth day she paid her bill and caught the late afternoon train to Bradford Station, and hired a taxi to the Merlewood cemetery.

'Please, wait for me,' she told the driver.

'Yes, Miss,' the man replied, stunned by the beauty of the tall, slim young woman making her way to the church-yard, holding in her gloved hands a sheaf of red roses.

Dusk was falling when, discovering the mound of newly dug earth beneath an elm tree, Gina placed her offering of red roses on Owen's grave. Overcome with grief, kneeling beside the grave, she covered her face with her hands. ' "They say a made a good end," ' she whispered.

Suddenly came a voice from the past. 'Georgina! Is it really you?'

Rising swiftly to her feet, facing the owner of the voice, 'Harold!' she cried warmly, extending her hands in greeting, forgetful of the past which had caused them both so much pain. 'Oh, Harry, I'm so pleased to see you!'

'And I you!' He clasped her hands, wondering what the hell the wasted years had been about; why he had allowed this lovely creature to slip through his fingers.

Marriage to Susanna had not brought him the happiness he had expected. Things had gone badly wrong from the beginning. His bride had proved both self-centred and demanding, robbing him of tenderness towards her. Even on their honeymoon, he had realized the extent of her selfishness; wanting everything her own way in the matter of lovemaking. Her lack of modesty had vaguely shocked him, then she had laughed at him, calling him a prude; laughter which had soon turned to irritation by his lack of initiative in bed. Of course he had wanted her, but not experimentally, like a performing dog learning new tricks.

'How did you know I was here?' Gina thought that time had not treated him kindly from a physical aspect – and yet he seemed kinder in other ways, gentler, more forgiving.

'I saw you getting out of the taxi. I drove past you on my way home,' he explained. 'Georgina, I need to talk to you.'

'The taxi's waiting.'

'Please, send it away. I'll drive you.'

'Very well.' She did as he asked.

He opened his car door for her. 'Where are you going?'

'I'm not sure.'

'Not Elmhurst?'

'No. Cowardly of me, I know.' She smiled. 'I hardly think they'll put out the red carpet.'

'You weren't at the funeral?'

'No. I came home from New York when I knew my father was ill.' Her voice shook slightly. 'I arrived too late. I read his obituary in *The Leeds Mercury*. Oh, Harry!'

He said decisively, 'I'll take you to the Queen's Hotel in Bradford. We can talk over dinner.'

'But you were on your way home. They'll be expecting you.'

'It isn't important. I often work late at the mill.' Keeping his eyes on the road, 'A lot of water has flowed under the bridge since our last meeting.'

'That day in church,' she said quietly, 'the day your banns were read, I want you to know it wasn't planned. I wouldn't have been there had I known. You looked so angry.'

'I *was* angry. I'm sorry, Georgie. Perhaps it was the shock of seeing you again in that particular place. For what it's worth, I'm sorry about a lot of things – the way I treated you when you came to return the engagement ring, for instance. Blame my inflated ego for that. I realized, too late, that I should have taken the time and trouble to talk to you.' He smiled ruefully. 'Just as well you left me at the altar. I'd have made you a rotten husband.'

'That's all in the past now,' she said. 'Far better to forget.'

'That's the trouble, I can't forget. I've never been able to get you out of my mind. At first I couldn't believe that the famous Gina Brett was the same girl who once threatened to kick my shins on the sands at Scarborough.'

'I know. I can scarcely believe it myself at times. It's hard to explain. I often feel I am two different people rolled into one, living in two different worlds.' Tears filled her eyes. 'If you knew how homesick I've been for the heather in bloom, the valley below. It's hard being separated from the people one loved, the places one knew as a child.'

'Is it true that you have a child?' he asked as the lights of Bradford came into view.

'Yes. A son, Oliver.'

'But you never married?'

'No, I have never married.' A slight pause. 'Tell me, Harry, have you any children?'

'Unfortunately, no,' he said stiffly. 'My wife never wanted any. At least, the circumstances proved – difficult for her. She is rather highly strung, I'm afraid.'

What circumstances? Gina wondered, as Harold drew up the car near the Queen's Hotel.

At dinner, he said, 'I think you should know that your brother paid me a visit after your father's funeral.'

'Tommy? Why?' Gina frowned.

'He intends selling the mill. He gave me what is known, in common parlance, as the first refusal.'

'*Sell* the mill! But he *can't*. He *mustn't*.' Deeply shocked, she stared at Harold across the table. 'My great grandfather founded the mill. My father lived for it. Harry, if what you say is true, it means the end of everything he fought so hard to maintain throughout the war years.' Wide-eyed,

254

'Remember how your father, and mine, struggled together to keep the looms in production? How they turned to the manufacture of shoddy as a means of income and support for the workers and their families?'

'I remember,' Harold said quietly, 'but the mill belongs to Thomas now, and if he chooses to squander his inheritance, there's little to be done about it, I'm afraid.' He added gently, 'At least if I decide to take over, you may rest assured that it will still be known as the Brett-Forsyth Mill.'

'Tell me, Harry, what value did Tommy place on the mill in monetary terms?' Gina asked.

He said uneasily, 'The sum of £50,000 was mentioned.'

The hotel, in close proximity to Bradford Station, catered mainly for businessmen. Gina had no trouble in booking accommodation for an unspecified length of time.

She and Harry drank coffee together in the lounge, over which he told her of his father's illness, and Josie's ill-fated marriage. 'Josie and Letty had a double wedding,' he said reflectively. 'Both seemed deliriously happy at the time. Letty's still happily married, with children, two boys and a girl. Poor Josie was not so lucky. Unfortunately her husband had psychological problems stemming from his captivity in a German prison camp during the war.'

'I'm so sorry,' Gina said.

'Apparently Josie's husband had a violent streak in his nature which resulted in physical abuse. She returned to Merlewood an embittered woman. Now her time is devoted to caring for Father. Without her help, I imagine that he would have been carted off to some nursing home or other to be looked after.' His voice held a trace of bitterness. 'My wife cannot stand illness or disability in any shape or form.'

This said it all, so far as Gina was concerned. A wife who could not stand illness or disability would scarcely have welcomed becoming pregnant.

'But tell me about yourself, Georgina,' Harold said eagerly. 'Why did you decide to become an actress?'

'Not now, Harry. It's late, and I'm tired.' Rising to her

feet, extending her hand, she said warmly, 'Thank you for this evening. Thank you for being so understanding.'

Holding her hand, he said, 'I never knew, until it was too late, how much I loved you.'

'Please, Harry.' Withdrawing her hand, 'We were never more than friends. Please don't let our present circumstances blind you to reality.'

He said, 'Promise me one thing, Georgina, that you will not go away without saying goodbye to me.'

'Very well, Harry, I promise.'

When he had gone, alone in her bedroom, Gina knew that tomorrow she must go to Elmhurst, to face what must be faced there, for better or worse.

Chapter Twenty-One

Walking up the drive, Gina saw Elmhurst not simply as a Victorian stronghold built to withstand the forces of Nature, but the prison-house of a jealous, unreasonable woman whose bitterness had tainted the lives of so many people. It was this stronghold she must enter if she hoped to salvage something which her father had valued, from the wreckage of his life.

Owen had loved his home for its memories of past happiness, when the rooms were filled with love and laughter. And Elmhurst had retained much of that laughter during her own childhood, especially when the Bickleys came to visit on special anniversaries, and there had been birthday tea-parties and Christmas celebrations, picnics and outings. Perhaps there had been undercurrents of jealousy even then, but children did not notice such things.

Mounting the front steps, she rang the bell. When a maid appeared, Gina gave her name and asked to speak to Mrs Brett-Forsyth. 'If you'll wait in the library, I'll tell Madam you're here,' the girl said, 'but I doubt if she'll see you.'

Entering the room, memories of her father flooded in on Gina. Blinking back tears, she saw on the desk his pipe and tobacco pouch; a book of poetry she had given him one Christmas long ago. Picking up the book, the pages fell open at his favourite poem, 'Dover Beach'. A numbing sense of grief overwhelmed her. Until that moment, part of her mind had refused to accept that he was dead. Reading his obituary in *The Leeds Mercury*, even laying flowers on his grave, the full realization of his death had not struck her as forcibly as it did here, in this room, among his personal belongings.

She turned, hearing the door open, to see not her mother but Thomas standing on the threshold. 'I might have known the black sheep would turn up eventually,' he said abrasively. 'Come to gloat, have you?'

'I don't know what you mean.' She looked at him uncomprehendingly, scarcely able to believe that this grossly overweight man was really her brother. 'Gloat over what?'

'The old man's will, of course. The fact that he left his money to that bastard of yours!'

Colour drained from Gina's face. She faced her brother in stunned silence for a moment. 'I knew nothing of this,' she said in a low voice, 'you had better tell me about it.'

His bullying instincts at full throttle, 'Don't play the innocent with me. You coerced the old man, didn't you, into leaving the mill to me, a fortune to that blasted kid, and making certain I couldn't lay my hands on the deeds of this bloody house? You even made sure you'd get your share of things! Why didn't you ask him for *all* the furniture instead of the contents of this one room? If you'd been a bit cleverer, you could have had the whole bloody shooting match, the house, the mill and the money, and turned Mother and me on to the street to live!'.

'You are talking nonsense, Thomas,' Gina said wearily. 'I know nothing except that you are planning to sell the mill. I talked to Harold Bickley last night.' Sick at heart, drained of emotion, worn out after her long, fruitless trip from New York, the death of her father, the nagging pain of her affair with TJ Power, and with her physical strength at a low ebb, the last thing she needed was a hostile confrontation with her brother.

'Oh, so you talked to Bickley, did you? Wonders will never cease! Pals again, are you, after the rotten trick you played on him?'

Suddenly, Thomas' swaggering attitude struck sparks of anger in Gina. A mental image of a small, bullying child destroying the Bickley girls' sand-castles on the beach at Scarborough invaded her mind. Colour returning to her cheeks, standing tall and proud, she said coldly, 'Sit down, Tom. Stop acting like a child and start behaving like a man.'

Bewildered by the sudden shift in position, he sank down

in his father's chair. This was a Georgina he had never seen before. The presence of the red-haired girl he had always resented seemed to fill the room. Her clothes, though simple, were well cut, of the finest quality, he noticed. Obviously acting was a well paid profession, he thought greedily.

'Tell me, Tom, why do you want to sell the mill? Can't you see that would be like killing the goose that lays the golden egg?'

'A fat lot you know!' His thick underlip protruded in the way it had as a child, when he wasn't getting his own way. 'I hate the mill. I always have. Father treated me like an office boy. He should have retired years ago. But no, not he. He never gave me credit for anything, he didn't even pay me a decent wage. How do you think I felt? The boss's son. A laughing stock more like. Five hundred quid a year he allowed me. I ask you. Five hundred measly quid. How the hell did he expect me to live as a gentleman on that pittance?'

'You mean five hundred pounds apart from your salary?'

'Oh, sure. His idea of a bloody Christmas present!'

Reading between the lines, putting two and two together, Gina guessed the reason for her brother's uncontrolled outburst was his bitterness over money. She said quietly, 'You're in debt, aren't you? Seriously in debt? Don't play games with me, Thomas. I want the truth.'

'It's none of your damned business!'

'That's where you're wrong. That you are about to squander your inheritance is very much my business! Don't be a fool, Tom. Can't you see what will happen if you lose the mill?' Coming to a quick decision, 'How much do you need to pay off your creditors?'

Eagerly wetting his lips, 'Two thousand quid,' he said hoarsely.

'*Two thousand!* My God, Tom. Did Father know?'

'Of course not.' Heatedly, 'He was the last person I could turn to.' Beginning to blubber, 'You don't know what it's been like for me this past year with everyone clamouring for payment, and the interest on the loan mounting up month by month.' Covering his face with his hands, 'Now those loan sharks have threatened me with the bailiffs if I don't pay up by the end of the week.'

Getting out her cheque-book and pen, 'I'll get you out of trouble,' Gina said, 'on one condition.'

Lumbering to his feet, 'I'll do anything you say!'

'Very well, then. You must promise me that you will not sell the mill. You wish to live like a gentleman, now you must act like one. I want your word of honour, as a gentleman, that you will do as I ask.'

'Yes, of course,' Thomas would have promised anything in his desperation to lay hands on the cheque. Light-headed with relief, he stuffed it in his breast pocket.

'Now, I want to see Mother,' Gina said.

Tom smirked. 'You can forget it. She doesn't want to see you.'

'How can you be sure of that?' Impatiently, 'Look, Tom, it's high time this quarrel was laid to rest.'

'Try telling the old girl that.'

'I shall, given the opportunity. Is she in her room?'

'It's no use going up there,' he said quickly. 'She won't see you.' Then, carelessly, 'Oh, what the hell. It's no skin off my nose.' The cheque for two thousand safely in his possession, he couldn't care less about his mother or Gina. 'I'm going out. I have business in Bradford.' He strode from the room.

'Just a minute, Tom. Shall I see you again?'

'Hardly likely, I'd say.' Crossing to the hall cupboard where his outdoor things were kept, he shrugged on his overcoat, put on his trilby. The cheque was not crossed. The sooner he cashed it the better, in case Georgina changed her mind. A warning bell rang suddenly in his head, 'You're not staying on here, are you?'

'Is there any reason why not?' Mistrust of Thomas came uppermost. 'You *will* keep the promise you made me?'

'I gave you my word, didn't I?'

'Yes, of course.'

'About the furniture,' he said magnanimously, 'the

260

contents of Father's study. Anything I can do to help?'
Better keep on the right side of her.

'Thank you, that won't be necessary. Father's solicitor
will make the arrangements.'

'It's not worth much,' Thomas said, opening the
vestibule door.

'It is to me,' Gina said.

'Yes, well, you were always the old man's favourite.' Best
be off now, he thought, before he said too much, before
his hatred of her and that misbegotten bastard of hers came
welling from his mouth once more. But he hadn't finished
with her yet. He was far cleverer than she knew. She would
find out that to her cost when he contested the will. Monies
from the sale of the mill would give him the financial clout
he needed to bring the action to court. In any case, hadn't
he just conned her into giving him a thousand quid more
than he needed to settle his account with the money-
lenders?

'Stop acting like a child and start behaving like a man.'
Georgina's words burned into him as he settled himself
behind the wheel of his father's car and drove recklessly
towards Bradford.

Slowly Gina mounted the stairs towards her mother's room.
The house seemed curiously silent and empty, a mausoleum
rather than a home. Gone were the signs of her mother's
whip-cracking domination. Traces of dust lay on the landing table, the stair-rods had not been polished.

Lightly she tapped her mother's door. There was no
response. She knocked once again. 'Come in,' said a
querulous voice. Gina entered the room.

Agnes was in bed, propped up with pillows. Her formerly
strong, iron-grey hair was white now, and much thinner.
The passage of time and ill-humour had etched her face
with downward strokes. Lines from her nose had linked
up with those at her mouth corners so that the sunken flesh
had formed into dewlaps above the fabric of the high-
necked nightdress she wore. Her hands reminiscent of dried
leaves lay on the coverlet.

Filled with a deep sense of compassion, approaching the bed, 'Mother,' Gina said softly, 'I *had* to come. I so much wanted to see you again.'

'Go away,' Agnes said wearily, turning her face away, plucking at the coverlet with her dried-leaf hands. 'I want Thomas. Where is Thomas?' With a strangled cry, 'He promised to give me my medicine. I need my medicine!'

'Let me give it to you.' Gina looked at the medley of pills and medicine bottles on the bedside table. 'Which do you want?' The thought occurred that Agnes had not the faintest idea who she was or why she had come. The woman in the bed was no longer a force to be reckoned with, but a self-centred invalid who had long since ceased to function as the mistress of the house.

'No, no, not that muck!' Pointing a trembling finger at the wardrobe, 'Over there! Thomas keeps my medicine over there.'

Opening the wardrobe, Gina realized, with a sense of shock, that the half-empty whisky bottle she found there was the 'medicine' with Agnes so desperately craved, supplied by her son.

Strung on the horns of a dilemma, Gina knew that to withhold solace from her mother would be both cruel and fruitless, and so she poured her a small measure of whisky, gave it to her and watched, heartbrokenly, Agnes' eager swallowing of the draught, the subsequent nodding of her head on the pillows as she fell fast asleep, her mouth wide open.

Gina sat beside Agnes for a long time. The scene she had dreaded, a renewed onslaught of her mother's anger, a raking-up of the past, the opening of old wounds, had not happened, but she would have rather faced the old, domineering Agnes than see her as she was now.

Anger welled up in her. How long had Thomas been giving Agnes the drink she craved? The way in which her mother's lips had folded greedily over the rim of the glass told its own story. How could her brother have done such a thing? *Why* had he done it? What had he hoped to achieve by substituting whisky for the medicine which might have done her good?

Getting up, she moved about the room tidying her mother's belongings, folding items of clothing left scattered on the velvet chaise-longue: a dressing-gown, stockings, a whaleboned corset and a bust-bodice. Leaving the dressing-gown where it was, picking up the more intimate garments, she placed them carefully in the top drawer of the dressing chest in which Agnes' undergarments had always been kept among fragrantly scented lavender-bags. Whatever her faults, Agnes Brett-Forsyth had paid scrupulous attention to personal freshness and hygiene. In her right state of mind, she would have never allowed her room to remain undusted, Gina thought. Crossing over to the dressing-table near the window she saw the rose-pattered china ring-stand and powder bowls, and the morocco leather box containing her mother's jewellery, her *lavellière* pearl necklace, sapphire and diamond brooches; pearl, ruby and diamond rings and matching ear-bobs, bracelets, heavy gold chains and pendants.

Opening the box, Gina saw that it was empty of all save a few worthless items of costume jewellery. Here lay the answer to the questions that had teased her mind, the reason why Thomas had relied on the whisky bottle as a means of dulling their mother's intellect to the extent that she would not know about the systematic removal and sale of her jewellery, would not even care as long as she could have the 'medicine' she craved.

Sick at heart, angry beyond belief, she tugged the bell-rope. When the servant appeared, 'I want this room dusted at once,' Gina said coldly.

'Oh, you do, do you? And who are you to give me orders?' the girl said impudently. 'Tom said we weren't to dust in here for fear of disturbing the old girl. Not that she'd know or care. Not in the state she's in.'

'How *dare* you speak to me like that? You know perfectly well who I am! Now, do as I tell you at once, or you may pack your things and leave this house immediately. Is that clear? And while you're about it, you may also dust the rest of the rooms, *and* the staircase. Go, now, and get on with your work!'

In a towering rage, Gina oversaw the cleaning and polishing of the stair-rods, the thorough dusting of the rooms, performed by the three girls in her brother's employ, one of whom – the girl she had confronted earlier – appeared to be the cook-housekeeper, responsible for the preparation and cooking of the food in the kitchen quarters once reigned over by Mrs Crabtree. She discovered, later, her protagonist pouring fatty liquid from a bowl of stock into a saucepan.

The kitchen was filthy, the sink cluttered with a mess of unwashed dishes, the table littered with the remains of breakfast – crumbs of dry, uneaten toast, sticky marmalade and jam-jars, bottles of half-curdled milk, tea-stained cups and saucers, dirty spoons, knives and forks, a bowl of damp, tea-stained sugar.

Oh God, she thought despairingly, how could Thomas have allowed this to happen?

Then, 'What are you doing?' She looked with distaste at the coagulated fat floating on the pale contents of the pan.

'What does it look like?' The girl's cheeks flushed mutinously.

'I asked you a civil question, I expect a civil answer!'

'It's the mistress's lunch. Chicken broth. Not that she'll touch it. She never does,' the girl replied.

'I'm not surprised.' Gina wrinkled her nose in disgust. Crossing quickly to the larder, she found there a cold roast chicken, an uncooked leg of lamb and a muslin-covered dish of plaice fillets.

'Here, what are you doing?'

'What does it look like?' Gina set the dish of plaice fillets on the table, picked up a box of matches, and applied a light to the grill.

'But them fillets is for the master's dinner! You have no right to meddle!'

'I have every right. Now you may hand me that crock of butter, and set your mistress' tray.'

*   *   *

When the fish had been grilled to perfection, Gina went upstairs to her mother's room, carrying the tray.

Agnes, awake now, stared at her daughter with lacklustre eyes as she sat on the edge of the bed and began feeding her morsels of fish and thinly cut bread and butter. The eagerness with which she accepted the food brought tears to Gina's eyes. The poor soul was starving. Lacking proper food and medicine, no wonder she had been reduced to a shadow of her former self.

Gina said softly, compassionately, when Agnes lay back against her pillows, 'Don't worry, Mother. I'm here now. I'll take care of you.'

Tomorrow, Gina decided, she would make the necessary arrangements to have Agnes removed from Elmhurst to a private nursing home in Bradford; from there, when she was fit enough to travel, to Welford House.

To her life's end, Gina would remember that Agnes had said weakly, as she stood on the threshold of her room, 'I'm sorry for all the trouble I've caused you.'

Daylight was fading. There was still no sign of Thomas' return. Gina ordered a taxi to take her back to the Queen's Hotel.

Too tired and upset to confront Thomas for a second time in one day, she would return to Elmhurst the first thing tomorrow morning, she decided. In the meantime, she must contact her father's solicitor and seek his advice regarding her mother's transfer to a nursing home. The terms of Owen's will were far from clear in her mind and she had to be sure of her ground before tackling her brother.

With luck, Mr Caulfield would grant her a private interview after office hours, when she had had time to bathe and change.

At the Queen's, she telephoned Mr Caulfield. Delighted to hear from her, and to save her trouble, he came to dine with her at seven o'clock that evening.

'My dear Georgina,' he said warmly, meeting her in the foyer, 'I had no idea that you were in Bradford until you

265

called.' His face saddened. 'I wish that we might have met in happier circumstances. As you know, I was a lifelong friend of your father. A fine man in every way. I shall miss him more than I can say.'

'So shall I, Mr Caulfield,' Gina said gently, deeply aware of the old man's grief. 'That was the reason why I knew I could turn to you for advice.'

'But of course, anything I can do to help or advise you in any way, I'll be only too pleased,' Caulfield said earnestly, as they made their way to the dining room.

Cock-a-hoop with his day's work, Thomas returned to Elmhurst to face the fury of Ellen's wrath that the fish and the roast leg of lamb she had cooked for his dinner had dried up long ago.

'Where the hell have you been?' she demanded angrily. 'You said you'd be back by six o'clock! It's now half-past ten. Well, I'm telling you here and now, I won't stand for it.'

'Shut your face,' he said foolishly, swaying on his feet, 'you are not the mistress of Elmhurst yet, not by a long chalk. You'd best remember that, Ellen, my girl.'

'And you'd best remember, Mr High and Mighty, that I wasn't born yesterday! It's *your* child I'm carrying, and I know enough about you to put you behind bars.' Her tirade continued, 'As for that bloody sister of yours. I'll get even with her one of these days. Treating me like a bloody skivvy. For two pins I'd have told her about the kid I'm having. But she'll get her come-uppance when she reads our wedding announcement in *The Leeds Mercury*, because I'll send her a copy, the stuck-up bitch.'

Tom's face darkened, his drunken mood switched from amiability to anger. Seizing Ellen's wrist, he twisted it until she cried out with pain. 'You *dare* to threaten me?' he demanded roughly. 'There'll be no wedding announcement. You think I'd marry a slut like you? Especially now!'

Writhing from his grip, pale and trembling yet still determined to have her say, consumed with curiosity, 'What do you mean – especially now?'

266

'Wouldn't you like to know?'

Born and brought up in the back streets of Leeds, possessed of an alley cat's instinct for survival, 'I have a *right* to know,' she screeched wildly, 'after all I've done for you. Letting you paw me whenever you felt like it; landing me in the family way. Oh yes, my fine gentleman, this bulge under my pinny was put there by you, make no mistake about that. And – and – if I'm a slut, you're nowt but a bloody lecher!'

'Oh, go to hell!' Turning on his heels, clutching the edge of the table for support, dizzy and bemused from all the whisky he had consumed, Thomas lurched unsteadily from the kitchen and went upstairs to his room.

Sinking down on his bed, stuffing the pillows beneath his head, loosening his tie, and breathing heavily, he re-lived the triumphant moment when Harold Bickley had bought the Brett-Forsyth Mill. Everything legal and above-board.

They had met that afternoon in the presence of Bickley's solicitor, a hastily contrived meeting convened by Thomas, who had rung Bickley earlier to issue the ultimatum that it was now or never. Clever of him to have thought up that phrase, Thomas considered, feeling in his waistcoat pocket for his cigarettes and matches.

The deal accomplished, he had gone to his favourite pub in Bradford to celebrate, with a group of cronies, the fact that he was now a very rich man, a *very* rich man indeed.

How much he had spent on drink that night, he neither knew nor cared. Cashing the cheque his sister had given him, his wallet was loaded with money. Now he was free, wealthy and independent. Free to travel the world if he so wished. Visions of a new, unfettered life rose up before him. He applied a match to his cigarette and watched, with a kind of hazy delight, the smoke-rings puffed from his thick lips rising towards the ceiling.

Smiling, his eyelids drooped and closed. The lighted cigarette dropped from his fingers on to the floor, a billowing curtain from the half-open window lifted lazily to brush the glowing cigarette butt, a ripple of flame ran up the curtain . . .

* * *

Harold Bickley entered the hotel foyer early next morning. The night porter, about to go off duty, regarded him balefully. 'Now, sir,' he enquired testily, wondering if these toffs had no home to go to, 'what can I do for you?'

Harold said bleakly, 'I must speak to Miss Brett as quickly as possible. It's very urgent.'

'But it's only six o'clock, sir,' the man admonished. 'She'll scarcely welcome being awakened at this hour of the morning.'

'God dammit, man,' Harold muttered angrily, 'do as I ask at once! This is an emergency!'

Until his dying day, Harold Bickley would never forget his night-long vigil on the lawn of Elmhurst; watching the flames from the burning building fan the night sky; the stench of smoke in his nostrils.

He had wakened around midnight to the strange feeling that something was wrong. Getting up, he had put on his dressing-gown and gone to the window to look out. Seeing the lurid glow in the sky, he had hastily pulled on his clothes and hurried out to the car. Firemen were already at the scene, pumping water on to the blaze. It was a scene of confusion, of incredible noise as the men called out to each other above the hiss of the water, the crackling of the fire. Hosepipes snaked and writhed across the lawns, there was the clamour of engines as more fire-fighters arrived on the scene from depots as far removed as Leeds and Wakefield. Screams could be heard from the house as the servants trapped inside cried for help. A safety-net was spread, a woman jumped from a second storey window.

Pushing his way towards her, his thoughts in a turmoil, he saw that she was no more than twenty, pregnant by the look of her, a pitiful sight with smoke-blackened face and streaming eyes, gesticulating wildly towards the house, unable to speak, half demented with terror.

'Get back, man!' Roughly, one of the firemen shouldered him aside. 'Make way for the stretcher bearers!' He had never felt so helpless in his life. 'Can't you see she's trying to tell us something?' he shouted. 'God dammit, I may be able to help. I know this house, the people who live there.'

'You're in the way,' the man said brusquely. The girl had gone into a paroxysm of coughing. A wailing sound, like that of a banshee, emerged from her throat as she fought for breath, a terrible sound, as though her soul was being torn from her body. He watched in fascinated horror as the stretcher bearers lifted her on to the strip of canvas between the shafts, covered her with a blanket, and hurried her to a waiting ambulance.

The fireman said, less brusquely, 'If you have something to say, tell it to the chief. No use telling me, I'm not in charge. Happen you'll find him down there, near the gate, directing operations.'

Hazily, he had turned away from the conflagration, his ears filled with the dreadful hissing and roaring, the crackle of the flames, his eyes smarting from the smoke, his brain reeling with the dreadful possibility that others may still be trying to fight their way out of the burning building, except one person . . . ! Agnes Brett-Forsyth, who would not have strength enough to put up a fight for survival.

Finding the chief of the fire brigade at long last, he blurted out his fears concerning the woman he had once regarded as a courtesy aunt, knowing that nothing else mattered except getting her out of the house.

'You are perfectly sure that Mrs Brett-Forsyth is inside the building?'

'Yes, I am. Absolutely sure.'

Everyone sinned, made mistakes during a lifetime. Harry remembered, with a deep sense of shame, the reason why he had never replied to any of Georgina's letters written to him during the war. The truth was, he had not been involved in the fighting at all. He had spent his time in the army as a junior officer at a headquarters well behind the trenches. A kind of glorified clerk, he thought bitterly, dealing with routine requests for sick or compassionate leave. More disgracefully, he had not wanted to be involved in the fighting.

'I believe that Mrs Brett-Forsyth's son may also be in

269

there,' Harold told the chief. 'His room is on the second floor, his mother's on the first.'

'I see. And what about the servants? How many?'

'I've no idea. The ones I remember have gone now. There used to be a gardener and his son living in a staff cottage to the rear of the house.' Again the helpless feeling enveloped him as the man strode away across the lawn. The thought crossed his mind that he should warn Georgina, tell her what was happening. He couldn't do it. Not yet. What would be the purpose of bringing her here to witness this horror?

Axes were being used now to break down the front door. He could see from a distance the firemen silhouetted against the glare of the flames, and found himself praying that the stairs had not been engulfed by the fire. Never physically brave or imaginative, he realized nevertheless what it must feel like to be trapped in a burning building, blinded by smoke, choking, gasping for air, stumbling helplessly to find a means of escape. Despite the cold night air, his hastily donned clothes clung to his body with trickling rivulets of sweat. He had heard the saying, 'sweating with fear', and knew that the clammy perspiration trickling down his face was fear-induced.

In the chilly night air, he had waited, and prayed, and sweated.

In the early hours, he returned briefly to Merlewood to bathe, shave and put on clean clothes, a dark suit, a collar and tie. In the kitchen he drank a cup of scalding hot tea and wolfed a slice of toast.

Josie came into the room in her dressing-gown. 'What on earth are you doing up at this hour?' she asked. Never had she known Harry to make a pot of tea before, much less toast. 'What's wrong?'

He told her.

When he had gone, Josie sat down at the kitchen table, staring into space, conjuring up memories of happier times before the war, when Elmhurst had been a second home to herself, Harry and Letty; long before bitterness and enmity had changed the pattern of their lives. Strange to think that Elmhurst was no more, a smoking ruin peopled with the ghosts of those who had lived once beneath its roof – Owen Brett-Forsyth, Agnes and Tom. Suddenly, she began to cry.

Chapter Twenty-Two

Harry was in the foyer when Gina came down from her room. She had slept badly; there were brushmarks of weariness beneath her eyes. How to tell her what he had come to say? How to break it to her that her past life, her home, her family had been wiped out in a single night?

Looking into his pale, set face, she knew that he had come to bring her bad news. Harry would scarcely have come to the hotel at this hour unless something untoward had happened.

The porter who had given her the message that a Mr Bickley wished to speak to her urgently, was standing near the reception desk. 'Shall we go to the lounge, Harry?' she said quietly. Turning to the porter, 'May we have some tea, please?' Her concern was for Harold, not herself. She could only think that his father had died suddenly, that she must keep calm for his sake.

When the porter came in with the tray of tea, Gina was sitting upright in an easy chair, her hands lying like pale butterflies in her lap, her face as pale as her hands; eyes fixed on the lightening sky beyond the window, as if fascinated by the dawning of a new day. As though she was sitting very still to have her photograph taken, the man thought, setting down the tray, mumbling his thanks for the pound note the gentleman handed him, telling him to keep the change.

The tea remained untouched, however. Georgie's stillness frightened Harold. He had expected tears, some show of grief or emotion; instead, she seemed frozen, incapable of tears, robbed of speech.

Perhaps he had used the wrong words, had been too hasty or too clumsy in breaking the news to her. He had tried to be gentle, had paved the way by saying that something terrible had happened.

'Is it about your father?' she asked quietly.

Deeply shaken, thrown off his stride, 'No,' he said harshly, 'it's your mother, and Tom.' And then he had blurted out the truth. The trouble was, he had never really understood how to treat women. His motives concerning the opposite sex had been purely selfish, male-orientated. As a child, his male ego had been firmly rooted in the belief that, as the heir apparent of the Bickley mill, he was the most important member of the household. As a boy he had been carelessly patronizing of his sisters' weaknesses. As a man he had failed miserably to father the son he longed for to carry on the Bickley name. Now he had failed as a comforter to the woman who might have become his wife, the mother of his children. He said slowly, 'I must tell you that Tom called a meeting yesterday afternoon.' He paused briefly, uncertain of his ground, unwilling to add to her misery. 'The fact is, I have bought the mill.'

She stirred then, and looked at him. 'So there is really nothing left, is there? Everything my father cherished has gone. *Everything*.'

'Not quite everything,' Harry reminded her. 'He cherished you most of all.'

She said, 'I haven't thanked you for coming, for what you did last night. It must have been terrible for you. Thank you for telling me yourself. I couldn't have borne to hear it from a stranger.' Her lips trembled. 'I'm sorry, I must go now. I . . .' Words failed her. She got up slowly from the chair and laid her hand on the back of it for support.

'Let me help you.' Crossing swiftly towards her, holding her arm, he felt the shaking of her body, as though a throbbing engine deep inside her was tearing her to pieces. Placing his arm about her waist, he led her from the room, shaken by his emotion towards her, as though he too was being torn apart by the overwhelming feeling of compassion which flooded through him like a tide, washing away every vestige of his deeply rooted egoism, false pride, and meanness of spirit.

273

'I'm all right now, Harry,' she said quietly, at the foot of the stairs, laying her hand on the banister. 'I just need to be alone for a little while. You understand?'

'Yes, of course. But if there is anything I can do to help . . .'

'You might contact Mr Caulfield, the solicitor,' she said wearily, 'if it's not too much trouble. He'll know what to do, how to advise me.'

'I'll do everything in my power to help you.' Harry clasped her hand. 'I'll be near you every step of the way.'

Alone in her room, Gina grappled with the horror of what had happened. Her mind seemed incapable of grasping the full extent of the tragedy. She desperately needed Mr Caulfield's help and advice to steer her through the grim days ahead. The old lawyer would know how to set about solving the many legal problems involved in a calamity of this nature. There was bound to be an inquest, an inquiry regarding the start of the fire. But above and beyond these considerations lay a welter of terrifying thoughts and emotions incapable of solution; questions to which there could never be any clear-cut answers.

Nightmare visions of the fire tormented her. Huddled on the bed, her vivid imagination gave rise to pictures of a helpless woman fighting for breath, a young man engulfed in flames, desperately clawing at any means of escape.

That Thomas had gone back on his word, had sold the mill despite his promise, scarcely mattered now that he was dead. Perhaps it was better so. Harold Bickley, she knew, would honour his promise to keep the Brett-Forsyth banner intact in the valley, and take care of the workforce, for her father's sake. She simply prayed that her mother and Tom had died as quickly, as painlessly as possible in that funeral-pyre of burnt-out rubble which had once sheltered the disparate members of the Brett-Forsyth family. But how could she be sure that they *had* died painlessly? And this, she knew, was the burden of doubt that she must carry with her for the rest of her life, along with the many other burdens gathered and shouldered along the way – the death of her father, the abortive ending of her love affairs with Rab Romer and TJ Power.

And yet, she thought, fighting her way back to normality through a nightmare haze of tears and regrets, she still had her son Oliver to love and to care for. 'Oliver!' She spoke his name aloud in the silence of her room, drawing comfort from the thought that nothing could ever destroy the loving relationship between them, that for his sake she must remain strong.

The thought of Oliver remained her lodestar during the dreadful days that followed, the frightening days of the inquest in particular. The boy's future was secure. Her father had seen to that. She clung to little shreds of comfort to make bearable the present ordeal. Her mother had been spared a nursing home, being cared for by strangers, living under a strange roof. Thomas had escaped his creditors, nor would he have to live with the knowledge of what he had done.

Two of the young servant girls had died in the blaze. The third, Ellen, had made a statement to the effect that Tom had come home drunk on the night of the fire. They had quarrelled, and he had gone up to his room in a bad mood. They had been on intimate terms, and she was expecting his child, the statement went on, so she could vouch for his habits. He had invariably smoked cigarettes in bed. On the night of the fire she had smelt smoke and gone to his room. He was in bed, propped up with pillows, fast asleep. The curtains were alight and the room was full of smoke.

She had done her best to rouse him, to no avail. The fire had begun to spread rapidly. She had run upstairs to tell the other girls that the house was on fire, but they had not responded quickly enough to her warning and had been trapped in their rooms on the third floor. She had not gone to Mrs Brett-Forsyth's room on the first floor because of the rapid spread of the fire and the thickness of the smoke. She had found her way to a room on the second floor, smashed a window and called for help. Someone must have reported the fire because the engines began to arrive. The firemen had spread out a net, and she had got out of the window onto a ledge, and jumped.

Unfortunately, the young lady, Ellen Jacklyn, had lost her unborn child, the coroner told the court of enquiry, and she was still in hospital recovering from her ordeal. Her written statement had, however, cleared up the possible cause of the fire, and he was satisfied that it had been started accidentally, not maliciously. He deeply regretted the loss of life, and extended his sympathy to Miss Georgina Brett-Forsyth, the surviving member of a well-known and respected family.

What happened next caught Gina completely off-guard. Leaving the coroner's court on the arm of Mr Caulfield, she had found herself facing a battery of flash-bulb cameras, a horde of newspaper reporters.

'There she is!' Pushing towards her, notebook at the ready, 'Tell me, Miss Brett, how does it feel to play the leading role in a real life drama?' one reporter asked, standing so close that she could smell the beer on his breath.

Jostling for pride of place, pressing in on her, they fired their questions. 'Did you know about your brother and the servant girl?' 'Did you know he was up to his ears in debt?' 'Why weren't you at your father's funeral Miss Brett? Why did you stay at the Griffen until it was over?'

'Gentlemen! This is preposterous!' Caulfield cried out in alarm. 'A totally unwarranted invasion of my client's privacy. I shall protest most strongly to your employers regarding this matter.'

Undeterred, the reporters continued their verbal assault. 'Is it true, Miss Brett, that you were once engaged to marry Harold Bickley? And is it true that you had an illegitimate child by him?'

Covering her face with her hands, Gina stumbled towards the waiting car, pushing her way blindly through the throng of newshounds and photographers, Caulfield's hand on her arm.

*　　*　　*

The morning papers dwelt in detail on the famous actress, Gina Brett's, involvement in the tragic fire which had robbed her of her mother, Mrs Agnes Brett-Forsyth and her brother, Thomas. Lacking factual evidence, the reporters had dealt in damning innuendo. 'When asked if she knew of her brother's liaison with the servant, Ellen Jacklyn, Miss Brett refused to answer,' one of them had written. 'Indeed, Miss Brett seemed disinclined to answer any of the *bona-fide* questions put to her by the gentlemen of the Press, which pre-supposes the most vital question of all – what is she trying to hide? The fact perhaps that although unmarried, she is the mother of a 10-year-old son!'

There followed a verbal account of Ellen Jacklyn's written statement to the court of enquiry, in which she had openly confessed that the child she had aborted as a result of the fire, had been fathered by Thomas Brett-Forsyth, whom she had hoped to marry in the fullness of time, despite his sister's antipathy towards her on the day preceding the fire.

Gina cared nothing for the gutter-press reportage of Ellen Jacklyn's sworn statement from her hospital bed, the flash-bulb photographs of herself on the steps of the coroner's court. All she cared about, and bitterly resented, was the muck-raking over her son, the implication that Oliver had been the result of a love affair which had shattered her happy relationship with her father. 'Why else,' the beer-swilling reporter demanded of the readers, 'should Miss Brett have neglected to attend her father's funeral if they had been on conciliatory terms at the time of his death?' The man had somehow got hold of a copy of her hotel bill, which had been published beneath the headline, 'Actress Goes to Ground as Father is Buried.'

Sick at heart, why had they done this to her, she wondered. Above all, how had this so-called 'gentleman' of the Press known about Oliver, whom she had so far managed to protect from the glare of publicity? Who hated her enough to have brought his existence to the attention of the gutter Press?

*   *   *

Angrily throwing aside the morning papers, facing his wife across the breakfast table, 'My God,' Harold said bitterly, 'how could you have done such a thing?'

'Done what? I don't know what you're talking about,' Susanna replied coolly, buttering a slice of toast.

'You know damn well what I mean! Don't lie to me. It was you who spread this vicious gossip about Georgina. I can guess *why*, but *how* did you do it? Did you go to the newspaper office to blab your filth? Or did you meet the reporter of *The Wakefield Clarion* in some seedy back street pub? You would scarcely have had the guts to write a letter – unless you did so anonymously. Yes, of course, that's how it was done. You wouldn't have had the common decency or the courage to sign your name.'

Rising strongly to her feet, leaning towards him, her hands outspread like talons on the table; face contorted, 'Yes!' she spat out, 'I *did* write a letter. Why not? How do you think I felt watching you make a bloody fool of yourself over that woman? It was *you*, remember, who told me that she was an unmarried mother, the night you came home late and dared to tell me that you had spent the evening with the red-haired bitch!'

She laughed scornfully. 'How innocent you made it all sound! God, Harry, what a pathetic worm you are. I suppose you imagined that filling in every detail of your conversation would blind me to what really went on between you. It's an old ploy, Harry, but it didn't work with me. I could sense your excitement, your guilt. I knew that this was the thin end of the wedge, and I was right. The night of the fire, the next day, and every day since then, you have been with *her*, not *me*. Even when you were lying beside me in bed, I knew what you were thinking and feeling. You didn't care tuppence about me. But I'm your *wife*! I did what any woman would have done in the circumstances. Everything I wrote in that letter to *The Wakefield Clarion* was the truth. In my opinion, your fine friend Gina Brett is nothing more than a common or garden slut!'

Harry struck, and struck hard. The impact of the blow

across her face with the flat of his hand sent her reeling backwards against a side-table. 'Get out! Get out of my house,' he said hoarsely, sweeping aside cups, plates and cutlery, 'before I choke the bloody life out of you. I mean what I say. Pack your things and go. *Now!*'

When she had gone from the room, weeping and trembling, he put on his outdoor things and drove to the mill. The morning was fresh and fair. Seated at the wheel of the car, he felt suddenly calm and free, a man in charge of his own destiny at last.

Thinking clearly, he knew that his love for Georgina would never be reciprocated, that their destinies lay poles apart, and yet . . . It pleased him to think that in keeping alive the Brett-Forsyth Mill for her sake, and her father's, he would retain a special place in her heart; that he had done something worthwhile for a change, had made up for his sins and omissions of the past.

The breeze from the open window brushing his face, he breathed in the scent of the valley, the tang of rich loam and wind-rippled grass and saw, rising from that rich earth, the solid stones and the tall chimney stacks of the two great mills of which he was now the master.

He had not meant to attack Susanna. His temper had got the better of him. No doubt she would make him pay dearly for his physical abuse of her. He did not care. Their marriage had been a mistake from the start. She had been an evil influence at Merlewood. His father, Josie and the servants would rejoice at her departure. Now he would be free to support Georgina on the day of the funeral, to stand firmly by her side when her mother and Tom were laid to rest, and to hell with what the 'gentlemen' of the Press read into their relationship.

Georgina had never looked more beautiful, he thought, than she had done then – dressed all in black – standing erect in the Merlewood churchyard, her face as pale as ivory, her emerald green eyes sparkling with tears beneath the veil of her close-fitting hat.

Harry wondered what she was thinking as the parson intoned the words of the burial service, and the many people who had come to pay a last tribute to the wife and son of Owen Brett-Forsyth gathered together beneath the rustling leaves of the great elm tree near the gate.

Gina thought how beautiful the sunlight looked streaming down through the branches of the tree, dappling the ground beneath with moving prisms of light. Those facets of light would continue to shine down in constantly changing patterns for as long as the tree existed, through many a coming springtime and summer, in winter, even, on those bitterly cold days when the sun stained the sky above the smoky valley with its pure, clear light.

Drawing comfort from the simple evidence of life after death in the springing daisies about her feet, the continuation of life in the singing of the birds above, the fact of Oliver's existence after the death of Poppy, she stepped forward to scatter flowers on the coffins, firm in the belief that her mother and Tom were free now of their earthly cares, no longer in bondage to the violent emotions, the greed, the fruitless ambitions, the lust, the false pride and the petty jealousies which had marred both their lives.

And yet, as she scattered the flowers, and silently repeated her inward litany of hope, Gina knew that later would come an outpouring of the held-back tears, a period of utter loneliness and despair when the funeral was over, when she was alone in her room at the Queen's Hotel, packing her suitcase in readiness for her return to London.

Harold Bickley would remember, jealously, the stranger who had entered the churchyard after the scattering of the flowers – a tall, distinguished-looking man – to whom Gina had turned with a glad cry of recognition, 'Oh, James! I'm so pleased to see you!' A man who, enfolding her in his arms, had led her gently towards his chauffeur-driven limousine parked on the Merlewood village green.

Chapter Twenty-Three

James Adley had received news of Gina through Madame Gautier, whom he had met by chance in Bond Street. Accepting his luncheon invitation, she confirmed his suspicions that all was not well.

Using her hands expressively, 'The poor child,' Madame said, 'to have had her Broadway début snatched away from her so abruptly was too cruel!' Sir James listened intently. 'Such a waste of time and effort,' Giselle went on. 'If only she had been in time to see her father before he died. She was grief-stricken when I spoke to her on the telephone.' Madame shook her head sadly. 'God alone knows how she must be feeling now in face of this new tragedy. I heard it from Bridget Donovan.'

'What new tragedy?'

'Her home burned to the ground. Her mother and her brother died in the fire. She has lost every member of her family, the poor darling. And that wretched man let her travel home alone. I shall never forgive him for that.'

'You mean TJ Power?'

Giselle's eyes flashed angrily. 'His place was with Gina. He should not have remained in New York. What possible excuse could there be for such ungentlemanly behaviour? But then, he has always been a law unto himself. Charming, yes, when he feels like it. But ruthless, even calculating at times. Have you not felt this also?'

Sir James refused to be drawn on the subject. Giselle scarcely noticed his silence. Lowering her voice, 'As for those dreadful reporters, how could they have treated her so badly? What had she done to deserve all that muck-raking? Bridget Donovan was in tears on the telephone when she told me what had been said about Gina in some disgusting rag of a newspaper.'

Deeply shocked, James Adley knew that he must go to Gina at once, and laid his plans accordingly.

How James had come to be there when she needed him most, Gina had no idea, nor had she been aware how much she needed him until she saw him at the church gate.

Inviting him to the reception at the Queen's Hotel, she had introduced him to her guests as they came into the private room she had engaged for the occasion, and he had been gravely courteous towards them, imparting a feeling of confidence to face this ritual of the funeral-meats which tradition demanded of the bereaved.

Aware of his comforting presence, she had managed to push to the back of her mind the reason why so many old friends and colleagues of her father were gathered together in this stuffy room to sip sherry and eat the cold food she had ordered.

Making polite, meaningless conversation with people whose faces she scarcely recognized, Gina knew that Harry resented James Adley's presence at the reception, and guessed why. Poor dear Harry. But she had meant what she said when she told him not to let present circumstances blind him to reality. She had come to value his friendship more than she could say, but she was no more in love with him now than she had been that May morning long ago when, picking up the skirts of her wedding dress, she had left him standing at the altar.

Even so, she had promised not to leave the West Riding without saying goodbye to him. Honouring that promise, when the reception was over, holding his hands in hers, 'Goodbye, Harry,' she murmured, her eyes bright with tears. 'Thank you for everything. The future of the Brett-Forsyth Mill is in your hands now, and I'm glad.'

He said hoarsely, 'Sir James Adley! Tell me, Georgina, are you in love with him?'

Startled, 'Love doesn't enter into it,' she said quickly, defensively. 'All I want now is peace of mind, time to come to terms with the past and decide what to do about the future. James Adley is my friend, nothing more. Believe me,

282

Harry, the last thing I need right now is to bother about love!'

Upturning the palms of her hands, kissing each in turn, Harry murmured, 'Goodbye, Georgie,' and hurried away.

No sooner had he gone than a tall, good-looking man came up the steps towards her. 'Miss Georgina,' he said, pulling off his cap, 'I had to see you, to tell you how sorry I am about what's happened.'

'Peter! Peter Dickenson,' Gina cried warmly, shaking his hand, 'I wondered what had become of you and your father.'

'Aye, well, Mr Thomas gave us the sack after the master died.' He spoke without rancour. 'It came as a bit of a shock to Dad, but Mr Owen left us a nice bit of money. It was leaving the cottage that upset him, but like he said, he's neither use nor ornament these days.'

'And what about you, Peter? Have you found other employment?'

'Nay, not yet, but I'm on the look out.' He grinned awkwardly.

'I want to thank you for keeping in touch with Bridget,' she said. 'I wouldn't have known that my father was so ill if it hadn't been for you.'

'I only did what was right and proper. I knew how much the master meant to you.'

The passing years had added stature to Peter Dickenson. The angular frame of the boy she remembered so well, who had driven her to church that May morning, had fleshed out and broadened considerably, yet remained trim, hard-muscled, energetic. But despite his boyish smile, his air of self-confidence, Gina guessed that he was deeply worried, as he might well be with an ageing father to care for, and with no firm prospect of future employment.

'Tell me, Peter,' she said quietly, 'where are you living now, you and your father?'

'Oh, we're lodging with a lady in Greenfield Street. She looks after us pretty well on the whole.'

Gina knew the street he mentioned – a row of terraced houses in a seamy area of the town – gardenless, with small yards to the rear. Poor old Adam Dickenson, who had lived for the Elmhurst garden and the greenhouses where he had pottered happily, nurturing seedlings for the kitchen garden and bringing on the great batches of luscious, red-gold tomatoes and green and purple grapes to grace the dining-table, would hate the confines of the house in Greenfield Street.

She said briskly, 'You may be just the person I'm looking for.' She spoke convincingly, 'I am sadly in need of a gardener-cum-handyman at my house in London.' Opening her handbag, 'Here is my card. Of course I should also need your father's help, if he would consider coming with you.'

Peter said carefully, 'Thanks, Miss Georgina, but you don't really need us, do you? You're just being kind, like your father before you.'

'You are wrong, Peter, if that's what you think. I need you and Adam more than I can say. Far more, perhaps, than you need me!'

'In that case, miss, I'll ask Dad, and let you know, if that's all right.' Squaring his shoulders, 'It'll be just like the old days, won't it?' Putting on his cap, he walked away with sunlight in his step, revitalized with a renewed sense of purpose in life.

When the trauma of the funeral and the reception were over, after Gina had slept for a little while, had bathed, changed and walked with him to the dining-room, 'I want you to come with me to Scotland, to Craiglachan,' James said.

'But that's impossible. I must go back to London.'

'Why?' he asked imperturbably. 'Your son is at school and you, my dear, are in need of a holiday, a complete change of scenery.' He added persuasively, 'Craiglachan is very quiet, very beautiful at this time of the year. You would find peace there, and solitude, not to mention an old friend of yours, Daisy Crabtree.'

'*Daisy?*' Gina smiled reflectively, feeling more relaxed than she had done since the fraught moment when, standing alone on the deck of the *Berengaria* she had seen the lights of Manhattan Island fast fading into a dim and dusky twilight, as though the vast city of New York had ceased to exist, as if the bright lights of Broadway had been swallowed up and extinguished by the dark waters washing against the sides of the ship.

In going with Sir James Adley to Craiglachan, what had she to lose that had not already been lost beyond her power of recall? Remembering she had told Harold Bickley that all she wanted now was peace of mind, time to come to terms with the past and decide what to do about the future, 'Very well, James,' she said quietly. 'I will go with you to Craiglachan.'

There was something she needed to do, she told James early the next morning, after they had breakfasted and their luggage stowed away in the boot of the car.

'Please, my dear, I think that would be unwise of you,' he said quietly. 'To see the place, as it is now . . . Wouldn't it be better to remember it as it used to be?'

'You don't understand. I need to see Elmhurst just once more.' How to explain that this final look at the house was necessary to her peace of mind? Akin to the bringing down of the curtain on the closing night of a play. Otherwise, she would go through life regretting that she had lacked the courage to look upon the ruins of her childhood home, had not paid silent tribute to all that it had meant to her father, his father before him, and old Thomas Brett-Forsyth who had built the house.

James waited in the car as she walked to the gate and stood there silently for a little while, staring at the ruins. Curiously, some of the chimneys remained standing, parts of the roof, and the solidly built entrance with its shattered front door. There were even tentacles of ivy clinging to the stonework in places, she noticed. Most of the windows of the ground floor rooms remained intact, as if the fire, surging upwards, had chosen what and what not to destroy as the flames fanned out against the night sky.

'Goodbye, my dear ones,' she whispered. Then, turning

away from the scene of destruction, she walked back to the car, to the comforting warmth of the travelling rug James tucked about her legs. The chauffeur nosed the shining bonnet of the limousine down the long road overlooking the Calder Valley.

I shall never come here again, she thought, as the morning sun bathed the valley with its pale, clear light. It would be better so.

Craiglachan, with its heavily slated roof and dunce-cap towers, set among rolling hills, appealed strongly to Gina. Possibly the austerity of the house, which remained much as James' father had left it, touched a chord of response in her present need of solitude.

There was a solidity and strength about the great rooms which she found comforting. Craiglachan, like Elmhurst, had been built to withstand the elements, and she could understand why an old man, tired of the world, had chosen this place as a retreat. But how remote and unfriendly it must have seemed to James' wife, a beautiful woman, forced by illness to accept her removal from the London she loved.

At dinner James sketched in something of his father's background. They were seated at one end of the long refectory table. A log fire burned in the massive stone fireplace. Candlelight cast flickering shadows on the tapestry-hung walls. 'Father loved this house,' he said. 'Of course it was far too big for him, but he found peace of mind here after the death of my mother.'

He smiled. 'Twice a year, at Christmas and the grouse-shooting season, he would invite the tenant farmers and their families, the vicar and the water bailiffs to a party. Otherwise, he remained pretty much a loner, content with his books and music. I think you'd have liked him. He would certainly have liked you.'

'Oh. Why?'

'He admired beautiful, talented women. Mother was both, which is why he adored her. When she died, he couldn't face living in London without her.' He paused. 'This I understand. I dreaded returning to the house in

286

Eaton Square after Caroline died. Oh, I used to stay there on business trips to Town, but that was different. I used the house as a *pied à terre*. It was when I returned to London, after the funeral, that loneliness struck me so devastatingly. It was hard, trying to pick up the pieces. There were times when I almost decided to come back here to Craiglachan, to live in seclusion like my father before me. I'm glad now that I did not. Otherwise, I would not have met you.'

'I'm so sorry about your wife.' She didn't know what else to say.

'And I'm sorry about TJ Power. Giselle Gautier told me he had decided to stay on in New York.'

'Yes. Apparently he reached that decision after a meeting with his ex-wife.'

'You mean that he has gone back to her?' James drew in an imperceptible breath of relief. Realizing that he had fallen deeply in love with Gina, he had regarded TJ Power as a stumbling block to their relationship.

'It's for the best. You see, he had never really stopped loving her.'

'You are very understanding,' James said.

'Not really. We quarrelled rather bitterly I'm afraid.'

Looking across the table at her, dwelling on the loveliness of her face, and knowing he wanted Gina for his wife, James also knew that this was neither the time nor the place to disclose his feelings towards her. He must give her time to come to terms with the tragic loss of her family.

He said gently, 'You must be very tired, my dear. I suggest that you have breakfast in bed tomorrow morning; stay in your room for as long as you wish. I shall not disturb you in any way.'

Going upstairs to her room, how kind he was, how generous and understanding, she thought, glad of the warm fire in the grate, the flowers on the dressing table, the books on the bedside table, the lavender-scented sheets and pillowcases, the billowy eiderdown on the tester bed where she lay down to sleep.

But sleep would not come.

Staring up at the ceiling, she remembered sitting beside

her father in the Alhambra Theatre on her fourteenth birthday; playing on the beach at Scarborough with the Bickley children; the horror of the war years; working at the mill as her father's secretary. No easy option, when her fingers had often felt too cold and stiff to hit the right keys of the typewriter, and she had hurried to work down roughly cobbled streets, her breath whirling away like smoke in the icy, sleet-laden air.

Then came memories of the recent past, so terrible that she could scarcely breathe for the lump in her throat, the tight feeling of misery in her chest. With a conscious effort of will, she turned her mind to her first meeting with Poppy Hewitt; saw in her mind's eye that saucy, wide-eyed face of hers, her all-embracing smile; the battered straw hat she wore at a rakish angle atop her mane of dark brown hair.

She thought then of Rab, who had been her first love, and remembered the first time she had seen him standing there in his studio, that slow-dawning smile of his . . . Rab, who had coloured her life with his presence, who had painted, on the canvasses of memory, unforgettable pictures of what it felt like to be young and in love. So in love that everything following his sudden departure from her life had seemed lacking in substance.

There had been other men in her life since then, whom she had met during the course of her career. Actors, theatre managers, playwrights, who had invited her to dine with them occasionally, none of whom she had cared for very deeply. Men who had sought her company for a variety of reasons, mainly because she was an actress. Some she had found interesting simply because they were part of the theatre background, and spoke her language. Others she had dismissed abruptly when it became clear they had much in common with that office Romeo, Basil Petch.

All these brief encounters had led to a longing for one man capable of filling the empty space in her heart.

Awake early next morning, she walked alone in the grounds of Craiglachan. Birds were singing in a spinney of larches near a burn of clear, bubbling water. Young bracken curled about her feet. The air was like wine. James had suggested having breakfast sent up to her room, but she could not have borne to stay in bed a moment longer.

Returning to the house, she made her way to the kitchen where Daisy Crabtree was busily engaged in making porridge.

'I thought I'd find you here,' Gina said softly, strangely comforted by the presence of her friend.

'Oh, Miss Georgina!' Turning away from the stove, leaving the porridge to take care of itself, Daisy held out her arms. 'My precious girl! My lamb. There now, don't cry. Daisy's here to look after you.'

In a little while, holding Gina at arm's length, 'But how thin you are. Why, there's scarcely a picking on you. No wonder, after all you've been through. Sit down, I'll make you something to eat in two shakes of a lamb's tail.'

'Thank you, but I'm not hungry.'

'Of course you're hungry! You're starving. Anyone with two ha'porth of sense could see that. What you mean is, you can't swallow properly for the lump in your throat. I know. I couldn't face food for a month after my sister died, but that's no way to go on. You must keep your strength up. See this nice fresh egg? Well, I'm going to whisk it up, add a knob of butter, a touch of pepper and salt, a dash of cream, cook it slowly, and you are going to eat every mouthful. You'll see, it will slide down a treat.'

Daisy hovered like a hawk as Gina ate slowly, albeit painfully, the scrambled egg she had prepared for her. 'There's a good girl,' she said, when the last mouthful had been swallowed. 'Now I'll make you a slice of hot buttered toast and a pot of tea . . . Feeling better?'

'Much better! Thank you, Daisy.'

'Look, love, for what it's worth, Sir James Adley is a very nice man. A gentleman. You have nothing to worry about on that score. He'll not make a nuisance of himself, if that's what's worrying you.'

'I wouldn't have come here had I believed otherwise,' Gina said.

'No, I'm sure you wouldn't. But watch out for that

daughter of his, Miss Leonora. Just bear in mind she worshipped the ground her mother walked on.'

Ten days later, at Gina's request, James drove her to Edinburgh to refurbish her wardrobe.

There she bought Harris tweed skirts, warm twinsets, leather walking shoes, a fine wool dress; jumpers for Oliver, Cairngorm brooches for Bridget and Daisy, a silk scarf; a set of gold cufflinks for James, which she handed to him over lunch at the Cockburn Hotel.

'My way of thanking you for all your kindness to me,' she said quietly, as he opened the package.

That evening, she came down to dinner wearing the wool dress. The rich caramel colour suited her to perfection. She smiled, noticing he was wearing the cufflinks.

After dinner, they relaxed in deep leather armchairs flanking the drawing-room fire, and drank their coffee by fire and lamp-light. Gina, he noticed, was smiling slightly as she watched the flickering tongues of flame lapping the pine logs on the hearth.

'What are you thinking?' he asked.

'Oh, just how much this holiday has meant to me. How grateful I am that you invited me here at a time when I badly needed help and support.'

Knowing the time for truth had arrived, he said carefully, 'You realize, of course, that I should like nothing better than to help and support you for the rest of my life?' His eyes met hers. 'I am asking you to marry me.'

'Marry you? But I . . .' Her smile faded. 'I'm not in love with you.'

He smiled ruefully. 'I know that, but we have a great deal in common, and I would never stand in the way of your career. Besides which, I am very much in love with you, and I think I'd make you a good husband.'

'Of that I have no doubt. But would I make you a good wife?' Her hands trembled as she set down her coffee cup and saucer.

'That is for you to decide. All I can possibly say is, I love you with all my heart. I loved you the first moment I saw you on-stage as St Joan. I loved you even more that evening I stood beside you watching the twilight deepen over Eaton Square. I love you to the extent that, if you married me, I should want children by you. Make no mistake, my darling, I should want you in every way that a man could possibly want a woman. Fully, and forever.'

Had he made a movement towards her at that moment, had he attempted to hold her, to kiss her, she might have reacted very differently towards his proposal. She could not have borne physical contact with any man just then, smarting as she was from the memory of her brief liaison with TJ Power in a hotel bedroom; her much deeper, hidden memories of Rab Romer.

But this man was by no means an insecure human being whose moods changed as easily as the wind swayed a weathercock. James Adley would make any woman a perfect husband. His caring attitude towards his late wife, the depth of his intellect, his charm, his bearing, could not be faulted. Besides which, she owed him a debt of gratitude for the way he had taken care of her since the day of the funeral.

Being totally honest, 'I don't love you, James,' she said slowly, 'but I *do* care for you.'

'Enough to marry me?'

She saw, by firelight, the look of love in his eyes, and thought of all he had to offer her, not only a proud name, security, a shared love of art, music, the theatre, but tenderness and understanding.

In a clear moment of perception, she knew that she needed, in particular, his understanding, that she cared for him enough to share her life with him, to bear his children. Painfully relinquishing her past memories, holding out her hands to him, 'Yes, James,' she said.

He drove her to a jewellers in Edinburgh to choose her engagement ring, an Aladdin's cave of shining gems; diamond and sapphire necklaces, emeralds, rubies; ropes of milky pearls. The pads of blazing solitaire diamond rings, half-hoops and clusters, held no appeal for her. Finally she chose a square-cut emerald for its colour and simplicity.

'You're quite sure this is the one you want?'

'Yes. It's lovely.' She held out her hand to admire the ring.

'Shall we choose the wedding ring?' James asked. Gina shook her head. 'Not today.'

'Just as you wish, my dear.'

'I'll wait outside for you.'

A thin rain was falling. A plume of grey smoke billowed upward as a train entered Waverley Station. Mist shrouded the battlements of the castle on the hill. People were putting up umbrellas. She heard a newspaper seller shouting his wares: 'Famous conductor attacked by Fascists'.

Buying a paper, she read with horror that Maestro Arturo Toscanini had been beaten for refusing to play the Fascist anthem 'Giovanezza' at a festival in Bologna. The attack had taken place outside the theatre attended by high officials of the Fascist movement. The maestro's passport had been confiscated, and he had been placed under house arrest.

'My dear, what is it? What's wrong?' James hurried to her side. She handed him the paper. 'How could such a thing have happened?' Her lips trembled. 'I thought we had seen an end to such barbarism.'

'An end? I'm afraid not. This could be a new beginning,' he said grimly.

His words sent a chill of fear through her. 'You don't think there could be another war?'

'I think it highly likely there will be, the way things are going,' he admitted.

She had accepted James' ring, but she would not agree to a formal announcement of their engagement until Leonora and Oliver had been brought into the picture. The fear that Leonora may not take kindly to her father's remarriage lay at the back of her mind. Nor did she wish Oliver to be handed a *fait accompli*.

She had no reason to suppose that her son would not

292

take to James, but she had to be sure. When she explained, James said, 'I promise you, my darling, that Leonora will not stand in the way of our happiness. Why should she? She is grown up now, living her own life in London. As for Oliver, possibly he could spend some time with us during the half-term vacation? You say he's artistic, interested in books, so he would probably enjoy a visit to my publishing house.'

'Yes, I'm sure he would, but—'

'Look, darling, if it will make you feel happier, I'll telephone Leonora, arrange a meeting when we return to London.'

'And – if she doesn't take to me?'

He said, with a touch of impatience, 'Of course she'll take to you! Why ever not? Leo's a sensible girl. I'm sorry, darling, it's just that I'd like you to take a more positive attitude towards our marriage.'

Gravel spurted beneath the wheels of Leonora's sports car as she savagely applied the brakes. Dark hair ruffled by the breeze, eyes blazing, she ran up the steps of Craiglachan. Barging unceremoniously into the hall, she tugged viciously at the bell-rope near the fireplace. An elderly manservant appeared in answer to her summons.

'Miss Leonora,' he said in bewilderment. 'I had no idea you were expected.'

'I'm not,' she retorted brusquely. 'See to my luggage, will you? Before you go, my father has a house-guest, I believe. Where is she?'

'In her room, I imagine.'

'Which room?'

'The Stuart Room, Miss.' Deeply shocked by her incivility, he turned his back on her. Never before, during his twenty-years' service at Craiglachan, had he been spoken to in such a fashion.

Taking the stairs two at a time, Leonora arrived, panting, at the door of the Stuart Room. Not bothering to knock, she flung open the door to find Gina seated at the dressing table, brushing her hair.

Startled, Gina stared at the dishevelled figure confronting her. 'Who are you? What do you want?' She rose hurriedly to her feet.

'Can't you guess? I am Leonora Adley. And you are the calculating bitch who thinks she can take the place of my mother! Well, you're wrong. You can't.'

'You don't know what you are saying!' Gina backed away slightly.

'Oh, don't I? Well, I know your sort. Ha. I see you're wearing an engagement ring. My father's ring, no doubt! Tell me, how many times did you have sex with him before you managed to persuade him to marry you?' She laughed bitterly. 'I imagine he was mad for it after all the years he'd gone without it.'

'You must be mad to even suggest such a thing,' Gina said, deeply shaken.

'No, Miss Brett, I am not mad. *You* are, if you think I'll stand by and watch him making a bloody fool of himself over some second-rate actress.'

'*Leo!*'

The girl turned at the sound of her father's voice.

'I'm glad you're here,' she cried unashamedly, 'to hear what I have to say to this – this—'

'Be silent! How dare you behave in such a fashion? You will apologize at once to Miss Brett.'

'Apologize for speaking the truth? I've been making enquiries about her. I called her second-rate and she is, morally speaking. I can't vouch for what she does on-stage, never having witnessed a performance. It's the way she performs off-stage that gets me. Look at these!' She flung down a handful of newspaper cuttings on the dressing table. 'She's an unmarried mother. Did you know that? She's using you to give her bastard a name. *Our* name.'

'*Enough!*' Eyes blazing, Gina flung down the brush she'd been holding with such force that a perfume bottle went spinning, splintering a cut-glass tray. In a towering rage, she took a step towards Leonora, her anger unleashed by the use of the word bastard in connection with Oliver. Oliver who meant more to her than James Adley ever could.

She knew that now. She must have been out of her mind to have even thought of settling for second best; marrying a man she was not in love with for the sake of her son, because she had wanted him to have a father-figure to relate to.

Snatching off her engagement ring, she flung it down amid the welter of broken glass. 'Let's get this straight, shall we, Miss Adley,' she said in a clear, ringing voice. 'Your family name does not interest me. Your reference to my son as a bastard *does*! Oliver is mine by adoption. His real mother was a far greater lady than you'll ever be. How dare you have burst into my room to lay tongue to all that filth about sexual intercourse between myself and your father? By what right did you come here to assault me verbally with your lies and innuendo?'

'Gina,' James said in a shocked tone of voice, 'I'm sure Leo didn't mean what she said.'

'Oh no? She meant every word of it, this "sensible" daughter of yours, who came here for the sole purpose of making trouble. I congratulate her. She has succeeded, beyond her wildest dreams, in bringing me to the realization that I have, thank God, my own life to live, that my future lies in my own hands from now on.'

Turning abruptly, 'Now, if you will accord me the courtesy of leaving my room, I have some packing to do.'

'Gina!' James interposed quickly. 'You can't leave like this!'

'Oh, can't I? Just watch me.'

Leonora laughed unpleasantly. 'God, what a performance. All we need now are the violins. Can't you see what she's up to? She'll ask you to drive her to the station. There she'll frame you into a tender reunion. The next thing you know, that bloody engagement ring will be back on her finger, there'll be a quick, quiet wedding ceremony in Craiglachan Church, she'll be Lady Adley, and I'll be the villain of the piece. I just hope, Daddy, that your conscience, and hers, won't get the better of you when you walk past Mummy's grave.'

Gina smiled grimly. 'Bravo, Miss Adley. Remind me to

give you an introduction to Tyrone Guthrie. You'd make a wonderful Katharina in *The Taming of the Shrew*!' She continued packing. 'Now, James, would you be kind enough to telephone for a taxi to drive me to Edinburgh.'

'Gina,' he said helplessly, 'for heaven's sake be reasonable. You too, Leo.'

Turning to look at him, deeply aware of his distress, unable to switch off her feelings towards him in a matter of seconds, and knowing at the same time that their brief, romantic interlude was over and done with, she said, 'Please, James, do as I ask. Can't you see that there could never be any kind of future for us now? We are poles apart. We always were. In one sense I am grateful to Leonora for reminding me how little I have to gain from becoming your wife.'

Her towering rage had abated now. She simply felt sick at heart that another affair had ended so disastrously. 'Just one more thing, before you go. Would you send Daisy Crabtree to see me?'

'Of course,' James replied.

When Daisy came to her room, 'It's all over,' Gina said briefly. 'I'm going home, to London. The reason I asked to see you is that I should like you to come to me, one of these days, when you're tired of Craiglachan.'

'Truth to tell, Miss Georgina,' Daisy admitted, 'I've been sick and tired of it for some time past. It's a dead house, nowadays, without my lady. Oh, don't get me wrong, I've nothing against Sir James, but it was my lady I really cared for. When she died, things were never the same for me.' She added grimly, 'As for that daughter of theirs, I can't think who she takes after. Not her mother, that's for sure.' Puckering her forehead, 'I'm sorry, in a way, that you're leaving, but I can't say I'm surprised. If you'll forgive my saying so, it seems so unfair that you have never found the right man to make you happy. God knows you deserve to be happy after all you've been through.'

'So you will remember, Daisy, that you'll always have a home with me?'

Kissing Gina warmly, throwing her arms about her, 'I will that! In fact, I'd pack my duds right now and come with you. But that wouldn't be fair on Sir James. I'll have to stay on here until he finds someone to replace me.' She smiled awkwardly. 'That's only right and proper, isn't it?'

'Yes, Daisy, it is. Well, I must go now. The taxi's waiting.'

Slowly, with dignity, without a backward glance, Gina left Craiglachan.

London. Maytime. Homecoming. And yet the cold, empty feeling of loss lay at the core of Gina's heart.

Landis had found her a new agent, hopefully a more reliable agent than TJ Power. Even so, she missed Power from the pattern of her life, as she missed her father and James Adley.

Oliver, thank God, would soon be home for the summer vacation. In the meanwhile, she wrote him long, affectionate letters, and walked alone in the garden at dusk, catching the fragrance of the herbs she had planted in memory of Poppy, longing for – she scarcely knew what.

Her new agent, Charles Prendergast, had arranged an audition for her in a revival of Ibsen's *Ghosts* at the Adelphi Theatre, in which she would appear, if successful, opposite an exciting new actor, John Gielgud.

Leaving his office, she walked past Grosvenor Square towards the Bond Street restaurant where she had arranged to meet Giselle Gautier for lunch. The pavements were crowded. So crowded that, had she not been forced to sidestep the tide of humanity flowing about her, she might never have noticed the gallery, the window, the grey silk drapes, the exhibition of paintings in the window, the raw, almost crude vitality of those paintings of men at work in a Cornish tin mine. Might never have seen the 'Not for Sale' notice attached to the easel on which was mounted the portrait of a girl with red hair. The artist, Robert Romer's 'Portrait of Gina'.

The gallery was equally crowded. People were studying

intently the pictures on display, some standing back a little to catch the overall effect of paint on canvas. A kind of energy emanated from the subject matter, men engaged in hard physical labour. One could feel the driving force necessary to the hewing of rock. It was all there, depicted in the straining forearm muscles, the beads of sweat on their faces, the weariness of the eyes underscored by lines of fatigue, a sense of hopeless dedication to a task which filled neither their own bellies nor those of their children.

The brushwork was marvellous, colours necessarily understated except where the artist had added touches of light, from lantern or candleglow, to illuminate the faces and figures of the miners, The composition of the paintings was outstandingly brilliant, a symphony of movement within a confined space as the artist had portrayed their every stance and posture: the turn of a head to ease aching neck muscles, the arching of the back to mitigate the strain of prolonged bending, so that one understood the misery, the pain of confinement underground – and something more, the strength and comradeship of those men, portrayed in a glance, a half smile, the outstretching of a hand with dirty fingernails.

Only Rab could have painted these pictures. Only he could have imbued each canvas with so much life, reality and compassion, Gina thought as she entered the gallery, her heart no longer empty but filled with renewed hope and joy, as though she had travelled a long, hard road towards this, her journey's end, feeling now as she had done long ago when she had hurried up the stairs to his studio to find him there smiling, awaiting her coming. 'Journeys end in lovers' meetings,' she thought, edging her way through the crowd towards a group of newspaper reporters and photographers clustered in a knot about the man she longed to see again after the empty years without him.

A table had been set with sherry glasses and *canapés*, at the far end of the room, behind which hovered a wine waiter. There was a tall, iron flower-holder from which cascaded an arrangement of hot-house blooms. An elegantly dressed man, presumably the gallery owner, was talking to a woman wearing an écru lace two-piece costume surmounted with a wide-brimmed, pink straw hat.

She saw Rab in profile at first. He was talking to the reporters, ill-at-ease in these surroundings. Sensing his restlessness, Gina realized that he had not changed all that much during the past years. Despite the grey strands in his still abundant crop of dark hair, and the fact that he had lost weight, he still possessed that air of bottled up energy and awareness she remembered so well.

Standing at the back of the crowd, she knew that her feelings towards him had not changed. Looking at him, she experienced all the long-suppressed emotions of the studio days in Scarborough, an outflowing of love as valid now as it had been then.

Her mind raced towards the moment when, alone together, she would confess to him how much she still loved him, when she would tell him about Oliver. She might have known that things were never that simple.

The photographers were now moving in on him, cameras poised. The gallery owner said, in a clear voice, 'Just a moment, gentlemen! Mrs Romer wishes to be photographed with her husband.' Holding out his hand to the woman in the écru lace dress and jacket, he led her forward, smiling, to take her place beside Rab.

In a fraught moment of decision, Gina knew that she must leave the gallery. Her mind in a turmoil, how could she have been so blind, so stupid to imagine that she and Rab could ever come together again in the way she had envisaged? His wife had seemed unreal to her before. Now Marguerite Romer was no longer a shadow but a living, breathing, curiously attractive woman, wearing a pink straw hat, standing beside her husband, looking up at him with adoration in her eyes, clasping his arm, posing for the cameras, artlessly proclaiming by the smile on her lips, the look in her eyes, 'This man is mine. All mine.'

Turning away, Gina moved quickly towards the door, paused momentarily to look back. Her sudden movement had caught Rab's attention. Their eyes met briefly across the crowded room. And then she was gone.

Deeply shaken, standing on the pavement, looking at the Portrait of Gina, she thought it unlikely that anyone would even recognize her now as the girl Rab had portrayed in the springtime of her life. It was as if that girl no longer existed, had died a long time ago.

And yet she had known, in that brief moment when Rab's eyes met hers, that he was still in love with her. Just as she, God help her, was still in love with him.

Chapter Twenty-Four

He had to see her again. The years without Gina had been akin to a cancer of the spirit, an incurable longing which had haunted him night and day throughout his time in Cornwall.

And yet, had it not been for the time he had spent at the Marquiss Vor, his deep involvement with the men with whom he had hewn the tin-bearing rock from the bowels of the earth, he would not have set brush to canvas to depict the respect and admiration he felt for them in art form. Those tired yet strong miners, warm-hearted, rough-tongued, had been his friends, had come to accept him as one of themselves once their initial mistrust of him had been overcome. Then they had shared with him their flasks of cold tea and bread-and-dripping butties, their laughter and snatches of song.

Painting late at night or in the early hours of the morning, when his eyes ached with fatigue and his torn hands could scarcely hold the brush, he had released a torrent of pent-up anger against Phillip Marquiss, slapping the colours haphazardly onto the canvas, working from the rough sketches he had made of his fellow miners at the rock face, so that the paintings possessed the raw vitality of the men he portrayed.

Soon he had discovered a steady market for his work via an art gallery in St Just, the owner of which he trusted implicitly to pay him the agreed fifty per cent commission. Nor had his trust in the man been misplaced. It was that gallery owner, a connoisseur of art, whose enthusiasm for his paintings had persuaded Rab that the time had come to concentrate solely on Art as a means of livelihood, who had encouraged him to break away from the restric-tive confines of Bourne House and find a place of his own where he could paint to his heart's desire.

And so Rab had followed John Christopher's advice. By this time the two men had become firm friends, to the extent that Rab had confided fully the nature of his emotional dilemma concerning Marguerite. 'Despite an improvement in health,' he told Christopher, 'she is still far from cured. I'm not sure if I could face the responsibility of taking her away from her family to live with me in a place of our own.' With a shrug of the shoulders, 'I have to face certain facts, John. The best I could afford at the moment would be a rented cottage. Could I reasonably expect to take care of my wife in such a place?'

John Christopher said quietly, 'Why not ask Marguerite? She is the only one capable of answering your question.'

A battle of wills ensued when Rab told Phillip Marquiss that he was leaving Bourne House, taking Marguerite with him. The cottage he had rented for them was small, unpretentious, set on a headland overlooking the sea, close to a fishing village with red-pantiled houses cascading down narrow streets to the harbour below.

'Are you out of your mind?' Marquiss raged. 'Do you imagine that I would allow a daughter of mine to live in such a hovel? Or perhaps you want Marguerite's death on your conscience?' But Marguerite, charmed by the idea of being the mistress of even a rented house, settled happily into her new surroundings. Less febrile and highly strung since Rab's return to Cornwall, and the specialist treatment which had proved successful in controlling her wild, manic outbursts, she would sit for hours on end watching her husband at work, content to be near him, sometimes getting up to gaze out of the studio window at the great expanse of sea beyond the headland, a slight, girlish figure despite the premature greying of her mass of dark hair, and the papery texture of her skin, her face seamed with the finely-etched lines of a prolonged illness; touching Rab's heart with compassion for her vulnerability, her utter dependence on him for the rebuilding of her shattered life.

The first time he made love to her, she had trembled like a trapped bird in his arms, and whimpered softly like a small animal in pain, had wept afterwards, her tears wetting the tendrils of hair about her pain-etched face – tears of joy because their marriage had at last been consummated, because she was now his wife in the truest meaning of the word. Then Rab had blamed himself for his long denial of her physical needs which had brought her so much suffering.

In one sense, she reminded him of Poppy Hewitt, whose need for the ultimate expression of affection had been imbued with a similar desperation. Poor Poppy; he often wondered what had become of her.

Now, here in London, Cornwall seemed a far country, mysterious and remote. The rented cottage was his now, and he would go back there to paint whenever the need for freedom came uppermost. In the meanwhile, he had rented a Victorian house in St John's Wood. The honeymoon period over, Marguerite had become restlessly aware of the isolation, the silence of the cottage, which had begun to get on her nerves; complaining that he thought more about his work than he did about her, constantly badgering him to take her to London to live, hankering after the bright city lights, talking of taking up music once more, now that she was cured of her illness and ready to face the world.

He hadn't the heart to tell her that she was far from cured. The signs of mental instability were all too evident in the shrillness of her voice when she was angry with him for not paying her enough attention, the rapid blinking of her eyelids, the twitching of a muscle in her right cheek, her habit of running her fingers wildly through her hair, her sudden lapses into complete silence when she would stare moodily into space for hours on end, when nothing he could do or say would break her trance-like reverie. Not until he had acceded to her demands for a house in London. Then she had thrown her arms about him in an excess of affection and told him how much she loved him, how proud he would be of her when she made her concert début at the Wigmore Hall.

Thankfully, his steadily increasing financial stability had

enabled him to provide a cook-housekeeper, a companion and a maid for Marguerite. Whatever the expenditure, he would have gladly paid more for the sheer relief of seeing her happy once more, flitting about the rooms like a pale butterfly; exclaiming with joy over the drawing-room piano, the red velvet curtains, the ornate overmantle, the broad staircase with its stained-glass landing window, the master bedroom with its solid mahogany furniture and rose-bedecked wallpaper. 'Oh, Robert,' she whispered ecstatically, 'this is heaven! We'll be so happy here. You'll see.'

He had not shared her enthusiasm. How could he? Who knew how long it would last?

It had taken every ounce of self possession not to go after Gina. In that split moment of recognition, his heart had lifted suddenly with a singing sensation of joy.

Common sense warned him not to betray his feelings. Her jealousy aroused, Marguerite would give him no peace. She was jealous of his Portrait of Gina, forever asking him who the girl was, if he had had an affair with her. God help him if she discovered that the woman who had left the gallery so abruptly was the girl in the painting.

Giselle noticed how drained Gina looked. The last thing she needed was the reappearance of an old love to add further complications, a fresh moral dilemma.

'Consider all that has happened to you since you left New York,' she said over lunch. 'One heartache after another. Now this man – this Robert Romer has cropped up again. Believe me, *chérie*, I know how hard it must have been to walk away from him, but what else could you have done? The pity is that he saw you. *Mon Dieu.* Why could not he have been looking the other way? *Men!*' Spreading her hands in a helpless gesture, 'Now he knows that you are here in London, my guess is he will not rest until he finds you, and then what? The man is married, living with his wife. They are sharing the same roof, presumably the same bed. Where is the sense or reason in laying yourself open to more hurt? Look, *chérie*, Oliver will be home soon. Why not take him abroad for the summer?'

'But have I the moral right to deny Oliver knowledge of his father?' Gina looked unseeingly at the passers-by in the street beyond, her mind in a turmoil. 'I know Rab is married, but does that give me the right to keep Oliver a secret from him?'

'Perhaps not,' Giselle conceded, 'but have you considered his wife's feelings if she found out that her husband had a child by another woman?'

'Of course I have. But things were different before today. I couldn't have told Rab about Oliver. I didn't know where he was. If he had kept in touch with the maestro, if I had known his address, I might have written to him.'

'To what purpose? None of this was your fault. What is the saying, let sleeping dogs lie?'

'It's Oliver I'm thinking about. The boy needs a father.'

'Perhaps. But does he need all the trouble connected with this man?'

'I know what you're saying, but this is something I must come to terms with in my own way. You see, I'm still in love with Rab.'

'All the more reason why you should take my advice and go abroad for the summer. To the south of France perhaps.'

Gina smiled sadly. 'I don't think running away is the answer. In any case, Peter and his father will be coming to London in a week or so, and Charles has arranged the *Ghosts* audition. I'd really like to tackle the role of Mrs Alving. It's a part I've always wanted to play.'

As she spoke, she knew that a deeper motive underlay her reluctance to leave London – the hope of seeing Rab again.

Chapter Twenty-Five

George seemed inordinately pleased with himself this morning, Giselle thought. 'You'll never guess what,' he said, in great good humour. 'I've received a letter from my old friend Rab Romer. Haven't heard from him in years!'

'Really? So why now?'

'He's in London. Doing well by the look of it. Hmmm,' he glanced through the letter, 'he's showing at the Regent Gallery in Bond Street. So he's made good at last. I knew he would. He's a damn fine artist.'

Giselle seethed inwardly. 'A better artist than a friend, it appears.'

'Eh?' George frowned. 'Oh, because he hasn't kept in touch?' Wondering why Giselle seemed so upset, 'That was my fault. He did write to me once a long time ago, just after he'd moved down to Cornwall. I meant to reply, but the letter went missing. You know how these things happen. At any rate, the important thing is that he hasn't forgotten me. He'd like to renew our friendship.'

'I bet he would,' Giselle said sourly.

'Tell you what, let's invite him to dinner next Saturday. He adores French cuisine. You could rustle up one of your Gautier *spécialités de la maison*. *Boeuf en daube* would be nice, and profiteroles.'

Giselle turned on him in a fury. 'I'll do no such thing! This man is trouble,' she burst forth.

Landis stared at her in amazement. 'Trouble in what way? You don't even know him. He happens to be a friend of mine. Surely I am allowed to invite a friend to dinner without calling down the wrath of God on my head. What's the matter with you?'

'More to the point, what's the matter with *you*? Oh, you men. You are all alike. So blind, so – stupid!'

'What the hell are you on about?'

'I'll tell you! Where has this "good friend" of yours been all this time?'

'I thought I'd explained all that.'

'Can't you see that he has an ulterior motive in getting in touch with you after all these years?'

'I don't know what you mean.'

Giselle snorted. 'The man's no fool! He wants you for one purpose only – to find out about Gina.'

'Gina? What about her?'

'You'll discover that soon enough.' She could say no more without revealing a private conversation. She would have cried off the evening except that her curiosity got the better of her.

Prepared to dislike Rab intensely, she had to admit that her pre-conceived notions had been wide of the mark, and wished afterwards that she had taken more trouble with the meal instead of chopping the vegetables haphazardly and flinging them in the earthenware pot on top of the chicken, hurrying round the corner to buy a fruit tart from the bakery.

Throughout dinner she watched him covertly, trying to pinpoint the source of his charisma. He was not handsome in the accepted sense of the word. His attractiveness lay in something far deeper, far more potent than physical perfection; a devastating combination of intellect, sensitivity and natural charm, so that nothing about him seemed forced or false.

She liked the way his thick dark hair grew back from his forehead, apart from one strand which he pushed back occasionally with the comb of his fingers, the smile that came as fleetingly as the sun after a summer storm, as though smiling had become a forgotten art of late. She admired the compactness of his body, the expressive use of his hands, his knowledge of art, music, the theatre, the fact that he had complimented her on the excellence of the meal in her own language, had treated her as a woman should be treated to bring out the best in her.

Finally, she had understood why Gina was in love with this man, why the memory of him had endured throughout the years, so that every other man had seemed a pale reflection of him in the mirror of her mind.

She might have felt differently towards him had he attempted to pump the maestro about Gina. He did nothing of the kind. After dinner, drinking coffee in front of an open window in the sitting-room, it was George who said conversationally, 'By the way, Rab, do you remember a girl called Gina Brett?'

'Of course. How could I forget her?'

'She's famous now.' George opened a bottle of wine. 'I knew from the start that she would be, of course.' He sighed reflectively, 'God, what talent. Have you seen her on-stage?'

'No, but I've followed her career every step of the way; kept newspaper cuttings about her,' Rab said.

Giselle's heart went out to him. 'You intend to see her again?'

He glanced across at her, 'I must. There's so much I want to say to her.' He paused. 'Do you know where I can find her?'

Giselle had been afraid of this, a question she preferred not to answer directly, for Gina's sake. 'Perhaps.' She smiled.

'But you'd rather not tell me?'

'Shall we say I'd rather you found out from someone else?'

'Good God, Giselle!' George exploded. 'Why all the secrecy? Rab's a friend of hers, for heaven's sake, not some star-struck youth in search of her autograph.'

'That's all right, George. I understand. Madame is simply protecting Gina's privacy. Rightly so. I should not care to have my whereabouts made public.' Returning Giselle's smile, 'I've had my share of newshounds, photographers, autograph hunters and their ilk.'

'Oh lord, I'd forgotten,' George said wisfully, 'you're famous, too! Seems everyone's famous except me. Wonder where I went wrong?'

'I shouldn't have any more to drink, if I were you,' Giselle advised him.

The clock chimed eleven. Rab rose to his feet.

'You're not leaving so soon, are you?' George looked hurt.

'I'm sorry, I'm afraid I must. I promised my wife I'd be home early,' Rab said quietly. 'Thank you for a delightful evening. Please, George, don't get up. I'll see myself out.'

George, who couldn't have got up anyway, said warmly, 'Come again, dear chap! Come as often as you like.'

'Thanks, George, I shall.'

'I'll see you to the door,' Giselle said. 'You may not be able to find the light switches.'

Standing beside him on the front step, she knew she owed Rab an apology. Whether he knew it or not made no difference. She said hesitantly, 'Please forgive me if I have seemed difficult tonight. The truth is, I was angry at first. I mistrusted your motives in writing to George after all this time. I thought you were using him as a means of finding Gina, that and nothing more. I was prepared to dislike you intensely.'

'Because of Gina? Because you felt that my seeing her again might hurt her in some way?'

Giselle said softly. 'Don't forget that you are married to someone else.'

'You love her very much, don't you?' Rab asked.

'Yes, I love her, as dearly as if she were my own flesh and blood. I thought she'd be far better off without you. Now I'm not so sure. It was what you said about the newspaper cuttings that changed my mind. After all, who am I to play God?'

'You think I resent the fact that you would not divulge her whereabouts, is that it?' Rab said. 'If so, please forget it. She must have an agent. There must be someone who could help me to find her.'

'I doubt if Gina's agent would tell you her address,' Giselle admitted. 'It's a kind of unwritten law, to protect a client's right to privacy.'

Rab smiled. 'I take it, then, that I shall have to join the crush of stage-door johnnies at the Adelphi Theatre? In which case, so be it.'

Laying her hand on his arm, 'No,' Giselle said kindly, 'that will not be necessary. Gina lives in Hampstead.'

'Thank you, Giselle!'

Raising her hand from his arm, he brushed it gently with his lips.

Marguerite had been coldly angry when Rab told her he had a dinner engagement with an old friend of his. 'A woman, of course!' she flung at him contemptuously.

'No, not a woman. A man I knew in Paris before the war,' he said patiently.

'Then why can't I come with you? Are you so ashamed of me that you want to keep me hidden away in this beastly house of yours?'

Speaking quietly, as to a recalcitrant child, 'This is not my house. It is ours. Our home. In any case, I shall not be late. You are tired, my dear. Why not go to bed? Have an early night?'

Eagerly wetting her lips with the tip of her tongue, 'Yes. Perhaps I shall. I'll go to bed early; stay awake for you.' Her angry mood forgotten, 'See what a good wife I am. I *am* a good wife, aren't I?' Throwing her arms about his neck, covering his face with kisses, 'Tell me you love me,' she said thickly, running her fingers through his hair, clinging to him. 'Tell me you love me as much as I love you!'

Sick at heart, he uttered the words she longed to hear, dreading what might happen if he did not do as she asked. He had lived through moments like this all too often before, had listened to her wild threats of doing away with herself if he failed to give her the affection she demanded.

Letting himself into the house, he walked slowly upstairs to the bedroom he shared with his wife, hoping against hope that she had fallen asleep; that he could make his way quietly to the spare room along the landing so as not to disturb her. Reaching the top step, his heart sank. The light was still on, filtering beneath the door.

He saw Marguerite, in his mind's eye, propped up with pillows, awaiting his coming; knowing she would not sleep until he had satisfied her lust.

Christ Jesus! How could he bear the thought, much less the reality of physical intimacy with Marguerite when his thoughts were all of Gina? His flesh recoiled at the prospect of what lay ahead as he opened the bedroom door.

But Marguerite was not in bed, as he had imagined she would be. She was standing in the middle of the room, her arms outstretched, completely naked apart from a diaphanous white *peignoir* wide open to reveal her childlike body, her frugal breasts, and the bush of black pubic hair at her crotch.

Swaying slightly, as if dancing to music that only she could hear, she came towards him, smiling, and wound her arms about him, drawing him towards the bed, whispering that she wanted him to hurt her when he made love to her, to beat her first, to make her cry out with pain. 'Punish me,' she begged him. 'Bad little girls deserve to be punished.'

Disgusted by her wantonness, he blamed himself for consummating the marriage from a sense of pity. Throughout the traumatic escape from Germany, he had refused to take advantage of her. She was a child in his eyes, a frightened little girl in need of a protector, and yet she had clung doggedly to the romantic notion that he had married her because he loved her – to the extent of conjuring up a phantom pregnancy.

Little wonder that Phillip Marquiss had seen him as a man incapable of self-restraint, a deflowerer of innocence, whose wickedness had driven his daughter to the brink of insanity.

Now Rab wondered if Marguerite's madness had been a ploy to ensure his return to Cornwall. Gently but firmly he prised open her arms and held her away from him, repelled by the expression of lust he saw in her eyes, the flickering of her tongue across her lips, the orgiastic movements of her body. Suddenly, 'Stop it, Marguerite!' he cried hoarsely. 'For Christ's sake, stop it! You're my wife, for God's sake, not a whore in a brothel.' Snatching up her nightdress, 'Here. Put this on. At once, do you hear me!'

Enraged, she began screaming at him that she would rather be a whore in a brothel than the wife of man who did not love her, had never loved her. Backing away from him like a cornered animal, baring her teeth, running her fingers wildly through her hair, she screeched how much she hated him, that she wished she were dead. Dead! Dead! That she had never been born! 'Get out of my sight,' she burst forth in a frenzy of tears. 'Get out! Get out! Get out, you bastard!'

Deeply shaken, he left the house. The moon was riding high in a blue velvet sky. Lamplight laced the summertime trees with threads of gold. Drawing in gulps of air, he walked alone, unseeingly, not knowing or caring where he was going – thinking of Gina. His love. His life. His reason for living.

He returned to St John's Wood in the early hours, and went upstairs to his studio on the top landing, an attic room with a wide dormer window overlooking the rooftops, which he had furnished with work-benches, odd chairs, and a couch reminiscent of his Scarborough days.

Flinging himself on the couch, he wondered if he had subconsciously chosen the secondhand furniture as a reminder of the St Nicholas Street studio. Possibly, but the two bore a merely superficial resemblance. He doubted his ability to paint here in any case. Art demanded concentration, inspiration. How could he concentrate on art with his mind in a vortex? Had coming to London been a mistake? He experienced once again the feeling of corruptness connected with money, as he had done painting the portrait of Harriet Cohen.

Looking back at his life, he knew his happiest times had been spent as a poor student in Paris, in the relaxed atmosphere of the Steiner home before the war, above all at the Scarborough studio where, despite his poverty, he had known a deep feeling of spiritual release, an enrichment of the senses when Gina had entered his world.

He knew, now, that he should not have left her. He should have told her the truth about Marguerite, that their marriage had not been consummated. He should have fought with every weapon available to free himself from the clutches of the Marquiss family. His conscience had been his undoing, his burden of guilt that an innocent young girl had been driven to the brink of madness because of him. Every letter received from Phillip Marquiss had hammered home to him his responsibility towards his daughter. Little wonder that he had seen his brief sojourn in Scarborough as an oasis of freedom blossoming between the horror of his wartime experiences and the arid desert of the future. But what of Gina? Had Madame Gautier been right in saying that she might have her own reasons for not wanting to see him again? In which case, what right had he to pursue her? None whatever. Except – he had known that day in the gallery, when she had turned to look back at him, that she was still in love with him.

Landis had spoken with pride of her achievements, her many standing ovations, her first appearance onstage when a coterie of hard-headed theatrical entrepreneurs had been stunned by her performance of Ophelia, and Rab remembered that he too had been stunned that day in the studio when she had read Shakespeare's *Cleopatra*.

Looking up at the ceiling, tormented with memories of Gina, he knew that he must see her again. His life, his future depended on that meeting. If she still loved him, he would ask her to go away with him. If she did not love him, if she turned him away, then he would return to Paris, rent a studio in Montmartre, put the past behind him. As for Marguerite, he would give her every penny he owned; make sure she was well provided for. More than this, he could not give her.

Nothing on earth would ever persuade him to live with her again, to suffer her stranglehold on his life, her moods, her tantrums – her lust, which had nothing whatever to do with love as he had known it in the quietude and peace of one woman's smile. A love which had been enriched, not decimated by the lack of physical contact, so that it had remained as pure and clean as moonlight on the sea, as warm as springtime, as haunting as a Viennese waltz.

Suddenly there came a babble of voices, a commotion from somewhere deep within the house, the urgent calling of his name, 'Mr Romer, Mr Romer! Come quickly!'

Hurrying downstairs to his wife's room, brushing past the servants gathered together on the landing, he saw that Marguerite was lying face down on the bed, her body contorted with spasms of pain; hands outspread, her fingers like talons, as if she was clawing for air.

'Well don't just stand there! Send for the doctor!'

Kneeling beside the bed, Rab saw that his wife's eyes were open and staring, that bubbles of saliva had formed at the corners of her mouth.

Lifting her up in his arms, he turned her on her side and covered her naked body with the eiderdown. Then, smoothing back her hair, he sat beside her, holding her hands, until the doctor arrived. By that time, her breathing had become easier, her body had stopped twitching, her fingers had relaxed.

His wife, the doctor told him, had suffered an attack of epilepsy – *grand mal* – symptomatic of some underlying nervous disorder involving a temporary loss of consciousness, convulsions and muscular spasms.

'Now,' the doctor said, 'she needs complete rest and quiet, peace of mind. Careful nursing.' Scribbling the necessary prescription, 'There is no cure as such, but the condition can be stabilized. You must, however, be watchful at all times.' He glanced at Rab thoughtfully. Having attended Mrs Romer since her arrival in London, he had formed an impression of a misalliance between two totally unsuited partners.

So much for the future he had mapped out in his mind, Rab thought dully. Going wearily upstairs to sit with Marguerite, he saw the house as a prison, his gaoler a sick woman whom, for reasons of conscience, he could not forsake in her hour of need.

Chapter Twenty-Six

Oliver watched, fascinated, the builders at work on the garden flat. Soon he was busily engaged in helping them to carry bricks and mix the mortar, full of questions about Adam and Peter Dickenson whose home it would be.

'I wish I could live there too,' he told Gina. 'It would be special, like living in a tree-house.' Next day she had a word with the architect who drew up plans for a small extension to the building, with its own entrance and sliding glass doors which would overlook and lead to the jungly part of the garden, as Oliver called it, recognizing the need of a growing boy for his own space when he came home from school, a place where he could dream and draw to his heart's content.

His face lit up with joy when she told him that he could furnish his *pied à terre* as he wished, and sleep there if he liked. 'You mean I could sleep in a hammock, and have proper bookshelves? Gosh! And are we really going to have a greenhouse, and will Adam grow lots of exciting things? And will Peter make a rockery and a border with tall plants? But you won't let him cut down the trees, will you, or the birds will have nowhere to live.'

He was growing so tall, she thought, watching him carrying buckets of water for the builders, and so handsome – a taller version of his father, with the same dark hair and olive complexion: Rab's slow-dawning, devastating smile, and his talent for art. But his eyes were Poppy's, shining with an unquenchable thirst for life, and his warm, happy, compassionate nature was hers too, the legacy she had bequeathed to him.

Watching him, she realized that no part of him was really hers, except his love. Then came once more, for the

316

thousandth time, the troubled thought that Oliver had a right to know the truth about his father, that he was a well-known artist, living here in London, married to a woman who might well resent the fact of his existence, if she knew of it. The nature of Gina's dilemma lay rooted in the fear of burdening a child with adult decisions and responsibilities, in destroying his happiness in his present well-ordered way of life for the sake of her own conscience. But how would she be able to live with her conscience if she condemned the boy to a tug-of-war existence? How could she be sure that if Rab knew he had a son, he might not only take him away from her, but refuse her further access to the boy? Would the memory of a long gone love affair hold sway against a father's natural desire to foster his own flesh and blood?

She had seen Rab fleetingly that day in the Bond Street Gallery, and thought he had scarcely changed at all. But how could she be sure? How could she be certain that fame had not blunted the edge of his sensitivity, that marriage to a possessive woman had not chained his spirit? He had, after all, married the woman of his choice. For whatever reasons, money or sexual attraction, he had married the woman in the pink straw hat. But that had not prevented him from making love to Poppy Hewitt in that bed beneath the stars, impregnating her, then leaving her alone to face the consequence of his betrayal.

The sun warm on her face, closing her eyes, God, what a fool she'd been all these years, Gina thought. How could she have been so blind, so stupid, as to imagine that Rab had been in love with her? Why had she felt herself in need of a second rate affair like that? And yet, as the thought occurred, she knew that she was powerless to rid herself of the memory of a love which had coloured all the days of her life since she had walked into the studio, to discover him standing there as if he had been awaiting her coming. That day when the arrow of his smile had pierced her heart with the knowledge of what it felt like to be in love, not for just a moment, a second, an hour, a day, a year, but always. For ever.

He had engaged a nurse to be with Marguerite during the long hours of the night, to administer the tablets the doctor had prescribed for her. Meanwhile he had taken to sleeping on the couch in his studio. *Sleeping?* Scarcely that. Since the onset of his wife's illness, Rab had scarcely slept at all; had arisen each morning at the crack of dawn to watch the sun coming up over the housetops, willing himself to face a new day of hopelessness and despair, until he could no longer endure his feeling of imprisonment.

Hampstead Heath, he knew, covered a wide area, but it was there he longed to be, in the faintest hope of seeing Gina again.

And if by some miracle they met again, face to face, what would be her reaction? Fame had added a lustre to her beauty, a certain style, elegance and sophistication. Had it also robbed her of that innocence he remembered so well? Madame Gautier said that Gina had been hurt a great deal. But how? He wished Madame had been more forthcoming.

Common sense told him that Gina must have met many attractive men: actors, theatrical entrepreneurs, members of the aristocracy, during the course of her career. Had she married one of them? That was a strong possibility. He had to *know*. This uncertainty was driving him mad. If it meant combing every inch of Hampstead Heath from dawn till dusk, he *must* find her!

The boy was sitting under a tree, crayon in hand, a sketch-pad resting on his knees. A dark-haired young woman was seated close by, reading a newspaper. 'May I look?' Rab asked the boy.

And, 'Yes, if you like,' he answered, 'but it's not very good.' The woman looked up sharply, suspiciously.

'On the contrary, it is very good,' Rab said, looking at the sketch, 'except that you've got the perspective slightly wrong. Now, if you were to imagine a dot on the landscape, and narrowed the path until it disappeared into that dot, you would add the dimension of distance to your drawing. Do you see what I mean?'

'Oh yes,' the boy said breathlessly, 'of course.'

Rab smiled disarmingly at the woman, apparently the child's mother. 'Forgive me,' he said, 'but the boy has talent. Tell me, has he had lessons?'

'Well, they teach art at the school he goes to,' Bridget said, stuffing the newspaper into her shopping bag, 'but drawing has always been a hobby of his – hasn't it, Oliver?' Still suspicious of the stranger's motives, 'Anyway, it's time we were off now. Say goodbye to the gentleman.'

'I do have lessons,' Oliver blurted, 'but nobody told me about perspective before.' Reluctantly closing his sketch-book, 'You see the art master isn't a proper teacher. What I mean is, he's really a parson who comes in once a week to take choir-practice.'

Curiously drawn to the boy, 'What is the name of your school?' Rab asked.

'St Bede's. It's in Berkshire. We play lots of sport. But my mother said I could have proper art lessons if I wanted, from a bone . . . a bony teacher.'

Rab smiled, so did Bridget, who was not averse to talking to good-looking men as a rule. 'You mean *bona fide*, Master Oliver,' she corrected him. Rab glanced at her in surprise. So she was not the boy's mother?

Intrigued by the stranger's unorthodox apparel – corduroy trousers, cashmere sweater, sandals, and a leather waistcoat, 'Are *you* an artist?' Bridget asked.

'Well, yes,' he replied. 'At least I have some knowledge of the subject.'

'You mean you're a teacher?' Oliver asked breathlessly.

'I have taught occasionally,' Rab said lightly.

'Could you teach me?'

'Oliver! Apologize to the gentleman at once.' Bridget spoke sharply.

'I'm sorry. But could you? I'm sure my mother wouldn't mind.'

'Oliver! I'm surprised at you. Come along now, this minute.'

'We live at Welford House,' Oliver said desperately as Bridget laid a firm hand on his arm. 'I'm sure my mother would be ever so pleased to see you, and I could show you my drawings of birds. Please say you'll come.'

'I'll think about it,' Rab said, aware that the boy reminded him of someone – himself when young. Indeed, photographs of himself as a boy bore an uncanny resemblance to Oliver.

Turning away, Rab thought how proud the mother must be of her son. He imagined the woman as dark-haired, slender, quite young, possibly a widow, since the boy had made no mention of his father. She must also be quite well-off to be able to afford a nursemaid for her child, a gregarious, outgoing person, he imagined, who would not mind discussing her son's artistic talent with a complete stranger.

As for himself, he could think of nothing he would enjoy more than fostering the artistic talent of the boy called Oliver.

Returning to St John's Wood, he discovered Marguerite sitting up in bed, damning the servants and the nurse to perdition, demanding that her sister Eleanor should come at once. The only person in the world she could trust to take care of her.

Quietly asking the servants to leave the room, he approached his wife, speaking to her gently, begging her to keep calm, desperately afraid that her outburst might result in another seizure.

'Keep away from me!' she shouted. 'This is all your fault. I hate you. I loathe and detest you. I want my sister. I want Eleanor.'

'Very well, I'll send for her.' He turned away.

'Wait till she hears how you have treated me. That's right, turn your back on me. Well, I don't care. Get out of my sight. Go back to Cornwall. Do what you hell you like, you selfish bastard!'

*   *   *

320

Later that day, he went to Welford House. Bridget let him in. 'You'd better wait in the drawing-room,' she said. 'Mind you, I'm not promising the mistress will see you. She doesn't like being dropped in on!'

Rab smiled. 'I'm sorry, I would have written or telephoned, had I known her name.'

'You mean you didn't know that Oliver's mother is famous? Well, that's a relief. You'd be surprised the tricks people get up to for a close look at her.'

Something stirred at the back of Rab's mind, a vague feeling of hope, a kind of tingle. His heartbeat quickened imperceptibly.

'I'll tell Miss Brett you're here,' Bridget said. 'Who shall I say is calling?'

'My name is Robert Romer.' His voice shook slightly.

'I say, sir, are you all right?'

'Yes, I'm fine, thanks.'

Bridget shot him a puzzled look as she left the room. He could almost read her mind. Possibly she had heard his name before. Almost certainly she thought he was crazy. He *felt* crazy. Crazy with joy, the relief of having found Gina at last. Crazy with anticipation, his strong desire to hold her in his arms once more, to feel the warmth of her body against his.

It had been such a long, long time. Now the waiting was nearly over. He wondered what he would say to her. What could he say except, 'I love you'? But she already knew that. She *must* know, must have seen the way he looked at her that day in the gallery.

They had both known, in that fleeting second when their eyes met across a crowded room, that nothing had changed between them. It had seemed, in that moment, that the empty years of loneliness had danced away like spindrift from a wave.

At the sound of footsteps, his body taughtened. As tense as a coiled spring, he awaited the opening of the door. Suddenly the footsteps wavered, then stopped.

Heart pounding, Gina had hurried from her room. Now she stood uncertainly in the hall, incapable of the

321

simple act of turning a doorknob. So much was at stake. Entering that room, her whole life might change in a matter of minutes, even seconds. She knew she would not leave it without telling Rab the truth about Oliver.

Why the memory of a trapped sparrow should have entered her mind just then, she would never know. It had taken a great deal of courage to run up the aisle of the Merlewood village church that May day long ago, to face an unknown future, a future which had led inescapably to this moment of decision when she must face, with every ounce of courage she possessed, the possibility of losing her son.

But how to deny the fast beating of her heart, her strong desire to see Rab again, to be held by him, kissed by him, loved by him? Drawing in a deep breath, laying her trembling hand on the doorknob, she entered the room, and stood there on the threshold, her pale, unsmiling face framed by her auriole of shining red hair.

'Gina, my love.' Slowly, Rab came towards her, overwhelmed by his love for her, seeing her as the girl whose portrait he had painted in the springtime of her life. Now, his heart told him, she was not that girl at all. No longer a trusting, immature child, but a woman – still beautiful, but changed imperceptibly by some sadness or pain she had recently endured.

Making no attempt to touch her, he said simply, 'I had to come. I had to see you again.'

'I know.' With a shuddering sigh, she entered his arms.

Holding her close, he breathed in the familiar fragrance of her hair; felt the uprush of an age-old desire of a man for the woman he loved in the suppleness of her body against his, the slenderness of her waist, the uplift of her breasts.

He began kissing her then, tracing the curve of her cheekbones, her nose, eyelids, her throat, as though he were painting a portrait of her with his lips, until, at last, covering her mouth with his, he felt the wetness of her tears upon his face.

'Don't cry, my darling,' he said tenderly, 'now that I've found you, I'll never let go of you again. But there is something I must say to you. Something that has weighed on my mind for a very long time. I shouldn't have left you the way I did. Can you ever forgive me?'

Gina's moment of truth had arrived. Withdrawing gently from his arms, 'You left someone else, too. Remember?'

Rab frowned slightly, 'You mean Poppy? Poppy Hewitt? Oh yes. Poor little Poppy. I've often wondered what became of her.'

After a long pause, 'She died,' Gina said quietly, 'giving birth to a child. *Your* child.' Her voice faltered. 'Oliver is mine by adoption, but he is your son, yours and Poppy's. Your own flesh and blood.'

The doorbell rang at that moment. There was a commotion in the hall, the sound of voices; laughter. Bridget knocked at the door. 'Miss Georgina,' she cried excitedly, 'Mrs Crabtree's here!'

'Thank you, Bridget. I'll be there in a minute.'

Rab said hoarsely, 'What you've just told me. Is it really true? Is Oliver my son?' Her heart went out to him when, bowing his head, covering his face with his hands, 'Why didn't she tell me?' he asked brokenly. 'Why didn't Poppy tell me she was pregnant?'

'Because you weren't there to tell,' Gina said. 'Now, I really must go.' She held out her hands to him, 'I'm sorry, I can't say any more just now. Perhaps we can meet again soon?'

'Yes, we must. There is so much more we need to say to each other. But that's not the only reason. I want you, Gina. I have never stopped wanting you.'

'I really must go now.'

'Of course.' Letting go of her hands. 'When? When shall we meet?'

She said, 'Tonight? There's an iron staircase leading up to my room.'

* * *

Alone with Rab, she knew that she would be powerless to deny the strong tide of passion running between them. But did she want to deny it? She loved him with all her heart. It was as simple as that . . . Simple? But Rab was married. What of his wife? What of her own conscience?

She recalled her scathing comment to TJ Power: 'Do you really think me capable of having an affair with a married man?' How smug and complacent she'd been then.

Now, watching darkness fall beyond her bedroom window, her heart beating like a drum, awaiting her lover, she wondered how it would feel to lie beside him, warm and naked in his arms. She had no way of knowing. Would she react to Rab's lovemaking as she had done to Power's? At the supreme moment of entry, would she fight against making that total commitment of loving? Would thoughts of his wife, of Poppy, Oliver, come uppermost in her mind at the last moment?

She knew herself so well. Of necessity, she had learned to come to terms with the fiercely burning flame of independence deep within her. How else could she have survived as an actress in the cut-and-thrust world of the theatre? What if she suddenly discovered that a long-held dream of love had no real substance or meaning beyond the scope of her imagination?

He came to her a little after midnight.

Hearing his footsteps on the wrought-iron stairs, she opened the balcony window and let him in.

Realizing at once her nervousness, her apprehension, he said quietly, 'If you've had second thoughts, my darling, I'll leave now.'

'No. You were right when you said we needed to talk. Above all, about Oliver. The boy needs a father.'

Rab said, 'There is a solution. I have a cottage in Cornwall. Oliver could spend his summer vacations there, with me. I could teach him how to fish, to draw, to paint.' He smiled, thinking how lovely she looked in her gold-girdled hostess gown. 'It would be even more wonderful if

324

you came too. Imagine how happy we'd be, the three of us together.'

Gina's heart lifted suddenly to the possibility of spending long, lazy summer months with Rab and Oliver; turning her face to the sun; relaxing on some sandy beach watching the tide coming in on the shore. But she knew this could never be. She said, 'I'm sorry, Rab. We are too well known. The gentlemen of the Press would have a field day. I could never subject Oliver to that kind of muck-raking.'

Moving towards her, overwhelmed by his love for her, he murmured, 'The gentlemen of the Press are not here now, my darling.'

'I know,' she said softly, 'but have we the right?'

Taking her hands, he led her gently towards the bed. 'I want you to know about my marriage. You have a right to know. Perhaps it will help you to understand why things happened the way they did.' Quietly, haltingly, he told her about the Steiner family, a frightened girl who had clung to him for help, whom he had married as the only means of bringing her safely out of Germany. How the Marquiss family had held him responsible for Marguerite's mental breakdown, their refusal to believe that the marriage had not been consummated, his reasons for going back to Cornwall in the hope that his presence there might alleviate her suffering.

'Please, Rab, there's no need to say any more. I understand.'

Kissing the palms of her hands, his voice hoarse with emotion, 'It was always you, Gina,' he said. 'Only you. You were never out of my thoughts for a moment.' He looked up into her eyes. 'You asked have we the right? I believe we have, but only you can decide.'

'I love you, Rab,' she said in a low voice. 'Please, my darling, kiss me.'

His skin was soft and warm to the touch, the colour of pale coffee; unblemished. How curious, she had never realized before how beautiful a man's body could be, or how vulnerable.

She noticed the way his hair curled at the nape of his neck. The face she loved seemed lit from within as he lay with her, gently caressing her body with his sensitive fingertips until a flame of desire, searing in its intensity, rippled through her.

When his lips met hers, she remembered the Song of Solomon: 'Let him kiss me with the kisses of his mouth: for thy love is better than wine.' Remembered, too, the many lonely nights she had spent imagining herself in his arms, being loved by him. She knew now that all the imagination in the world could never compare with this reality; her passionate response to his ardour – the exquisite moment of surrender.

When Eleanor Marquiss arrived at St John's Wood, Rab met her and, as a matter of courtesy, escorted her to Marguerite's room. Her attitude implied that she would be in charge from now on. Rab had no objection to this. Eleanor could throw her weight about as much as she liked, just as long as he was well out of the way.

Cornwall beckoned. He would return to the cottage with its panoramic view of the sea, the comforting sight of the fishing cobles coming home at dusk, their riding lights glowing like fireflies as darkness fell. The thought of having his son there with him shone like a beacon before him as he packed his cabin trunk.

He had not wanted his 'Portrait of Gina' displayed in the Regent Gallery window. The owner had persuaded him that the portrait would prove his versatility as an artist. Reluctantly, Rab had agreed on condition that the portrait must be returned to him when the exhibition was over. The picture now stood on an easel near the studio window, covered with a protective dust-sheet.

When the time came to place the portrait in his cabin-trunk, drawing aside the cover, he saw that it had been slashed to ribbons.

The wantonness of a jealous woman's attack on the painting he prized beyond any other, shocked him deeply. How could Marguerite have done such a thing? He felt no compunction now, no sense of guilt in returning to Cornwall.

The fact remained that he was still married to her. He also knew that, sooner or later she would make him pay for his temporary escape to happiness.

PART THREE

Chapter Twenty-Seven

It seemed to Rab as if those long, slow days of summertime would never end. And these were the gifts he and Gina had given to their son, as precious as the pearl necklace a father had once given to his daughter on the day of her confirmation. Time in which Rab would grow closer to Oliver with every passing day they spent together at the cottage.

How eagerly the boy had responded to his mother's suggestion, that first summer, that this might be the perfect opportunity to take the art lessons he longed for. She had not told him that Rab was his father, wanting their relationship to develop naturally, as it had done the day when Oliver said wistfully, liking Rab so much, 'I wish that *you* were my father.'

They had been together on the beach at the time, watching the tide come in, gathering shells, laughing as the water foamed about their feet. Then, placing his arm about the boy's shoulders, overwhelmed with a deep sense of wonder, 'I *am* your father,' Rab said quietly.

Never would he forget his son's acceptance of that simple confession. How right Gina had been, Rab thought, in asking him not to rush things, to give Oliver as much time as he needed to reach his own conclusions, not to burden the child with enforced knowledge of their father–son relationship, rather to wait, to be patient, until the right moment occurred.

As daylight faded, and the half-moon of sand was swallowed up by the incoming tide, man and boy had returned to the cottage on the headland in companionable silence, where Rab cooked their fish supper in a skillet over a glowing kitchen fire, while his son brought to the table the knives and forks, the loaf of bread and the slab of Cornish butter they had bought that morning in the village.

When the meal was over, Oliver said, 'I think I should like to go to bed now, Father.'

Keeping his emotion in check, 'Very well then, son,' Rab said. 'Good night, and sleep well.'

Turning on the threshold, the boy had rushed back to him like a hummingbird in flight. 'I'm very glad you're my father,' he said breathlessly, flinging his arms about him. 'Promise you won't go away and leave me. Promise you'll take me fishing tomorrow!'

Wide awake until the early hours, watching the glittering path of moonlight on the sea, Rab wished that Gina could be there with him, sharing the magic view from the window on this night that was made for love. But for Oliver's sake they must put aside their own feelings and desires, Gina had said when he asked her again to come to Cornwall for the summer. He remembered her words: 'The best we can hope for, my darling, is happiness not for ourselves, but your son.'

'*Our* son.' Holding her gently. 'I think of Oliver as our child, yours and mine.'

'Thank you for that.' Her eyes misted with tears. 'Then will you help me to face what must be faced? Going our separate ways for his sake? I love him too much to allow a breath of scandal to spoil his life. I know how cruel newspapermen can be, how they can twist and turn innocence into something ugly.'

'Our separate ways,' he echoed dully. 'You mean that you want me to live a lie with Marguerite? I'm sorry, my darling, I'm not sure if I could face that. My wife doesn't either want or need me any more. She has made that abundantly clear.'

'But you are still married to her, and she needs all the help and support you can give her.'

A note of bitterness entered his voice, 'And while I'm helping and supporting Marguerite, where will you be? What will you be doing?'

'My job,' she said simply, 'earning my living. Learning lines; moves; rehearsing the same lines, the same moves, the same scenes over and over again until the final dress-rehearsal, before the opening night of whatever play I happen to be in at the time. Exactly where I'll be is more difficult to predict. It could be Manchester, the West End, New York. Wherever, my love, you must let me go with the realization that nothing can come between us now that we have found each other again. Do you understand, Rab, what I'm trying to say? That wherever we go, whatever we do from now on, there will always be an invisible cord between us?' Looking up at him. 'That cord has always existed. It is even stronger now, because of Oliver, at least that's how I feel. But how do *you* feel?'

'The way Arthur must have felt when he drew Excalibur from the stone,' Rab said, with that slow-dawning smile of his.

That first summer he had taught his son how to stretch and prime a canvas. Watching his father paint, Oliver wanted to do the same, and daubed away happily, mixing paint on a cracked kitchen plate, learning which brushes to use, which colours to choose.

From then on, throughout those Cornish summers, Rab had watched his son grow from a child into a straight-limbed, handsome young man. And when summertime was over, he would go back to London to fulfil his responsibilities to Marguerite, to take up the burden of their strange half-life together, holding memories of those long, happy days of summer close to his heart, worrying about the future; world events which he viewed as an inescapable pattern leading to the coming Armageddon in which a generation of young men like Oliver would be cut down before they had begun to live.

Hitler's rise to power had brought about the confiscation of Jewish property, Nazi barbarism towards those of non-Aryan blood. The writing on the wall, Jewish artists of the calibre of Schoenberg, Erich Kleiber, Otto Klemperer and Stefan Zweig, along with other men of art, music and letters, had fled Germany in face of the coming pogrom.

Hitler's stormtroopers had marched into Austria in the spring of last year. Prime Minister Neville Chamberlain's return from Munich in the autumn, waving a scrap of paper, declaring 'Peace in our time', had all the hallmarks of a sick political joke. This autumn, air raid shelters were being dug in Hyde Park.

A deep melancholy invaded Rab's heart during those final days in Cornwall, when he and Oliver were clearing up the cottage against their departure, an overwhelming feeling that they would never come here again.

Sensing his father's despair, Oliver sat with him near the fire on the last evening, aware that he knew next to nothing about Rab's past; his relationship with his mother. These things had never seemed important to him before. Now he needed to know.

Slowly, the truth unfolded. Sitting over the embers of the fire until the early hours of next morning, Rab told his son about the Steiners' home in Germany, their wide circle of friends and their unorthodox lifestyle, the liberality of their political views which, linked to their refusal to accept dictatorship, had led to their deaths.

He spoke then of Marguerite whom he had married, as a matter of expedience, in order to bring her to safety. How, leaving her in Cornwall with her family, he had joined British Intelligence as an interpreter.

Holding nothing back, he told his son how, after the war, he had gone to Scarborough where he had met Poppy Hewitt.

'Tell me, Dad, did you love her?' Oliver asked.

'No-one could help loving Poppy,' Rab said. 'She was all heart. She cared deeply for her fellow beings. It's hard to explain our relationship. All I can possibly say is that she brought happiness, laughter into my life at a time when my luck seemed to have run out.' He paused. 'Then one day she brought her friend Gina Brett to meet me.'

'It's all right, Dad. You needn't say any more. I understand. You fell in love with her?'

'Yes. I knew then that I had never been in love before, had never begun to understand the meaning of the word.' Making no attempt to elicit his son's sympathy, 'I behaved badly,' he said, staring into the dying embers in the grate.

'I have never forgiven myself for that. I never shall. For what it's worth, I had a price to pay for my cowardice. I am still, to some extent, paying that price.'

His lips curved in a rictus smile of regret for the wasted years of his life as a member of the Marquiss household, tied to a woman he was not, and never had been, in love with.

As the last spark of the fire went out, he continued, 'One thing I shall never regret – these summertimes I've spent with you. Everyone on earth needs something or someone to cling to when the going gets rough.

'Your mother, in her wisdom, knew how much it would mean to me to bring you here, to teach you how to fish, to swim, to paint. If I'm sad now, it's because I think this is the last summer we'll spend together for a very long time.'

'Because of the war, you mean?' Oliver said quietly. He paused. 'I think I should tell you, Father, that if and when war comes, I shall need to be a part of it, to fight for the things I believe in. How did Shakespeare put it? "This earth, this realm, this England".' He smiled and got up to light the lamp. Laying his hand on Rab's shoulder, 'Thanks for everything, Dad. All these summers which have meant so much to me. I'll make you proud of me one of these days.'

Next day, locking up for the last time, Rab turned to look back at the cottage. The scene he had painted so often would remain framed in the gallery of his mind. He saw the slate-tiled roof and whitewashed walls, the scrap of garden where autumn flowers grew in a profusion of colour: the marigolds Oliver had planted that first summer, now toughly rooted in the moist earth, the clumps of Michaelmas daisies and sea-pinks. He saw the vast expanse of sea beyond the headland, as calm as a mill-pond in the clear light of a warm August morning, and thought of the tawny sand below, of the tide foaming in on the beach where a man and his son had walked and laughed together. And all these memories he would hold close to his heart as a talisman – akin to the Victorian threepenny-bit he had found, one day, on the beach at Scarborough, which he had carried with him ever since, as a good luck charm.

Much had happened in the years leading up to the war . . .

Gina had sailed to New York in the summer of 1936, on the newly commissioned *Queen Mary*. Rab had understood her reasons for wanting to return to America. This was a challenge she must face for Owen's sake, the repayment of a debt of honour to Alwyn Jefferson, who had cabled her: 'To hell with St Joan. Come over and play Cleopatra.'

New leading ladies had burst upon the West End scene about that time. The charming young actress, Peggy Ashcroft, had received rave notices for her Juliet; Wendy Hiller had scored a direct hit in *Love on the Dole*. Rab had wanted Gina to carry the banner for England from the West End to Broadway. His encouragement had given her the confidence to accept Jefferson's offer.

Oliver had been enthralled at the idea of his mother sailing to America on Britain's ultimate in luxury liners. 'Don't forget to send me lots of postcards,' he said.

'Sure you don't mind my going away for a little while?'

'Of course not, Mother! In any case, Dad and I will be off to Cornwall soon, and there'll be lots to do in the garden before then.'

Inviting Daisy Crabtree to go to America with her had been an inspiration on Gina's part. Daisy had fitted so well into the Hampstead house that she had stayed on to make herself useful in many unexpected ways, taking a particular pride in Gina's wardrobe, making sure that her gowns were kept neatly pressed, her lingerie hand-laundered and laid in her chest-of-drawers among tissue paper and muslin bags of pot-pourri. Daisy would make a wonderful travelling companion, a marvellous dresser, but the offer must be made on a business footing, the nature of the job explained fully beforehand: the long hours involved, the quick changes between scenes, the responsibility of having everything to hand, the personal props, shoes, jewellery, wigs, and so many other things besides – dealing tactfully with over-zealous fans after a performance, standing by with needle and thread in case of a sudden tear, the loss of a button, or a missing hook and eye.

Daisy had not batted an eyelid. She would have gone to the ends of the earth and back for Gina.

Standing at the ship's rail, Gina remembered her first visit to New York. Nothing had changed. The Statue of Liberty still stood guard over the harbour, the Hudson River was still alive with tug-boats. There was the same churning air of excitement as the great liner sailed majestically towards its berth. But something was missing. TJ Power was missing. How protective he had been, understanding her sense of awe. Now she was being protective towards Daisy.

Alwyn Jefferson would be on the dock to meet them, she felt sure, but she could not see him anywhere as they walked down the gangway, carrying their personal luggage.

'My goodness, it's just like the pictures,' Daisy remarked. An avid cinemagoer, she loved Hollywood movies depicting ship-board romances. 'I just hope there aren't any gangsters, that's all.' She giggled nervously. 'All we need is George Raft blasting away at us with a tommy-gun!' She paused to straighten her hat. 'Oh, I don't know, though, I quite like George Raft. Did you see him in *Bolero*? Anyone who can dance like that can't be all bad.'

'Hello, Gina. Welcome back to New York!'

Turning her head at the sound of a well-known voice, heart hammering, Gina saw TJ Power standing beside her, holding a bouquet of long-stemmed roses.

'These are for you,' he said softly. 'A peace offering.' Handing her the flowers, 'I am deeply sorry about what happened the last time we met. Can you forgive me?'

Daisy sniffed audibly as Gina introduced them. So this was the TJ Power Bridget had told her about? Tall and handsome he may be, but she attached no importance to physical appearance. Mistrustful of his motives, what was he up to, she wondered? But of course she knew. He had designs on her ewe lamb.

A jostling group of reporters and photographers were

waiting as Gina left the Customs' buildings. She posed for them, smiling, holding her bouquet, as they fired their questions, 'How was your trip?', 'Think you'll make Broadway this time, Miss Brett?' 'How about Hollywood, Miss Brett? Any plans to make motion pictures?', 'Say, Miss Brett, is it true the King of England is going to marry Mrs Simpson?'

Power waded into the breach. 'As Miss Brett's agent, I can confirm her appearance as Cleopatra. Rehearsals will begin the day after tomorrow. And yes, there is a strong possibility of a Hollywood contract. Now, Miss Brett is rather tired after her journey, and would like a little peace and quiet. Thank you, gentlemen. That will be all for the time being.' His car was waiting.

Insensitively perhaps, Alwyn Jefferson had booked rooms for Gina and Daisy at the Gotham Hotel. Walking into the foyer, memories of her former visit returned to her in full force. 'This wasn't my idea,' Power assured her.

'It doesn't matter,' she said wearily.

'You will dine with me tonight?' he asked. 'The Renaissance Room? Say eight o'clock?'

'Thanks Power. I think not. Daisy and I will have something to eat in the Alpine Grill around seven. All right with you, Daisy?'

'That suits me fine,' Daisy said with grim satisfaction, glad that Gina had given her escort the brush-off. Just who did this TJ Power think he was anyway? She would take the artist fellow, Rab Romer, any day of the week. She knew well enough the difference between dross and gold.

Apparently, so did Gina.

She would look back on *Antony and Cleopatra* as the highlight of her career. The words of her most poignant speech: 'Give me my robe, put on my crown; I have Immortal longings in me . . . I am fire, and air; my other elements I give to baser life', seemed a reflection of her innermost feelings, a statement of her own emotions.

Never had she felt so in command of her destiny. Free at last from self doubt, secure in the knowledge of Rab's love, that invisible cord which linked his heart to hers, her power as an actress had never been more potent or illuminating.

Imbuing the role with the human qualities of a woman in love, a woman torn between love and duty, she took Broadway by storm, bringing audiences to their feet after the final curtain, standing alone, centre-stage, in the magnificent cloth-of-gold robe she wore in the last act, holding a single red rose.

Every night since the play began, a red rose had been brought to her dressing-room, bearing the simple message, 'I love you'. Every night, taking her curtain calls, she had carried the rose on-stage with her as a talisman, a reminder of Rab's unfailing love for her.

Night after night, TJ Power watched her hungrily from the wings, unable to pinpoint the change in Gina.

More beautiful than ever despite the passage of time, he discerned in her a new strength and maturity far more potent than physical beauty – a timelessness, an enrichment of the personality born of experience, suffering, perhaps. Whatever the causes, he knew that she had secured her place among the legendary leading ladies of Broadway.

Eaten up with jealousy and remorse, if only she would trust him once more. But Power knew to his cost that trust, like faith, was not easily regained. He had failed her miserably. For what?

He might have known that his liaison with Ruth would end, as their marriage had done, with bitterness and recrimination. They had lived together for a while in an apartment overlooking Central Park, getting on each other's nerves; quarrelling violently in the morning; making love in the afternoon if they felt like it, during which time they had failed to reach a closer understanding of each other, so that their relationship had seemed like the 'El' railway system racketing above the streets of downtown New York, arriving at the same destination over and over again. Until the act of love had seemed as wearisome and predictable as a carousel ride on which the brightly painted horses went round and round in an endless circle. Until he had begun to loathe the sight of Ruth's naked body astride his, the futility of her endless, unproductive orgasms.

He needed to get Gina alone, to talk to her about the future, but she had been caught up in a whirl of activity since her arrival in New York – activity which intensified whenever he had suggested their lunching together, leaving him in no doubt that she did not wish to resume their former relationship. He realized that he should have asked her permission before telling those reporters that he was her agent and mentioning the possibility of a Hollywood contract. She had said, in the car, on the way to the Gotham, 'I had no idea that you had appointed yourself my agent. What a lot of trouble you've been to on my behalf. I imagine it was your idea to publicize my arrival, to feed the reporters misinformation about a Hollywood contract?' He had noticed that she was no longer holding the bouquet he had given her as a peace offering. Her refusal to dine with him that evening had set the seal on her disapproval of his high-handedness. He had not realized, at the time, that the starry-eyed girl of long ago no longer existed. He knew now.

The trouble was, he was still in love with her. And so he watched her, night after night, from the wings of the Bijou Theatre, awaiting his chance of a moment or two alone with her.

That chance came one night after the show, when the rest of the cast had gone to late-night supper and Gina was alone in her dressing-room. Alone, apart from the redoubtable Daisy Crabtree who answered his knock, scowled, and told him that Miss Brett was busy and did not wish to be disturbed.

'It's all right, Daisy,' Gina sealed the letters she had finished writing to Rab and Oliver, 'ask Mr Power to come in.' Useless, she considered, to defer her confrontation with TJ indefinitely. Daisy understood. 'I'll make myself scarce, then, shall I? But don't you put up with any of *his* nonsense.' So saying, she put on her coat, jammed on her hat, and sailed out of the dressing-room.

'Obviously your dresser has a poor opinion of me,' Power observed when Daisy had gone, slamming the door behind her.

'I wonder why?' Gina said coolly.

'OK. So I deserve the punishment you've handed out to me since your return to New York. I admit it. I'm sorry. What more can I say?' Running his fingers through his hair, 'God dammit, Gina, we once slept together, remember?'

She said quietly, 'Remember? Of course I remember. How could I ever forget the way you turned your back on me afterwards? But that is all in the past.'

'Is it, Gina?' Pulling her into his arms. 'I don't believe that. I loved you then. I'm still in love with you.' Drawing a deep breath, 'I'm asking you to marry me, to be my wife, to let me take care of you from now on.'

There could be no mistaking his sincerity, his passionate avowal of love, and she would have been less than a caring human being had she coldly dismissed the feelings of this man, even though he had taken her with no real understanding, in a series of desperate, upward thrusts which had nothing whatever to do with love. Nothing to do with gentleness or compassion.

Withdrawing from his embrace, 'I'm sorry, Power,' she said. 'I would have married you once, had you asked me. You were so strong an influence in my life, I thought, mistakenly, that I couldn't do without you. But that was a long time ago.' She paused. 'You weren't there when I needed you most. If you had taken the trouble to talk to me then, things might have been different.'

He said angrily, 'Oh, I see. So the great Gina Brett is now a tower of strength! What happened to change you from a clinging Ophelia into a domineering Cleopatra, I wonder? Fame? Fortune? Revenge?'

Understanding his anger, 'None of those things,' she said simply, laying a hand on his sleeve. 'Be honest with yourself, Power. You know as well as I do that you were still in love with Ruth, that you are still in love with her, and always will be. You see, that's the way love is, or should be. All or nothing!' She smiled wistfully, glancing at the red rose on her dressing table. 'I know because I have been in love with one man all my life, for better or for worse. And that's the way it is. If I have changed it has nothing whatever to do with fame, fortune, or revenge. Only with love.'

He said bitterly, 'You are wrong about Ruth. Our relationship is over and done with. She's in Washington now, working for *Vogue Magazine*. Frankly, I couldn't care less what the hell she's doing. It's you I care for. You, and only you!'

Gina said compassionately, 'If the dinner invitation still stands, we might find a vacant table in the Renaissance Room. I'm starving.' She smiled. 'Just give me a moment to put on my glad rags.'

He would always remember the way the diners applauded her entrance; how gracefully she had stood on the threshold of the Renaissance Room, a shining presence in a white satin gown stabbed with a single red rose, and the orchestra had played Jerome Kern's 'Lovely to Look At'.

But he had known, as he escorted her to their table, that he had lost her somewhere along the way, that he would regret, for the rest of his life, exchanging gold for dross, starlight for moondust.

Even so, he continued to stand in the wings of the Bijou Theatre until the closing night of *Antony and Cleopatra* the following December. December the twelfth to be exact, when the American nation had listened, with bated breath, to a recording of Edward VIII's renunciation of the throne to marry Wallis Warfield Simpson.

Returning to England, Gina had planned an exciting Christmas for Oliver, with lots of holly and mistletoe, a giant Christmas tree, fairy-lights, brightly wrapped presents, the traditional turkey and plum pudding.

Hurrying along Regent Street, doing the last minute shopping, buying gifts for George and Giselle, Peter and Adam, Daisy, Oliver and Bridget, she wished that Rab might join in the celebration. She longed to see him again, to tell him about her trip to New York. Never had their enforced separation seemed so irksome. If only she dare send him a message, ring him, hear his voice on the telephone; but messages could be intercepted, and what would happen if Marguerite answered the phone?

She might have known that Rab would find a way.

The church was filled for Midnight Mass, aglow with candlelight, ablaze with flowers. She was there with Daisy and Oliver.

'Once in Royal David's City'. Turning her head to watch the procession of choirboys down the aisle, suddenly her eyes met Rab's. He was standing a little way back, across the aisle. Smiling, he mouthed the words, 'I love you.' Misty-eyed, she returned his silent message.

Knowing Rab, he would leave before the service ended. She could not bear the thought of him slipping away into the shadows without a word. As the congregation rose for the final hymn, noticing that he had gone, she hurried up the aisle and down the path to the gate. 'Rab,' she called out to him. He turned. She ran into his arms. 'Won't you come back to the house with us?'

'I wish to God I could. I'm afraid it's not possible.' He looked weary, she thought, drained of vitality. 'Marguerite has taken it into her head to entertain. The house is filled with people I scarcely even know, apart from Phillip and Eleanor Marquiss . . . Oh God, Gina, you'll never know how much I've missed you, how much I need you.'

She said quietly, 'Remember that garden entrance? The iron staircase? I'll always be there for you, my darling. What other solution is there? Given the choice, I'd walk arm-in-arm with you down the Mall to Buckingham Palace.'

He knew what she meant, that she hated the thought of a clandestine relationship as much as he did. Even so, his heart warmed to the idea of a sanctuary of the heart, a peaceful oasis to be treated with respect.

The service over, people were beginning to leave the church. Holding her close, kissing her, 'I must go now,' he said. 'God bless you, my darling, and – thank you. This is for you, by the way. I hope you'll like it.'

343

She unwrapped Rab's Christmas present to her in the silence of her room. It was just a small package, but nothing in the world could have meant more to her. The miniature had been mounted in an oval, butterfly-wing frame. The sun-kissed, smiling face of Oliver, painted against a background of blue sky and sea, looked up at her from the soft folds of tissue paper surrounding it.

The intervening years had brought with them fresh challenges, new roles for Gina to conquer, new pictures for Rab to paint. But always, at the back of their minds, lay the knowledge of an escape-route to happiness via a garden gate and a flight of iron steps leading up to a balcony window.

Chapter Twenty-Eight

'I have decided to go back to France,' Giselle said proudly. 'Back to my roots. Back to where I belong.'

'But *why*, Giselle? Why now?' Gina asked in amazement.

'Because I can no longer bear the humiliation of knowing that I mean less to the maestro than the dust beneath his feet.'

Her pride dissolved suddenly into tears. She burst forth, 'All these years I have gone on hoping, praying that he would one day say something kind to me. One little word of appreciation would have meant so much to me. But no!' Fumbling for a handkerchief, 'I loved him once. Now I hate him! He is so blind, so stupid, so – insensitive!

'I gave up my career for that unfeeling *cochon*. For his sake, I came to England to help him establish his School of Dramatic Art. You know why? Because he once kissed me and told me I was beautiful, and I thought he loved me! Loved me? Ha! Well, I was beautiful then. Now look at me.

'All the students imagined that I was his mistress. *Pah!* Never once, during all the years we have spent together under the same roof, has he come to me for anything save a good meal.

'Night after night, year after year, I have lain in my bed willing him to cross that strip of landing, to come to me – not for food, but love: because he needed me as much as I needed him!' Drying her tears, 'Well, that's all over and done with now! He doesn't love me. He never has. Now I have my own future to think about. You see, Gina, I don't want to die, unloved, in a foreign country.'

'Have you told him?' Gina asked sympathetically.

'Told him? No, of course not. Why should I?' Latching on to her stiff-necked pride once more. 'All he'll get from me is a note of goodbye, wishing him luck for the future, hoping he'll find another fool like me to cook his food and train his students.'

Then, her pride deserting her, Giselle said wearily, 'It's just that I feel so old, so useless nowadays. I can't go on like this any more. Waking up in the morning, looking at my face in the mirror, all I want to do is escape from myself, and from him, go back to my family and friends, people who remember me as I used to be in my heyday, the toast of Paris. Do you know, students from the Sorbonne once drew my carriage along the Champs Elysées to the restaurant where I dined with the Maharajah of Ranchipur?' Tears filled her eyes. 'That was a night I shall never forget. To think I gave up all that for – what?'

They were in the drawing-room of Welford House at the time. Gina said carefully, 'I think you underestimate the maestro's feelings for you. Perhaps he takes you for granted because you have been together for so long.'

'*Too* long!'

'That doesn't mean he does not love you in his own way. You know as well as I that the maestro relies on you utterly, that you play an important role in his life.'

'I know that familiarity breeds contempt,' Giselle said stubbornly.

'But to leave him without a word of explanation.'

'I gather you don't approve. I thought that you, of all people, would understand. Apparently I was wrong.'

'I understand this much, Giselle. If you go away in anger, you'll live to regret it. You are tired, upset. Go away for a holiday if you must. Spend some time in France with your family and friends, but leave your options open.'

'No! I'm sorry, my mind is made up. I am leaving England for good.'

Moving quietly about her apartment in the early hours of the morning, packing her belongings, Giselle tore down the posters from the walls, crumpled them and threw them into the stove she had lit as a receptacle for the memorabilia she had gathered about her throughout the years, reminders of her life with George Landis: programmes, theatre tickets,

346

invitations, photographs, birthday and Christmas cards, which she now regarded as worthless junk. Hardening her heart, she watched them burn and shrivel in the heat of the fire.

She had taken her clothes from the wardrobe and laid them on the bed near the window, in which she had lain many a lonely night looking up at the stars, hearing the sounds of movement in the apartment across the landing, willing Landis to come to her, praying that he would come. He had not. Never. Not once in all the years they had been together had he come to her bed in need of the love and tenderness she had longed to give him. Never had they lain, night long, in each other's arms, or watched the sun rise over the rooftops across the way.

Opening her suitcase, it was not sexual fulfilment she had needed so much as warmth and companionship, Giselle thought, folding her dresses, her skirts, jumpers and lingerie into the case.

Her many books, paintings and ornaments, she considered, would have to be sent on later by a firm of carriers who would crate and despatch them according to her written instructions.

She was seated at her desk, pen in hand, when the door opened and Landis walked into the room. 'What the hell are you doing?' he asked in amazement.

'What does it look like?'

'I smelt burning,' he said. 'I thought the house was on fire!'

'No, George. Not the house. Just – rubbish.'

Bemusedly, 'Why are you packing?'

Getting up from the desk, 'I'd have thought that was obvious. I'm going away.'

'*Going away?* Where to?' He was wearing a plaid dressing-gown and carpet slippers. His hair was untidy. He looked stunned.

'To France. I'm leaving you, George.'

'*Leaving me?* But you *can't*! I mean, *why* for God's sake? What have I done?'

The moment for truth had arrived. 'It's not what you've

done, it's what you've left undone,' Giselle said hoarsely. 'All these years. I'm a woman, for Christ's sake, not a plaster statue.'

'But I thought—'

'*What* did you think, George? I'd really like to know. Don't tell me, let me guess. You thought that I was a permanent fixture, part of the furniture and fittings of this school of yours. Some kind of cipher, some bloody old has-been in need of nothing more than a roof over her head. But you were wrong. I needed much more than that. I needed to be told, now and then, that I was important to you. I needed warmth, companionship. Love!' She turned away from him, sobbing.

Laying his hands on her shoulders, he said quietly, 'I'm sorry, my dear. I thought you knew.'

'Knew *what*?'

'How much I love you. How much I have always loved you. You just seemed so out of reach, that's all. You were always the star. The great leading lady, the clever one. I – I never was much of an actor. Never much of a success at anything really. I've always been shy with women. It never crossed my mind that you would look twice at a ham like me.

'The nights I've paced my room wondering what you'd say if I came to you. I daren't take the risk of your turning me away, telling me to get out. I could not take the chance that you would – leave me.'

'Oh, George!' She turned to face him. Tears were streaming down her cheeks, 'Why didn't you tell me this before? All the time we've wasted! It doesn't bear thinking about.'

He said, 'Then let's not waste any more.' Handing her a handkerchief from his dressing-gown pocket. 'Let me think. We'll apply for a special licence, get married as quickly as possible, arrange the reception; take a couple of days off. Go to Oxford perhaps, stay at the Mitre—'

'God dammit! This is so typical of you. Well, the answer is no. Here. Take this, I don't need it.' She thrust the handkerchief back in his pocket.

'Now what I have done wrong?' His jaw sagged. 'I thought you would like the idea of marriage.'

'I do!'

'Then why say no? I've just proposed to you, for heaven's sake, thinking that's what you wanted.'

'Oh, is that what it was? A proposal? It sounded more like a railway timetable to me.'

'What did you expect? That I would get down on one knee, place my hand on my heart: say "Darling, I love you. Will you marry me?" '

'Yes! That is exactly what I expected.'

'In my dressing-gown and slippers?'

'Precisely. Do it, George.'

'I'm damned if I will! You'll have to make do with this.' Clasping her hands, he drew her close to him. Catching the fragrance of her hair, overwhelmed by a feeling of tenderness towards her, seeing her as *La Dame aux Camélias*, he murmured, 'I love you, Giselle. I have always loved you, and I want you for my wife. Please say you'll marry me. My life would be meaningless without you. Please, darling, will you marry me?'

Smiling up at him, 'Yes, of course I will,' she said softly.

Giselle decided that she would wear a cream lace dress and carry a bouquet of camellias. Both she and George wanted a quiet church wedding with a few close friends about them. George had asked Rab to be his best man. As a matter or courtesy, Marguerite could not be overlooked.

Strung on the horns of a dilemma, Giselle went to see Georgina. Deeply worried, 'I never realized, until I started writing the invitations,' she said, 'what an impossible situation it would be for you and Rab! Dare I *not* invite Marguerite?'

'Of course you must invite her,' Gina said.

'But she is a jealous, possessive woman. And she has seen his Portrait of Gina.'

Marguerite shopped extensively for the wedding. In her unbalanced state of mind she had chosen a dress more suitable for a girl than a mature woman; a hat of Pari-buntal straw bedecked with flowers. On the wedding day, she entered the church on Rab's arm, her high heels clicking on the grey stone slabs, her face flushed with excitement.

'But I want to sit with you,' she cried petulantly, as Rab led her to a pew, made sure she was safely ensconced, and moved quietly away to speak to George. 'I'm *going* to sit with you!' Getting up, she clawed at Rab's sleeve. 'How *dare* you leave me on my own? I'm not sitting among strangers.'

'Please, Marguerite. You forget, I have a duty to perform,' Rab said quietly.

'I'd have thought your first duty lay in looking after *me*. I *am* your wife.' Her voice rose shrilly. The organist looked round at the disturbance. George lumbered to his feet, visibly distressed, feeling he had enough to cope with without an hysterical woman to contend with into the bargain.

'Please, do sit down, Mrs Romer,' he said heroically, 'Sit next to me, if you wish. The bride will be here at any moment.' God grant, he thought wildly, that the stupid woman would not insist on standing by Rab's side throughout the ceremony.

Thankfully, she did not. Her tantrum over, seemingly drained of energy, she closed her eyes, a curious smile playing about her lips, as though lulled and hypnotized by the words of the wedding service.

Deliberately, Rab did not look at Gina throughout the ceremony. He dare not, lest his eyes betrayed his love for her. He was simply aware of her presence, a slim, cool figure in a pale green chiffon gown, standing close to the bride, clasping a bouquet of apricot roses in her gloved hands, her face framed by a green halo hat trimmed with apricot ribbon.

How serene she appeared, how strong. He wished that he could prevent the inevitable meeting of Marguerite and Gina at the wedding reception. He knew that he could not, and dreaded the outcome of that meeting.

*   *   *

Inured, from long experience of Marguerite's illness, to her every mood and whim, Rab laid a firm hand on his wife's arm as they entered the room where the bride and groom awaited the arrival of their guests.

Giselle reacted magnificently to Marguerite. 'My husband and I are so pleased that you were able to come to our wedding,' she said warmly, 'that we have the pleasure of meeting you at last.'

'Why? Did you think I wouldn't be able to come? Is that it?'

'No, of course not, my dear, I simply meant that we . . .'

But Marguerite was not listening. Catching sight of Gina, lurching unsteadily towards her, thrusting aside Rab's restraining hand on her arm, 'I've seen your face before,' she said accusingly. 'I'd know it anywhere! You're the girl in the portrait, aren't you? *Aren't* you? That bloody portrait my husband thought so much about that he couldn't bear to part with it.'

'You are wrong, Mrs Romer,' Gina said quietly, 'the girl in that portrait no longer exists. She died a long time ago!'

Returning home, she saw Peter Dickenson and Bridget Donovan standing close together in the garden, looking at each other with an intensity which could mean only one thing. They were in love.

A letter awaited her. The offer of a contract to star in a West End production of *Antony and Cleopatra*.

Staring into her dressing-table mirror, she uttered the lines: 'Give me my robe, put on my crown; I have Immortal longings in me . . .' Tears spilled down her cheeks. She knew the words were false. She was just a woman in love with a man who belonged to someone else. And yet . . . 'Immortal longings'? Yes, perhaps that much was true.

Would Rab send her a single rose with the message, 'I love you', before every performance, she wondered.

She might have known that he would.

Maytime brought the Coronation of George VI. London was a blaze of colour, packed with overseas visitors.

Excitement was in the air. Edward VIII's sad departure for France following the abdication had been forgotten in the delight of a new royal family.

Oliver was in Cornwall with his father when Adam died one night in his sleep. It had been a peaceful end to a long and useful life. They laid the old man to rest in the Hampstead cemetery, his coffin heaped with the flowers he loved.

Afterwards, Peter Dickenson asked Gina's permission to marry Bridget, to live in the garden flat after the wedding, which she gladly granted. They would wait awhile, he said, out of respect for his father. 'That is entirely up to you,' Gina said, 'though I think that Adam would not have wanted you to wait too long.' She could not have explained her misgivings at that moment, her fear of the future.

The coronation had pushed into the background the fact that Germany was re-arming. The Nazis had entered the Rhineland the previous year, Mussolini's Fascist troops had overrun Abyssinia in the autumn of 1935. These facts could not be ignored, and those who had lived through the horror of the First World War must be aware of history repeating itself.

If war came, Peter would be called on to fight for his country. She could not very well have said to him, 'Take all the happiness you can, while you can.' The same applied to Oliver. How could she bear it?

Rab shared Gina's disquiet about the future. Returning to London in the August of 1939, he realized that war was inevitable. Plans had already been made for the evacuation of children to places of greater safety. Air raid shelter signs were in evidence, government buildings had been sand-bagged, European refugees had begun to arrive in England in droves as the crisis deepened.

He viewed with horror the inescapability of suffering that war would entail; the lives of those he loved most, Gina and Oliver, shattered by the coming conflict. He knew Oliver had meant what he said about joining up, fighting for the country he loved, but how would Gina react to his enlistment? A nineteen-year-old boy with a promising future ahead of him? A boy? No that was unfair, derogatory. Oliver was now a man in every sense of the word: tall, strong, athletic, fair-minded, clear sighted – valiant – the stuff of which England was made. 'A body of England's, breathing English air'.

Rab also viewed with a deep feeling of weariness, an incalculable sadness of the spirit, what war would mean to him in terms of renunciation of his freedom, those Cornish summers which had given him the self-discipline to face wintertime with Marguerite. Summertimes during which, inspired by the presence of his son, he had painted as never before: pictures of fishermen at work on their nets; women gossiping; cobles coming home at eventide, their riding lights winking like fireflies in the dusk; moonlight on the sea. How would he be able to live, to work, to create, without spiritual freedom?

More importantly, how could he stand by doing nothing to mitigate the suffering of those old, well-loved friends of his, forced by their religion, into prisons, denied the right to human dignity? The answer to that was not yet clear, but there must be an answer.

With God's grace, he would find that answer.

Chapter Twenty-Nine

The outbreak of war would be forever linked, in the minds of the theatrical profession, with the sudden blacking out of the West End and provincial theatres, the closure of the cinemas; the grim spectre of unemployment.

'This is monstrous,' the maestro complained bitterly. 'As if this bloody war's not hard enough to bear without the government denying people the right to entertainment!'

'Calm down, George,' Giselle said soothingly. 'Remember your blood-pressure.'

'To hell with my blood-pressure! Talk about "Goodbye, Mr Chips", it's goodbye to Victory, in my view! I've a good mind to write a letter to *The Times*!'

Giselle knew he wouldn't. But someone else did: George Bernard Shaw! 'What agent of Hitler suggested that we should all cower in terror for the duration?', he demanded, in print: that towering, Irish wordsmith, speaking on behalf of a nation at war.

Gina had auditioned for, and had been awarded, the role of Miss Moffat in Emlyn Williams' *The Corn is Green* – a far cry from Cleopatra – nevertheless a role she found interesting and looked forward to playing, until suddenly the West End theatres had been plunged into darkness.

Even Ivor Novello's smash-hit musical, *The Dancing Years*, had ceased to dance when the cancellation notices were posted on the doors of Drury Lane, a theatre destined to remain closed, in one sense, until the Entertainments National Service Associations' staff moved into their newly established headquarters, after the blackout restrictions had been relaxed somewhat, to mastermind professional entertainment for HM Forces serving at home and abroad.

'Huh, what's the use of all this ENSA nonsense?' Landis said gloomily, throwing aside his copy of *The Times*. 'I know the director, Basil Dean, better than most. An impossible man to work with. Besides, what hope of a return to normality with a six o'clock curfew imposed on the West End theatres? *Six o'clock!* I ask you. The time babies are put to bed.'

'At least the West End companies are at liberty to perform in the provinces,' Giselle reminded him, still worried about his blood-pressure. 'That is something to be thankful for.'

'Oh, you think so, do you?' George fretted. 'You think it good enough that an actress of Gina's calibre should be forced to perform in run-down theatres the length and breadth of Great Britain? Well, I *don't!*'

Peter Dickenson had joined the Royal Navy at the outbreak of war. When his vessel returned to port for repairs, he had been granted compassionate leave to visit his wife; to see his newly-born son, Adam. A mere 48 hours to be with Bridget before he must return to his ship.

He came to see Gina in the early morning of his departure, a jaunty figure in a navy blue uniform with a laid back collar.

'I've just come to thank you for taking care of Bridget and the boy,' he said shyly. 'You're just like your father. He took care of people, too.' He smiled. 'You know, Miss Georgina, I think of this place, this house, as a second Elmhurst, with all the people I prize most around me. Daisy Crabtree. Above all, you, miss!' His eyes misted with tears momentarily, then he said stalwartly, 'Well, I'd best be off now.'

Clasping his hands, kissing his cheek, 'Goodbye, Peter, and good luck,' she murmured. 'And don't worry about Bridget and Adam. You know they will always have a home here with me.' She smiled crookedly. 'After all, they are part of my family. And so are you.'

She walked with him to the front door; turned away as he embraced his wife and child. And then he was gone, his duffle-bag slung over his shoulder, turning back to wave to Bridget who was standing forlornly on the front steps, watching him go, their infant son clasped tightly in her arms.

When he had turned the corner, 'They might have given us a few more days together,' Bridget said tearfully. 'Just a few more hours . . .'

Just a few more hours, Gina thought bleakly, leading Bridget indoors, hating this war which had carved up the lives of innocent people into precise segments of time, bound by officialdom into carefully controlled hours, minutes and seconds which had no bearing on the very real human emotions of people in love, giving no guarantee that two people in love would ever see each other again when the hours, minutes and seconds allotted to them, had run out.

Closing the front door, Gina knew that soon the time would come when she must say goodbye to Oliver.

She had been aware, ever since he had joined the army, that when his training was completed, he would be sent overseas. Even so, when the time came, she was unprepared for the pain of leavetaking.

The last night of his leave, they talked together until the early hours of the morning. Reminiscing.

'Do you remember taking me to feed the pigeons in Trafalgar Square?' he asked. 'The way you came to my room to kiss me good night before you left for the theatre? You always smelt so nice. What was that perfume you wore?'

'Eau de cologne, most probably.' She smiled.

He said, 'Dad knows I'm leaving tomorrow. I risked a phone call to St John's Wood. He's seeing me off at Waterloo.'

'I'm glad.' She paused. 'Do you want me to come, too?'

'I'd rather you didn't. Don't get me wrong. I'd rather remember you here, in this room, the firelight shining on your face.'

She turned her head away. 'Oh, Oliver!' Tears filled her eyes.

Suddenly he was at her feet, his arms about her, holding

her tightly. 'Don't cry, darling. You mustn't worry. I'll be all right, you'll see.'

'Forgive me. I made up my mind not to cry. Somehow, I can't help it. I meant to be brave. Now look at me.'

Standing up, he drew her into his arms, 'I *am* looking at you,' he said quietly. 'My St Joan. That's how I shall always think of you. Proud, courageous, indomitable. Just like Grandpa Owen. I loved him so much, and I love you!'

Bending down, he kissed her gently. She clung to him momentarily. 'Take care of yourself, my son.'

'I will. I promise.'

And then he was gone. Their time together had run out.

As much as she wanted to see him just once more, she knew that she must not spoil his memories of the night before. Experience had taught her the right moment to allow the curtain to fall.

She heard the arrival and departure of the taxi he had ordered to take him to the station. Then, very slowly, she stepped out onto the balcony, and walked alone to his garden room. There, she looked at his collection of treasures, his books and drawings, his paintings, seeing Rab's hand in their composition and subject matter. She saw his collection of shells carefully arranged on the shelves, and the special niche in which he had hung pictures of her as Ophelia, St Joan, *la Dame aux Camélias* – Viola, Roxanne, Desdemona, Juliet, Phèdre, Cleopatra, and the many half-forgotten roles she had played during her repertory season with the Barry Jackson Company: these alongside family snapshots taken on the terrace, at picnics and on school open days, at the seaside, and on Hampstead Heath; above a broad shelf on which lay his scrap-book full of press cuttings.

Opening a door, she saw his clothes hanging there, his school blazer and flannels, long outgrown, his Sunday suit and winter coat, his favourite dressing gown – the one he referred to as his 'Noel Coward'.

'To make one little room an everywhere' . . . Oliver had

done just that, had left in this, his special, private place, the imprint of his happy, multifaceted personality.

He had slept in this room last night. What had been his thoughts, she wondered, as he lay looking up at the stars? She had loved Oliver since the day he was born, but how well had she really known him? She had spent so much time away from him when he was little, of necessity, when she was working hard to earn a living.

Now, success had reaped its rewards. She was financially secure at last, well respected in her profession. But was this enough?

At the back of her mind lay the troubling thought that it was not. During the last war she had pulled her weight as her father's secretary, getting up each morning at the crack of dawn, to walk down to the mill, to play her part in the war effort, aggravating her mother by her refusal to roll bandages and knit Balaclava helmets under the auspices of the Ladies' Aid Society, as Josie and Letty Bickley had done.

Closing the door of Oliver's room, Gina knew that now the final curtain had been rung down on *The Corn is Green*, she must help, in some positive way, towards the war effort: relinquish her role as a leading lady of the theatre to wash up in a Forces' canteen, if necessary; drive an ambulance. Anything, just as long as she felt useful once more, as she had done on those wild winter mornings in the Calder Valley, hurrying to the mill, her face stung with the wind and the rain.

'Dad, what's wrong with your hand?' Oliver stared concernedly at the blood-soaked handkerchief tied haphazardly round his father's wrist.

'I cut it while shaving. It's nothing. Don't worry, I'll have it seen to later.'

His father looked tired, worried, Oliver thought. He hated station platforms, goodbyes, the bustle of departure, the ear-splitting steam-letting, clanking handbarrows, the feeling of time running out. He said, 'Remember the tide coming in on the beach? How we watched the sun come up over the sea? That's what I'll be thinking of. You and Mother. All the happy, peaceful things.'

'I have something for you.' Rab felt in his pocket. 'It's a coin I once found on the sands at Scarborough. A Victorian threepenny-piece. I've kept it ever since – a kind of talisman, a good luck charm.'

'Thanks, Father. I'll give it back to you one day.'

The train was due to depart. Time had run out. He gave Rab a brief hug then got into the carriage. The guard came down the platform, slamming doors; glancing at his watch. He couldn't say the word goodbye. His lips felt frozen, unnatural. He tried to smile. He felt the tiny silver coin his father had given him pressing into the palm of his hand as he raised it in a wordless gesture of farewell.

When the train had disappeared from view, Rab walked unsteadily out of the station. Blood was running down his hand. He could feel the pulsing throb of the wound and knew that he must get it seen to. The razor had bitten deeply into his flesh. He had seen the dazzling sweep of the blade too late to prevent its descent. But far more shocking than the suddenness of the attack had been the look on Marguerite's face, the hatred in her eyes as he had wrestled with her for possession of the weapon. The same look, he imagined, as when she had shredded the Portrait of Gina to ribbons.

Following the attack, Marguerite had sunk to her knees and grovelled on the floor, uttering obscenities, beating her fists on the blood-stained carpet, her hair in disarray. Calling for the servants to take care of her, he had raced downstairs to ring for the doctor.

Glancing worriedly at the grandfather clock, he knew that he had exactly an hour and a quarter in which to get to Waterloo. Thank God the doctor had sensed the urgency of the call.

His diagnosis of Marguerite's condition had not been prolonged, nor his subsequent actions in any way indecisive as he asked permission to telephone for an ambulance. 'Your wife is seriously disturbed,' he said. 'I dare not take the risk of leaving her here a minute longer. For her sake as well as yours, I am taking her to my private clinic to be cared for by experienced psychiatric nurses until certain tests have been carried out.

'You needn't worry for the time being. She is under heavy sedation.' Hanging up the receiver. 'Now, you'd better let me take a look at that hand of yours.'

'May I see her?'

'Better not. I suggest that you leave her in my care for the next day or so. I assure you that she will be well looked after. Frankly, Romer, I would far rather you kept your distance in the present circumstances. Now, about that hand—'

'No! I'll come to your surgery later. I have an urgent appointment. Something that can't wait.'

On the way to Waterloo, his mind in a turmoil, Rab roughly bound his injured hand with a clean hanky. Immediately, the blood welled up again, staining crimson the white linen. The pain of it meant nothing to him compared with the imagined pain of not being in time to say goodbye to his son.

Walking out of the station, weak from loss of blood, Rab realized with a horror bordering on despair, that Marguerite had meant to kill him. Now she really was mad, God help her.

A deep feeling of pity for her suddenly overwhelmed him. He stared with unseeing eyes at the hurrying tide of humanity flowing past him in an endless stream, and heard the grinding roar of the traffic: remembered, as someone in a dream, the tide coming in on a crescent moon of a beach in Cornwall; the peace of a Cornish sunrise, his son's face framed by a railway carriage window of that train that would take him to God alone knew where in the theatre of war.

He came to in a clinically white hospital bed, his right hand expertly bandaged, feeling weak from loss of blood and the anti-tetanus jab he'd been given.

'So, you're back in the land of the living?' The nurse at his bedside was young, dark-haired, pretty.

'Where am I?'

'The Charing Cross Hospital. You were brought in by ambulance yesterday afternoon.'

'I can't seem to remember what happened.'

'I'm not surprised. You'd passed-out near the newsstand outside Waterloo Station. You'd lost an awful lot of blood.'

Rab frowned, trying to remember.

'From that gash on your hand,' the nurse explained patiently. 'The thumb was almost severed.'

'Ah, yes.'

'What had you been doing? Chopping wood?'

'Something like that.' He attempted a smile.

Plumping his pillows, 'Just as well you're not a concert pianist. You're *not*, are you?'

'No.' He knew what she meant. The curtailment of a career. The girl had made a light-hearted remark meant to cheer him. The odds against his being a concert pianist had been a million to one, and she knew it. But what of an artist with a damaged right hand?

The girl looked worried. 'I haven't said anything wrong, have I? It was meant as a joke.'

'I know. You needn't worry.'

'It's just that Matron hates us VADs. She'd have my guts for garters if she knew I'd upset you.'

'What's your name?' Rab asked gently.

'April. April Smith.'

'Tell me, April, where are my clothes? I can't stay here any longer.'

'You must! You can't leave until the doctor's given you the all-clear. There'd be a hell of a row, and I'd be held responsible.'

The poor child, Rab thought compassionately, understanding her distress. 'It's all right,' he said calmly, 'I'll abide by the rules.'

April Smith smiled tremulously. 'You will? Gee, thanks! They'll be serving breakfast in a minute. How do you fancy a bowl of warm porridge and a hard-boiled egg?' She laughed suddenly, her confidence restored. A kind-hearted lass who had gone into nursing primarily because she liked the uniform.

'Nurse Smith!'

April glanced anxiously towards the swing doors. 'Gotta go now,' she told Rab, *sotto voce*. 'Sister's on the warpath!'

When she had skated off down the ward, staring up at the ceiling he imagined the horror of never being able to hold a paintbrush properly again. Never again to know the joy of creation on canvas. But above and beyond that lay the memory of Marguerite's frenzied attack, her hoarsely uttered words: 'I'll kill her, that woman you're in love with. I'll cut her face to ribbons!'

He harboured no doubt that Marguerite had meant what she said. What if she had carried out her threat, had injured Gina? But no, he was not thinking clearly. Dragging his mind back to reality, he remembered that his wife had been taken to Dr Waverley's Richmond Clinic, under heavy sedation.

A ward orderly came in at that moment, pushing the breakfast trolley. 'Porridge, sir? A nice boiled egg? Toast?' he enquired cheerfully.

'No thanks. I'm not hungry.'

'Please yerself.' The trolley moved on to the next bed.

Rab remembered hazily that he had meant to go to Welford House last night to see Gina, to tell her that he had been at Waterloo to say goodbye to Oliver; to comfort her.

Last night, above all others, she would have been expecting his footsteps on the iron stairs leading up to her room, would have needed a shoulder to cry on. What must she have thought when there had been no word from him? No message?

He imagined her, alone in her room, crossing to the window occasionally to stare into the emptiness of the night, wondering why he had not come to her.

This was the pattern of his life, he thought bitterly, not being there for the woman he loved when she needed him most. And where, for God's sake, was the doctor in charge of the ward? The waiting was unbearable. So too was the searing pain in his right hand, now that the effects of the pain-killing tablets he had been given the night before were beginning to wear off.

The house seemed very still, very quiet, bereft of the febrile presence of Marguerite; her quick, flurried movements, high-pitched voice, the sound of the drawing-room piano on which she had played, over and over again, Chopin's 'Revolutionary Study'; continually striking wrong notes, not even aware that she had done so, lost in a crazy dream of a recital at the Wigmore Hall.

Wearily, Rab closed the front door behind him. His world seemed encompassed, at that moment, by the throbbing pain in his right hand.

'Oh, sir. You're home. We've been that worried!'

The maid had taken him by surprise. He had not even noticed her hurrying downstairs towards him.

'Have you? I'm sorry. I had no way of letting you know. I spent the night in hospital.'

'The thing is, sir, Madam's doctor has been trying to get in touch with you,' the girl said importantly. 'He said you was to ring him the moment you came in. The number's on the pad in the study.'

'Thank you, Elsie.'

Slowly Rab entered the study, picked up the phone, and asked the operator to connect him with the Richmond Clinic.

Chapter Thirty

Half out of his mind with worry, 'How did it happen? How could you have allowed such a thing to happen?' Rab demanded of Dr Waverley.

'I'm sorry, Mr Romer. You have every right to be angry. I accept full responsibility,' the doctor said heavily.

'God dammit, man, this is no time to talk about responsibility! Have you made a thorough search of the grounds? Have you notified the Police?'

'Of course I have. The minute one of my nurses discovered that your wife was missing from her room, I instituted a search party to cover every inch of the grounds. We looked everywhere. There was no sign of her. I then contacted the Police.' Waverley added, as a sop to his conscience, 'I did try to contact you several times last night. You were not at home.'

'For the simple reason I was in hospital. But that's neither here nor there. The only thing I give a damn about right now is discovering my wife's whereabouts! She cannot simply have disappeared without trace. I'll come as quickly as I can!'

His mind and movements seemed unco-ordinated as he went upstairs to change into a clean shirt and sweater. The fact that he was still suffering from shock and loss of blood, did not occur to him. He groaned with frustration trying, single-handedly, to button the shirt and struggle into a fresh jumper. He had asked the maid to ring for a taxi; had scarcely finished changing when the doorbell rang.

Gina had waited up until two o'clock. She had been so sure that Rab would come to her that night, just to be with her, to talk about Oliver.

It had been a long, difficult day. Restless and lonely, she

had gone for a long walk on the Heath that afternoon, thinking of Oliver, longing for night to come, in need of Rab's comforting presence.

Curious how time sped by towards a moment of leave-taking, how slowly the hands of the clock had moved that night as she waited alone in her room, her senses alert for the sound of footsteps that never came.

When the clock chimed two, she had locked the french windows and gone to bed. Exhausted as she was, she had remained on the *qui vive* for the ringing of the telephone on her bedside table; willing it to ring.

She must have fallen asleep then. Waking at five, she realized with a start that the bedside lamp was still on. Getting up, putting on her white dressing-robe, drawing back the curtains, she thought that the room resembled the stage-set of some second-rate drama – an amateur production at that, in which the cast had forgotten their lines.

As the taxi sped towards Richmond, Rab wondered how was it possible for a heavily sedated woman to have escaped the vigilance of the nurse in charge of her sick room? What had been at the back of his wife's mind when she had slipped out of the building into the darkness of the outside world? His head came up sharply. His brain began to function again. Gina! Of course. Christ, he thought, what if Marguerite had already harmed her in some way? Taken by surprise, Gina would be no match for a mentally deranged woman with murder in her heart.

He glanced at his watch. Two o'clock . . .

At two o'clock Gina, dressed for going out, picked up her gloves and handbag. Bridget was on the stairs. 'If Mr Romer should ring, tell him I've gone out,' she said, 'I have no idea when I'll be back.' She was carrying an overnight case.

The taxi sped up the drive of the Richmond Clinic. Rab noticed, with a feeling of dread, that two police cars were parked there. A uniformed officer came briskly towards him. 'May I have your name, sir?'

365

'Romer. Robert Romer.'

'Please follow me.'

Doctor Waverley, grey-faced, was standing in the hall of his expensively furnished nursing home. 'Thank God you've come,' he said hoarsely. 'Such a terrible tragedy.'

'Tragedy? What the hell do you mean? What tragedy?'

The police officer intervened. 'The body of a woman has been recovered from the river a hundred yards or so downstream, which we believe to be that of Mrs Marguerite Romer. I must ask you to make the formal identification.'

Gina went by tube to Golders Green, and walked from the Underground station to the School of Dramatic Art.

Giselle greeted her warmly. 'You did perfectly right to telephone,' she said. 'Come, I will make some tea, and you will tell me all about it.'

'I felt I'd go mad if I stayed in the house a minute longer,' Gina said wearily, as Giselle put the kettle on to boil.

'I know the feeling only too well, *ma chérie*. There are times when I could run away screaming.' Getting out the cups and saucers, 'It was unlike Rab not to contact you.'

'I know I am being stupid, petty. I just felt so let down, lonely, angry too – and jealous.'

'Jealous?'

'Of Marguerite!' The floodgates opened. 'Suddenly it all seemed so humiliating. I saw myself for what I am – the "other woman". Second best! It has always been there at the back of my mind, the guilt feeling, the secrecy. Last night I asked myself if I was being fair to Rab, myself or Marguerite. Suddenly the situation became unbearable.'

'Because you were too tired to think clearly, *chérie*.' Giselle sat down at the table. Taking Gina's hand, squeezing it tightly. 'Little wonder, after all you've been through. But second best? That is nonsense and you know it. It is you Rab loves. You and only you.'

Gina bit her lip, fighting against tears. 'I know he loves me. It's just that we have to live in the shadows all the time. We can never be like other people – free, above-board.'

'Remember the reason why this is so,' Giselle reminded

her. 'Ask yourself if it was worth denying yourself that kind of freedom, for Oliver's sake.'

George came in at that moment. 'Gina darling, it's lovely to see you. Ah, tea. I'm parched.' He was wearing a strange get-up, disreputable Oxford bags, an old shirt and a butcher's apron. 'I've been clearing rubbish from the attic,' he explained, catching Gina's puzzled expression. 'If an incendiary bomb came through the roof, we'd be grilled.' He sighed deeply. 'Ah, the treasures I've unearthed. The memorabilia of a lifetime!'

'Now, darling, you mustn't let sentimentality get in the way.' Giselle poured the tea. 'If I don't keep my eye on him, he'll simply remove everything from the attic to the cellar, then we shall end up barbecued!'

'Dear heart. You must leave me to decide,' George rumbled. 'This is a deeply emotional time for me. The end of an era, a dream.' He paused as only the maestro could pause – dramatically. 'At times like this, a man is best left alone.'

'Oh? In that case I might as well take a holiday,' Giselle said, tongue-in-cheek. 'What would you say, Gina, to a few days in the country? A remote cottage perhaps, or a farm somewhere. Long walks, old clothes. Silence. Fresh country butter. Hmmm. Seriously, why not? You wouldn't object, George, if Gina and I left you on your own for a little while? Gina?'

George beamed. Gina smiled. The idea of getting away from London appealed to her strongly at that moment. A phone call to Daisy that evening to find out if Rab had been in touch convinced her that she should take a break, when Daisy said, 'No, I'm sorry, my lamb, I'm afraid he hasn't.'

'Yes, that is my wife,' Rab said quietly.

'Thank you, sir. There will have to be an inquest,' the Police officer told him.

'Yes, of course.' He stood there looking down at Marguerite's body, filled with an overwhelming sense of pity that she had met so tragic an end. The words of a half-forgotten poem teased his mind: 'Her life was turning, turning, In mazes of heat and sound . . .'

Someone had had the decency to cover her flimsily-clad body with a coat after she'd been taken out of the water. If only they had carried her a little further up the bank so that her hair was beyond the reach of the river. Deeply distressed, he noticed the dark tendrils, spreading like seaweed, floating and lifting on the current, the bruised appearance of her skin, the trail of slime oozing from her lips.

It had been a hell of a day. He had not realized the questioning involved in a death from unnatural causes. He had begun to wonder, at one stage, if the police suspected him of murder.

The nurse in charge of Marguerite's sick-room had broken down and wept, admitting that she had gone to the staff room for a cup of tea and a cigarette, thinking her patient would remain unconscious for another hour or so at least.

Dr Waverley, badly shaken, said that Mrs Romer had been admitted to his clinic suffering from a complete nervous breakdown, and under heavy sedation. He would not have believed it possible that any woman, sedated to that extent, could have walked out of the building on her own two feet.

Returning to St John's Wood, Rab wondered if Eleanor's absence had been partly responsible for Marguerite's breakdown. She had reacted badly when Eleanor had returned to Cornwall to care for Phillip Marquiss, who had suffered a slight stroke. 'Father doesn't need you as much as I do!' she had screamed after her sister as she had walked down the front steps to enter a waiting taxi.

Now, clearly, the Marquisses must be informed of Marguerite's death. Sending the telegram, his heart sank at the very thought of Eleanor's return to London. A crumb of comfort lay in that Phillip Marquiss would not be with her.

At six o'clock he rang Welford House, longing for the

sound of Gina's voice on the line. Bridget answered. 'I'm sorry, Mr Robert,' she said, 'the mistress isn't here. She came home earlier, collected a few belongings, and went off again in a hurry.'

'Did she say where she was going?'

'No. I don't think she knew that herself. All I know is, she seemed a bit upset.'

'I see. Thank you, Bridget.'

He should have rung Gina the minute he had been discharged from hospital, Rab thought bleakly. If she was upset, it was his fault.

The farmhouse, well off the beaten track, with its 'Bed and Breakfast' sign affixed to the gate, caught Giselle's attention. 'What have we to lose?' she said brightly. 'If we don't like it, we can easily move on the first thing tomorrow morning.'

When morning came, they didn't want to move on. The farmer's wife had given them freshly baked scones, Devonshire clotted cream and strawberry jam for tea, a supper of ham and eggs. Their rooms were as clean as fresh paint; bathwater scalding hot, the view of the Devonshire countryside from their attic windows, absolutely breathtaking.

At breakfast, Giselle said mistily, 'The war seems a million light years away here. I had almost forgotten how good it would feel to be free of the sound of air-raid sirens, bombers droning overhead, newspapers. Bad news in general. Worried people with worried faces. Am I being very selfish, *chérie*?'

'If you are, so am I.' Gina smiled reflectively. 'It's a matter of perspective, isn't it? Of standing back a little from life.'

'*Wife of Famous Artist Dies in Mysterious Circumstances.*'

Details of the inquest on Marguerite Romer appeared in print.

'Well, I hope you're satisfied,' Eleanor Marquiss said stiffly, after a verdict of accidental death due to drowning had been recorded.

'*Satisfied?*' Rounding on his sister-in-law, his anger at full spate, 'How dare you suggest such a thing?' Rab demanded. 'I am far from satisfied. Had you and your father not been so blind, so blinkered, this tragedy might never have happened!'

'So now you are blaming Father and me for Marguerite's death?' Eleanor bridled. 'How typical of a man like you. A man who took full advantage of her youth and innocence—'

'No, Eleanor, that simply won't wash any more, and you know it,' Rab said quietly, his anger subsiding. 'I told you from the beginning that Marguerite and I were man and wife in name only. Did it never occur to you, when she underwent a phantom pregnancy, that our marriage had never been consummated? That she was play-acting? That she would have done everything in her power to ensure my return to Cornwall – including emotional blackmail.'

'But you did consummate the marriage eventually,' Eleanor reminded him, 'when you took her to that hovel at Talland Bay to live with you. I *know* because Marguerite told me so.'

Rab smiled grimly. 'May I accept, then, that you knew I was speaking the truth when I brought your sister back to England during the last war? When I told you that she was still a virgin?'

'Yes, I suppose so, but—'

'Spare me the "buts", Eleanor,' Rab said intently. 'To-morrow, for Marguerite's sake, we have no choice other than to attend her funeral together. When that funeral is over, I want you out of my house, out of my life, as quickly as possible. Is that perfectly clear?'

Walking the hills together, 'Do you realize,' Gina asked Giselle, 'that, had it not been for you, the maestro and Rab, I might be earning my living as a shorthand typist?'

'And would that have pleased you?'

'It might have been a lot simpler.'

Giselle laughed. 'If you wanted the simple life, you should not have left your lover standing at the altar. By this time, you would have been a boring, middle-class matron

holding dinner parties for your husband's business acquaint-
ances, worrying about your children's teeth and tonsils.
But think what you'd have missed; the applause, the
acclaim, the thrill of those opening nights; starring on
Broadway. No *chérie*, you were not born for the simple life.
You set your own seal on the future when you left – what
was his name? Harry Bickley? You must have known, even
then, that you wanted more from life than being a housewife
or a shorthand typist.'

Tucking her hand in Gina's elbow, 'He is still on your
mind, *n'est-ce pas?* Every minute of the day, he is there. He
is here with us now, is that not so?'

'Rab? Of course. He is never out of my thoughts for a
second, consciously or not. He never has been.'

'Then perhaps it is time that we went back to London.
You see, however ludicrous it may seem, George is never
absent from my thoughts either.' Giselle paused. 'You
knew, of course, that he was once madly in love with you?
Oh, don't look so shocked. It is quite true, I assure you.
Obviously you did not know. Neither, thank God, did you
realize the extent of my jealousy towards you at the time,
when he told me how exquisite you were.'

'Giselle, I give you my word. I had no idea.'

Giselle smiled. 'I told you that story to prove how
pointless, what a wasted emotion jealousy really is, unlike
love, which is never wasted, simply mislaid now and then.'

The few days in Devonshire had been a refreshing change.
Giselle was right in saying how wonderful it was to get
away from the constant tension of sirens and air-raids,
from worried-looking people and grim newspaper head-
lines. Even so, Gina returned to London with a sense of
relief. Stepping back a little from life, she had realized the
futility of attempting to run away from Rab; had seen her
anger, frustration and jealousy, as unworthy. The more she
thought about it, there must have been a strong reason why
he had not been in touch with her.

That reason became all too apparent when Daisy said
concernedly, 'That poor man! What a terrible time those

newspaper reporters have given him; hounding him day and night just because he's famous.'

'What do you mean, Daisy? What are you talking about?'

'You mean you don't know? You haven't heard?'

'Heard what?' They were in Gina's room at the time, she unpacking the clothes she had taken with her on holiday, Daisy picking out the garments that needed washing and ironing.

'About Mrs Romer.'

Gina stopped what she was doing. 'What about her?'

'She's dead! The poor soul was accidentally drowned. The papers have been full of it. Well, they would be wouldn't they?'

Gina sank down on the edge of the bed. The thought uppermost in her mind, that she had not been there for Rab when he needed her. She covered her face with her hands. Would Rab ever forgive her, would she ever forgive herself for her lack of trust in him at a time of crisis in his life?

'Oh, Daisy,' she sobbed, 'I've been so weak, so selfish.'

'Aren't we all, at times?' Sitting down beside her, Daisy cradled Gina's head on her shoulder. 'You mustn't take on so, my lamb. Everything will work out right in the end. You'll see.'

Raising her head, her eyes wet with tears, 'Tell me, Daisy, how long have you known that Rab and I were lovers?' she asked.

Daisy smiled. 'From that first time, I suppose, when he came in by the garden gate.'

'And you didn't mind?'

'Mind? Why should I? I'm not an arbiter of right and wrong. All I ever wanted was your happiness, and his. There's little enough of it in the world, if you ask me. I would never blame anyone for snatching a bit of it now and then.' She added fiercely, 'I'd have thought very differently if I hadn't known for certain that you were in love, if I had believed, for one moment, that you were wrong for each other—'

'Daisy, I must get in touch with him at once!'

She had never attempted to contact him when Marguerite was alive.

The maid who answered her phone call said that Mr Romer had left the house just after the funeral. No, he hadn't said where he was going. All he'd said was that the house would be re-let in due course.

'Frankly, madam,' the maid admitted, 'I don't blame him for wanting to get away from this house. I'll be glad to leave here myself at the end of the week.'

At last he had the peace and silence he craved.

After the funeral he had cleared the house of his personal belongings – surprisingly few, considering the length of time he had been in London; had paid the servants and contacted the agent from whom he had rented the house, to hand in his notice. Leaving that prim Victorian villa, he had not looked back. He never wanted to see or to think of the place again.

Arriving at the cottage, he experienced an overwhelming desire to sleep on a tide of forgetfulness. Sleep to the sound of the waves washing in on the shore.

Climbing the wooden stairs to his room, he sprawled on the bed fully dressed, too tired to think any more, feeling a great emptiness, a sense of detachment from all that had gone before.

How long he slept, he scarcely knew. He had fallen asleep in daylight, awakened to daylight. If night had come and gone in between, hours of darkness sandwiched between two slabs of day, he had not been aware of it.

Getting up stiffly, he looked out of the window. Talland Bay was veiled with rain. The roofs of the fishing village below the headland glistened dully; water ran in rivulets down the steep, narrow streets. Rain, like tears, trickled down the window panes.

At that moment, it seemed that God must be weeping for the world of His creation, the unhappiness, the waste of human life.

* · * *

373

How strange mankind's compulsion to satisfy the basic needs of existence, even when existence held no real meaning. He was hungry, therefore he must eat, cold, so he must light a fire, dirty, so he must wash and shave.

His hand was still painful, even though the stitches had been removed. Bringing in wood from the shed, he lit the fire, unpacked his belongings and walked down to the village for bread, milk, fish, tobacco and matches.

The woman behind the counter knew him well. 'Pleased to see you back, sir,' she said. 'Your son not with you this time?' When Rab explained that Oliver had gone overseas, 'It's a bad job, this war,' she sympathized, shaking her head. 'Take what happened last night in London, for example. We heard about it on the wireless. Those German bombers dropped hundreds of incendiaries and high explosives. They say the city's a shambles!'

The four mainline stations were almost at a standstill as a result of the Blitz. She had been lucky to find a seat on the Paddington–Penzance train, Gina realized; even luckier to find a train still running, however slowly. Perhaps she was setting off on a wild-goose chase, but her common sense told her that Rab must have gone to Cornwall. Where else would he have gone to find peace of mind?

Throughout the long, tiring journey, she wondered if this journey would end in a lovers' meeting. If Rab had gone to the cottage, would he be pleased to see her, or would he regard her appearance there as an intrusion of his privacy? Could she hope to bridge the barrier of misunderstanding she had built up between them?

Watching the passing scenery, her mind in a turmoil, she knew she must shoulder the blame for what had happened.

Darkness had fallen when she arrived at the cottage. Dismounting from the car she had hired at Polperro, she saw, with infinite relief, a faint glow of light behind the curtains. Light-headed with weariness and hunger, she stumbled down the path towards that light, uncertain of her welcome.

How could she have been so blind, so stupid not to realize that he had been physically unable to come to her that night? She knew, as she knocked at the door, that she would attempt no explanation of her behaviour. She would also know, the moment the door opened, if Rab still loved her. And if he did not, all the explanation in the world would not matter a damn.

Then she would simply walk back up the path to the waiting taxi.

The door opened.

'Rab,' she said simply, 'can you ever forgive me?'

'Darling!' His voice broke suddenly. He held out his arms to her. Wordlessly, he held her close to him. She felt the strong beat of his heart, and knew that he was weeping. Above all, miraculously, she knew that he still loved her.

They talked long into the night, by firelight, until the embers sank to ashes and the light of a new day filtered into the room. Then they walked down to the beach together to watch the spread of sunlight on the sea.

It was there, on that crescent moon of sand lit by the light of early morning, that Rab asked Gina to marry him; the sooner the better.

Sensing his urgency, 'Why the sooner the better?' she asked, suddenly afraid.

'Because, my love, there isn't much time left to us. I can't say more than that.'

'You mean that you are going away? But where?'

'I'm sorry, I'm afraid I can't answer.' Holding her close, 'It's just that I love you so much, my darling, and we have waited so long. Oh, Gina, I ask you again, please, will you marry me?'

She said huskily, 'Of course I will.'

Through tear-filled eyes, her head resting against his shoulder, his arms about her, she watched the relentless flow of the incoming tide.

'Wilt thou, Robert, have this woman to thy wedded wife, to live together after God's ordinance in the holy estate of

375

Matrimony? Wilt thou love her, comfort her, honour, and keep her in sickness and in health; and, forsaking all other, keep thee only unto her, so long as ye both shall live?'

It had been a simple ceremony. Bright sunlight bathed the altar, the scent of summer flowers filled the church. She heard the sound of the sea in the distance, the haunting lament of a seagull's cry as it swooped down to the harbour in search of food, felt the firm clasp of Rab's hand in hers as she mounted the steps of the beribboned, horse-drawn carriage that would take them to their wedding reception at The Mermaid, where she had stayed until the wedding, alive now with fiddle music, laughter; the camaraderie of the ordinary people who had gathered there to wish long life, health and happiness to the bride and groom.

That day would always seem to her as a few precious hours lifted from the dross of the war, something shining and bright to remember always with joy, a day untainted with sadness. Standing at the altar, she thought of Oliver, how joyful he would be when he knew that the two people he loved best had come together at last.

The villagers had taken it on themselves to provide the wedding reception. The landlord's wife had set the tables in the room above the public bar with the food she had cooked herself: miniature Cornish pasties, a whole salmon, mushroom patties. The room was long, raftered, with a view of the harbour, and a platform at one end for the musicians.

Smiling her gratitude, Gina knew that the preparations had been made in Rab's honour, because they respected him, regarded him as one of themselves. By the same token, they had accepted her also into their close-knit community, asking no questions, taking her at face value.

When the food had been eaten, the cake cut, the speeches made, the tables were pushed back and the music began. 'Well, go on sir, open the dancing,' someone called out. Laughingly, Rab complied. 'Will you do me the honour, Mrs Romer?' he asked, drawing her into his arms.

'What did you call me?' Smiling into his eyes, 'Would you mind repeating the question?'

'I love you, Mrs Romer,' he whispered.

Later, they had driven to Polperro for their brief honeymoon, to a small hotel overlooking the sea.

Again she had marvelled at the strength, compactness and beauty of his body, the framework of muscle, bone and sinew beneath the smoothness of the flesh, reminiscent of a sepia sketch by Michaelangelo for his finished masterpiece, David.

He made love to her ardently, intensely, with great tenderness, as he had never made love before, glorying in the physical perfection of her body, the power of his erection, his desire to make of this, their first lovemaking as husband and wife, something wholesome, rich and beautiful beyond compare; and knew, when at last they lay at peace in each other's arms, that they had reached a pinnacle of loving, of life itself. Now, whatever the future held for them, they would always remember this place, this room, this warm, moonlit night, the sound of the sea beyond the windows, the eternal movement of the waves reflecting the rhythm of their love.

Holding her close in his arms, Rab wondered how he could bear to leave her now. But the die was cast. His manhood, his beliefs, his loyalties, his command of the German language, had convinced him of the role he was destined to play in this war. No brass bands, no uniform, no flag-waving, simply a melting into the shadows of a war-torn Europe, the conveyance of secret messages to the Allied Headquarters in London; the threat of death lurking in every shadow.

Waking her with a kiss, he said quietly, 'Gina, my darling, I must leave you now. Please, my love, don't move; don't say goodbye. Just let me look at you, let me remember you the way you are now.'

Looking up at him, 'I had no idea it would be so soon,' she said brokenly. 'Oh, Rab! Why didn't you tell me?'

'I didn't want to spoil our wedding day.'

'Where will you go when . . .' Her voice shook with emotion, '. . . you leave here?'

'To an airfield near the Kent coast.'

'And then?'

'I don't know. My orders will be given to me there.'

'Oh, Rab! I'm so afraid.' She buried her face against his shoulder.

'You mustn't be, my darling. Promise me you'll go on with your life, your work. I'll need your strength, your faith, your belief that I'll come back to you when this war is over.' Lifting her hand, he kissed the wedding ring on her finger, 'I love you Gina,' he said tenderly – and then he was gone.

A letter from Oliver had arrived during her absence, giving an address to which she could write, from which her letters would be forwarded if his unit had been moved on in the meantime. *India*? What was he doing in India, she wondered. But at least he was safe and well, thank God.

Sitting up late, she wrote him a long letter giving him news of the wedding, writing as if she was talking to him, spilling on to the paper her thoughts and feelings, so that reading the letter he would know every detail of that wedding day, the colour of the dress she had worn, the flowers she had carried, the way the sunlight had slanted on to the altar through the stained glass window – even the waltz the musicians had played – 'When I Grow Too Old to Dream'.

She ended the letter, 'I never realized that such happiness was possible in the midst of war. I thank God for it, however short-lived. Rab and I had the briefest of honeymoons before he went away on active service. More than this I can't tell you. Knowing your father, you'll understand that he also wished to be in on the action. I miss you both more than words can express.'

A few days later, she received a phone call from her agent, inviting her to have lunch with him at the Savoy. He had something important to tell her. He sounded chirpy – unusual for Charles Prendergast – who had never been the proverbial 'ball of fun'. More of a 'suet-pudding' personality with his pasty face and heavy dewlaps.

'Why all the mystery?' she asked impatiently.

'I'll tell you tomorrow!'

Facing him across the table, knowing full well that the dish of the day, despite its fancy French delineation, meant fish pie, pure and simple, 'Well, Charles,' she said. 'What's on your mind?'

'I have managed to arrange a provincial tour of *The Corn is Green*, opening in Newcastle upon Tyne a fortnight from now!' he said triumphantly.

Gina's heart sank.

'Thereafter we'll be moving on to Leeds, Hull, Manchester, Sheffield, Bristol, Cheltenham, and—' Pausing abruptly, 'Why, what's the matter? I thought you'd be pleased!'

'No, Charles. I'm sorry. I'm staying here, in London, where I belong.'

'But you don't understand! I've moved heaven and earth to arrange the bookings. I thought you'd be delighted.'

'I suppose I should be, but I'm not.'

'I – I don't understand,' he reiterated helplessly.

Smiling to soften the blow, 'It's just that I've decided to take up war work of some kind.'

Daisy and Bridget listened in silence as Gina put forward her idea that they should take Adam to Cornwall for the duration.

'The cottage is small, a bit isolated,' she told them, 'but the people are friendly, and you'd be safe there. Well, what do you think?'

Daisy and Bridget looked at each other. Daisy spoke first. 'I'm all for Adam, bless him, being taken out of harm's way, but I'm staying here with you. You'll need looking after if you take up this war-work idea you're so keen on. Besides, we have the garden shelter. Not that I'd like that damned old Hitler to know he'd got Daisy Crabtree hiding in a hole in the ground. No sir!'

Gina smiled. 'And you, Bridget? What do you say?'

'The same as Daisy. London's my home, and Adam's. Holy Mother of God! Can you imagine me stuck away in a cottage in Cornwall? I'd go melancholy mad.'

She fiddled up her sleeve for a hanky, blew her nose hard. 'It's bad enough the men going away. What would happen if all the women went away too? What would they have left to come home to?' In the grip of a strong emotion, she went on, 'If I'm about to die, I'd rather do it here, with the people I love around me. That's why I'm staying. Besides, who'd look after the garden?'

The discussion had taken place in the drawing-room. When it was over, Gina crossed to the sideboard, poured three glasses of sherry, two of which she offered to her loyal companions in life, the bright-eyed Bridget and the plump, comfortable Daisy Crabtree, who had stood by her through thick and thin.

Then, raising her own glass, she said proudly, 'Let's drink a toast, shall we, to – Victory? To the future! To Peter, Rab and Oliver, where ever they may be, who are fighting to make that future possible.'

Rising to her feet, Daisy said huskily, 'Now I'd like to propose a toast to you Gina, for all your kindness.'

'No, please, Daisy, I'd rather you didn't.'

'I'll drink to that.' Bridget said. 'Here's to you, Miss Gina! You'll never know what it has meant to us, all of us, Peter, Adam, Daisy and me, to be close to you.'

The room was long and low, dimly lit, filled with the uniformed men and women who had gathered there in the basement of a Methodist church, to while away a few hours playing billiards and table-tennis; drink tea or coffee, and dance to the music of a wind-up gramophone.

'Please do remember, Mrs Romer,' the plump, officious lady in charge of the canteen told her, 'only *one* level spoonful of sugar per person, if they take sugar, that is. And if they start complaining about the food, remind them there's a war on!'

As if they would need reminding of that, Gina thought,

taking up her position behind the counter: pouring, with shaking hands, her first cup of tea from a huge metal teapot – not just because she was nervous – the teapot weighed a ton.

'Hey, you're new here, aren't you?' The fresh-faced young soldier she was serving glanced at her admiringly. 'A bit out of your element, aren't you, slumming it in a dump like this?'

'Do you take sugar?' Her eyes twinkled.

'Yeah, two spoonfuls!' He twinkled back at her. 'Go on, I *dare* you!'

Gina accepted the dare. 'There,' she said lightheartedly, 'but that's it. Don't come back for more.'

'No, I won't.'

She knew what he meant. He and his pals gathered about the billiards table would never come here again after tonight.

She returned home at midnight, her head throbbing to the music played over and over again on the wind-up gramophone, 'Begin the Beguine', a tune that would remain with her for the rest of her life, which, whenever she heard it played, would resurrect exact memories of war-time, of blacked-out windows, blue cigarette smoke, the click of billiard and table-tennis balls: the smell of slightly rancid fat from the kitchen, the occasional whiff of rotten eggs shoved into a bucket under the sink: flaccid sausages and limp chips, a gargantuan lady in a white overall ruling the roost like an oversize pouter-pigeon, who obviously regarded the soldiers, sailors and airmen, and their female counterparts who came to her canteen for relaxation, conversation, and something far more important – understanding – as riff-raff.

She would also remember the battle royal she had engaged in with that lady before the pouter-pigeon received her marching orders; her feeling of triumph when at last she had brought about a new régime of cleanliness and efficiency to the canteen kitchen, ensuring that the food served to the men and women who came there would at least be hot and appetizing, adhering strongly to the belief that even a common-or-garden sausage, properly cooked, served with piping hot chips, was a meal fit for heroes, a point of view based on her deeply held conviction that every member of the fighting forces who came to the canteen deserved to be treated as a hero.

In the ensuing months, the canteen had become a way of life. In charge of the place, she had gone there every day to clean and reorganize the kitchen. Dressed in her oldest clothes, her face devoid of makeup, she had got down on her hands and knees to scrub the floor, had washed down the walls, cleared out the cupboards, thrown out sticky sauce bottles – the contents of which had long since dried up – and blitzed the grease-caked gas-cooker with buckets of scalding hot water laced with soda-crystals.

Encouraged by her whirlwind activity, her band of helpers had buckled in to clean the club-room and the counter from which the food and refreshments were served. A large tea-chest was dragged into the centre of the room, and into which were thrown the chipped and cracked cups, the bent spoons and the tattered tablecloths which Gina considered an insult to what she laughingly termed 'the clientèle'.

When the premises had been cleaned to her satisfaction, she had set about organizing a small sewing and mending group of women willing to darn socks and sew on buttons; had set apart a small room in which the men and woman who came to the canteen could sit quietly, if they wished, to read or write letters.

This accomplished, she had contacted local trades-men in the area to ensure daily deliveries of fresh food, decent potatoes, sausages and meat pies, whenever poss-ible. Carrots, it seemed, were always readily available, so was dried egg powder. Better by far, Gina considered, to use powdered egg than so-called fresh eggs imported from overseas, so rotten by the time they were cracked that the stench was unbearable. Hoarding like a magpie, she filled the kitchen cupboards with the tinned food, spam and bully beef she had managed to appropriate in aid of her clientèle.

And whalemeat, she'd discovered, tasted fine, as long as no-one knew what they were eating.

Sooner or later, Daisy was bound to get in on the act. 'If you speak to me nicely,' she said, 'I might be persuaded to make whalemeat cottage pie for your boys and girls. We're not short of carrots or potatoes, and what about the parsley, sage, rosemary and thyme on the patio? They'd end up thinking they were dining at the Ritz!'

Bridget butted in, 'And I could start digging for Victory. I could grow all manner of things: onions, spring greens – carrots!' She burst out laughing.

Despite the misery of the war, clothes rationing, the battle for survival, they were together, and that was all that mattered. Three women bearing each other's troubles and anxiety against a background of world-shattering events; living each day as it came, taking encouragement from Winston Churchill's familiar V-sign, his voice on the radio.

Letters were slow to arrive. Every morning brought the trauma of awaiting the thud of mail on the doormat, the hope and expectation of news from abroad, the underlying fear of a telegram from the War Office. Gina at least knew the whereabouts of her son. Soon after the arrival of his first letter, his unit had been posted to North Africa. Bridget was not so lucky. No telling where Peter Dickenson might be from one day to the next. Throughout, Daisy Crabtree remained a tower of strength, cooking their food, providing a shoulder to cry on when necessary, keeping them going with her inbred humour and compassion, her gutsiness and London pride, her unfailing belief in the triumph of right over wrong.

Chapter Thirty-One

One day, in the summer of 1942, Gina received an unexpected visitor. Sir James Adley's daughter, Leonora.

This was a very different Leonora from the girl who had confronted her so savagely in her bedroom at Craiglachan, Gina realized.

'Come in and sit down.' Leading her into the drawing-room, 'Would you care for a glass of sherry?'

'No. No thanks. Do you mind if I have a cigarette?'

'Of course not.' Gina handed her an ashtray.

'This isn't easy for me,' Leonora said sharply. 'Admitting that I was wrong about you, I mean.'

'Wrong? In what way?' Gina sank down in the chair opposite.

'Oh, don't pretend. You know exactly what I'm trying to say.'

'No, I'm sorry, I don't.' Gina frowned perplexedly. 'That day at Craiglachan, you made it abundantly clear that you wanted rid of me as quickly as possible, and I knew why. Did you really believe that your father and I stood the remotest chance of happiness when you were prepared to do everything in your power to ensure that we would never be happy together?'

'I know,' Leonora admitted, 'because I was desperately jealous at the time. Afraid that you would take Daddy away from me, that he would love you more than he loved me. Well, all that doesn't matter any more. You see, Miss Brett, my father is dying, and it's all my fault.' Throwing aside the unlit cigarette, she covered her face with her hands. 'The truth is, he has never got over losing you!'

Rising quickly from her chair, placing her arms round the weeping girl's shoulders, Gina said compassionately,

'Tell me, Leo, how can I help? What exactly is it that you want me to do?'

Uncovering her face, Leonora said hoarsely, 'I want you to go to him. Please say you will.'

Remembering how much James Adley had once meant to her, 'Of course,' Gina said quietly.

'James,' she said, entering the drawing-room of the Eaton Square house, moving swiftly forward to clasp his hands in hers, 'I'm so pleased to see you again.'

'Gina, my love!' He looked up at her, his heart in his eyes. 'Can you ever forgive me?'

'Forgive you for what? There's nothing to forgive.'

'Ah, but there is. So much. If only I had been less easily swayed. But I still love you, my darling.'

'I understand you've been ill. Leonora told me. She came to see me.'

'So I believe.' He had lost a great deal of weight, Gina noticed, and that old, vital spark was missing; and yet illness had not detracted from his handsomeness. Indeed, his loss of weight had sculpted his face to the resemblance of a finely-chiselled mask by Rodin. 'I think my daughter has reason to regret her high-handed actions of the past. Unfortunately, she learned humanity the hard way. Her fiancé was killed in action three months ago. She is still bitter about that, but she is more understanding, more tolerant now than she was before.'

'I'm so sorry.' Gina paused. 'But what about you?'

He shrugged dismissively, 'My doctor tells me I'm doing fine.' He smiled, but the smile did not reach his eyes. Gripping her hand, 'The thing is, my darling, the time that is left to me, I'd like to spend with you.'

Glancing towards the french windows, she remembered that evening long ago when she had stood beside him looking up at the London sky, aglow with stars and a slip of moon; his words, 'That glow in the sky will still be there when darkness deepens. A reminder of the world out there. Your world, Miss Brett.'

She said quietly, 'I'm so sorry, I'm afraid that's not possible. You see, I'm married now.'

His breeding came uppermost, the charm of a born and bred English gentleman. She could only guess the effort that went into his shrugging aside of the rug tucked about his knees, the pain he suffered in rising to his feet to kiss her hand. 'Then I wish you all the happiness in the world, my dear.'

'Please, James,' she said, 'I can't leave you like this. I need to talk to you, to explain.'

Sitting beside him when he had sunk back in his chair, Gina pondered the strange undercurrents of her life which had led to this moment, the quirks of fate which had guided her destiny to its ultimate conclusion – her marriage to Robert Romer – the only man she had ever truly loved or desired. And yet she had loved James Adley, too, as she had loved TJ Power, in different ways, and for different reasons. But both men had added lustre to her life, a depth and meaning without which her life would have been less rounded, far less rewarding, and she wanted James to know and understand that, had she married him, she would have remained faithful to him always.

Rewarded by his look of understanding, the smile that finally reached his eyes, bending down, she kissed him gently on the cheek. Then, realizing that he was very tired, half asleep, she moved silently out of the room, pausing momentarily to look back at him, and the Monet painting over the mantelpiece which reminded her of – Rab.

Six months later, she read the announcement of Adley's death in the obituary column of *The Times*, and wept for the passing of someone dear to her.

But life must go on. Apart from her sadness at the death of Sir James, her mind was shredded with worry over Rab, from whom she heard nothing since he had left her alone in that hotel room in Polperro, and Oliver, presently engaged in desperate battle against Rommel's heavily armoured tank divisions thrusting forward against the British positions near Benghazi.

At a low ebb, emotionally and spiritually bankrupt for the time being, Gina wondered *why* life must go on. For what purpose, what reason? And yet she continued to stand on her own two feet, to fight her own, silent inner war of attrition against the tiredness and frustration, the day-to-day grind that threatened to overwhelm her initial courage and resolution, not knowing, not realizing, that this was the greatest courage of all, to keep on fighting in the face of adversity, when the brain and body cried out for rest: deep, untroubled sleep – forgetfulness of the horrors of war. But truly, she thought, night after night, tossing in fitful sleep, it was not herself she cared about. She could not give a damn about herself as long as those she loved came through this war unscathed. But where was God amid this holocaust? Where was His voice, His presence, His reality?

Then, rising from her bed as dawn broke over the City of London, opening wide the windows, leaning her elbows on the sill, hearing the chatter of nesting birds in the garden below, looking up at the pearl-grey sky above the chimney-tops, noticing the first rays of sunlight slanting through the clouds of the departing night, she would hear His voice, welcome His presence, accept His reality as a vital part of her own self and being, and go on living.

Night after night, day after day, the silence of the desert was shattered by the droning of aircraft, the sound of gun-fire, the whine of explosive shells fired from the turrets of the rapidly advancing tanks of Field Marshal Rommel's Panzer divisions thrusting against the Allied-held fortress of Benghazi.

During a brief respite from the shelling, battle-stained and weary, lying flat on his back, looking up at the stars burning brightly in a black velvet sky, Oliver recalled the words of his favourite poet, Rupert Brooke: 'Hear am I, sweating, sick, and hot, And there the shadowed waters fresh Lean up to embrace the naked flesh.' And then, 'God! I will pack, and take a train, And get me to England once again! For England's the one land, I know, Where men with Splendid Hearts may go.'

England! He missed every square inch and acre of it: saw it continually in his mind's eye as the ultimate goal, the highest level of achievement when this bloody awful war was over, to which he would always return – no matter how far he travelled.

He recalled, with a deep sense of shame, telling his father that if war came, he would want to be a part of it, to fight for the things he believed in. Christ, how pompous he must have sounded with his tub-thumping and misty-eyed idealism, his schoolboy ego and sense of importance in the scheme of things entire. Now here he was, shattered, dirty and disillusioned.

No, he thought, rolling over on his side. Shattered and dirty maybe, but disillusioned? *Never!* One of these days, whatever the odds stacked against him, he would return to England. All he had to do was stay alive, tomorrow, the next day, and the day after, *ad infinitum.*

He yawned then, stretched his limbs, and fell fast asleep beneath the stars, the silver threepenny bit his father had given him tucked safely in the breast pocket of his battle-dress.

Sometimes Daisy and Bridget went to matinée performances at the local cinema, from which Bridget would, oftener than not, come home in floods of tears saying how much she'd enjoyed herself. *In Which We Serve* was her favourite 'fillum', closely followed by *Mrs Miniver*. 'Oh, that Greer Garson,' she enthused, drying her eyes, 'she reminded me of you, Miss Gina, the way she coped with everything.'

Gina laughed. 'I don't cope, Bridget. I just muddle through.'

'Mind you,' Bridget commented, 'Greer Garson didn't get down on her "chart in heaven" to scrub floors. Hers seemed a more ladylike kind of war.'

'Well it would, wouldn't it?' the more practically-minded Daisy observed, getting the tea ready. 'That's all make-believe, the American version of the war.'

'I know that. I'm not daft. All I'm saying is . . .'

Leaving them to their argument, Gina went to her room to write to Rab, as she had done every day since he went away, in the form of a diary, with no way of knowing if ever he would read what she had written. This was her way of keeping faith with the man she loved.

Today she wrote, 'My darling, on such ordinary little things our life here revolves – shopping, making our rations spin out, rejoicing over a few fresh eggs, the unexpected bonus of a tin of salmon, a few age-spotted bananas. Queuing has become a part of our daily routine. Daisy's a marvel at this. Off she goes every morning to the village with an empty shopping bag. Back she comes, in triumph, with all manner of things. This morning she came home with a fillet of cod, enough for a pie, and half-a-pound of butter. Butter, mark you, not margarine!

'Oh, my love, how bored you'll be reading this drivel. We'll laugh about it then, when you come back to me. Where are you now, I wonder, at this precise moment in time? Oliver writes, in every letter, "Give my love to Father". How I wish I could do just that, and give you my love, too. But you know, don't you? Wherever you are, you must feel our love reaching out to you.'

Gina and Giselle had continued to meet occasionally at their favourite restaurant. The School of Dramatic Art had ceased to exist since George and Giselle had moved down to the ground-floor, and the maestro had dismantled his mini-theatre. Now George had taken up paid air-raid warden duties, and Giselle had joined the auxiliary Red Cross as an ambulance driver.

'How things have changed,' she mused over lunch one day. 'Remember the glory days, the bright lights, the applause, the parties, the lovely dresses we wore in Paris? Ah, Paris! Poor, beautiful Paris. I can't bear to think of it now. No more laughter or gaiety; swastikas everywhere. I can't bear ugliness, waste, desolation. There is so little joy left in the world.' She sighed, 'Look at us now. I in this dreadful uniform, those lovely hands of yours ruined. Don't you ever wish that you had gone on tour in *The Corn is*

Green? It seems all wrong that an actress of your calibre should spend her time washing up greasy dishes in a Forces' canteen. Why did you do it?'

Gina smiled. 'It's hard to explain. I suppose I've always looked on acting as a kind of self-indulgence. During the first war, helping my father at the mill, I realized the effect of war on the lives of my fellow workers. There was nothing in the least glamorous about getting up at the crack of dawn, facing hard physical labour. Most of the women wore clogs and shawls. I admired those women more than I can say. They were tough, resilient, plain-spoken, down-to-earth, with no time or money to waste on fripperies.' She paused. 'I suppose, when it came to the question of staying on in the theatre or doing a hard, unglamorous job of work, I chose the latter as being closer to reality, more necessary to the war effort. Does that make sense?'

'Of course. But don't forget that people need entertainment, too. A touch of glamour now and then to make them forget about reality,' Giselle reminded her.

The great German offensive had begun. As Rommel's Panzer divisions launched their attack on the British 8th Army, German dive bombers swooped down from the sky to blast the Allied forward positions.

Tobruk lost, the British retreated into Egypt, to their old defence lines at Sidi Barani. The British naval bases at Alexandria and Cairo were now under threat from the enemy onslaught.

Tired and dispirited, the men of Oliver's unit tasted the bitterness of defeat. It was then he remembered his favourite play, 'Henry V' – that 'little touch of Harry in the night'. Good old Will Shakespeare! He did not say: 'O! for a Muse of fire, that would ascend The brightest heaven of invention'. His men would have hustled him off to the camp doctor if he had. He simply talked to them of their homes and families, imbuing each with a renewed feeling of pride in themselves and each other, knitting up the ravelled sleeve of care, bringing laughter to their lips, renewed courage to their hearts. 'This is just a temporary set-back,' he said cheerfully. 'You'll see. We'll get the better of those German bastards yet!'

His prediction came true. Days later, in a battle royal for supremacy, the British 8th Army beat back the German offensive. General Claude Auchinleck's forces struck hard at the Axis forces ranged against them. The Germans moved back eastward to regroup. Fresh British troops and new equipment were sent into battle. The British line at El Alamein held firm.

Then came the news that General Bernard Montgomery had taken over command of the 8th Army, an aggressive type of soldier whose Spartan methods of training and will of iron had gained him the reputation of a martinet.

Soon they would have reason to bless the cold, clear-sightedness of Montgomery of Alamein who, under the pale gold of a full desert moon, one night in October 1942, ordered one thousand guns into action, the tanks under his command to move forward, backed up by aerial bombing and line after line of steel-helmeted men with rifles at the ready, bayonets fixed, leading his troops to a glorious, resounding desert victory.

On the 15 November, the bells of victory were suddenly ringing out throughout the length and breadth of England, from the towers of great cathedrals. The first time that bells had been heard since the threat of a German invasion in 1940. Peal after peal rang out from the bomb-shattered Coventry Cathedral, where the spire and bell-tower were still standing amidst the rubble created by those German bombers which had almost razed the city to the ground in December, 1940.

An announcer, broadcasting on the BBC's World Service, asked: 'Did you hear those bells in Occupied Europe? Did you hear them in Germany?'

A seemingly illiterate, dirty, unshaven citizen of the Third Reich, sitting on a filthy mattress in a damp, rat-infested cellar in Berlin, listening intently to that broadcast, suddenly raised his head and smiled, his eyes misty with tears.

* * *

Joy swept the nation. People danced and hugged each other
in the streets of every village and city in England as the
bells rang out. This was the good news they had longed
for. Glasses were raised to 'Monty' of Alamein, the men of
the 8th Army, the 'Desert Rats', who had given them this,
the first resounding victory of the war so far.

Bridget Donovan-Dickenson hurried down to the Catholic
Church in the village to light a candle to the Virgin Mary;
crossed her breast and offered up a prayer of thanks for the
triumph of good over evil.

In the kitchen of Welford House, Daisy took from the
oven the carrot cake she had baked to celebrate the victory,
at the same time keeping an eye on young Adam, who was
into everything these days.

Sitting at her desk, writing a letter to Oliver, Gina looked
up suddenly, slightly startled, as the doorbell rang.

Getting up, calling out to Daisy not to worry, that she
would answer the door, wondering who on earth it could
be calling at five o'clock in the afternoon, she scarcely
noticed the telegraph boy on the doorstep. All she saw, with
a sinking feeling deep inside her, was the buff envelope
bearing her name: Mrs Robert Romer.

'Sign here, please,' the boy said. He added kindly, 'Hope
it's good news. Well, I mean, this is good news day, isn't
it?'

Opening the envelope with trembling fingers, she
read: 'The War Office regrets to inform you that your
son, Lieutenant Oliver Brett-Forsyth is missing, presumed
dead.'

Chapter Thirty-Two

Oliver had not been involved in the El Alamein campaign as Gina had imagined. A letter from his commanding officer had arrived just before Christmas, from which she gathered that he and two other men had been instructed to report to headquarters on 22 October, to undergo special training. The aircraft they had boarded had been reported missing, since when nothing more had come to light regarding the plane, the crew, or its passengers. The letter, necessarily brief, brought no shred of comfort. That Christmas was the worst she had ever endured.

Night after night she went to his room, seeing in everything about her the evidence of Oliver's full and happy life. How could someone who had loved life so much, possibly be dead?

After the war, he'd told her, he wanted to travel, to Africa, South America, countries rich in wild life, to study and paint animals in their natural habitats, to write about his travels using his own illustrations. Not long-winded text books, but something akin to the book of birds she had given him when he was 10-years-old. His Grandfather Owen had been very much in his thoughts at the time: appreciation of the money Owen had left him which would enable him to travel. It seemed a bitter quirk of fate that he had gone to Africa not to write or to paint, but to sacrifice the life which had brought him so much joy.

Deeply worried about Gina, one bitterly cold night in January, Daisy padded down to the garden room muffled in what she termed her shelter gear. Grief, she knew, was best shared, not kept bottled up, and Gina was grieving inwardly. Besides, she was working far too hard. Entering the room, 'I thought I'd find you here,' she said.

'Oh, *Daisy*.' Gina attempted a smile. 'Couldn't you sleep?'

'I haven't had a decent night's sleep since we heard about Oliver.' Knowing the time had come to speak her mind, 'And I'm not the only one by the look of it. You can't go on like this, you know. You'll make yourself ill.' Daisy sat beside Gina on Oliver's bed. 'It can't be good for you sitting here alone every night, worrying your soul out.'

'What would you have me do? Pretend that nothing has happened?'

'But that's exactly what you are doing! You've scarcely mentioned his name since that telegram arrived.'

'So you'd have preferred me to keep harping on about it, making other people's lives a misery?'

'No of course not. All I'm saying is, it's as if you'd shut him out of our lives so we can't talk naturally about him any more.'

Gina looked at Daisy in surprise. 'Have I *really* done that? I didn't mean to. I thought, with Peter away, things being what they are, Bridget wouldn't want reminding that he, too, is in danger.'

'You think she doesn't know that? Georgina, my lamb, we are *all* in danger now. Every time the air-raid sirens start wailing, none of us knows for sure if we'll still be alive and kicking when the All Clear sounds. This is everyman's war. But we can't fight it alone, in isolation. We need to draw strength from each other.'

'Yes, you are quite right, Daisy.' Gina's eyes filled with tears. 'It's just that I feel closer to Oliver here in this room. Rab, too.' Feeling for a handkerchief, she dried her eyes. 'I'm sorry. My mind's in such a muddle I don't seem able to think straight at the moment.'

'Because you're tired out. That's why.' Grasping the nettle, 'Why don't you take a holiday? Go away somewhere for a bit of a rest and a change of scenery?'

'That's not possible. I'm needed at the canteen.'

'Stuff and nonsense! That Mrs Turnbull you speak of so highly would be pleased to stand in for you for a week or two, I'm sure. I mean, it's a voluntary job after all.' A thought struck Daisy. 'Why don't you go to Scarborough for a breath of sea air? Or your husband's cottage in Cornwall?'

'No. Not the cottage. I don't think I could bear that right now.'

'Scarborough, then?'

Gina smiled reflectively, 'Yes. Perhaps.' Eagerly, 'We could *all* go, you, Bridget and Adam and I! What do you think?'

'It sounds like a great idea to me.'

Bridget had demurred at first. Who knew what letters or telegrams might arrive at Welford House during their absence? On the other hand, the sea air would do young Adam a world of good, the poor little kid, whose life so far had been encompassed by the limitations of a walled-in garden; visits to Hampstead Heath, the smoke, fog and grime of London, the wailing of air-raid sirens; nights spent in an Anderson shelter as the German bombers droned overhead.

In the event, it was Easter-time when they arrived in Scarborough, to find the town not deserted, as Gina had imagined it would be, but crowded with visitors. Tired of restriction, ignoring the Government's appeal not to travel, people had flocked from the industrial cities to the seaside as a means of relaxation, a respite from their worries.

'My word, this is something like!' Hands outspread on the railings edging the Esplanade, gazing at the wide expanse of the South Bay, Daisy filled her lungs with clean air while Bridget, standing beside her, holding Adam in her arms, told him ecstatically, 'Look, darling. All that water out there. That's the sea. And that yellow stuff is sand.'

Gina said nothing. She could not have spoken for the lump in her throat, the conjuring up of happy memories of herself and Poppy walking along the seashore together; sitting on a bench to eat their sandwiches. Two ghosts from the past.

Most of the big hotels had been commandeered by the

Army and the Royal Air Force, but Gina had managed to find a small, privately-owned hotel in Esplanade Road, a stone's throw from the promenade. The weather was brilliantly sunny and warm. She experienced a deep sensation of freedom away from London, a feeling of peace, of homecoming, and knew how much she had missed this town which meant so much to her.

From where she was standing, she could see the gaunt ruins of the Norman castle, the harbour beneath the rocky promontory on which the fortress had been built, the parish church of St Mary, Catlin's Arcadia, the Foreshore; St Nicholas Gardens; ice-cream parlours, the zig-zagging paths leading up to St Nicholas Cliff; the Royal Hotel. And, was it her imagination, or was that area of glass glinting in the sunlight the skylight window of Rab's studio?

Were the confetti paint splashes still on the floor? she wondered.

That afternoon, they walked through the cliff gardens to the seafront. Trees were coming into leaf, the grassy banks were starred with daisies. Easter was late this year; Maytime just around the corner. Lifting her face to the sun, Gina breathed in the familiar tang of salt air and seaweed, a fragrance more precious to her than any costly French perfume.

Unaccustomed to walking so far, Daisy sank down on a bench to rest her feet and watch the world go by. 'Don't bother about me,' she said. 'You two do whatever you've a mind to. I'll be all right here until you come back for me.'

'In that case,' Bridget said, 'I'll take Adam as far as the harbour, and buy him some ice-cream, if that's all right with you, Miss Gina?'

'Of course,' replied Gina, 'this is your holiday too, and I want you to enjoy it.' She paused. 'By the way, after all the time we've been together, I think we might dispense with the "Miss", don't you?'

'Well, I don't know, I'm sure.' Bridget had never lost her wild-rose colouring. Her cheeks flushed a deeper pink. 'I'd feel a bit awkward. I'd sooner call you Mrs Rab, if you don't mind.'

'I'd like that very much,' Gina said warmly. With a wave of her hand, she walked quickly to the penny tramway to town, to St Nicholas Cliff, to re-live old memories. With a fast-beating heart, she saw the Woodall Gardens, the Royal Hotel and, next to it, the house she had visited so often with Poppy, on the top floor of which was Rab's studio.

Her heartbeat quickened when she saw that the house was for sale.

The estate-agents, she realized, would be closed for the Easter weekend, re-opening on Tuesday morning. Meanwhile, she must restrain her impatience, do everything in her power to ensure that Daisy, Bridget and Adam had a marvellous weekend.

Tomorrow was Saturday. She would take them to Peasholm Park in the afternoon, she decided, where Adam could feed the ducks, and Daisy could listen to music played by the Royal Marines' Band, and rest her feet at the same time if she wished. Or, knowing Daisy, she may prefer to spend the afternoon at the Odeon Cinema. Freedom was the name of the game. Freedom to do whatever they chose, so perhaps it was wrong of her to make plans on their behalf.

As for herself, she would be quite content to sit in the sunshine looking out to sea, attempting to get her life into perspective. But planning her own future right now would, she realized, prove as fruitless, possibly as unrewarding, as planning the day ahead for Bridget and Daisy. And yet, deep in her heart, she knew that this little space, this feeling of freedom away from the shattered city of London, had imbued her with renewed hope, a different, more optimistic approach to life, as if the sea air, the sunlight, the laughter of the passers-by had relieved the tension of the past few months, reminding her that happiness, like memories, remained, or was still possible, however fleeting it may be.

A foolish notion of hers, perhaps, to want to see Rab's studio again. Even so, the first thing on Tuesday morning, when the Bank Holiday crowds had dispersed leaving the streets of Scarborough bereft of their laughter, she walked into town through the cliff gardens, across the Spa Bridge to St Nicholas Cliff, along St Nicholas Street, and turned right into Newborough, passing the house where she and Poppy had once lodged, to the estate-agents' office in Queen Street.

If the junior partner felt surprised that an attractive, middle-aged lady expressed a wish to look round the St Nicholas Street house, he kept his feelings to himself. No need to point out its defects. She would find out soon enough. The place was in a dreadful state of repair since its temporary Army occupation last winter – a cold, draughty barn of a house in his opinion, which seemed likely to remain on the books indefinitely, at least until the Ministry of Works coughed up the money to repair the damage caused by the soldiers they had billeted there.

His feeling of surprise deepened when, about to put on his outdoor things, she said, 'There is no need to show me round the house. If you don't mind. I prefer to go alone.'

'Very well, madam. Just as you wish.' He handed over the keys, added anxiously, 'You will let me have them back as soon as possible?'

'Of course.'

Closing the front door behind her, she saw the staircase up which she and Poppy had walked so often to the top floor; recalled a swirl of laughter, Poppy's voice saying, 'Better take a deep breath, it's a fair old climb.'

Funny, she had never thought of the house as an entirety before, simply as a staircase leading to the stars. She had never wondered what the other rooms were like. Even when she had lived there with Poppy, she had never seen inside the landlady's private apartment on the ground floor, although she had gone often along the passage to the shed in the yard to bring in fuel for the pot-bellied stove.

Now, with a curiosity sharpened by a desire to keep the best till last, she looked into all the rooms, realizing, as she did so, what a lovely house it must have been once, before those high-ceilinged rooms, with their deep skirting-boards and plaster mouldings, had become age-spotted with neglect and misuse.

Finally, her eyes misted with tears, standing on the top landing, she opened the door of Rab's studio . . .

Nothing had changed. Sunlight glanced through the skylight window onto the dusty floor beneath. Only the furniture was missing, the two farmhouse tables, the shabby couch in front of the old black stove.

Stepping inside the room, looking down at the floor where Rab's easel had once stood, scuffling aside the dust with the toe of her shoe, she saw the confetti-like splashes of dried paint which time had not erased. It was then she knew beyond a shadow of doubt that it was here she truly belonged, and always would; in this place, in this room with all its memories. In this house.

Suddenly her tears overflowed and spilled down her cheeks.

It was madness, of course, to even contemplate buying such a rabbit-warren of endless passages and mouldering rooms. It would cost the earth to repair, and yet she wanted it as she had seldom wanted anything before.

Closing and locking the front door behind her, holding the keys in her hand, she walked slowly across the road to the Woodall Gardens and stood there for a little while looking out to sea, thinking of Rab and Oliver, of Poppy. Poor, charming Poppy to whom she owed far more than she could ever hope to repay except, perhaps, in this way – in giving her spirit a secure resting place, a place it could call home.

With a sudden overwhelming clarity of vision, looking out to sea, hearing the hoarse cries of the gulls wheeling overhead, catching the scent of springtime in the air, Gina knew that she belonged, also, to the theatre. Why else would Oliver have pinned up on the walls of his garden room those photographs of her in the heyday of her youth and beauty? To him she had always been his leading lady, his St Joan, facing life, even death, serenely, unafraid as he had been, of either living or dying.

*   *   *

On their return to London, Gina contacted Charles Prendergast; invited him to lunch.

'ENSA? You want to join ENSA?' He looked as stupefied as if she had said she wished to jump off London Bridge. His dewlaps sagged. 'I don't advise it. What put that idea into your mind?'

'I'd like to go to the Middle East,' she said calmly.

'My dear girl! Have you any idea what you'd be letting yourself in for? Touring's a nightmare at the best of times. Can you imagine the horror of one-night-stands in make-shift theatres, being pestered with mosquitoes, bumping over rough terrain in an army vehicle, arriving at your destination to find there's no running water, no proper sanitation? Often as not, no dressing-rooms. I strongly advise you to think again.'

'I have thought, Charles, and it's what I intend doing.'

'But dammit all, you're not an entertainer, a juggler, a singer; you're an actress!'

'But they are putting on plays, aren't they?' she insisted.

'Well, yes. I believe Don Sinden and Ian Carmichael, Nigel Patrick and James Mason are on tour at the moment – without much success, I hear.'

'*Charles.*' She smiled, replenishing his wine glass. 'Stop being obstructive. You have your ear to the ground. And, after all, you *are* my agent.'

Looking as unhappy as he felt, Charles sighed deeply. 'Oh, very well then. They're auditioning for *Private Lives* at Drury Lane next week. But be sensible, Gina! Frankly, you're no Gertrude Lawrence. You can't even sing.'

'How do you know? You should hear me in the bath.'

'You know quite well what I mean. You're a dramatic actress, not a musical comedy star.'

'Your faith in me is touching!' She laughed.

'But you've never done comedy before.'

'I could learn.'

'But comedy requires an entirely different approach, split-second timing, a kind of "over the top" quality, if you see what I mean.'

'I understand perfectly what you are trying to say. Even so, I'd like a bite at the cherry.'

Knowing when he was beaten, 'You say you could learn?'

'I believe so, with Giselle Landis' help. Don't look so worried, Charles. Have some more wine.'

'Why I entered this profession, I'll never know!'

'Because of your ten per cent, perhaps?' she asked, tongue-in-cheek, eyes sparkling with mischief.

'Huh, ten per cent of an ENSA actress's salary wouldn't keep me in toothpaste,' he said gloomily. 'Believe me, Gina, it won't keep you in toothpaste either!'

'Perhaps not.' She added, more seriously, 'But this has nothing to do with money. This is something very personal which I need to do for reasons I can't explain right now.' Her eyes glistened suddenly with tears. 'You will help me?'

'Of course. I'll arrange an audition for you as quickly as possible.'

'Thank you, Charles.'

Daisy came into the dining-room at that moment. 'It's fish pie and carrots,' she said, plonking the dishes on the table. 'Home-grown carrots. Good for your eyesight!'

Chapter Thirty-Three

'You're going to do *what*?' Giselle stared in amazement. 'Are you out of your senses? Why the Middle East, of all places? And why Coward?'

'The Middle East because of Oliver,' Gina said quietly. 'Coward because I hardly think the boys out there would relish the notion of *Hamlet*. In any case, they're auditioning for *Private Lives*, not Shakespeare. Amanda, not Gertrude.'

'But you've never done lightweight comedy before.'

'All the more reason why I should add comedy to my repertoire, don't you think?'

'My God, Gina, you *are* an amazing woman.' Giselle laughed.

'You will help me?'

'Of course I'll help you. But ENSA! Do you realize what you are letting yourself in for?'

'I've a rough idea. But my mind's made up. Besides, the Americans are sending over the cream of the crop – Dietrich, Hope, Crosby . . .'

'All right! You've convinced me. The sooner we get to work the better. Have you brought the script? Good.'

'No, no, no! Look, *chérie*, you're timing's all wrong. You must allow time for the laughs. And for heaven's sake relax. Now, let's go through that scene again. Remember that Amanda is a glamorous woman of the world, not a village schoolmistress drumming knowledge into the head of a Welsh miner.'

Later, 'That was much better. You're beginning to get the hang of it now. The auditions are when?'

Gina told her. Giselle ran her fingers through her hair distractedly. 'What the hell shall we do about your hands? Gloves. You must wear gloves. I take it you have something

402

decent to wear? Or have you given away your clothes to the poor and needy?'

Gina laughed. 'No, not quite. I still have my wedding dress and jacket.'

'Thank God for small mercies. And you will do something about your hair? You must sail into the Old Vic with all flags flying. Remember you're a star.'

Following Giselle's advice, Gina had been given star treatment, and the role of Amanda – to Daisy's relief.

'Thank goodness you're not going back to that canteen,' she sighed. 'It didn't seem right, somehow, Cleopatra scrubbing floors. I'll see if the chemist can let me have something for your poor hands.'

Bridget said excitedly, 'Is it true you'll be in uniform? Wouldn't Oliver be proud if he knew? I'm sorry, I didn't mean—'

'It's all right, Bridget.' Gina smiled. 'I'm doing this for him, and others like him. My way of keeping faith.'

'And all I can do is light candles.'

Rehearsals took place in a dilapidated church hall near the Charing Cross hospital, which boasted a tinny piano, a stage and the usual kitchen facilities. Windows had been shattered in places and boarded up, reminiscent of the East End canteen.

At first, Gina had sensed a certain withdrawal in the attitude of her fellow actors, which puzzled her until she realized they were treating her as someone apart from themselves – a star performer – calling her Miss Brett. The first clue came when the young actress playing the part of Louise said nervously, 'I've never worked with a famous West End actress before. All I've done so far is repertory.'

They were drinking tea from chipped enamel mugs at the time. The girl, Dodo Brown, said, 'You shouldn't be drinking from that thing, Miss Brett. I'll find you a proper cup and saucer.'

Gina laughed. 'No thanks, love. This is fine.' She paused, knowing the other members of the cast were listening. 'And my name is Gina, if you don't mind.' The ice was broken.

She knew the risks she was taking. Troop-ships, convoys, were sitting targets for German U-boats, and she would be travelling, in convoy, aboard a troop-ship, towards a theatre of war, therefore certain legalities must be observed in the event of her death. Rab had made certain that his affairs were in order, had appointed an administrator to look after his cottage in Cornwall; arranged for his most recent canvases to be stored in a place of safety, and drawn up a will in her favour before the wedding. Now she must do the same. Make certain that Daisy, Bridget and little Adam, would be provided for if anything untoward should happen to her.

She anticipated leaving England some time in July. There was much she wanted, needed to do before then.

First she settled the details of her will, then, taking a few days leave of absence from rehearsals, she travelled to Scarborough to find out if progress had been made on the house. The news was good. The Ministry of Works had agreed to pay for the damage, and a firm of builders would begin the repairs as soon as possible.

Young Mr Keenan, the estate-agent, grandson of the Mr Marshall who had been a friend of Cecil Colebrook, was delighted to see Gina again. Frankly, he had not thought for one moment, the day she came to borrow the keys, that she would make an offer for the St Nicholas Street white elephant. He admired enormously the fact that she had driven a hard bargain – albeit in such a charming way that he had found himself agreeing to her provisos, although he could not imagine why she wanted the attic room at the top of the house kept locked, and he had not dared to ask.

Matters pertaining to the sale of the house, the transference of the deeds and so on, she had placed in the hands of the firm of solicitors now known as Colebrook and Partners. Even though old Cecil Colebrook had been dead these many years past, his family retained a guiding influence and refused to consider a change of name.

Gina's business affairs had been undertaken by Mr Mainwaring, now lacking even the fringe of hair which had seemed to cling as assiduously to his high-domed head as the wilting flower in his buttonhole had clung to his lapel.

'I don't suppose you remember me, Mr Mainwaring,' Gina asked as he shuffled the papers on his desk.

'No,' he murmured, peering at her through his gold-rimmed glasses, 'I'm afraid not. Ahem, should I?'

'I used to work here in Mr Colebrook's time,' she said. 'Well, no matter. A lot of water has flowed under the bridge since then. But perhaps you remember Miss Hewitt? Poppy?'

'Ah, yes.' Mr Mainwaring sighed. 'Yes indeed. Little Miss Hewitt. She died, you know. Such a pity. She was so young, so pretty. I attended her funeral. Now, Mrs Romer, I gather that you wish me to act on your behalf regarding . . .' His voice had droned on.

About to leave the office, she had seen behind the reception desk a plain, fat, elderly-looking woman with scragged-back hair, sniffing at a nasal inhaler, whom she recognized as Patience – the office junior of long ago, whose catarrh had obviously not improved with age.

Walking down the stairs to the street below, she wondered what had happened to Jimmy, the cheeky young office boy who had lost his father in the first war, whom Poppy had befriended.

Lost in thought, she had bumped into a tall, handsome, immaculately dressed man who begged her pardon profusely.

'Not at all, I am entirely to blame,' she said apologetically. Then, looking down at her, smiling like a sunburst, he exclaimed excitedly, 'Forgive me if I'm wrong, but aren't you Georgina Brett? Poppy's friend?'

'Jimmy! What on earth are you doing here?'

'Believe it or not, I'm a so-called junior partner. Not that I'll be here for very much longer. I'll be joining up very soon. The RAF. Well, I always was a bit of a high-flier.' Clasping her hand, 'But tell me about yourself. God, you

405

look marvellous!' He laughed. 'If I wasn't a married man with two kids and another on the way, I'd give you a hug for old time's sake.'

'And if I were not a middle-aged married woman, I'd give you this.' Standing on tip-toe, she kissed his cheek. He reminded her of Oliver. 'Well, goodbye, Jimmy, and good luck, until we meet again.'

Now there was something else she must do before leaving England. Something which had haunted her day and night ever since she had left the West Riding in the belief that she would never go back there. A feeling borne of cowardice, perhaps, a deep-seated refusal to accept that her family were dead and gone; her father no longer a part of the living world. She thought differently now. Owen had lived on in countless different ways through herself and Oliver. Unseen, but a vital part of their thinking and believing. Now she needed to make her peace with the past before embarking on the future.

She saw a visit to the cemetery at Merlewood as a necessary rounding of the circle of life, a tucking-in of stray threads, a suturing of old wounds concerning Agnes and Tom.

While in the area, she called briefly on Mr Caulfield, old now and shaky, but still alert, and with whom she dined at the Queen's Hotel where she was staying. 'This brings back memories,' he said. 'Life has not been easy for you, my dear, but you have had wonderful success.' He smiled. 'I have followed your career with considerable interest. Your father would have been so proud of you.'

She asked him about the Bickleys. 'Jack Bickley passed away some time ago,' Caulfield told her. 'Harry and Josie are still at Merlewood. A sad business when one considers what might have been had their marriages been successful. But Letty has done well, I understand. Her husband is now a Member of Parliament. A bitter pill for poor Josie to swallow. They were such bright young things, so carefree and attractive, Josie in particular, I thought. Although Letty had the sweeter nature of the two, Josie had more intelligence.

'It is Harry I feel sorry for, however. The woollen industry had been in decline before the war, and who knows what its future will be when the war is over?' He sighed deeply. 'I'm sorry, my dear, perhaps I am being too pessimistic. A sign of old age. I cannot help wishing that Harold Bickley had a son to succeed him. It is sad to contemplate the end of an era, the dying out of a well-respected name.'

She had been uncertain whether or not to contact Harry before returning to London. Now she knew she must complete the circle. Harry, Merlewood, the mills, were a part of her life which she could not put aside or forget. She had gathered from her conversation with Mr Caulfield that things were far from well with Harold and Josie. Nor could she shake off the feeling that she was partly to blame for the Bickley family's misfortune.

Having made up her mind to contact Harry, she jibbed at the idea of asking him to meet her somewhere for lunch. That would be tantamount to taking the coward's way out.

History seemed to be repeating itself as she walked up the drive to Merlewood at dusk, and rang the bell.

A manservant, whom she recognized as Johnson, answered the door. With a strong feeling of *déjà vu*, she said, 'I should like to speak to Mr Harold Bickley.'

'Very well, madam, I'll see if he's at home. Whom shall I say is calling?'

'Mrs Robert Romer.'

'If you'd care to wait here, madam.'

The wheel turned full circle as Josie came downstairs, clutching the banister, and stood staring down at her. '*You!* What the hell are you doing here?' she demanded.

'Josie?' Gina frowned. The voice had not changed, but the woman had. Wispy grey hair framed a face scored with the lines of a Topolski drawing. She was wearing a shapeless skirt and cardigan. A vision arose of the attractive young girl who had waltzed into Elmhurst one May morning long ago, wearing a dress of lemon taffeta and a wide-brimmed hat bound in green satin ribbon. Deeply shocked by the change in her, 'I'm sorry, Josie. I had hoped that you might be pleased to see me again after all this time.'

'You thought wrong, then! Did you expect me to welcome you with open arms?'

'Not exactly, I just thought—'

'You'd come to gloat. Is that it?' Josie came down to the hall, as she had done once before, to confront Georgina. 'The successful actress paying a visit to all the old, familiar places? Well, take a good look! If you're wondering where the grandfather clock, the paintings, the silver, has gone, I'll tell you – the saleroom.'

'Please, Josie, don't. I can't bear it.'

'*You* can't bear it? Huh, that's rich. *I* can't bear it, either. Harold can't bear it.'

Harry emerged from the drawing-room. 'What on earth is going on?' He looked old, bewildered. '*Georgina!*'

'It's all right, Harry, I'm not staying. I just came to say goodbye, to wish you well, you and Josie.'

'But you must stay! Josie, what have you been saying to her?'

'Just telling her a few home truths, that's all. My God, Harry, what a worm you are. Forgive and forget, let bygones be bygones, is that it? Well, that won't wash with me. I hold Georgina responsible for all that has happened to us, beginning with the death of our mother.'

'Josie. That's not fair, and you know it,' Harry interrupted hoarsely.

'Oh, isn't it? My, you've changed your tune, haven't you? Am I mistaken, or was it you who burned the wreath the Brett-Forsyths sent to Mother's funeral?'

Harry groaned. 'That was years ago, for God's sake.'

Moving quietly towards the front door, her hand on the knob, Gina turned to look at Josie. 'Before I go,' she said, 'I want you to know that I loved your mother, and I think she liked me. Knowingly, I would not have harmed a hair of her head.

'Tell me, Josie, do you also blame me for the break-up of your marriage, the death of your father, the bitterness that is ruining your life, all the anger and hatred that you have kept bottled-up inside you for the better part of a lifetime? Or is it simply that you need a whipping boy for your own mistakes?'

Opening the door, she walked out into the sweet-scented dusk and down the drive to the gate, hearing the piercing notes of a blackbird in the dark blur of the Merle Woods beyond the garden.

Harry came after her. 'I'm so sorry,' he said confusedly. 'Josie's not herself. You must forgive her.'

'I do, Harry, believe me. I just wish that she could find it in her heart to forgive me.'

'When the war is over,' he said, 'if we are spared, we are going to Australia, Josie and I, to make a new beginning. It will mean the end of the Bickley and Brett-Forsyth mills, the end of an era, the end of Merlewood. I have no choice other than to sell up. You understand?'

'Of course, Harry. And I wish you all the luck in the world.'

Holding her hand, 'I shall never forget you, Georgie,' he said. 'A part of me will always belong to you – to all this.' Keeping a tight rein on his emotion. 'You came to say goodbye. Where are you going?'

'Abroad,' she explained, 'to the Middle East. I'm not sure where.'

'And you are married now. Tell me, Georgie, are you happy?'

'Not very. Not at the moment. Perhaps I shall be again, one day. Who knows?' Gently unclasping his hand, 'I must be going now, make an early start in the morning.'

At that moment, the front door opened and closed, betraying a momentary fragment of light. A dark shape hurried down the path towards them, a hoarse voice called out, 'Georgie! Please wait!'

Tears streaming down her raddled cheeks, Josie stumbled blindly into Gina's outstretched arms, knowing that everything she said was true. She *had* allowed bitterness, anger and hatred to ruin her life.

Gina's arms about her shaking body, Josie suddenly felt

whole again. Absolved. At peace. Hopeful of the new beginning she and Harry would make after the war.

Early next morning, Gina returned to London to face inoculation against yellow fever, typhoid and cholera, which meant that she would soon be on her way to the Middle East, sailing from Liverpool aboard the troop-ship *Samaria*.

On her last evening at home, she called Daisy and Bridget into the drawing-room to tell them the plans she had made on their behalf if she should not return, wanting them to know that, whatever happened, they would remain safe and secure – or as safe and secure as the war allowed.

But even if Welford House was razed to the ground, she explained, she had set up a trust fund for them to ensure their survival.

'But what if the house is destroyed and we're inside it?' Bridget enquired tearfully.

Daisy said, 'Well then, no need to worry; at least we'll be buried in style!'

When Bridget had gone to see to young Adam, 'Now the time has come,' Daisy said softly, 'I wish you weren't going. I wish you were still at the canteen.'

'Oh, come on, you can't have it both ways.' Gina smiled at Daisy in the fireglow. 'At least my hands are better now!'

'I know. But I can't bear the thought of you aboard that troop-ship, facing God knows what.'

Gina said with a smile, 'Don't fail me now, Daisy. Not now, when I need you so much.' Her eyes tender by firelight, 'We go back a long way, you and I, remember?'

'Oh yes,' Daisy said proudly, 'I remember!'

'I'm entrusting everything to you,' Gina said. 'And I want you to know that when I return, you will always have a home with me, if you so wish.'

Daisy said stalwartly, 'I'm not a very good Christian, but I remember the story of Ruth and Naomi: "Whither thou goest, I will go".'

Chapter Thirty-Four

There came times in the secret war when the human soul cried out for companionship, the lost facets of civilization – music, books, the benison of hot baths, dreamless sleep, good food – freedom. Times when the constant threat of danger became a burden almost too hard to bear, when the brain seemed incapable of cohesive thought, the under-nourished body incapable of decisive action. And yet, underlying all, remained the knowledge that every message relayed to the Allied Headquarters in London, however insignificant, added something to the total of information garnered to bring about the defeat of Hitler's Third Reich. And so one kept on surviving, playing one's part. In Rab's case, that of a semi-literate, mentally retarded hospital porter whose work included swabbing the operating theatre floors, stoking boilers, burning blood-stained dressings and bandages.

British Intelligence, he knew, was a complicated network divided into different sections, sub-divided into numerous circuits. He also knew that he was not really alone, except in the deep chasms of the mind when, unable to sleep, he lay in the darkness of a rat-infested cellar worrying about Gina and Oliver, wondering how they were, where they were, if they were alive or dead.

At such moments of unhappiness bordering on despair, he would turn his mind to his Portrait of Gina, the way she looked when she sat for the portrait, a young girl at the height of her beauty, and thought that, one day, God willing, he would paint another portrait of her, not of a girl, but a woman – his wife – the way she had looked on their wedding night.

Then his thoughts would turn towards his cottage in Cornwall, the happy times he had spent there with his son.

And these thoughts, these memories, would give him the courage to get up, at the dawn of a new day, to stoke the boilers, to pick up his bucket and mop, to walk the hospital corridors beneath the noses of the Germans who saw him as a mumbling fool beneath either their pity or contempt, simply as a means of swabbing up the mess the surgeons left in their wake. If they only knew . . . And, *Heil Hitler*, he would venture as the Germans passed by, smiling foolishly, backing against the wall as he did so, hearing the click of their jack-boot heels on the corridor.

Every night he would go to a working men's café to drink beer and eat sausages and sauerkraut, knowing the importance of establishing an ordered routine to fit the persona of the man he had become. Sitting alone at a rough wooden table, he would eat and drink with noisy relish, wiping his shaggy moustache with the back of his hand, and smile foolishly at those who taunted him for his inability to string two words together without stammering, who tapped their foreheads and laughed at him because he was not as they, ostracized by his stupidity. Then, tired of goading the idiot, they would leave him alone to slobber over his beer, and hunch together to talk of this and that, spilling information as easily as the fool at the next table spilt his drink.

He would get up to leave the café at nine-thirty precisely, a shambling figure in shabby clothes, with closely shaven head, his ragged moustache almost covering his mouth – a moustache which had earned him the soubriquet 'the Walrus'. Turning, the men would jeer at him as he shuffled towards the door: 'Look, the old walrus is off to bed! But whose bed? Which brothel tonight, Walrus?' And Rab would grin stupidly and sketch the outline of a woman with his dirt-grimed hands. The men would roar with laughter, 'How long is it, Walrus? An inch and a half? Two inches?' Then Rab would spread his hands to indicate twelve inches, and they would rock with mirth.

In the darkness of the outside world, the old walrus would lurch unsteadily along the pavements, aware that his life may depend on keeping up appearances; living his role of Klaus Kessler, a hospital porter with a healthy sexual appetite, a frequenter of brothels, a man of habit who returned to his cellar at the hospital on the stroke of midnight, hazy with drink, too foolish and confused to remember which brothel he had visited earlier that night.

It would be far too risky, he had discerned, to relay messages from his room, and so he had evolved a complicated system of moving the transmitter from place to place under cover of darkness, melting into the shadows, his ears attuned acutely to sounds of danger which might mean the end of his usefulness if the Germans discovered the source of his signals to Allied Headquarters.

Once he had lain frozen to immobility beneath a shrubbery of rhododendron bushes, as German soldiers scoured the area, thrusting their bayonets into the thickets until the search had been called off. Then, mud-caked and weary, he had emerged from his hiding place to stagger back to the hospital, knowing how close he had come to death when a gleaming bayonet had delved into the shrubbery a fraction of an inch from where he lay.

Initially, he had been flown from the Kentish airfield to a training establishment near Beaulieu, to be taught tradecraft: how to live under cover, how to cope with interrogation, police controls and searches. Above all, how to use a transmitter radio. This training had, of necessity, been hard and thorough, involving the memorizing of codes and signals, the code-names of other agents, the siting of safe-houses, assault course training, parachuting. The art of disguise.

His cover had been carefully planned. Photographs of the real Klaus Kessler had revealed a man in his fifties, hunch-shouldered, with closely-cropped hair and a drooping moustache, the mentally retarded son of a German couple, devout followers of Adolf Hitler, who had been killed in an Allied air-raid on Cologne. Possibly Klaus had been killed in the same air-raid. He had however risen Phoenix-like from the ashes, to seek employment in Berlin. The man's forged papers were a miracle of invention, the dossier on his life based on irrefutable fact from the day he was born: which schools he had attended, which clinics, his hobbies, his preference in food and drink, including his penchant for prostitutes with large breasts . . .

And so Rab had assumed the character of Klaus Kessler, had grown a moustache, shaved his head, and walked throughout his training period with stooped shoulders, feet splayed slightly, to enhance the impression of a man both mentally and physically retarded.

Catching sight of himself in a mirror one day, he wondered if Gina would applaud his performance, if she would even begin to recognize him as the man she had married, in whose arms she had lain, night long, in that hotel room in Polperro.

Amid the bustle and noise of departure, watching the casting-off of the shorelines, the creamy wake of the troopship *Samaria* fanning out towards the shore as the vessel left Liverpool, Gina wondered if she would ever see England again, her 'sights and sounds, dreams happy as her day, her laughter learnt of friends, and gentleness . . .'

Don Sanderval, who would play the role of Elyot Chase to her Amanda, came to her side at that moment. 'Quite an adventure, isn't it?' he said softly.

'Yes, it is.' She had come to like Don enormously during rehearsals. 'I can't believe that we are really on our way.'

'I wonder why I keep on thinking about the *Titanic*?' He laughed.

'I doubt if we'll come across any icebergs where we're going.' She joined in his laughter. 'Mines, possibly. Icebergs no!'

He said, more seriously, 'You're a wonderful woman, Gina Brett.' He paused. 'I must admit that I was scared stiff of you at first, or rather the thought of acting opposite a leading lady of your calibre. But you've been marvellous. It must have been damned hard for you to change tack from Shakespeare to Coward.'

They were joined by the other members of the cast, the director and the pianist, at that moment. As they stood talking excitedly together, Gina looked at the rapidly diminishing shoreline of England. Strangely disorientated, she thought of all the people she had left behind, all the days and nights, the rich pattern of the years which had led to this moment of sailing into an unknown future. She thought of Walt Whitman's, 'Now, Voyager, sail thou forth to seek and find'. If only she could find the two people she loved most on earth, if this journey might end in lovers meeting. She knew it would not. Then, as the girl Dodo Smith, who was standing beside her, laid a trembling hand on her arm, Gina looked at her and smiled, understanding her emotion as the great ship swung round to join the convoy. 'I never dreamt it would be like this,' Dodo said in a low voice. 'So overwhelming.'

In time to come, Gina would look back on that period of her life as a play within a play, set against a backdrop of vivid colours and impressions, or a painting by Monet, Degas or Pissarro in which the colours, at times, seemed blurred by fatigue; slightly unreal, yet overlaid with the practicalities of travelling from one place to another, with the attendant miseries of heat, mosquitoes, mislaid luggage, inadequate sanitation and faulty generators.

But every night, however exhausted, she wrote up in her diary her impressions of the day. For instance: 31 July, 1943, 'Dinner and dance at the Officers' Club, Ismailia. Lovely spot, fronting on Lake Timsah. Sailing out there in moonlight. "Begin the Beguine" was playing on shore, recalling memories of the East End canteen.'

Her diary continued to record her first sighting of a camel, a mirage on the way from Ismailia to Fayid, a heavenly blue sea, palms and hills, playing the Tek Hospital and dancing afterwards at the US Club, half dead with fatigue. A matter of *noblesse oblige*.

Later, re-reading her diary, had she really lived all those experiences she had recorded faithfully, night after night, Gina wondered? She must have. How, she was not quite certain. A question of mind over matter, she supposed, of walking the extra mile – or rather dancing the extra mile – when all she had wanted, after her performance as Amanda, was to fall into bed and sleep. But how could she possibly have disappointed the men, fighting a war under the direst circumstances, by absenting herself from their Mess parties? She was there, as she had constantly reminded herself, to do a job of work.

Thereafter, she had overcome her weariness by pretending that Oliver was seated in the audience, watching her performance, that he would be present at the Mess parties afterwards, willing her to shine as brightly as a star in the velvety darkness of a desert night.

'Someday I'll find you, Moonlight behind you, True to the dream I am dreaming . . . Make it all come true, Say you love me too. Someday I'll find you again . . .'

She was surprised to discover how many of the older men she danced with remembered her as St Joan, how many of them wanted to ask her about England, the London Blitz, her career, her appearance on Broadway; even more surprised to realize that her name meant something to the officers and men of the 8th Army who gave her a standing ovation when she appeared on-stage, no matter how rickety or makeshift that stage might be. The same thing occurred whenever she entered the Mess quarters after the show.

At first she had felt bewildered by the adulation, undeserving of the attention her presence invoked, until Don Sanderval had taken her aside and told her not to be so modest, so self-effacing. 'Don't you see, Gina,' he said earnestly, 'that Dodo, Abby, Simon, Shaun, Wesley and I love basking in your reflected glory?'

'You do?'

Sanderval, fair haired, fiftyish, slightly built, who walked with a slight limp, and bore a passing resemblance to the Master – Noel Coward – said, in his Elyot Chase voice, 'Of course we do, dahling. We're all simply potty about you, or hadn't you noticed?' Then, in all sincerity, speaking naturally, clasping her hands in his, 'We love you, Gina, and so do the men out there. You are a star, my dear.' He paused. 'Don't be afraid to shine. We all need a little starlight now and then.'

416

Her diary continued: 'Qassaim. Played base. First difficult audience so far. The men got carried away by Dodo Brown and Abby's charms. Understandably so. They hadn't clapped eyes on young attractive women for six months or more. Even I attracted my fair share of wolf-whistles. Shaun quickly rang down the final curtain, whilst Wesley played 'God Save the King' on a mouth-organ, then we packed up in a hurry and headed for the transport truck, still wearing our makeup. Not a good night.'

'Packed for Palestine. Walked along front. Saw fishing fleet and de Lessep's statue. Cocktail party in the Officers' Mess before boarding the ferry at Cantara. The transport truck broke down en-route. Arrived at Gaza in the early hours of next morning. Cypress trees, orange groves, and peace, perfect peace, at last. Slept all day. Awoke refreshed, in time for the evening performance.'

'Never knew such rain was possible anywhere apart from London! Looking out of the window next morning, the sea seemed red from the clay the rain had brought down from the hills. Thought of the parting of the Red Sea in the Bible; Moses and the Israelites. The theatre was good, for a change. Too bad that the rain beat so hard on the tin roof it drowned the dialogue and ruined my song. The boys, bless them, appeared not to mind as they stamped their feet in rhythm with the rain. They opened a bottle of champagne in the Mess afterwards.'

'Travelled towards Jerusalem, the Holy City. Why is it, wherever I go, I am reminded of the Bible? Reminded of faith and hope in a world gone mad with fear and repression? I ask myself, in the dark and lonely hours of the night, why I came here, to what purpose? To play Amanda, when the soul of me cries out to speak the words of the Sermon on the Mount, the doxology, or the *sanctus*. Great words reflecting the glory of life as life was meant to be lived; with love, not fear, with faith and hope at the root of all creation. So I think and believe. Meanwhile, the show must go on. Letters from home. All is well, thank God.'

'Travelled to Ein Sheimer. Heavy road blocks en-route. Haifa fairly quiet. Billeted at the Malcolm Club. Fresh morning air and a glimpse of far distant hills. Don and I played tennis while the rest of the cast lolled around sipping lime juice and soda. I may be wrong, but I think that Don and Dodo are in love.'

'Malta. What a journey! No leave. Sailed on the *Arundel Castle*. Met some of the boys from 58 ME at Gaza and Ismailia on board. Best news of all, Don and Dodo are engaged to be married.'

'On leave in Cairo, staying at the Windsor Hotel. Heavenly cakes! The sphinx and pyramids much smaller than expected. Wonderful news! Italy has surrendered unconditionally to the Allies! Great excitement in the Officers' Mess. Wine flowed like water.' The date of that entry in Gina's diary – 8 September 1943.

In November came the first of 'Bomber' Harris' devastating air-raids on Berlin, following his solemn declaration that the stronghold of Hitler's Third Reich would be bombed until the heart of Nazi Germany ceased to beat.

On 25 November a certain hospital porter with a close-cropped head and a drooping moustache left Berlin for Frankfurt. Boarding the train, he was elbowed aside by a man carrying an attaché case and a brown paper parcel.

'Out of my way, idiot!' the man snarled, dropping the parcel.

This was Rab's contact, code-name Wilhelm. In the ensuing confusion of the collision, Rab picked up the parcel containing a change of clothing, scissors, soap and a razor; fresh identity papers.

In the toilet compartment, Rab worked quickly, methodically, to alter his appearance, according to instructions from Allied Headquarters. First he shaved off, albeit painfully, his walrus moustache, and trimmed his eyebrows, wishing the train would slow down a little to make easier the trimming and shaving rituals. No such luck.

Having changed his clothes, he wrapped up the hospital porter's cast-off garments which he wrapped in the brown paper. Then, methodically, he shredded Kessler's documents which he flushed away at intervals.

Minutes later he emerged from the toilet to mingle with the crush of people in the corridor, to all intents and purposes a pharmaceutical salesman, Anton Brandt, returning from a brief stay in Berlin to visit a sick relative whose clothing he had brought away with him to have cleaned.

The exchange of the parcel and the samples case would take place in a gents' lavatory at Frankfurt Station. Clear instructions had been given, the plan seemed straightforward enough. Even so, Rab felt uneasy.

Alighting from the train, he saw Wilhelm pass through the barrier ahead of him. So far so good. He walked briskly to a news-stand where he bought a paper. Strange how naked he felt without his walrus moustache. Glancing towards the barrier he noticed a couple of men – Gestapo agents, one could spot them a mile off – scanning the faces of those passing through the barrier, mainly grim-faced men and women, Berliners frantic to escape the bombing.

His feeling of unease grew stronger. Beyond the barrier he could see a contingent of SS men armed with revolvers.

Wilhelm had entered the gents' lavatory. Relaxing his shoulder muscles, Rab folded the paper and walked towards the barrier. Relief washed over him. He had not been challenged, and yet the feeling of danger persisted.

According to plan, his contact had propped up the case of samples near the stem of a wash-basin. A line of urinating men at the far end of the room had their backs to them as Rab put down the brown paper parcel close to the samples case, and began washing his hands in the basin next to Wilhelm's. Not a word passed between them. Not even a glance, and yet there existed between them a feeling of comradeship and respect. The 'Silent Army', Rab thought

419

as his contact picked up the parcel and headed towards the exit.

Minutes later, after carefully and unhurriedly drying his hands, Rab picked up the case and walked towards the door.

His sense of danger had proved correct.

The cold grey eyes of the Gestapo agent chilled Rab to the bone. 'Ah, at last we have you, Herr Kessler,' he said smoothly, 'you and your compatriot. Now you will accompany me to headquarters where you will be given a warm welcome, I assure you. A very warm welcome indeed.'

Chapter Thirty-Five

It seemed, in the springtime of 1944, that the tide of war was beginning to turn at last in favour of the Allies. American forces had stormed ashore at Anzio. 'Bomber' Harris had rained thousands of tons of high explosives on Berlin, the Russians had smashed the German siege lines at Leningrad; British forces had landed in Burma, the German spine of resistance had been broken at Monte Cassino.

Letters from Daisy remained cheerfully optimistic. Peter had been home on leave in February, now Bridget was pregnant once more and as happy as Larry, whoever Larry may be.

By this time, the cast of *Private Lives*, the director Shaun King, and Wes Bowen, the pianist and general factotum, were becoming jaded, physically exhausted, and more than a little homesick. Don and Dodo, now married, complained bitterly that they seldom had a minute alone together. Gina understood their frustration over the sleeping arrangements – the three women in one room, the four men in another – besides which, they had not even had a proper honeymoon.

One day, finding Dodo in tears, Gina, who seldom if ever spoke about her private life, told the weeping girl about her own short-lived honeymoon in Polperro. 'I didn't even know you were married,' Dodo said, drying her eyes. 'Where is your husband now?'

'I don't know.' Gina smiled sadly. 'I don't even know if he is still alive.'

'But that's terrible! You mean you've never heard from him?' Dodo's face crumpled. 'God, what an ungrateful wretch you must think me. At least I have Don here with me all the time. Honestly, I'll never complain again. It's just that I'm sick and tired of the play, packing and unpacking. Tired of the heat, the sun, those interminable Mess parties after the show. What I'd give for the scent of lilacs after a shower of rain.'

'I know. But we have a job of work to do,' Gina reminded her gently, 'along with the men and women who are fighting this war. I imagine they are homesick too.'

That night, after writing up her diary, lying in her bunk, gazing through the uncurtained window at the stars ablaze in the desert sky, Gina gave way to the grief she had fought so hard to control every moment of this tour.

Where was Rab now? Where was Oliver? The stars had no answer to give her, and yet their clear brilliance in an immutable, mysterious heaven brought a modicum of comfort to her grieving heart, a feeling of eternity far beyond the limits of earthly life.

At Gestapo Headquarters in Frankfurt, Rab and Wilhelm were made to stand against a wall until late afternoon, with no food or drink. Later they were put into separate cells, scarcely more than a width of a human being, with only a board to lie on.

In the early hours of next morning, Wilhelm was taken from his cell to the torture room. Heart pounding, Rab awaited his return: saw, to his horror, that the man's clothing was covered with blood, his face twisted with pain, his eyes glazed with the suffering he had endured at the hands of the Gestapo inquisitors.

Soon it would be his turn to undergo the same kind of treatment, Rab realized. Lying in the narrow confines of his cell he thought of Gina, his wife, his only love, and knew that he must keep on thinking of her and her alone, however terrible his suffering may be at the hands of his enemies. He had no fear of death, simply of leaving behind him the woman he loved to face life without him, never knowing what had become of him; casting a dark shadow over the rest of her life.

When the guards came for him, to escort him to the torture room, Rab rose strongly to his feet to meet them.

Gina wrote in her diary: 'Woke to see Mount Hermon, snowcapped, and the purple hills beyond Syria and Transjordan. Most people here are Arab sympathizers. Afraid for the first time as news filtered through of the slaughter of a Jewish community not far from here. Show cancelled. However, Peninsular Barracks asked us to Mess there. They certainly needed cheering up! Intermittent rifle fire throughout the performance. It seems so awful, the thought of men dying somewhere out there, struck, perhaps, by a sniper's bullet. God grant this war will be over soon!'

The Gestapo, relentless in their methods of worming out the truth from their victims, led Wilhelm from his cell in the early hours of a May morning. Clinging to the bars of his prison Rab watched, with a heavy heart, the grim execution ritual.

Too weak to walk unaided, the man Rab knew only as Wilhelm, was half-dragged, half-carried to the execution post in the prison yard, the wall behind which was blood-splattered, riddled with bullet holes – a terrible reminder of all the brave souls who had died there for their beliefs of justice and freedom.

Wilhelm, Rab realized, must have broken down under torture, God help him. Now, his usefulness at an end, the Gestapo had signed his death warrant, as they would surely sign his own if they succeeded in dragging from him the names of his compatriots, the siting of those safe houses known to British agents working undercover in Germany; the nature of his mission.

He watched, with a sick feeling of horror, the shackling of Wilhelm's wrists to the post as the firing squad, lined up in the courtyard, awaited instructions from their senior officer. Rab began silently to pray: 'The Lord is my Shepherd, I shall not want, He maketh me to lie down in green pastures, He leadeth me beside still waters. He restoreth my soul . . .'

Suddenly the shots rang out. He saw, through tear-dimmed eyes, the fluttering of pearl-grey wings as a flock of pigeons rose from the roof of the prison in a startled upsurge of flight.

A month later, Allied troops stormed ashore in Normandy. The Tricolor fluttered over the Port of Cherbourg.

Listening to the news on the BBC's Overseas Service, Shaun King opened a bottle of wine in celebration, raised a toast, 'To Victory! A speedy end to the war!' He added, in a voice thick with emotion, 'Tonight, my dears, I feel that we should celebrate this victory in a special way.'

'Anything specific in mind?' Don asked.

Shaun said, 'Why not a series of poetry readings; community singing, based on the theme "Forever England"?'

'Great,' Dodo butted in, 'I could do my impersonation of Marie Lloyd singing all the old music hall favourites.'

'And I know, "Home Thoughts from Abroad", "England, my England", "Loveliest of Trees, the cherry now," and Henry V's speech before Agincourt, like the back of my hand,' Don enthused.

Abby interposed eagerly, 'Simon and I could sing, "We'll Gather Lilacs", "London Pride", and "A Nightingale Sang in Berkeley Square", couldn't we, Simon?'

'And you, Gina. What about you?' Shaun asked quietly.

'Don't worry, I'll come up with something,' she promised.

That evening's quickly cobbled-together show was a great success catching, as it did, the euphoric mood of the audience whose spirits had soared to a peak of pride in the England they loved, for which they had fought so courageously beneath a blazing sun, with sand beneath their feet, the throbbing of enemy aircraft overhead, the rapid fire of ack-ack guns shattering the stillness of those mysterious desert nights which seemed strangely immune to the racket of modern warfare, as if the desert would simply swallow up their footprints in the sand when the war was over.

Dodo, in a quickly run-up dress made from blackout material, with a flounced hemline, a feather boa and a wide-brimmed hat decorated with artificial roses, sang, 'Hold your hand out, you naughty boy', 'Don't dilly-dally on the way', and 'The boy I love is up in the gallery', to ecstatic applause and wolf-whistles.

Abby and Simon, in their first act of *Private Lives* gear, sang 'We'll Gather Lilacs', 'I'll be Seeing You', and 'A Nightingale sang in Berkeley Square'. The hall was packed to overflowing. The audience of soldiers and Waafs crowded together on trestle seats, those at the back of the hall sat on tables, or stood near the wall. The stage was reasonably good, of the English church hall variety, with curtains, far superior to some of the stages on which they had performed *Private Lives*. Apart from the sound of sporadic firing in the distance, they might well be in an English village hall, thought Gina, waiting in the wings as Wes, seated at his piano, led the community singing.

How strange that, even now, after all her experience of the great stages and theatres of the West End, she felt the same chewing sense of nervousness she had experienced at the time of her first-ever audition. A feeling born of anxiety that her contribution to the evening's entertainment might prove an anti-climax.

She was wearing the white satin evening gown she wore in the balcony scene of *Private Lives*. As slender as a girl, her auburn hair swept back from her still lovely face with its delicate, age-defying bone structure, she awaited her entrance. Tears filled her eyes as she listened to Wesley's closing number, 'Keep the Home Fires Burning', the full-throated roar of approval when he stood up to take his bow.

Shaun, acting as compère, stepped forward, hand raised to quiet the applause. 'And now, ladies and gentlemen,' he said huskily, 'it is my honour to introduce to you a great leading lady of the British Theatre. A lady who has thrilled audiences in England and America with her superb portrayal of the great classic roles, St Joan, Cleopatra, Camille, Ophelia. I give you – Miss Gina Brett!'

The curtains parted, the applause died away. The audience waited expectantly.

She began to speak very quietly: 'And Jesus said unto His disciples, "Therefore I say unto you, take no thought for your life, what ye shall eat; neither for the body, what ye shall put on. The life is more than meat, and the body is more than raiment . . . Consider the lilies of the field, how they grow; they toil not, neither do they spin; and yet I say unto you that even Solomon in all his glory was not arrayed like one of these . . .".'

Her voice deepened imperceptibly. Then came the glorious moment of truth in which she became the vessel of the living word, that divine uplifting of the spirit as the words flowed from her as water from a spring, as effortlessly as rain falls from the sky.

'My God,' Shaun murmured shakily, 'she's magnificent!'

Sanderval made no reply. He couldn't have spoken if he had wanted to, for the lump in his throat, the tears in his eyes, the rightness of it all as Gina spoke the final words of the Sermon on the Mount: ' "Fear not, little flock; for it is your Father's good pleasure to give you the kingdom." '

There occurred a moment of stunned silence before the audience rose to applaud the beautiful woman whose magnetism and humility had touched them to the heart.

'Just listen to that applause,' Shaun said, brushing his hand across his eyes. 'Christ! She's even got me crying. I wouldn't have thought it possible. Frankly, Don, if I'd known beforehand she intended spouting words from the Bible, I'd have begged her to reconsider. I'd have told her they were the last thing a tough audience of soldiers and Waafs wanted to hear.'

Don smiled. 'You'd have been wrong, then, wouldn't you? I reckon Gina knew exactly what they *needed* to hear. Trust Gina. She knows what she's doing.'

Gazing towards centre stage, he saw Gina as a shining sword, a burning flame, steel-true, radiant, incandescent, and knew that here was the star, the leading lady whose natural modesty cloaked the blazing talent, carefully concealed until the necessary moment of truth occurred. Then came the metamorphosis of woman into actress, stripping her of inhibition, strangely altering even her

426

physical appearance. Now, without the aid of lighting, props or added makeup, drawing herself to her full height, lifting her head and, with an imperious gesture of the hand, she became Elizabeth, Queen of England, addressing her subjects at Tilbury, before the Armada. Her words rang out clear and strong:

' "Let tyrants fear. I have always so behaved myself that, under God, I have placed my chiefest strength and goodwill in the loyal hearts and goodwill of my subjects; and therefore I am come amongst you, as you see, at this time, not for my recreation and disport, but being resolved in the midst and heat of the battle to live or die amongst you all; to lay down for God, my kingdom and for my people, my honour and my blood, even in the dust . . .

' "I know I have but the body of a weak and feeble woman; but I have the heart and stomach of a king – and a king of England too . . . We shall soon have a famous Victory." '

Rising to their feet, the audience surged towards the stage, reaching up to clasp her hand, to touch her dress; begging for her autograph. 'My God,' Shaun cried bemusedly, 'they'll tear her limb from limb! What the hell shall we do?'

'Do nothing,' Sanderval advised him quietly. 'Leave this to her.'

'Hell's teeth!' Shaun gasped in amazement, 'She's going down amongst them.'

'And why shouldn't she? Stop fussing man.'

'But she'll be hustled to death in that crowd.'

'Not she. They have too much respect for her. They just want to be close to her, that's all, so they can tell their grandchildren that they once actually met the great actress, Gina Brett. Take a look at their faces. They adore her.'

'I must admit,' Shaun confessed, wiping his forehead with the back of his hand, 'I never realized what a really great actress she is until tonight.' He grinned awkwardly. 'What bugs me, how could she have borne to play Amanda all this time?'

'I expect she had her reasons,' Don said.

This was Gina's happiest night of the tour. There was something special about it. She had never felt so relaxed. The warmth of the audience, the community singing, the feeling that the war was drawing to an end, had all lightened her heart. She talked animatedly to the men and girls crowding about her. One man asked if she would return to the West End stage when the war was over. 'I hope so,' she said, and knew with a warm feeling at heart how much she had missed the thrill of those London nights, the richness and variety of the roles she had played, the surge of goodwill – love, almost – which flowed so richly from the audience to the players.

When the hall had cleared, the commanding officer suggested a celebratory drink in the officers' quarters, where they would be staying overnight before moving on to Isdud early the next morning.

As Shaun switched off the hall lights, and they walked into the starry night, Gina shivered involuntarily despite the heat. The distant firing had stopped now. Everything was quiet. Almost too quiet. Suddenly, Abby gave a startled cry: 'My God! Out there on the road! What is it?'

Weird shapes were moving silently along the dusty track beyond the compound. The Commanding Officer said, 'Not to worry. They pass this way every night. They are Arab boys with their donkeys on their way to the shaduf in the village a mile or so from here.'

Abby laughed nervously, 'Oh, is that all? I thought . . .' Her words gave way to a shrill scream of terror as the silence of the night was broken by the sound of rifle fire, the whine of bullets fired at close range, the sounding of the emergency klaxon.

'Quickly! Indoors!' The CO spoke urgently, forcefully. 'Get the ladies inside at once, King!' More shots rang out, answered by rapid fire from the sentries. The klaxon continued its racket. Abby, hysterical by this time, standing as if rooted to the spot, was seized by Shaun and dragged towards shelter. 'For Christ's sake, hurry!' he shouted to the rest of them, struggling to hasten Abby who seemed incapable of movement on her own accord. 'Simon!

428

Where's Simon?' she screamed. 'It's all right, darling, I'm here,' he said tautly. 'Leave her to me, Shaun. I'll take care of her.'

King thankfully handed over his burden. Turning quickly, he saw Dodo and Don, Gina and Wes, running towards the officers' quarters. 'Come on,' he urged them. Don had his arm protectively around Dodo's waist, Wes had Gina's hand tightly in his. 'Not far now,' he cried encouragingly.

Forever afterwards he would recall that terrible moment when her fingers loosened their grip on his, and she slumped to the ground, when he saw the white dress she was wearing stained crimson with blood from the bullet-hole in her back.

Curiously, at that moment, he remembered her stirring speech from the platform earlier that evening, her strangely prophetic words: ' "To lay down for God, my kingdom and for my people, my honour and my blood, even in the dust." '

Chapter Thirty-Six

Hazily, she heard the throbbing drone of aircraft engines. Someone was sitting beside her – a woman. 'We're taking you home,' she said.

'Home?'

'To England.' The woman, a nurse, smiled. 'You must sleep now.'

She dreamed of a city, narrow streets, silversmiths at work in the shade, Moorish architecture, brightly coloured mosaics, a profusion of flowers, veiled Arab women. But which city? The answer lay beyond her power of comprehension. She was lost. Alone in a strange place. In pain.

The bullet had been removed at the base hospital near Isdud in the early hours of the morning. The 20-mile journey had been a nightmare of heat, dust and bumpy roads over rough terrain, Shaun King recalled.

The Medical Officer had treated Gina initially, but he had not the skill or the equipment to perform a delicate operation, and so the decision had been taken to risk the journey to Isdud. There was really no choice. Gina would die if the bullet was not removed. She might die anyway, King thought, sitting beside her in the ambulance, feeling that he had aged 10 years in the space of a few hours. Recalling the old saying, 'The show must go on', this was one show that would not go on, he thought bitterly. Last night had been its swan song. The girls, the men, were in a state of shock. He was in a state of shock. They were pulling out of here, the sooner the better.

Thank God for the Royal Air Force! Thank God they were all going home.

The Press had got wind of the story. 'Famous Actress Injured in Shooting Incident. ENSA party returns to

England.' How the crafty devils knew so much remained a mystery to King. They had even named the Charing Cross Hospital, outside which reporters, photographers and crowds of people had gathered to witness the arrival of the ambulance.

Soon, flowers began to arrive. Huge bouquets and baskets of flowers. Roses, carnations, lilies, asters, dahlias – so many flowers that the room in which Gina lay resembled a bower.

'What it is to be famous,' the ward sister remarked to one of the nurses. 'Not that I envy her. She has a long, rough road ahead of her.'

'Have you ever seen her on-stage, Sister?' the girl asked.

'Oh yes,' the woman smiled. 'I've seen every play of hers so far. I've queued up in the rain to see her.'

'Do you think she'll pull through?'

'Of course she'll pull through! She's a fighter. A survivor.'

The ward sister had no idea that soon the grey old City of London would face a new peril: Germany's long-range V-2 rockets, 15 tons in weight, carrying one-ton warheads, the first of which had fallen on Chiswick, causing a blast wave felt for miles around, in the pellucid autumn of 1944.

During her long stay in hospital, Daisy and Bridget had taken turns to visit her. Bridget, whose baby was due in November, looked well and happy. 'If the baby's a girl,' she confided, 'Peter and I would like to christen her Georgina, after you, if that's all right.'

'All right? Bridget, I'm honoured! But are you sure?'

'Certain sure.'

'And if it's a boy?'

'In that case, we'll call him Oliver.'

'Oh, Bridget.' Gina's eyes filled with tears.

'There now, don't cry, Mrs Rab. The war's nearly over, and you'll be coming home soon, praise be to God.' Bridget's warm Irish brogue had never deserted her.

Giselle and George, too, had come as often as their duties allowed, and so had Shaun King, Wes, Don and Dodo, Abby and Simon. These dear and good friends of hers had helped Gina through the long, difficult days of tests and X-rays; a series of further operations deemed necessary by the surgeons to repair the internal damage caused by the bullet; intensive bouts of physiotherapy to restore the use of her limbs.

The day she left hospital, her arms filled with flowers, the reporters and Press photographers were on the steps to record the event, along with a crowd of well-wishers who clapped, cheered and called out to her as she walked, slowly and upright, to the waiting taxi, with Daisy beside her and members of the hospital staff grouped behind her, smiling. Each one of them, from the surgeons to the lowliest porter, had received a personal gift and a note of thanks for all they had done for her.

She turned and smiled at one woman in particular who called out to her, 'Go it, St Joan! Show 'em what it means to be British!'

She saw, from her balcony-room window, the terrace edged with its terracotta pots of parsley, sage, rosemary and thyme, the line of trees at the garden's edge, the windows of Oliver's room – the room which had been his special and private sanctuary.

Somehow she could not bring herself to believe that Oliver and Rab, the two people she loved beyond all telling, would never come back to her, that she would never see them again, hear their voices, feel the touch of their hands in hers.

At that moment, the future seemed to her a dark void of despair, a limitless desert on the sands of which the human footprint left no trace.

Bridget's baby, a girl, was born in November.

Watching Gina closely, the woman she still thought of as a girl was not picking up as quickly as she had hoped, Daisy thought worriedly; as if some inner light had been extinguished; as if that burning flame within her had suddenly gone out. Of course she knew why.

How strange, she thought, that a woman so deserving of happiness had had happiness doled out to her in such small measure, like caviar on fingers of toast. Dry toast. Never the whole meal.

Christmas came and went. In the kitchen of Welford House, Daisy rendered down the fat from the goose she had managed to winkle from her friend the butcher. Giselle and the maestro had been invited to share their Christmas. She had hoped and prayed that the maestro would not dwell on the theatre as a topic of conversation. So much for prayer! A ham in need of curing, that one, she thought wickedly, pouring the fat from the goose into jars.

Had he not the sense to realize that Gina, her ewe lamb, was not strong or well enough to even contemplate a return to the theatre?

What she needed was a complete rest, a change of scenery. A new interest in life far removed from those blessed buzz-bombs sailing overhead every hour of the day and night. What kind of man was that bloody Hitler anyway to endanger even the lives of innocent children?

One day she broached the subject uppermost in her mind. 'I've been thinking,' she said artlessly. 'Isn't it about time you went to Scarborough to find out how the house is getting on?'

'Perhaps. But I thought I might wait until you and Bridget can come with me for a holiday.'

'Well, that's a thought,' Daisy conceded, 'but travelling would be awkward for Bridget until she's finished breast-feeding.'

And so Gina packed her bags and travelled north. Tall and slender, plainly but immaculately dressed, her hair, she noticed, was flecked with silver threads. Pinning on her hat, she saw that her face bore traces of the heartbreak and suffering she had endured since the death of her son, the long, anxious hours she had lain awake worrying about Rab.

But life, like the show, must go on. Just how or why, she was not quite certain as she stepped from the train that cool April evening in 1945. Then she knew . . .

The house seemed to welcome her with open arms. The moment she crossed the threshold, she felt a sense of homecoming.

There was much to be done. Furniture, carpets and curtains to buy. Wandering through the empty rooms, she knew exactly which colours, the kind of furniture she wanted to bring those rooms to life.

Haunting the local salerooms, she bid for heavy, old-fashioned Victorian wardrobes and chests of drawers, brass-knobbed bedsteads, marble-topped wash-handstands, a long mahogany dining-table and chairs. Deep, comfortable settees and armchairs upholstered in warm crimson velvet; basins, ewers and ring-trays in fine bone china embellished with a pattern of blue trelliswork and pink roses – the kind of furniture which had once graced Elmhurst.

At last she came upon two long, scrubbed farmhouse tables and a sagging cretonne-covered settee, which she bought for a song because no-one else had bid for them, no-one else wanted them. But *she* wanted them, plus the single iron bedstead the auctioneer sold for half-a-crown, to be rid of it.

Was it morbid, wrong to try to re-create the studio as she had known it in the springtime of her life? Perhaps. Nothing in earth or heaven came as it came before, but she needed something to cling to, and memories were all that were left to her now.

The death of Adolf Hitler, the man whom Churchill had described as that 'bloodthirsty guttersnipe' came as a shock. Hearing the news on the wireless, Gina, and millions of other people besides, could not at first grasp the fact that the man who had plunged the world into war had taken the coward's way out, had died a despicable death – like a rat caught in a trap – a steel and concrete bunker in the heart of Berlin. The madman whose dreams of world domination had condemned to death millions of innocent men, women and children, had ceased to exist.

Switching off the wireless, trembling from head to foot, Gina thought of the shattered lives, hopes and dreams of those left to carry on in a world robbed of grace and beauty.

But she was wrong. Beauty did still exist. Beauty beyond the power of mankind to destroy. Looking out of the studio window, she saw pink cherry blossom in bloom in the Woodall Gardens, the calm blue sea beyond.

She had left the front door open for the saleroom porters. Hearing footsteps on the stairs, quickly drying her eyes, 'I'm coming,' she called out. 'I'll be with you in a minute!'

She hurried towards the door; stopped suddenly, pressing her hand to her lips. The footsteps continued. Just one man's footsteps. *One* man's footsteps! Suddenly, with an instinct older than time, she knew to whom they belonged.

Robbed of the power of movement, she waited as those footsteps came closer and closer. Scarcely able to breathe, her heart fluttering like a trapped bird, she waited, her eyes fixed on the door. Never till her life's end would she ever forget those fraught moments of waiting.

Was the music she heard real or imagined as Rab entered the studio? It seemed to her that she heard the sweeping chords of a great symphony as, stumbling towards him, she came to rest in his arms. Then, his lips on hers, she felt that the world had suddenly stopped turning, and they were encapsulated in a shining rainbow of happiness which had no beginning, no end.

Chapter Thirty-Seven

The loving came first, that passionate need and longing for one another which could not be denied. Clinging together, they rediscovered the power and passion of physical love, the tenderness of each other's lips, the warmth and beauty of the human body at the exquisite moment of surrender.

Afterwards, lying at peace in Rab's arms, seeing his sleeping face upon the pillow, Gina knew that he had been tortured. There were scars on his body which had not been there before. Holding him close in her arms, she had traced those scars with her fingertips. Man's inhumanity to man. Tears filled her eyes. There were scars on her body, too. Would those scars ever heal? Scars of the mind as well as the body.

Staring into the future, Gina wondered if it would ever be possible to come to terms with the death of their son? Or if, in years to come, despite their love of one another, they would grow a little apart, nursing their grief over the death of Oliver until one day they might not be able to speak of him at all – the shining boy who had been the mainspring of their existence.

Strung between dreams and wakefulness, Rab re-called the day he awoke in his cell to find the door standing open.

Sensing a trap, he had emerged slowly into the grim prison corridor to find that he was not alone. Other inmates were wandering about the building in a state of bewilder-ment, not knowing what to do, where to go; painfully thin, frightened people, all of whom had suffered torture at the hands of the Gestapo. Young, once-pretty girls with staring eyes and trembling limbs; older women, half-fainting, with crippled hands and feet. Men, like himself, with horrific burn marks on their bodies, who had also been branded with red-hot irons.

It had taken some time to realize that the Germans had gone, that they were free. They had broken down and wept, then, those pathetic survivors of the torture room, and he had thought how ironic that those brave souls who had withstood so much pain had finally been broken by the feel of soft summer rain on their faces.

By firelight, cradled in each other's arms, watching the slow sinking of the embers, they talked quietly of Oliver.

'If only I knew what had become of him,' Gina said bleakly. 'Somehow I can't believe that he is gone. Not Oliver.' Tears streamed down her cheeks.

'Hush, my darling,' Rab whispered, holding her trembling body close to his. 'You see, the last time I saw him I gave him my talisman, that Victorian threepenny-bit I found once on the sands here in Scarborough. Remember? He promised he'd give it back to me one day, when the war was over. And I believed him. After all, our son never broke a promise in his life before.'

'I know, my love, but if he was prevented in some way from keeping that promise, what then?'

The aircraft had landed in the desert a couple of hours after take-off, he would remember much later, when his memory returned, slowly and painfully, along with his power of speech.

Then, frighteningly, he would experience once more the rushing sensation of a strong wind blowing beneath the wings of the crippled aircraft, the blinding glare of light on the sea of sand beneath: the bucking of the plane, the grinding sound of twisting metal as it ploughed into that sea of sand which jetted up like water on either side of the fuselage.

But sand was not water. Sand was gritty, choking stuff as deadly as a morass, capable of swallowing men alive – or dead. He knew. He had seen it happen once before, during the El Alamein campaign: the slow sinking of an aircraft into a sucking, clawing waste of desert sand.

He had also known, before he had blacked out completely, that he was the only survivor of the crash, that the crew of the aircraft and his two fellow officers were dead.

Vaguely he remembered wondering, much later, how long he could continue to survive in a twisted metal coffin in a sea of sand. Strange to think that he owed his survival to an Italian tank patrol whose vehicles were known derisively as 'self-propelled coffins'. Not that he had known at the time, when they had dragged him from the wreckage, bleeding from a deep gash on his forehead.

Regaining consciousness in a prison camp hospital, he had not the faintest idea who he was or how he had come to be there. He had no form of identification. His pay-book had been in the pocket of his uniform jacket, which had been left on the plane. All he had by way of a personal possession was a small silver coin.

Emerging from unconsciousness, he had been aware of noise and confusion, running footsteps, hoarse shouting in a foreign tongue, the sound of heavy gunfire in the distance. Desperately thirsty, he had asked someone, presumably an orderly, for water. The man had rolled his eyes, muttered something incomprehensible and hurried away, gesticulating wildly.

Shortly afterwards, several wounded men were brought in on stretchers, by which time he had lapsed into a semi-conscious state, aware of a deep, throbbing pain at his temples. Had he been wounded in battle? He could not remember. It hurt him to even try. Memory would return slowly, like the pieces of a jigsaw puzzle. Meanwhile, he answered to the name Tony, short for Antonio. 'Oh, oh, Antonio, he's gone away. Left me all alonio, all on my ownio'.

Slowly he pieced together that he was in Italian hands, a prisoner, a man lacking identity. The language barrier had proved insurmountable. He was unable to speak above a whisper in any case during the interminable days and nights of his hospital incarceration. Not that the orderlies were harsh or unkind in any way. 'Hey, Tony,' they would say to him when they came to dress his wound and perform other, more intimate rituals necessary to his cleanliness and well-being.

One day he and his fellow prisoners, mainly Greeks and silent, dark-skinned Abyssinians, had been carried to waiting transports, from which they had been placed aboard a troopship bound for the port of Reggio on the Italian mainland. Eventually they had been taken by truck to a prison camp near Potenza. There, he could sense fear in the air.

The camp on the mainland was different, harsher, but blessed in one respect: there were British prisoners. He could have wept for the simple fact of communication; hearing his mother tongue once more, although he had felt more inclined to laugh for joy when a burly highlander clapped a hand the size of a ham shank on his shoulder, and said: 'Weel, Jock, mon, we'll no be here long I'm thinkin'. We've got these Eye-Tie buggers on the run. Then it's hame tae Bonnie Scotland I'll go, just as fast as ma wee legs'll carry me.' A pause, then, 'What's your name, ma wee laddie?'

Memory flooded back as though a sluice-gate had been opened.

'Oliver Brett-Forsyth,' he said.

Summer had begun to mellow to autumn. The house was almost finished. They had shared the joy of creation. Rab had been to Cornwall to see to the crating of his canvases, and to bring home his hoop-topped cabin-trunk.

In time, perhaps he would sell the cottage, but not yet. It held too many memories of Oliver. Marigolds had continued to bloom in the garden despite the war. They reminded him of Oliver – bright, shining, indomitable.

The studio looked much as it had done in the Maytime of 1919. He had set up an easel beneath the skylight window. Stone jars of brushes, tubes of paint, charcoal, turpentine, littered one of the long farmhouse tables. The pictures he had painted of Cornwall at the height of his fame glowed upon the walls of this, his own and Gina's special room of the house.

He had managed to find a throne closely resembling the one on which Gina had posed for him in the springtime of her youth and beauty.

Now the time had come to find out if he still possessed the power to paint, if he was still capable of holding the tools of his profession in his damaged right hand, capable of recapturing the clarity of vision he had known as a young man, when he had painted that blue light shining through the stained glass windows of Sainte Chapelle.

Soon, Daisy Crabtree would be coming to Scarborough to live with them. Peter would be home any day now. He and Bridget would be happy to make Welford House their home, to act as caretakers in her absence.

One day, perhaps next year or the year after, she would return to the West End, or possibly she would decide never to return to the stage. She could not be sure of anything at the moment except the happiness of this place, this house so full of memories – of being with Rab once more. She needed him so much, needed his strength, his quiet wisdom and compassion. His love. That slow dawning smile of his which had never changed throughout the years. That smile which had captured her heart the first moment she set eyes on him. The smile which made her feel as she had done the day Poppy had called out 'Coo-ee' on the landing. Poppy who, unknowingly, had altered and re-charted the whole course of her life, without whom she would never have known the joy of mothering a boy called Oliver; might never have become an actress.

Dear Poppy, to whom she owed so much. Far more than she could ever hope to repay. Who, dying, had made her richer gifts than gold, who would always remain an integral part of her life – and Rab's.

He had refused to let her look at the portrait until it was finished.

One day in October, when the trees in Woodall Gardens were beginning to shed their mantle of gold and crimson leaves, holding out his hand to her, 'You can look at it now,' Rab said. 'I hope you won't be disappointed, my love.' He uncovered the canvas.

Stepping forward, not knowing quite what to expect, she drew in a sharp breath as she looked at Rab's new 'Portrait of Gina'.

The face he had depicted on canvas was no longer young, untroubled, but that of a beautiful middle-aged woman whose eyes reflected the courage of someone who had known suffering, yet still regarded the future with a sense of hope and fulfilment.

He had not been kind to her, nor cruel. He had simply painted, with great skill and artistry, despite his crippled right hand, a picture of the woman he loved as she now was – as she now knew herself·to be – a woman with a lifetime of experience behind her, a lifetime compounded of sorrow and joy intermingled. Above all a *woman*, painted by an artist whose genius blazed upon canvas for all the world to see, a man who had battled through all the odds stacked against him, to come through his personal hell of pain and self doubt to paint a masterpiece.

The next morning was misty, overlaid with a thick sea-fret. The weather had changed suddenly. Waking to the sound of the fog-horn, sitting up in bed, Daisy would be coming today, Gina remembered. But where was Rab?

Shrugging on her dressing-gown, she met him at the door of their room. He seemed aglow, curiously excited. His hair was damp. 'Have you been out?' she asked, bemused with sleep. 'On a morning like this?'

'Why not?' He laughed. 'It's a lovely morning! Get dressed, darling. Let's go for a walk along the beach.'

Rab had been alone in the house when the phone call came. He had wondered at first why Bridget was ringing up at four o'clock in the afternoon, why the scarcely-veiled excitement in her voice.

'Is that you, Mr Rab?' she asked conspiratorially.

'Yes. Why? What's happened? Is anything the matter?' He imagined that Peter had come home unexpectedly, that she wished to impart the news to Gina. 'Mrs Rab's not here at the moment. Shall I give her a message? Ask her to ring you when she comes in?'

'No. The fact is, someone here wishes to speak to you.'

'Oh?' The someone must be Daisy Crabtree, he thought, to tell him her journey from London had been delayed for some reason; possibly little Adam who adored speaking to people on the telephone. He smiled and waited.

A strong, vibrant, familiar voice came on the line. 'Hello, Dad,' Oliver said.

They had had a long conversation. Oliver had arrived at Welford House at midday. Now he hoped to snatch a few hours sleep before catching a late train from King's Cross, the so-called 'milk' train, due to arrive in Scarborough in the early hours of next morning.

He said huskily, 'Selfish of me, I know, to want to be there as soon as possible. You understand why I'm catching the milk train?'

'Yes, my son. Of course I understand,' Rab said.

'The thing is, this may come as a bit of a shock to Mother. Promise you'll break the news to her gently?' He paused. 'The last thing I want is a formal homecoming, you know the kind of thing I mean?'

'I know exactly what you mean.'

'Goodbye, then, Dad, until tomorrow!'

The beach was still and empty, possessed of a melancholy beauty which reminded Gina of the moors above the Calder Valley, wet with rain, with a strangely diffused light filtering through the mist. Thank heaven the barbed-wire barriers had been removed.

As she and Rab walked together near the sea's edge, she heard the soft wash of the outgoing tide, the haunting cry of the sea-birds overhead, the plaintive, insistent clamour of the fog-horn from the lighthouse pier.

Seeing the implosion of their footsteps in the wet sand, she quoted softly, ' "Lives of great men all remind us, we should make our lives sublime. And, departing, leave behind us footprints on the sands of time." '

Rab stopped walking. Drawing her close to him, looking deeply into the eyes of the woman he loved, he said quietly, 'Remember the silver threepenny-bit I gave to Oliver? The one he promised to return to me after the war?'

Frowning slightly, 'Yes. Of course I remember. But why?'

'Hold out your hand.'

Staring at the coin, 'I don't understand,' she said, frowning. 'Where did it come from? Who gave it to you?'

'Oliver gave it to me,' Rab said gently, 'when I went to the station to meet the early morning train.'

'*Oliver?*' Her eyes betrayed her uncertainty. 'But that's not possible!'

'Gina, my love, in this life everything is possible. Look. The fog is beginning to lift.'

'You mean that Oliver is not dead? That he has come back to us?' Tears streamed down her cheeks. Looking down at the tiny silver coin lying in the palm of her hand, she experienced a sudden uplifting of the heart, an overwhelming feeling of joy that the boy they both loved so much was still a part of the living world, not dead and gone as she had believed him to be, but miraculously, still gloriously alive; a living member of the human race, not some remote star shining in a desert sky above a wilderness of limitless sand dunes; no longer a memory to sadden her heart, but a warm and wonderful reality.

But where was he, this son of theirs?

Glancing down, seeing a set of footprints in the sand leading towards the lighthouse pier, suddenly she knew . . .

Staring ahead into the dwindling mist she saw, in the distance, a tall familiar figure standing in a ray of unexpected sunshine breaking through the clouds, his arms

443

outspread to sweep her up into a new dimension of happiness.

Even so, she seemed incapable of movement until Rab, gently urging her forward, murmured, 'Go to him, my love. He is waiting for you!'

THE END

THE SMOKE SCREEN
by Louise Brindley

Sarah Vale had let herself go. Plump and ill-dressed, she was nevertheless shocked when her husband, Faulkner, announced that he was leaving her for a nubile young executive who was expecting his child. Rejected by her grown-up children, who blamed her for the break-up, Sarah decided that the time had come to make some drastic changes in her life.

Embarking on a new life in the lovely old cathedral city of York, Sarah discovered success in her work and also found herself being admired by two very different men: Nicholas, young, rich and mysterious, with a tragic family background to escape from, and Ralph, a nervous schoolmaster living a lonely bachelor existence. Sarah, newly slim and with a wardrobe of smart clothes, found that even Faulkner wanted her back – and the decisions she had to make about her life forced her to come to terms with her past.

0 552 13829 0

SPINNING JENNY
by Ruth Hamilton

At eighteen Jennifer Crawley led a strange and lonely life
– her days in the spinning room of the cotton mill, her
nights with possessive – and slightly mad – Aunt Mavis.
Jenny didn't even know who her parents were. Aunt
Mavis never spoke of them.

Then came the chance to better herself – to work as a
servant at Skipton Hall. And there Jenny found a household as dangerous and weird as the one she had left
behind. Mrs Sloane, the terrifying housekeeper, was as
cruel as she was ugly, taking pleasure in bullying and
frightening the young maids. Henry Skipton was an
embittered, solitary man who took care never to see his
invalid wife. And Eloise Skipton lay bed-ridden, a beautiful woman in a beautiful room, feeding on hatred and
plotting vengeance on the man she had married. When
she first set eyes on young Jenny, she realized she had
found the perfect weapon for revenge.

But Jenny, for the first time in her life, had a friend.
Maria Hesketh, a gutsy, talented Liverpudlian, her
character as fiery as her hair, was determined that she
and Jenny would make something of their lives, would
succeed in spite of everything.

O 552 13977 7

SWEETER THAN WINE
by Susan Sallis

The quarrel had begun many years before – in 1850 on a West Indian sugar plantation – but although Charles Martinez and Hanover Rudolph had been dead a long time, the resentment and grudges of that old enmity still separated the two most important families in Bristol. The Rudolphs and the Martinez disliked each other intensely – until the Michaelmas Ball of 1927.

There, Jack Martinez, handsome roué and gambler, danced with spoilt, precocious Maude Rudolph and a spark was kindled. The two young lovers, scandalizing respectable Bristol, forced the families to unite and an uneasy truce was formed in time for their child to be born.

But there were others in the feuding families who were to be drawn into the subtle, confusing, and emotional bonding. For Maude had a brother, a tense, silent, moody man called Austen, who still couldn't forgive the Martinez family, even though he thought Jack's sister, Harriet, the loveliest and most gentle girl he had ever seen. As the families fused, blended in the most tragic and unexpected ways, so Austen and Harriet found themselves trapped in a complex union of passion, lies, and frustrated love.

0 552 14162 3

A SELECTED LIST OF FINE NOVELS
AVAILABLE FROM CORGI BOOKS

☐	14036 8	MAGGIE MAY	Lyn Andrews	£4.99
☐	13984 X	RACERS	Sally Armstrong	£4.99
☐	13648 4	CASTING	June Barry	£3.99
☐	13829 0	THE SMOKE SCREEN	Louise Brindley	£3.99
☐	13952 1	A DURABLE FIRE	Brenda Clarke	£4.99
☐	13255 1	GARDEN OF LIES	Eileen Goudge	£4.99
☐	13688 3	THE OYSTER CATCHERS	Iris Gower	£4.99
☐	13977 7	SPINNING JENNY	Ruth Hamilton	£4.99
☐	13872 X	LEGACY OF LOVE	Caroline Harvey	£4.99
☐	13917 3	A SECOND LEGACY	Caroline Harvey	£4.99
☐	13976 9	RACHEL'S DAUGHTER	Janet Haslam	£4.99
☐	14104 6	LOVE OVER GOLD	Susannah James	£3.99
☐	13708 1	OUT TO LUNCH	Tania Kindersley	£3.99
☐	13880 0	THE VENETIAN MASK	Rosalind Laker	£4.99
☐	13674 3	THE SPINNING WHEEL	Claire Lorrimer	£4.99
☐	14001 5	THE SILVER LINK	Claire Lorrimer	£4.99
☐	13910 6	BLUEBIRDS	Margaret Mayhew	£4.99
☐	13904 1	VOICES OF SUMMER	Diane Pearson	£4.99
☐	10375 6	CSARDAS	Diane Pearson	£5.99
☐	13987 4	ZADRUGA	Margaret Pemberton	£4.99
☐	13921 1	ALICE DAVENPORT	Audrey Reimann	£4.99
☐	13636 0	CARA'S LAND	Elvi Rhodes	£4.99
☐	13870 3	THE RAINBOW THROUGH THE RAIN	Elvi Rhodes	£4.99
☐	13934 3	DAUGHTERS OF THE MOON	Susan Sallis	£4.99
☐	14162 3	SWEETER THAN WINE	Susan Sallis	£4.99
☐	14106 2	THE TRAP	Mary Jane Staples	£4.99
☐	14154 2	A FAMILY AFFAIR	Mary Jane Staples	£4.99
☐	13838 6	A ROSE FOR EVERY MONTH	Sally Stewart	£3.99
☐	14163 1	THE SNOWS OF SPRINGTIME	Sally Stewart	£3.99
☐	14118 6	THE HUNGRY TIDE	Valerie Wood	£4.99